PELICAN BOOKS

JAMES CONNOLLY:
SELECTED WRITINGS

James Connolly was born in Edinburgh in 1868, the third son of an Irish immigrant. He started work at the age of ten, enlisted in the army when he was fourteen and served for nine years, mainly in Ireland. In 1892 Connolly discharged himself and returned to Edinburgh where he married Lillie Reynolds, a girl he had met in Ireland. He became actively involved in the Scottish Socialist Federation and in 1896 the Dublin Socialist Club offered him a full-time job as organizer. Within a few days of his arrival in Ireland he founded the Irish Socialist Republican Party and he spent the rest of his life working for Irish socialism and trade unionism; he was a supporter of women's rights and a life-long catholic. He wrote many pamphlets, articles and books including *Erin's Hope and Labour in Irish History*, the first Marxist analysis of Irish history. In 1903 financial difficulties forced him to emigrate to the U.S.A. with his family; he worked at a variety of jobs and became active in the American trade union movement. In 1910 he returned to Dublin and became the organizer of the Socialist Party of Ireland. He was an outspoken opponent of Irish involvement in the First World War and was one of the leaders of the Easter Rising in 1916. He was wounded in the fighting and, following the surrender of the insurgents, was court-martialled and executed on 12 May 1916. Peter Berresford Ellis is a journalist and author. He has written several books on the history and political development of the Celtic peoples, including *The Scottish Insurrection of 1820* (with Seumas Mac a' Ghobhainn), 1970, and *A History of the Irish Working Class*, 1972.

D1410048

JAMES CONNOLLY:
SELECTED WRITINGS

•

EDITED WITH AN INTRODUCTION BY
P. BERRESFORD ELLIS

PENGUIN BOOKS

Penguin Books Ltd, Harmondsworth, Middlesex, England
Penguin Books Inc., 7110 Ambassador Road, Baltimore, Maryland 21207, U.S.A.
Penguin Books Australia Ltd, Ringwood, Victoria, Australia

—

Published in Pelican Books 1973

—

Introduction and Selection copyright © P. Berresford Ellis, 1973

—

Made and printed in Great Britain by
Hazell Watson & Viney Ltd,
Aylesbury, Bucks
Set in Linotype Plantin

This book is sold subject to the condition
that it shall not, by way of trade or otherwise,
be lent, re-sold, hired out or otherwise circulated
without the publisher's prior consent in any form of
binding or cover other than that in which it is
published and without a similar condition
including this condition being imposed
on the subsequent purchaser

CONTENTS

INTRODUCTION

CONNOLLY: HIS LIFE AND WORK

JAMES CONNOLLY was one of the leaders of the 1916 Easter Rising in Ireland. He was named as vice-president of the Provisional Government of the Irish Republic when it was proclaimed from the steps of Dublin's General Post Office building at noon on 24 April, and was Commandant-General of all the insurgent forces fighting in the Irish capital. After the defeat of the insurgents by British Government troops, and a summary court-martial, forty-eight-year-old Connolly was executed. He died on 12 May 1916 in front of a firing squad while strapped to a chair because the wounds he had received during the fighting would not allow him to stand. This much is known and recorded of Connolly in every history of the foundation of the modern Irish State. His execution shocked the socialist movements of the world for Connolly was known as a Marxist, a militant socialist whose trade union activities were widely recognized and praised. His pamphlets and articles were read and discussed from the USA to Russia and from Ireland to Australia. Both Lenin and Trotsky were familiar with his writings and admired them. Connolly is considered to be the most profound mind and the greatest theoretician among the men whose actions in 1916 gave birth to the modern Irish state.

Connolly was a man of high ideals, a man who lived and died for other people. His entire life was spent in fighting for the poor, the exploited, the alienated, not only in Ireland but in Britain and the USA; he fought for the rights of those who were the tools of greedy, powerful men in a corrupt and corrupting society. Because of the part he played in the 1916 Rising, he has been accorded a prominent place among the heroes and martyrs of Ireland's struggle for national emancipation. So much is he revered that every Irish politician, of no matter what political philosophy, finds it necessary to pay lip-service to him. It is

largely because of the multitude of differing Irish political
philosophies which have conjured his ghost to their banners that
the thoughts and teachings of Connolly have, through the years,
often been distorted and lost. Writing of Wolfe Tone, the Irish
revolutionary leader of 1798, Connolly commented: 'Apostles of
Freedom are ever idolized when dead, but crucified when living.'
It was certainly true of his own life but, more tragically, while
today Connolly the man is idolized, his political philosophies,
which made him the man he was, remain crucified. As early as
1919 an attempt was made to discredit Connolly's political
beliefs; it was said that he had 'allowed himself to be obfus-
cated by German philosophical doctrines [Marxism] which
he either misunderstood or interpreted in a sense different
from their authors.' (*Irish Monthly*, August 1919.) In 1966,
during the Golden Jubilee commemoration of 1916, the then
Irish Taoiseach (Prime Minister) Seán Lemass, dismissed
the relevance of Connolly's thought to the modern Irish State
with the comment, 'even many of the views of James Connolly,
revolutionary though they were considered in his time, seem
out of date in the circumstance of today.' It is significant,
however, that, during the past decade in Ireland, there has been
a tremendous growth of interest among the radical young in
the political thought of Connolly. It is also significant that during the guerrilla struggle in Northern Ireland not only the Irish
tricolour flew over the Republican ghettoes but alongside it
flew the 'Plough and the Stars' – the flag of Connolly's Citizen
Army.

It is, perhaps, strange that in a country where all political
parties pay homage to Connolly there is no complete edition of
his writings, for Connolly left behind him a body of writings in
newspapers, periodicals and pamphlets which leaves no doubt as
to his political objectives and programme. Scholars, Owen
Dudley Edwards the historian for example, are pressing for the
formation of an editorial board to compile a comprehensive
edition of all Connolly's works to be published in chronological
order, to be edited in the best tradition of historical scholarship
on much the same lines as the USSR have issued the collected
works of Lenin or the USA have edited the collected works of

Benjamin Franklin and Thomas Jefferson. Since Connolly's death only a few selections of his writings and a number of his pamphlets have been published. The purpose of the present volume is to provide a general introduction to Connolly's life and thought. For this purpose this introduction is divided into two sections: first, a brief biographical sketch and, second, an introduction to the main points of his work.

HIS LIFE

James Connolly was born on 5 June 1868 at 107 Cowgate, Edinburgh, Scotland. He was the third son of John Connolly, an Irish immigrant, and of Mary McGinn, whose parents came from Co. Monaghan. At the time of his birth his father was working as a manure carter for the Edinburgh Corporation but was promoted shortly afterwards to lamplighter. The area where the Connolly family lived was over-crowded and plagued by the physical and social diseases of all slums. We can only guess at the environment which drove young James to work at the age of ten or eleven in order to help support his family. He found a job with his brother Thomas, two years older than himself, who was working as a compositor's labourer on the Edinburgh *Evening News*. A year later a factory inspector discovered James's real age and he was sacked. He worked in a bakery and then in a tiling factory until, at the age of fourteen, like so many from the same background seeking security, he enlisted in the 1st Battalion of the King's Liverpool Regiment.

The regiment was counted as Irish, with dark green uniforms and a badge composed of an Irish harp surmounted by a crown. It was, perhaps, among the soldiers of this regiment that Connolly developed his Irish national consciousness, for the regiment had been infiltrated by the revolutionary Fenian Movement so well that during the Fenian uprising of 1867 all its arms were placed under lock and key in the depot in case the regiment defected to the insurgents. The regiment was similarly disarmed during the Land League troubles in 1881. In July 1882 it was felt safe to send the battalion to Ireland and the young Connolly saw his father's country for the first time. He served with the regiment at Youghal, Castlebar, The Curragh and Dublin, until its return to Aldershot, England, in February 1889.

It was in February 1889 that Connolly's father suffered an accident and was summarily dismissed from his job. Later the Edinburgh Corporation relented and found him work as a caretaker of a public convenience in Edinburgh's Haymarket. Connolly was worried. Although he had a further four months to serve in the army he 'discharged himself' and left for Scotland. He was never arrested. Apparently in the transfer from Ireland his battalion's records had been lost and his desertion was not discovered.

Lying low in Perth, Connolly became involved with John Leslie, a Scottish poet of Irish descent, who drew Connolly into socialist politics. With Leslie as his mentor, Connolly began to give himself a firm grounding in Marxism. On 13 April 1889 Connolly married Lillie Reynolds whom he had met while in Ireland. By 1892 Connolly was extremely active in the Scottish Socialist Federation and his eldest brother John (six years his senior) was secretary of the movement. It was in 1892 that Connolly took over the secretaryship from his brother and began to contribute articles to *Justice*, the journal of the Social Democratic Federation which drew its inspiration from Marx. Connolly consulted his wife in matters of grammar, spelling and punctuation; as a self-educated man he wanted his articles to be word perfect. He was also beginning to study the art of oratory.

In November 1894 he came third out of four candidates when he stood as a socialist for St Giles Ward in the Edinburgh Municipal Elections. Connolly found, however, that he had lost his job as a carter with the Edinburgh Corporation and he tried to set up business as a cobbler. In April 1895 he was again defeated in the Poor Law elections, once again standing for St Giles Ward. His articles in *Justice* and *Labour Leader* were attracting favourable attention from fellow socialists but Connolly, now with three daughters, Mona, Nora and Aideen, found himself in grave financial difficulties. He accepted promptly, therefore, when the Dublin Socialist Club offered him a full-time job as organizer in May 1896.

Within a few days of his arrival in the Irish capital, Connolly formed the Irish Socialist Republican Party and drew up a programme which the historian D. R. O'Connor Lysaght has described as 'too advanced for its time'. Connolly headed his programme with the aphorism of the French revolutionary Camille Desmoulins: 'The great appear great to us only because we are on our knees: let us rise.' The object of Connolly's programme was:

Establishment of AN IRISH SOCIALIST REPUBLIC based upon the public ownership by the Irish people of the land, and instruments of production, distribution and exchange. Agriculture to be administered as a public function, under boards of management elected by the agricultural population and responsible to them and to the nation at large. All other forms of labour necessary to the well-being of the community to be conducted on the same principles.

Connolly presented a ten-point programme: 1, nationalization of railways and canals; 2, abolition of private banks and money-lending institutions and establishment of state banks, under popularly elected boards of directors, issuing loans at cost; 3, establishment at public expense of rural depots for the more improved agricultural machinery, to be lent out to the agricultural population at a rent covering cost and management alone; 4, graduated income tax on all incomes over £400 per annum in order to provide funds for pensions to the aged, infirm and widows and orphans; 5, legislative restrictions of hours of labour to forty-eight per week and establishment of a minimum wage; 6, free maintenance for all children; 7, gradual extension of the principle of public ownership and supply to all the necessaries of life; 8, public control and management of national schools by boards elected by popular ballot for that purpose alone; 9, free education up to the highest university grades; and 10, universal suffrage.

Money was still scarce for Connolly and his family, living in one room in a tenement block. His wage as an organizer was irregularly paid and he took work as a labourer, shipyard worker and publisher's proof reader. During long periods of unemployment, which the family survived by selling and pawning their belongings, Connolly spent hours at a time studying in the National Library. His first major political essay, *Ireland for the*

Irish, appeared in three instalments in the *Labour Leader* beginning in October 1896. He also edited excerpts from the writings of the radical Young Ireland leader James Fintan Lalor. He formed a '98 Club' to commemorate the 1798 uprising – the rising by which the United Irishmen sought to establish a radical Irish Republic – and also edited some of the important radical writings of the United Irishmen leadership. His increasingly outspoken attacks on British imperialism in Ireland began to bring him into conflict with English socialists who believed the cause of Irish independence was 'a mere chauvinism calculated to perpetrate national rivalries and race hatreds'. Replying in the *Labour Leader* of January 1898 Connolly maintained:

> ...under a Socialist system every nation will be the supreme arbiter of its own destinies, national and international; will be forced into no alliance against its will, but will have its independence guaranteed and its freedom respected by the enlightened self-interest of the social democracy of the world.
>
> The statement that our ideals [Irish national independence] cannot be realized except by the path of violent revolution is not so much an argument against our propaganda as an indictment of the invincible ignorance and unconquerable national egotism of the British electorate, and as such concerns English Socialists more than Irish ones.

In March 1897 Connolly's first major theoretical work, *Erin's Hope,* was published – an uncompromising statement of the socialist case which contained the embryo of the theme he was to develop in *Labour in Irish History* – the conflict between the common ownership of land held under the Irish clan system and the feudal system introduced by the English conquerors. A lot of ideas in *Erin's Hope* are still valid, some are out of date, and others Connolly himself revised. For example, Connolly wrote 'no revolutionist can safely invite the co-operation of men or classes whose ideals are not theirs and whom, therefore, they may be compelled to fight at some future critical stage of the journey to freedom.' Later he came to Lenin's conclusion that 'Whoever expects a "pure" social revolution will never live to see it.' And Connolly agreed that 'the true revolutionist should ever call into action on our side the entire sum of all the forces and factors of social and political discontent.'

In March 1898 came Connolly's only experience of the agrarian struggle. A famine threatened the west of Ireland. Once again the potato crop had failed and Connolly foresaw a recurrence of the terrible famine of 1845–9 when a million Irish people died of starvation and the disease that accompanies malnutrition, and a further million had been forced to emigrate. The tragedy was that the famine had been an artificial one in that there had been enough food in Ireland adequately to feed the starving people but the peasants were forced to sell their produce to pay their rents to absentee landlords. Charity ships from the European mainland, racing into Irish ports with food for famine relief, were surprised to see six times their number of ships heading for England bearing cargoes of grain, wool and flax. Connolly determined that such a situation should not arise again and issued a manifesto entitled *The Rights of Life and the Rights of Property* in which he pointed out that

... in 1847 our people died by thousands of starvation, though every ship leaving an Irish port was laden with food in abundance. The Irish people might have seized that food, cattle, corn and all manner of provisions before it reached the sea ports, have prevented famine and saved their country from ruin, but did not do so, believing such action to be sinful, and dreading to peril their souls to save their bodies. In this we know now they were entirely mistaken. The very highest authorities on the doctrine of the Church agree that no *human* law can stand between starving people and their right to food including their right to take food whenever they find it, openly or secretly, with or without the owner's permission.

Connolly spent three weeks in Co. Kerry reporting on the famine for Daniel de Leon's *Weekly People,* the journal of the Socialist Labour Party of the USA. Connolly found that the main cause of the famine was the 'failure of the system of small farming, restricted mental horizon of peasants who could have prevented blight if they had co-operated. In these circumstances state action was necessary to prevent disaster.'

In July 1898 Connolly was in Scotland raising money to launch a journal for his Irish Socialist Republican Party. His friend Keir Hardie donated £50 and on 13 August the *Workers' Republic* was launched. In January 1889 Connolly's party put forward an unsuccessful candidate at the first election to be held under the Irish Local Government Act, one of a series of Conservative measures to 'kill Home Rule with kindness'. Connolly had now achieved a reputation by lecturing throughout Ireland and also in Scotland. He had bought a small press and was the editor, contributor, composing room staff, machine room staff as well as the printers' devil of the *Workers' Republic*.

On 27 August 1899, Connolly, under ISRP auspices, organized the first public protest against the Boer War, which was a war 'enabling an unscrupulous gang of capitalists to get into their hands the immense riches of the diamond fields'. One anti-war meeting was prohibited by the police and the carriage transporting the speakers to the meeting was stopped by a police cordon. Connolly took the reins and drove the carriage through the police ranks, scattering them. At the meeting place the speakers only just had time to make their speeches before the police squads arrived and took them to Store Street police barracks. Connolly had been arrested once before, in 1898 when leading a demonstration against the celebrations of Queen Victoria's Diamond Jubilee. This time Connolly and his fellow speakers were detained a few hours only. But on arriving at the ISRP offices Connolly found that the police had raided the place in his absence and smashed his cherished printing press. Nevertheless, Connolly's campaign against the morality of the Boer War brought recruiting for the armed forces in Ireland to a standstill.

The International Socialist Congress met in Paris in 1900 and Connolly's ISRP sent two delegates, E. W. Stewart and J. J. Lyng. The Congress became the first ever international meeting to recognize Irish nationhood. It was at this Congress that the paths of 'revolutionism' or 'reformism' were heatedly debated. The debate arose from the fact that a French socialist deputy, Millerand, had entered the French Government (which included General Galliffet the 'butcher of the Commune') on the pretext that he could use his influence to make reforms. In the final analysis the British, German and Austrian delegations favoured 'reformism', the Polish, Italian and American delegations were divided, and only the Bulgarians and Irish unanimously condemned the action, placing themselves on the 'revolutionary' side of the International.

During 1901 Connolly published *The New Evangel*, the second major theoretical work to come from his pen. While in places there are confusing ideas which, when his thought had matured and crystallized, he corrected in his later work, its publication endorsed Connolly's emergence as a theoretician. Of the essays contained in the work 'Socialism and Religion' marked the beginning of Connolly's attempt to make Catholics understand that there was nothing incompatible between their Catholicism and socialism. During the same year Connolly's growing reputation in England increased when he made a lecture tour under the auspices of the Social-Democratic Federation. Returning to Dublin in mid-October he was elected to the Dublin Trades Council as a nominee of the United Labourers Union. Standing for the ISRP as a candidate for the Wood Quay Ward in the Dublin Municipal Elections, he suffered from a campaign of slander and vilification. Sermons were preached in which he was branded as an anti-Christ and priests ordered that no Catholic was to vote for him under pain of excommunication. He won 431 votes while the successful candidate achieved 1,424 votes.

Declining an invitation to become secretary of the Builders' Labourers Union, he crossed to Scotland for a lecture tour and then accepted an invitation to go on another in the USA and Canada where his pamphlet, *Erin's Hope*, republished by the American Socialist Labour Party (SLP), had been warmly greeted. He spent four months touring, lecturing and contributing articles to the *Weekly People*. Before leaving the USA, in January 1903, Connolly remarked, significantly: 'The United States is the country on which the emancipation of the workers of Europe depends.' Arriving back in Dublin he again unsuccessfully contested the Wood Quay Ward in the municipal elections. The same month the *Workers' Republic* carried the first instalment of his magnum opus, *Labour in Irish History*, the first Marxist analysis of Irish history.

As usual life was financially difficult for the Connolly family, now consisting of Mona, Nora, Aideen, Ina, Maire and

Ruaidhre (Roddy). Frustrated with the continual bickering of Irish socialists and the lack of any progress, Connolly decided to emigrate to the USA where, in 1903, he took a job as an insurance collector in Troy, New York. In August of the following year his wife and children joined him but tragedy had struck the family. Connolly's eldest child, Mona, had died, aged thirteen, from severe burns following an accident. Connolly had joined the American Socialist Labour Party and was in demand as a lecturer. He lectured at Clark's Hall, in New York. He was coming into conflict, however, with the SLP leader Daniel de Leon, who was vehement in his attacks on the Catholic Church. Connolly replied to de Leon's attacks in the 9 April 1904 issue of the *Weekly People*, in a piece entitled 'Wages, Marriage and the Church'. De Leon's socialist dogmatism and general intolerance of those of differing views made the conflict a bitter one.

Meanwhile Connolly was learning Italian (he had already mastered French and German) and was soon able to translate articles on socialism from journals such as *Il Proletario* into English.

In America Connolly was again drifting in and out of jobs, taking positions as a machinist, filer and once more as an insurance collector. It was while Connolly was so engaged that the Industrial Workers of the World (the famous 'Wobblies') were born in Chicago out of Eugene Debs' American Labour Union. An affiliated union – the Western Federation of Miners – had struggled for nearly a year against impossible conditions. They literally had to defend themselves gun in hand against mineowners' private armies and hired thugs. They had found that their strength lay in a union of all trades and so, with the Industrial Workers of the World (IWW), was launched industrial unionism and the concept of workers' control. The IWW was born at a time when the idea of industrial unionism or syndicalism was challenging the old Marxist concept that parliamentary democracy was the way to implement the Socialist State. The syndicate or trade union was to be the tool by which to seize control of power. Connolly observed that industrial unionism was

. . . simply the discovery that the workers are strongest at the point of production, that they have no force available except economic force, and by linking the revolutionary movement with the daily fight of the workshop, mill, shipyard, factory, the necessary economic force can be organized. Also that the revolutionary organization necessary for that purpose provides the framework of the Socialist Republic.

Connolly immediately launched himself into the movement and together with a fellow Irishman, Patrick Quinlan, he formed a branch of the IWW in Newark, New Jersey. He became organizer and secretary of the Building and Constructional Workers Industrial Union in Newark, but he was soon organizing tramwaymen, moulders, garment workers, milkmen and dockers. He was also elected to the National Executive Committee of the Socialist Labour Party, still dominated by de Leon, but the conflict between them forced his resignation in October 1907. On 29 March 1907 Connolly launched his Irish Socialist Federation (ISF) among Irish-American workers. As the New York correspondent of the *Industrial Union Bulletin*, he was becoming widely known in the American labour world. Amidst a flurry of activity he finished *Labour in Irish History*, published a volume containing some of his verse as *Songs of Freedom* and launched a new journal *The Harp* as the paper of the ISF.

Early in 1908 Connolly formed the IWW Propaganda League, the purpose of which was to aid recruiting to the IWW by explaining the philosophy of industrial unionism. He went on a lecture tour of the USA, helped to organize the 'Eugene Debs for president' campaign and was a delegate to the fourth IWW Convention in Chicago. In December Charles Webb of Chicago published *Socialism Made Easy*, Connolly's theoretical work on industrial unionism and the first of his pamphlets actually to earn him money. In May of the following year Tom Mann and Australian syndicalists incorporated the expository section of the work, under the title 'The Axe to the Root', in the year book of the Australian syndicalist One Big Union Movement. The work was also distributed in Britain although it was not published there until an edition was put out by the Socialist Labour Press of Glasgow in 1917. In their book *Industrial Democracy in Great Britain*, authors Ken Coates and Tony Topham acknowledge the importance of Connolly in pioneering the ideas of industrial unionism in Britain.

But by 1908 Connolly confided in his friend William O'Brien, who formed a new socialist party in Dublin in 1909 called Cummanacht na hÉirann (Socialist Party of Ireland). 'I may confess to you that I regard my emigration to America as the great mistake of my life, and I have never ceased to regret it.' Momentous things had been happening to labour in Ireland during Connolly's absence. In January 1907, a firebrand trade union organizer, James Larkin, a Liverpool Irishman, had arrived in Belfast to organize the dockers. His successes were spectacular. For the first time since the Establishment had played the 'Orange Card' in order to divide and rule Protestant and Catholic Irish and defeat national self-determination, Protestants and Catholics united behind Larkin's banner and remained united in spite of frantic efforts by northern capitalists to split the union's stand into sectarian strife. Larkin moved like a whirlwind through Ireland organizing and consolidating. But he was frustrated by the lack of knowledge and sympathy shown by the union head office which was, like so many unions in Ireland, London-based. The English leaders of the trade unions in Ireland understood little of Irish conditions. By 1906 employers in England had been forced to concede the right of combination to workers, but Ireland, despite her early start in trade union organization, was still twenty years behind. The basic right of combination for workers had to be fought out in Ireland town by town: Belfast in 1907; Dublin in 1908; and Cork in 1909. The London-dominated trade unions failed to see the differing national problems. Trotsky, writing in *Nashe Slovo* in 1916, commented. 'The young Irish working class ... clashed with the egoistic, narrow minded, imperial arrogance of English trade unionism and naturally swung between nationalism and syndicalism, uniting both tendencies in their revolutionary consciousness.' Indeed, in disgust Larkin formed the Irish Transport and General Workers Union (ITGWU) – 'one big union' for Irish workers as Connolly was to see it. And while Connolly fretted in the USA the ITGWU began a struggle for its existence not only against the Irish employers but against the English-based trade unions who

saw the creation of independent Irish organizations as 'perpe-
trating national rivalries and race hatreds'.

Connolly continued his work in the USA, being appointed
national organizer of the Socialist Party of America, assigned to
the mid-west, in June 1909. In June 1910 *The Harp* was trans-
ferred to Dublin with Larkin as editor. In March of that year
Larkin issued an appeal for funds to bring Connolly back to
Ireland on a lecture tour. At the same time Connolly was taking
part in the famous Free Speech Campaign in New Castle,
Pennsylvania, led by 'Big Bill' Hayward, and editing the *New
Castle Free Press* when its editor McKeever was jailed.

On 26 July 1910 Connolly returned to Ireland to find Larkin
in jail, serving one year's hard labour on a trumped up fraud
charge, as the employers and English trade unions sought to
smash the infant ITGWU. Connolly immediately launched
himself into the arena, organizing petitions and demonstrations
which resulted in the release of Larkin within three months.
Connolly became organizer of the Socialist Party of Ireland,
establishing branches in Cork and Belfast. In August 1910 his
most famous work on the religious question, *Labour, Nationality
and Religion*, was published. This was followed in November by
Labour in Irish History in book form. The works did much to
establish Connolly's reputation as a Marxist theoretician as well
as a practical revolutionary.

In March 1911 Connolly took up residence in Belfast and
joined the ITGWU, becoming its Ulster district organizer and
secretary. He was soon proving his organizational powers once
again, leading the famous millgirls' strike in Belfast in October
of that year. In November he formed the Textile Workers' section of the ITGWU and became the union's delegate to the
Belfast Trades Council. In January 1911 he was asked to take
over the organization work during a lock-out in Wexford. In
August of the previous year two Wexford ironmasters decided
to close their works, locking out 550 members of the ITGWU
in an attempt to destroy the union's hold in the town. Other
employers, including the town's mayor, followed suit and all factories where members of the union were found were closed. The
local organizer, P.T. Daly, raised no objections to the men joining

any other union so long as employers recognized their right to join the ITGWU. The men held firm and police were called in to break up union meetings, using their batons freely. One worker died and many were injured. In January 1912 Daly was arrested and forcibly moved to Waterford. At this point Connolly arrived and proposed the men form the Irish Foundry Workers Union affiliated to the ITGWU. The employers eventually compromised and agreed to let the men join this new union, which was eventually merged in the ITGWU as an official branch. It was a significant victory for the union but merely a dress rehearsal for the great attempt to smash it during the Dublin Lock-Out of 1913.

Connolly was now proposing that an Independent Labour Party of Ireland should be formed 'as the political weapon of the Irish working class'. This was merely an extension of his belief in industrial unionism, mapped out in his *Socialism Made Easy* in which he suggested that as well as an industrial organization, a political party should act as the political branch of that organization. Connolly felt that a Labour Party should be firmly welded to the Irish Trades Union Congress.

The general election of 1910 had resulted in a return to Westminster of 314 Liberal/Labour MPs, 271 Conservatives and 84 Irish Nationalists holding the crucial balance of power. It now seemed certain that Ireland would get her long awaited Home Rule. Connolly, realizing 'some form of self government seems practically certain of realization', saw the necessity of a united socialist party being ready to enter the Irish Parliament. Writing in *Forward*, 27 May 1911, he made a plea for socialist unity in Ireland. On 3 June William Walker of the Belfast Independent Labour Party replied reiterating his belief in the union with England and Protestant ascendancy. Walker had stood as an ILP parliamentary candidate in North Belfast with Ramsay MacDonald as his election agent. He had embarrassed Ramsay MacDonald, who then believed in self-government for both Ireland and Scotland, by maintaining a completely sectarian attitude, expressing open support for the union and declaring that Catholics should not be allowed to hold office. 'Protestantism,' he maintained, 'means protesting against superstition, hence

true Protestantism is synonymous with labour.' Walker was three
times defeated in his bid to get into parliament. By 1912 he had
departed from the Labour Movement, accepting a Government
position under the new National Insurance Act introduced by
Lloyd George. Connolly at once joined battle against Walker's
pseudo-socialism, and the resulting exchange of views, which
have become known as the 'Connolly-Walker Controversy' (and
published under that title in pamphlet form by Connolly Books
in 1969), shows clearly the views of the Walkerite 'social-
imperialism' (Lenin's phrase) and of Connolly's anti-imperialist
views. In this exchange Connolly was trying to educate the
majority of English socialists who, using the catchphrase 'international socialism', opposed working class participation in anti-
imperialist struggles on the pretext that since the working class
interest was international it was opposed to all national struggles.

Connolly was also keeping his eye on the Home Rule Bill then
going through the House of Commons and demanding that,
incorporated in this Bill, should be 'proportional representation,
excision of a proposal for a senate and suffrage for women'. He
was appearing on many Women's Rights platforms throughout
the country. At the Irish TUC meeting in Clonmel, Connolly
was successful in moving that 'the independent representation of
labour upon all public boards be, and is hereby, included amongst
the objects of Congress.' In 1912, following the interest taken in
his *Labour, Nationality and Religion*, Connolly was involved in
a controversy revolving round the question of whether the
Catholic Church had been mistaken in political matters. Connolly's articles enlarged his reputation and brought him into
debate with Hilaire Belloc at the Irish Club in London. The
audience was astonished at the ease with which Connolly
trounced one of the leading intellectuals of Britain.

In January 1913 Connolly unsuccessfully contested Dock
Ward in the municipal elections in Belfast. He had been supported by the Belfast Trades Council. In August 1913, the
famous 'Dublin Lock-Out', the first great serious confrontation
of the twentieth century between organized labour and capitalism,
took place. William Martin Murphy, chairman of the Employers'
Federation, virtual owner of Dublin Tramways and owner of the

Irish Independent newspaper group, decided to lead a crusade against Larkin's union. He took the initiative by calling a meeting of his newspapers' dispatch department and told the workers that they must resign from the ITGWU or accept dismissal notices; employees were also asked to sign a declaration of their loyalty and an assurance they would not strike. The ITGWU retaliated by 'blacking' Murphy's newspapers and Murphy answered by locking out all members of the ITGWU. At 9.40 a.m. on Tuesday, 26 August, 700 employees of Murphy's tramways company walked off their trams. The Employers' Federation united to break the union and by September 3 some 400 employers had agreed to lock-out their employees. 25,000 Dublin workers were affected by 22 September. Larkin was arrested and Connolly hastened from Belfast to help organize. He too was arrested and refused to recognize the court, denying the right of the English to govern in Ireland. Sentenced to three months imprisonment in Mountjoy, Connolly was released after an eight-day hunger strike. On 12 September Larkin was released on bail and went on a fund-raising tour of England. He was taking a tough line: 'I am out for revolution!' Ireland's leading intellectuals were outspoken in favour of workers' resistance. These included Pádraic Pearse, W. B. Yeats, James Stephens, George Russell (AE), Pádraic Colum, Joseph Plunkett, Thomas MacDonagh, Seamus O'Sullivan and Susan Mitchell. The Government finally intervened on 26 September and set up a Board of Trade Inquiry. Connolly prepared the statement on behalf of the workers for submission to the inquiry which found that the onus for settlement was on the employers. Murphy and his colleagues refused to accept the result of the inquiry. Even the London *Times* was aghast at the attitude of the employers in their intent to starve the ITGWU into submission.

On 27 October Larkin was brought to trial and sentenced to seven months in Mountjoy and Connolly took over the leadership of the workers, speaking at a gigantic meeting in London's Albert Hall with George Bernard Shaw, Delia Larkin, Ben Tillet and George Lansbury in protest at Larkin's jailing. October also saw the birth of the Irish Citizen Army, which has been described as Europe's first 'Red Guard'. The workers had found themselves open to organized attacks by the police and the employers' hired thugs so Connolly and Captain Jack R. White D S O, a Protestant Ulsterman, formed an armed unit to protect the workers. But in Connolly's mind the Irish Citizen Army was the nucleus of an armed revolutionary force which would overthrow British imperialism in Ireland and establish a Workers' Republic. He wrote:

> An armed organization of the Irish working class is a phenomenon in Ireland. Hitherto the workers of Ireland have fought as parts of the armies led by their masters, never as a member of any army officered, trained and inspired by men of their own class. Now, with arms in their hands, they propose to steer their own course, to carve their own future. (*Workers' Republic*, 30 October 1915)

The death knell of the workers' resistance was being sounded and in the early months of 1914 the workers were returning to work on the condition that none of them 'remain or become in the future a member of the Irish Transport Workers Union'. The struggle had been left entirely to the workers of Dublin and while British trade unionists had initially expressed sympathy, sending funds, they refused sympathetic strikes and to commit themselves to an industrial war over a 'purely Irish' matter. By 1914, through lack of financial and sympathetic support, the Irish workers found themselves giving way to the employers. Writing in *Forward*, 7 February 1914, Connolly said:

> And so we Irish workers must again go down into Hell, bow our backs to the last of the slave drivers, let our hearts be seared by the iron of his hatred and instead of the sacramental wafer of brotherhood and common sacrifice, eat the dust of defeat and betrayal. Dublin is isolated.

Storm clouds were now gathering from another direction – Ulster. Home Rule seemed now a certainty and there was growing concern from the Irish industrial capitalists who were chiefly concentrated in the north-east of the province of Ulster. Since the Union of 1801 the capitalist industries of the north had been developed for the English imperial markets and so industrial capitalism had thrown its weight behind the union with England. The mainly southern petty capitalists, however, relied on the home market and needed to seal off the Irish market behind strong protective barriers in order to bring about a flourishing native manufacturing capitalism in Ireland. They therefore championed self-government which would have spelt disaster for the northern industrialists. To keep a considerable weight of public opinion behind them the northern capitalists had fostered and developed the religious differences in the country, pointing out that north-east Ulster was mainly Protestant while the rest of Ireland was mainly Catholic and that under Home Rule the Protestants could expect to be 'swamped'. 'Home Rule is Rome Rule' was the catchphrase. Led by a Dublin Unionist, Sir Edward H. Carson (later Lord Carson), a Protestant army called the Ulster Volunteers was formed in 1913 to prevent the north-east of Ulster becoming part of the Irish (Home Rule) state. To the average Ulster Protestant he was merely defending his religion and being loyal to the Crown of England but since it was imperative that the industrial capitalists had access to an imperial market, they sought another imperial power with which to ally themselves should they be 'cast off' by Britain. In August 1913 Carson lunched with the German Kaiser following which the Protestant *Irish Churchman* joyfully announced:

We have the offer of aid from a powerful continental monarch, who, if Home Rule is forced on the Protestants of Ireland, is prepared to send an army sufficient to release England of any further trouble in Ireland by attaching it to his dominion ...

In answer to the arming of the north and the birth of the Ulster Volunteers, the Irish Volunteers were formed on 25 November 1913 to defend Home Rule. Behind the establishment of the Irish Volunteers, however, were members of the Irish Republican Brotherhood who seized the opportunity to set up a military front organization which could be turned into a revolutionary force. In Europe the massive race for imperial gains, colonies and possessions was arriving at its logical conclusion. War was on the horizon and this made a settlement of the 'Irish question' urgent. A proposal for a partition of Ireland was made to provide exclusion of the province of Ulster from Home Rule. Ulster is a province of nine counties of which only four counties had 'loyalist' majorities. On 4 August 1914 war was declared on Germany and the question was immediately shelved. Carson pledged his Ulster Volunteers to fight for England and John Redmond, leader of the Irish Nationalists and a member of the ruling council of the Irish Volunteers, not to be outdone, made a similar pledge on behalf of the Irish Volunteers. Connolly commented:

> Full steam ahead John Redmond said
>   that everything was well chum;
> Home Rule will come when we are dead
>   and buried out in Belgium.

In October 1914, Larkin had set off for the USA, tired and exhausted by the Dublin struggle, with the aim of collecting funds for the Irish labour movement. In his absence James Connolly became acting General Secretary of the ITGWU, commander of the Irish Citizen Army and editor of the *Irish Worker*, the newspaper Larkin had launched in June, 1911. Connolly was horrified at the disintegration of the European socialist movement at the outbreak of the First World War.

What then becomes of all our resolutions; all our protests of fraternization; all our threats of general strikes; all our carefully built machinery of internationalism; all our hopes for the future? (*Forward*, 15 August 1914)

Like Lenin, Connolly completely denounced the imperialist holocaust. In vain he pointed out:

A great continental uprising of the working class would stop the war; a universal protest at public meetings would not save a single life from being wantonly slaughtered.

Connolly watched the very same socialists who had denounced his demands for national liberation as 'chauvinism' flocking to provide cannon fodder for the imperial banners.

Should the working class of Europe, rather than slaughter each other for the benefit of kings and financiers, proceed tomorrow to erect barricades all over Europe, to break up bridges and destroy transport services that war might be abolished, we should be perfectly happy in following such a glorious example and contributing our aid to the final dethronement of the vulture class that rule and rob the world. But pending either of these consummations it is our manifest duty to take all possible action to save the poor from the horrors this war has in store.

As early as 8 August 1914, writing in the *Irish Worker*, Connolly decided that Ireland should seize the opportunity to organize an uprising for national independence, to disown the imperialist war in Europe and by so doing 'set the torch to a European conflagration that will not burn out until the last throne and the last capitalist bond and debenture will be shrivelled in the funeral pyre of the last war lord.' Connolly realized that he must ally himself to the bourgeois nationalists, or rather, the most progressive section of them. These, led by Pádraic Pearse, sometime lawyer, schoolmaster, poet and playwright (in both Irish and English), had succeeded in splitting the Irish Volunteers. At a Dublin Convention of the Volunteer movement, the Volunteers had split into those who supported Redmond, going off to fight in Europe in the belief that by so doing England would grant Home Rule at the end of the war, and those who were determined to remain as a defence force in Ireland, resisting conscription and defending the unity of the nation and its right to self-determination. Those that remained in the latter category, retaining the name of Irish Volunteers, numbered only 12,000. Connolly's increasing involvement with the bourgeois nationalists brought forth strong criticism from the secretary of the Citizen Army, the future playwright Seán O'Casey, who resigned in disgust although he, himself, had once advocated that the traditional republicans and labour unite to achieve the national revolution.

Both the Irish Republican Brotherhood and Connolly determined that Ireland should strike out for its independence seizing England's involvement in the European war as a prime opportunity. Connolly applied himself diligently to learning all about street fighting and insurrectionary warfare and during 1915 he published a series of articles, now republished as *Revolutionary Warfare*, which classes Connolly as a proficient military scientist. Connolly fumed at the increasing delay by the Irish Republican Brotherhood at announcing a date for the uprising. From November 1915 to early January 1916 Connolly intensified his

campaign for an immediate armed revolution. In January the
Supreme Council of the Irish Republican Brotherhood decided
that the uprising was to begin on 22 April and Connolly was
immediately informed. He disappeared from 19 January to 22
January in secret conclave with the IRB leaders. He was made
a member of the IRB and co-opted to its Military Council, joining Tom Clarke, Eamonn Ceannt, Seán MacDiarmada, Pádraic
Pearse and Joseph Plunkett. Thomas MacDonagh was co-opted
later.

The plans for the rising relied on the entire Volunteer
movement and the Irish Citizen Army taking part. Dublin insurgents were to seize key positions in the city while insurgents
in the provinces were to surround garrisons and prevent troops
advancing on the city. A military provisional government would
be proclaimed with Pádraic Pearse as president, James Connolly
as vice-president and including Tom Clarke, Seán MacDiarmada,
Thomas MacDonagh, Joseph Plunkett and Eamonn Ceannt. A
civil government would also be named to look after specific
'civilian problems' during the rising which was to consist of
William O'Brien (a disciple of Connolly), Mrs Hanna Sheehy-
Skeffington, Seán T. Ó Ceallaigh, Alderman Tom Kelly and
Arthur Griffith (president of the Sinn Fein party). Pearse,
MacDonagh, Ceannt and Clarke were all to the left of the Irish
bourgeois nationalists. Pearse, although his writings show no
familiarity with socialist theory, was moving almost instinctively
towards a socialist stance. He had admired Larkin but with
Connolly he became friendly and accepted much of his teaching.
In his last major pamphlet, *The Sovereign People*, he began to
develop a theory that challenged the concept of private property.
Pearse had decided 'in substance that separation from England
would be valueless unless it put the people – the actual people and
not merely certain rich men – of Ireland in effectual ownership
and possession of the soil of Ireland.' Pearse felt that the 'right
to the control of the material resources of a nation does not reside
in any individual or in any class of individuals; it resides in the
whole people and can be lawfully exercised only by those to whom
it is delegated by the whole people, and in the manner in which
the people ordains.' Connolly's influence is evident in the draw-

ing up of the 1916 Proclamation (written by Pearse) which declares 'the right of the people of Ireland to the ownership of Ireland'. And goes on

... The Republic guarantees religious and civil liberty, equal rights and equal opportunities to all its citizens, and declares its resolve to pursue the happiness and prosperity of the whole nation and of all its parts, cherishing all the children of the nation equally and oblivious of the differences carefully fostered by an alien government ...

The Proclamation of the Republic mentions that the provisional government would hold the affairs of the nation in trust until a national government was elected by the suffrage 'of all her men and women'. It was not until 1918 that the British Government allowed the franchise to women over the age of thirty and not until 1928 that the age limit was lowered to twenty-one.

The Irish Volunteers and Citizen Army were ordered to take part in 'three days of manoeuvres' over the Easter Week. Even Professor Eoin MacNeill, *de jure* head of the Volunteers, was not told of the intention of the IRB leaders. A few days before the date of the intended rising Connolly delivered his last lecture on guerrilla warfare to his men: 'I'm going to fight the way I want,' he told them, 'not the way the enemy wants. It'll be a new way, one the soldiers haven't been trained to deal with.'

As the date for the uprising drew near, however, things started to go wrong. A German ship, the *Aud*, bearing arms and ammunition for the insurgents, was pounced upon by English warships and her captain scuttled her and the valuable cargo off Cobh (then Queenstown) on 20 April. On the same day the IRB envoy to Germany, Roger Casement, and two companions, landing from a German submarine at Banna Strand, were arrested. Eoin MacNeill, discovering the orders for 'manoeuvres' were, in reality, orders for the insurrection, issued countermanding orders, published in the *Sunday Independent*, calling off all parades. Lord Wimborne, the Lord-Lieutenant of Ireland, realizing that something was in the wind, had already issued orders for over a hundred leaders of various revolutionary groups to be arrested on Easter Monday.

Pearse and Connolly knew the insurrectionists would have to move or be crushed for another generation. At 10 a.m. on Easter Monday, 24 April 1916, only 1,500 men of the Dublin Volunteer Brigade and of the Citizen Army answered the call to parade. MacNeill's countermanding orders had been obeyed by the majority of the Volunteers. Outside Dublin a Volunteer force from Louth carried out a series of 'flying-column attacks' and severed the Belfast–Dublin railway line. In Co. Wexford 600 men under Commandant Robert Brennan occupied Enniscorthy until outnumbered when they retired to Vinegar Hill before surrendering. In Galway, Liam Mellowes led 1,000 men in destroying bridges, cutting telegraph wires and attacking barracks. They captured Athenry but were encircled at Moyvore by troops. Mellowes decided to stand and fight but priests persuaded his men to disperse and surrender and Mellowes took to the hills.

Connolly, as well as vice-president of the provisional government, was appointed Commandant-General and commander of all the insurgent forces fighting in Dublin. Michael Mallin, secretary of the Silk Weavers Union, was appointed Commandant of the Citizen Army. Miss Helena Molony, secretary of the Irish Women Workers Union, headed a women's nursing section of the army. The Citizen Army numbered 220 men of which 38 men and one woman, Connolly's secretary Miss Winifred Carney, were in the insurgents' GHQ in the General Post Office building in O'Connell Street.

The insurgents' plan was simple. The General Post Office in central Dublin was to be seized and the Provisional Government established there. The main road from Dun Laoghaire (then Kingstown), by which troops landing from England would have to pass, was covered by the Third Battalion commanded by the Dublin Brigade Adjutant, Eamonn de Valera. The First Battalion, commanded by Edward Daly, occupied the Four Courts buildings. Thomas MacDonagh and the Second Battalion occupied Jacobs Biscuit Factory while Kingsbridge Station, the terminus of the rail links to the south, was controlled from the South Dublin Union occupied by the Fourth Battalion under Eamonn Ceannt. The Citizen Army occupied St Stephen's

Green and Connolly, with a sense of humour, had his 'Plough
and the Stars' Citizen Army flag hoisted over the Imperial Hotel,
owned by William Martin Murphy. Smaller sections of insurgents occupied encircling positions at railway termini and other
strategic points. Connolly commented: 'From the moment the
first shot is fired there will be no longer Volunteers or Citizen
Army but only the Army of the Irish Republic.' As he left Liberty
Hall, the ITGWU headquarters, that Easter Monday, Connolly
whispered to his friend William O'Brien: 'We are going out to
be slaughtered.' O'Brien asked: 'Is there no chance of success?'
Connolly replied: 'None whatever.'

At noon on Easter Monday, 24 April 1916, the proclamation
of the Irish Republic was read to the amazed citizens of Dublin
while a transmitter on top of the GPO broadcast the fact to the
world.

The insurgents held stubbornly to their positions as thousands
of British troops poured into the capital. On Thursday, 27 April,
the British brought their artillery into play against the GPO, and
the insurgents' GHQ became cut off from the outlying positions.
Surrounded by burning buildings and a hail of gunfire and
artillery shelling, Connolly led thirty volunteers out into a street
at the rear of the building to erect a barricade. Directing operations he suddenly stopped in mid-order, paused, then resumed
command in the same firm voice. He stood for a few minutes to
to make sure the barricade was built correctly, then returned to
the GPO and went to the hospital section. He asked the medical
orderly, Jim Ryan, if they could go some place privately. Behind
a screen Connolly revealed he had been shot in the arm. After
having the wound dressed he told Ryan: 'Not a word about this
to anyone.'

He immediately returned to his men at the barricade and
organized them into an assault party to take a new position to
meet the British offensive. Standing in the open he encouraged
his men forward. After making sure they had reached their new
positions safely, he made to return to the GPO. A bullet suddenly hit the pavement, richocheted into his left ankle and he
fell. For a moment he was tempted to call for help but he realized
that this would attract British snipers, so, in agony, he began to

drag himself towards the GPO. Some of his men saw him and he was carried inside and placed in the makeshift hospital. A captured British army doctor applied a tourniquet and an attempt was made to sort out the jumble of bone fragments – the bullet had smashed the bone just above the ankle. Connolly was given a weak solution of chloroform and later morphine to stop the pain, although, despite the morphine, he kept waking. After an agonizing night Connolly insisted on having his bed wheeled into the main part of the GPO to be with his men. He also dictated a communiqué to his secretary, Winifred Carney, in an attempt to boost the insurgents' morale: 'Never had a man or woman a grander cause; never was a cause more grandly served.' Later, on Friday 28 April, as fires began to take hold of the GPO, Pearse delivered his final message to the insurgent troops in which he paid a special tribute to Connolly who 'lies wounded but is still the guiding brain of our resistance – if we accomplish no more than we have accomplished, I am satisfied. I am satisfied that we have saved Ireland's honour.'

With the insurgents' GHQ on fire a plan of evacuation was made, the women of the nursing auxiliary, the Cumann na mBan, were dismissed, but three women insisted on remaining – Winifred Carney, and two nurses, Elizabeth O'Farrell and Julia Grenan. The wounded, with the exception of Connolly, were also evacuated. At 8.40 p.m. the main body of insurgents evacuated the GPO. Pearse stood in the street, indifferent to bullets, and directed the evacuation as Connolly was carried across the street on a stretcher. On one side of him a young boy of the Fianna Eireann ran alongside sheltering Connolly with his own body while Winifred Carney sheltered his other side. A new GHQ was established at 16 Moore Street.

Connolly's leg, however, was becoming more gangrenous by the hour. There were also seventeen other wounded in Moore Street who, without proper medical care, would soon be vulnerable to complications. The insurgents were surrounded and cut off from their other positions and the British were about to launch an artillery attack on the Moore Street area where hundreds of civilians were sheltering as well as insurgents. Pearse and Connolly agreed to an unconditional surrender at 2.30 p.m.

on 30 April 'in order to prevent the further slaughter of Dublin citizens and in the hope of saving the lives of our followers now surrounded and hopelessly outnumbered'. Winifred Carney asked Connolly: 'Is there no other way?' Connolly replied: 'I cannot bear to see all these brave boys burn to death. There is no other way.'

Some 1,351 people had been killed or seriously wounded and 179 buildings in central Dublin alone had been utterly destroyed. The total damage costs were initially estimated at two and a half million pounds and a third of Dublin's citizens were demanding public relief. Ninety insurgents, including all the leaders, were tried and sentenced to death by secret court-martial. Thousands more were shipped off to prison camps in England. The executions began on 3 May when Pádraic Pearse, Thomas MacDonagh and Tom Clarke were shot. On 4 May Joseph Plunkett, Edward Daly, Willie Pearse (Pádraic's young brother) and Michael O'Hanrahan were shot. On 5 May John MacBride was shot. On 8 May Eamonn Ceannt, Michael Mallin, Seán Heuston and Con Colbert were shot. On 9 May Thomas Ceannt was executed in Cork.

By Monday 1 May gangrene had taken a firm hold on Connolly's leg and pain was precluding sleep, even with morphine. Connolly felt himself slipping away from life. In accordance with his religious beliefs as a Catholic, he sent for Father Aloysius, a Capuchin friar whose *aide-mémoire* on the interview was not published until 1942. Connolly retracted none of his political beliefs as was subsequently insinuated. He merely carried forward his own, oft-stated belief, that one could be a Marxist in politics and a Catholic in religion without any question of conflict. He accordingly received absolution. On 9 May the military authorities propped him up in his bed and court-martialled him. Connolly made no defence and merely contented himself with rejecting unjust allegations that he had ill-treated prisoners. He told the court-martial:

We went out to break the connection between this country and the British Empire and to establish an Irish Republic. We believed that the call we then issued to the people of Ireland, was a nobler call, in a holier cause, than any call issued to them during this war, having any connection with the war. We succeeded in proving that Irishmen are ready to die endeavouring to win for Ireland those national rights which the British Government has been asking them to die to win for Belgium. As long as that remains the case, the cause of Irish freedom is safe.

Believing that the British Government has no right in Ireland, never had any right in Ireland, and never can have any right in Ireland, the presence, in any one generation of Irishmen, of even a respectable minority, ready to die to affirm that truth, makes that Government for ever an usurpation and a crime against human progress.

On 12 May Connolly was carried on a stretcher to the yard of Kilmainham Jail, Dublin. Seán MacDiarmada, crippled with arthritis, was shot first. Then Connolly was taken from the stretcher, sat in a chair, to which he was strapped to keep him upright, and shot.

HIS WORK

Because of the drama of events of Easter Week 1916, Connolly has been known mainly for his synthesis of nationalism and socialism. At the time, with the significant exception of Lenin, who grasped the importance of the uprising, the world's socialist leaders looked on Connolly's part in a 'nationalist' uprising with almost total incomprehension. Among British socialists, who unfortunately never seemed to have grasped the problem of imperialism and nationalism when applied to their Celtic neighbours, there was a complete lack of understanding. In fact, Arthur Henderson, the British Labour leader, was a member of the Cabinet responsible for the executions. Tom Johnston writing in *Forward*, 6 May 1916, confessed '. . . it is all a mystery to me.' He added: 'He may, of course, have changed his views.' The idea that Connolly changed his beliefs was further endorsed by the playwright Seán O'Casey who, having resigned as secretary of the Irish Citizen Army, accused Connolly of stepping from 'the narrow by-ways of Irish socialism' to 'the crowded highways of Irish nationalism'. O'Casey maintained that 'the higher creed of international humanity' had lost Connolly. But had it? There was in fact no contradiction at all on Connolly's part in the 1916 uprising and the teachings he had propounded all his life. He had long taught that nationalism, by which he meant the advocation of the freedom of a nation from the cultural, political and economic exploitation by another nation, was inseparable from the achievement of a true socialist society. National and social freedom were not two separate and unrelated issues but were two sides of one great democratic principle, each being incomplete without the other. His part in 1916 was merely the logical progression of his life's work and teachings.

Early in his career, writing in the *Labour Leader*, January 1898, Connolly maintained:

> ... under a Socialist system every nation will be the supreme arbiter of its own destinies, national and international; will be forced into no alliance against its will, but will have its independence guaranteed and its freedom respected by the enlightened self-interest of the social democracy of the world.

During his famous controversy with Walker of the Independent Labour Party, Connolly, writing in *Forward*, May/June 1911, reiterated:

> The internationalism of the future will be based upon the free federation of free peoples and cannot be realized through the subjugation of the smaller by the larger political unit.

He had come to one of the basic precepts of Lenin's thought on the matter. In one of his major works on self-determination for all nationalities (*The Socialist Revolution and the Right of Nations to Self Determination*) Lenin wrote:

> Victorious Socialism must achieve complete democracy and, consequently, not only bring about complete equality of nations, but also give effect to the right of oppressed nations to self-determination, i.e. the right of free political secession. Socialist Parties which fail to prove by all their activities now, as well as during the revolution and after its victory, that they will free the enslaved nations or establish relations with them on the basis of free union – and a free union is a lying phrase without right to secession – such parties would be committing treachery to Socialism.

Writing the year after the 1916 uprising, Lenin made his message clear:

The principal condition of a democratic peace is the renunciation of claims of annexation. This must not be wrongly understood in the sense that all powers should recover what they have lost, but according to the only true meaning, which is that every nationality without exception in Europe and in the colonies should obtain freedom ...

With regard to the specific question of Irish independence, Marx had long ago felt

... it is the direct and absolute interest of the English working class to get rid of their present connection with Ireland ... The English working class will never do anything before it has got rid of Ireland. The wedge must be driven in in Ireland. That is why the Irish question is of such importance for the Socialist movement generally. (Marx's letter to Engels, 10 December 1869)

Although the majority of British socialists looked at Connolly's stand against imperialism with almost total incomprehension, there were, of course, some notable exceptions. One of the most prominent was the Clydeside socialist leader John Maclean (1879–1923), who was then a member of the executive of the British Socialist Party. In 1916 he was in prison for his anti-war propaganda. Maclean was to spend many years in prison for his beliefs and this imprisonment was eventually to cause his early death. Influenced by Connolly he tried to combine the national struggle in Scotland to the socialist struggle and formed the Scottish Workers' Republican Party in the year of his death. Among others who clearly understood Connolly's action was the English socialist historian T. A. Jackson. But while the majority in Britain did not understand, European socialists dismissed the rising merely as a 'putsch' (A. Kulisher in *Rech* no. 102). G. V. Plekhánov, the first exponent of Russian Marxism, whose speech at the first congress of the Second International in 1889 inspired many Russian revolutionists but who, due to increasing egocentricity, came into conflict with Lenin, dismissed 1916 as 'positively harmful'. In his article in *Nashe Slovo*, 4 July 1916, Leon Trotsky commented that Plekhánov's remarks were 'wretched and shameful' but 'the experience of the Irish national uprising is over ... the historic role of the Irish proletariat is just beginning'.

Already into this uprising, under an archaic banner, it has carried its class indignation against militarism and imperialism. That indignation, from now on, will not subside. On the contrary, it will find an echo throughout Great Britain. Scottish soldiers smashed the Dublin barricades, but in Scotland itself miners are rallying around the red banner raised by John Maclean and his comrades. Those very workers whom, at the moment, Henderson is trying to chain to the bloody chariot of imperialism, will revenge themselves against the hangman Lloyd George.

Only Lenin, writing in *Berner Tagwacht*, 9 May 1916, seems to have completely grasped Connolly's position.

The term 'putsch' in the scientific sense of the word, may be employed only when the attempt at insurrection has revealed nothing but a circle of conspirators or stupid maniacs, and has aroused no sympathy among the masses. The centuries old Irish national movement, having passed through various stages and combinations of class interests, expressed itself, incidentally in a mass Irish National Congress in America (*Vorwärts*, 20 May 1916) which called for independence, expressed itself in street fighting conducted by a section of the urban petty bourgeoisie and a section of the workers after a long period of mass agitation, demonstrations, suppression of the press etc. Whoever calls such an uprising a 'putsch' is either a hardened reactionary or a doctrinaire hopelessly incapable of picturing a social revolution as a living thing.

For to imagine that social revolution is conceivable without revolts by small nations in the colonies and in Europe, without the revolutionary outbursts of a section of the petty bourgeoisie with all its prejudices and semi-proletarian masses against landlord, church, monarchial, national and other oppressions – to imagine that means repudiating social revolution. Very likely one army will line up in one place and say 'we are for socialism' while another will do so in another place and say 'we are for imperialism' and that will be the social revolution. Only from such a ridiculously pedantic angle could one label the Irish rebellion a 'putsch'.

Whoever expects a 'pure' social revolution will never live to see it. Such a person pays lip service to revolution without understanding what revolution is.

Lenin argues:

... the struggle of the oppressed nations of Europe, a struggle capable of growing to the length of insurrection and street fighting, of breaking down the iron discipline in the army and martial law, will sharpen the revolutionary crisis in Europe more than a much more developed rebellion in a remote colony. A blow delivered against the British imperialist bourgeois rule by a rebellion in Ireland is of a hundred times greater political significance than a blow of equal weight in Asia or Africa.

However, Lenin felt:

The misfortune of the Irish is that they have risen prematurely when the European revolt of the proletariat has not yet matured. Capitalism is not so harmoniously built that the various springs of rebellion can of themselves merge at one effort without reverses and defeats.

While Connolly was trying to make socialists see the importance of anti-imperialist struggles, he was, at the same time, trying to make nationalists see the importance of tying their anti-imperialism to the socialist movement. Writing in *Shan Van Vocht*, January 1897, Connolly made what has become a profound prophecy for the modern Irish State.

If you remove the English army tomorrow and hoist the green flag over Dublin Castle, unless you set about the organization of the Socialist Republic, your efforts would be in vain.
England would still rule you. She would rule you through her capitalists, through her landlords, through her financiers, through her array of commercial and individualist institutions she has planted in this country . . .

Connolly's position is best summed up in an article he wrote for the *Workers' Republic*, 5 August 1899:

We mean to be free, and in every enemy of tyranny we recognize a brother, wherever be his birthplace; in every enemy of freedom we also recognize our enemy, though he were as Irish as our hills. The whole of Ireland for the people of Ireland – their public property, to be owned and operated as a national heritage, by the labour of free men in a free country.

And when Connolly talked about 'the freedom of Ireland' he made clear what it was he meant to free. Writing in *Workers' Republic*, 7 July 1900, he stated:

Ireland without her people is nothing to me, and the man who is bubbling over with love and enthusiasm for 'Ireland' and can yet pass unmoved through our streets and witness all the wrong and suffering, the shame and degradation wrought upon the people of Ireland, aye, wrought by Irishmen upon Irish men and women, without burning to end it, is in my opinion, a fraud and a liar in his heart, no matter how he loves that combination of chemical elements which he is pleased to call 'Ireland'.

In this collection I have selected seven essays which I believe introduces the reader to the essentials of Connolly's thought on the matter.

Perhaps Connolly's most important pioneering theoretical work was on the religious question. The son of Irish Catholics, a Catholic himself, Connolly lived in a country where the Catholic Church was an important factor in everyday life. As a man who believed strongly in the basic principles of Christianity, Connolly felt it ridiculous that the Church Hierarchy and clergy should be considered as possessing special status when making pronouncements on matters outside the theological realm and should therefore be exempt from analysis and criticism. Catholicism and Marxism are still held to be mutually exclusive and Connolly was much misunderstood and misinterpreted in his assertion that one could be a Catholic in religion while, at the same time, a Marxist in political ideology. For Connolly, socialism was a practical and economic question, a science like pure mathematics, whose validity could be discussed without involving questions of theism, atheism or the dogmas of institutionalized Christianity. Politics, as Connolly pointed out in *The New Evangel*, was a question of the stomach and not the brain. Socialism and religion could and must coexist.

By 1901, with the publication of *The New Evangel*, Connolly had already formed his basic theory:

Socialism, as a party, bases itself upon its knowledge of facts, of economic truths, and leaves the building up of religious ideals or faiths to the outside public, or to its individual members if they so will. It is neither Freethinker, nor Christian, Turk nor Jew, Buddhist nor Idolator, Mahommedan nor Parsee – it is only HUMAN.

Connolly's personal belief was that early Christian teaching proposed the same ethics as socialism and therefore he believed that for those who accepted the original Christian ethic the logical place for them was in the socialist movement. Connolly was well acquainted with the writings of the early Catholic Church leaders and he used their writings to good effect. He showed that it was not Pierre-Joseph Proudhon who coined the phrase 'Property is theft' in his book *What is Property?* which appeared in 1840 and so impressed Marx. St Basil said it centuries before and St John Chrysostom echoed it with the statement 'The rich man is a thief.' According to St Ambrose 'only unjust usurpation has created the right of private property'. He goes further:

The bread which the rich eat belongs to others more than to them. They live on stolen goods. What they pay comes from what they have seized ... You have gold dug up from the mines, only to re-bury it. And how many lives are buried with it! And this wealth is kept for whom? For your heir, who waits idly by to receive it ... It is not the poor who are cursed, but the rich. Scripture says of the rich, not of the poor, that the man who increased the price of corn will be cursed ... Who is the wise man? The one who shows compassion to the poor, who sees the poor as natural members of his family.

Early Christianity was clearly a struggle of the oppressed, the poor against the rich man and his exploitation. St Isidore warned that 'those who oppress the poor must know that their sentence is heavier because of those they try to hurt. The more they press their power over these wretched lives the more terrible their future condemnation and punishment will be.' The early Christian Church, to Connolly, was communistic in the broadest sense. It did not believe in the exclusive ownership of property and owned all things in common, the poor receiving what they needed from the common holdings. As Tertullian wrote: 'We who share one mind and soul obviously have no misgivings about community in property.' *The Didache* states: 'Share everything with your brother. Do not say "It is private property." If you share what is everlasting, you should be that much more willing to share things which do not last.' The liberation of the poor and oppressed was a cardinal tenet of Christian belief and practice but in the overthrow of the oppressors the weapon of non-violence was to be used. 'It is certainly a greater and more wonderful work to change the minds of enemies, bringing about a change of soul, than to kill them,' says St John Chrysostom. The Canonical decrees compiled by St Hippolytus order that 'Christians are not to become soldiers voluntarily ... He who carries a sword must be sure that he does not shed blood. If he does shed blood, he must not participate in the sacraments.' St Cyprian dryly commented: 'If a murder is committed privately it is considered a crime. But if it happens with the authority of the state, they call it courage!'

While Connolly was pioneering the idea that socialism was not anti-Christian but, on the contrary, had much in keeping with the original Christian ethic, a similar move to establish a synthesis between Catholicism and socialism was taking place on the Continent although it would seem Connolly was unaware of this. The Westphalian Wilhelm Hohoff (1848–1923), who had been ordained in 1871 and became parish priest of Petershagen, asserted that far from being the antithesis of each other, Catholicism and socialism could mutually support each other. Hohoff and Connolly differed in their approach in that Hohoff was merely a theoretician whilst Connolly, a worker writing for workers, did not divorce theory from practice. Hohoff and Connolly differed also over one conclusion. It was Hohoff's assessment that the Catholic Church had never admitted the justice of interest on money or capital but had merely tolerated it. Connolly's attitude was that the Church not only tolerated it but permitted, authorized and accepted interest on capital. His attitude was clear. He maintained that 'should the clergy at any time profess or teach doctrine not in conformity with the true teachings of Catholicity it is not only the right but it is the absolute duty of the laity to refuse such doctrines and to disobey such teachings'.

Again it must be emphasized that in religion Connolly was a Catholic and when he attacked the Church he did so with a disgust not for the ideology of its religion but for the way that religion had been debased, harnessed for the service of the aggrandizement of the few and re-interpreted in ways that insulted God and man. Connolly was horrified by what he saw as the prostitution of the Catholic Church in the interests of capitalism. Writing in *The Harp*, January 1909, he stated.

> It is not Socialism but capitalism that is opposed to religion; capitalism is social cannibalism, the devouring of man by man, and under capitalism those who have the most of the pious attributes which are required for a truly deeply religious nature are the greatest failures and the heaviest sufferers.
>
> Religion, I hope, is not bound up with a system founded on buying human labour in the cheapest market, and selling its product in the dearest; when the organized Socialist working class tramples upon the capitalist class it will not be trampling upon a pillar of God's Church but upon a blasphemous defiler of the Sanctuary, it will be rescuing the Faith from the impious vermin who made it noisome to the really religious men and women.

In this we find an echo of the teachings of Christ when he threw the money lenders and merchants, selling religious paraphernalia, out of the temple: 'Take these things hence; make not my Father's house an house of merchandise.' (John ii, 16) In fact, it would seem that Connolly was one of the most staunch defenders of spiritual values in a world hellbent on materialism. In his excellent analysis of Connolly's views on religion Dudley Edwards, in *The Mind of An Activist – James Connolly*, rightly points out that what is true of Connolly's day is even more true of our modern world where the materialistic ethic subordinates all else to its will. It is ironic that Connolly was denounced as 'materialistic' by those Church leaders who misunderstood the basic precepts of Marxism, while they themselves were perpetuating a system which sought to destroy true Christian values. It is worth pointing out that 'materialism' has a precise philosophical meaning and does not, when used by Marxists, refer to an emphasis on manufactured goods, financial success and physical pleasure. Not until the pontificate of John XXIII has recognition been given to the fact that Marxists have been more concerned with spiritual welfare in a way that should shame the pious 'spiritual leaders'.

Connolly's Catholicism made him revolt at the sanctimonious efforts of capitalism and its defenders to justify the exploitation of man by appealing to a divine plan – that, in reality, God was responsible for the enslavement of the working classes. Connolly, no more as a socialist than as a Catholic, refused to ascribe to God the crimes of man and saw God's place in history as a force that would rally man to hurl himself against mammon. Christ has clearly taught: 'You cannot serve God and mammon.' (St Matthew vi, 24) Connolly's remarkable concept of man's responsibility in history placed him greatly in advance of his contemporary fellow Catholics ... even of such intellectuals as G. K. Chesterton and Hilaire Belloc.

Connolly, naturally enough, was often accused of being anti-clerical because he treated the clergy as men prone to mistakes and misconceptions. Most Catholics would believe that a statement from a priest was a pronouncement from God. His fellow socialists did not attempt to alter this situation as many of them refused to discuss theoretical questions of socialism with priests on equal terms, basing their attitude on the assumption that a priest's cloth made him 'different'. Connolly regarded any man worthy of courteous discourse and it was such debates with priests that gave rise to many of his tracts on the subject of Catholicism and socialism, debates such as his reply to M. J. O'Donnell DD, Father Finlay SJ and, of course, his reply to the Lenten Discourses against socialism given by the Jesuit Father Kane which produced *Labour, Nationality and Religion*. I have chosen to include this work in its entirety as I believe it is Connolly's major theoretical work. It raises and answers a number of questions as to the nature of socialism with Connolly pointing out the similarities between the foundation of Christianity and of the socialist movement. Pursuing a line used by Friedrich Engels, in his essay on early Christianity, Connolly emphasizes that Christianity began as a struggle of the oppressed, reflected in the social doctrines of early Church leaders. Therefore, he maintained, for those who accepted the original Christian ethic the logical place for them was in the socialist movement.

The next most important group of writings are Connolly's ideas on trade unionism and industrial unionism. As one of the early members and organizers of the syndicalist Industrial Workers of the World, Connolly, especially through his *Socialism Made Easy*, pioneered the concepts of industrial unionism not only in the USA but in Ireland, Britain and Australia. His work in this field has been dismissed, even by his biographer C. D. Greaves, as merely a step in his mental evolution, the principles of which he afterwards abandoned. But Connolly never abandoned his views on syndicalism. He saw the Irish Transport and General Workers Union as the 'one big union' which could be used as both an industrial and military force by which to establish an independent socialist State in Ireland. His work in this field shows a bold creative thinking but has a certain weakness in an incomplete analysis of the nature of the capitalist state. Connolly felt:

> ... the enrolment of the workers in unions patterned closely after the structure of modern industries, and following the organic lines of industrial development, is *par excellence*, the swiftest, safest and most peaceful form of constructive work the Socialist can engage in. It prepares within the framework of capitalist society the working forms of the Socialist Republic, and thus, while increasing the resisting power of the worker against present encroachments of the capitalist class, it familiarizes him with the idea that the union he is helping to build up is destined to supplant that class in the control of the industry in which he is employed.
>
> The power of this idea to transform the dry detail work of trade union organization into the constructive work of revolutionary socialism and thus to make the unimaginative trade unionist a potent factor in the launching of a new system of society cannot be overestimated ... (*Socialism Made Easy*)

Connolly was advocating industrial unionism to within a few months of his execution and nowhere can I find evidence of him dropping or renouncing it. He advocates it in his *The Reconquest of Ireland*, published in 1915, in which he propounds the thesis that the chief task of the Irish working class is the reconquest of the country from British imperialism and its native allies. In this work, mapping out the approaching national and social struggle, Connolly maintains his belief in industrial unionism. This was, of course, criticized by Professor A. D. Kolpakov of Moscow State University in his introduction to the 1970 Russian translation of Connolly's work. Kolpakov dismisses it as 'his anarcho-syndicalist mistakes' from which Connolly 'gradually freed himself'.

Connolly was worried by the way trade unionism was developing in Britain and Ireland. He complained of 'the tendency in the labour movement to mistake mere concentration upon the industrial field for essentially revolutionary advance'. Growth and amalgamation was then rampant in unionism in Britain but, instead of hastening the advent of socialism, this only meant that trade unions were 'becoming engines for ... suppressing all manifestations of revolutionary activity'. Prophesying the future of trade unionism in Britain, Connolly wrote: 'The greater unionism is found in short to be forging greater fetters for the working class; to bear to the real revolutionary industrial unionism the same relation as the servile state would be to the Co-operative Commonwealth of our dreams.' In introducing Connolly's ideas on the subject I have included two sections from *Socialism Made Easy*, and the articles 'Old Wine in New Bottles', 'Industrialism and the Trade Unions' and 'The Problem of Trade Union Organization'.

Connolly was an avowed feminist and supporter of women's rights. He takes his place as a stronger advocate of female emancipation than most socialist theorists of his time. He was probably influenced in this field by Francis Sheehy-Skeffington, the Irish socialist, pacifist and crusader for women's rights. Connolly spoke on many a women's suffrage platform and his leadership of the Belfast millgirls' strike is well known. Countess Markievicz, the only woman to fight as a combatant in the 1916 uprising, as a lieutenant in the Citizen Army, was one of his most ardent disciples. She was to become the first woman elected to the United Kingdom Parliament in 1918 on the Sinn Féin abstentionist ticket and was the first Irish Minister for Labour in the revolutionary Dail of 1919. Connolly's chapter 'Woman' from *The Reconquest of Ireland*, included here, gives a clear statement of his views.

Because of the part he played in the 1916 uprising, it was alleged that Connolly 'suddenly ... ran amok for a bloody revolution' and that he was a militarist. Connolly passionately hated war. This much is evident from his writings. Pádraic Pearse wrote, in December 1915:

The last sixteen months have been the most glorious in the history of Europe. Heroism has come back to the earth ... the old heart of the earth needed to be warmed with the red wine of the battlefields. Such august homage was never before offered to God as this, the homage of millions of lives given gladly for love of country.

Connolly's reaction was 'blitherin' idiot'! Writing in *The Worker*, 30 January 1915, he said:

... there is no such thing as humane or civilized war. War may be forced upon a subject race or subject class to put an end to subjection of race, class or sex. When so waged it must be waged thoroughly and relentlessly, but with no delusion as to its elevating nature, or civilizing methods.

But while Connolly was anti-war he was also a political realist. Writing in *Forward*, 14 March 1914, he pointed out

To my mind an agitation to attain a political or economic end must rest upon an implied willingness and ability to use force. Without that it is mere wind and attitudinizing.

Believing only an insurrection was the next logical step in Ireland's fight for national and social freedom, he gave clear warning of his intentions: 'We believe in constitutional action in normal times; we believe in revolutionary action in exceptional times. These are exceptional times.' To prepare himself he made a study of insurgency fighting and, during 1915, published a series of articles by which to prepare his Citizen Army. These have subsequently been republished as *Revolutionary Warfare*. Of all the 1916 leaders Connolly showed himself to be the most prepared and practical as regards organizing military resistance. The fact that the insurgents managed to hold out for as long as they did is mainly due to the methods propagated in his studies, through his articles and lectures to the Citizen Army and the Volunteers. I have included his article on the 'Moscow Insurrection of 1905', the lessons of which are clearly underlined in 'Street Fighting – Summary', because the parallels to the Dublin insurrection are clear. It has been popularly stated that Connolly believed that British troops would not use artillery in Dublin because capitalists would hesitate to destroy capitalist property.

A reading of these excerpts from his studies on revolutionary warfare shows that Connolly could not have entertained any such naïve notion. Like Engels, who developed a knowledge of the science of warfare, Connolly displayed a talent as a proficient military scientist. He seems to have formed his own conclusions for there is no evidence that he studied Engels' writings in this respect. The basic concepts to which Connolly came have been used time and again in insurgency struggles throughout the world. I have divided his thoughts on warfare into two groups – 'War and Revolutionary Warfare' and his analysis of the 'First World War'.

Owen Dudley Edwards, writing on recent events in Northern Ireland, states:

> Connolly between 1968 and 1971 moved from the lecture room to the streets, and the insight his writings exhibited in the analysis of industrial Ulster proved all too relevant in the work commenced by courageous young people no longer content to leave Connolly in the shrine of inactive piety to which he had been consigned by their cautious seniors.

Connolly saw the partition of Ireland as a means of dividing the Irish working class. His analysis is as relevant today as ever it was and, in view of the guerrilla struggle in Northern Ireland, the inclusion of his views on the partition adds an important contribution to the understanding of the situation.

I have included in this volume Connolly's thoughts on the Irish language question. Ireland's language and culture had suffered under centuries of imperialist persecution so that its very existence was, and still is, threatened. Until the famine years of the 1840s it had been the majority language of the people; a language enshrining a vast literary wealth, containing Europe's oldest vernacular literature and being Europe's oldest written language after Greek and Latin. During the late nineteenth century various movements were organized to restore the language. In this respect Ireland became part of a general European movement of small dominated nations who began to go through a 'cultural rebirth', struggling to restore their languages and the culture enshrined in them. Many of these nations, Lithuania,

Latvia, Estonia, Armenia, Finland, Norway, Slovenia, Albania, the Faroes, etc., have succeeded in achieving successful language restorations. The linguistic struggles in many of these countries were spearheaded by socialists who saw the destruction of the people's language and culture as one of the most evil and most direct consequences of imperialism. Connolly's first judgement of the language struggle in Ireland, in 1898, was cautious and, although he saw the replacement of the Irish language as a fulfilment of Marx's observation that 'capitalism creates a world after its own image', he observed 'you cannot teach starving men Gaelic'. However, Connolly called upon the language revivalists to recognize the socialists as 'your natural allies'. In the *Workers' Republic* of March 1903, he wrote:

... those who drop Irish in favour of English are generally actuated by the meanest of motives, are lick spittles desirous of aping the gentry, whereas the rank and file of the Gaelic movement are for the most part thoroughly democratic in spirit.

While in the USA he crystallized his opinion that the suppression of one language by another was one of the most corrupting aspects of imperialism. In this again he found support from Lenin who believed language was one of the essential principles of nationhood and to those who ridiculed the idea that all languages, especially minority languages, should be safeguarded and education given through them, Lenin held up Switzerland as an example. By this he refuted the pseudo-internationalist argument which wanted all national differences stamped out as a prerequisite for social progress. Lenin showed this seemingly ultra-revolutionary argument was a perverted form of imperialism. Thanks to Lenin's work on the importance of language and culture it is the official policy of the USSR to encourage the continuance of all minor linguistic groups. While Russian, with 125 million native speakers, is naturally becoming more widely spoken in the countries of the USSR, linguistic minorities are actively encouraged from region to region to the extent that some previous unwritten country vernaculars have during the course of this century acquired literary status. For example, Chukchee, spoken by 12,000 people in the extreme north-east of Siberia, in the Krai region, first became a literary language in 1932 and Dargwa, spoken by 108,000 people in the Caucasus, only became a written language after the revolution. There are many other such examples and whatever motives may be ascribed to the Soviet authorities for this encouragement, in accordance with Lenin's ideas, it contrasts very strongly with the attitude of such countries as Britain, France and Spain towards the linguistic minorities within their State borders. It was after Connolly's return from the USA that he set about learning the Irish language and acknowledged that it was a revolutionary force. It is perhaps sad to relate that in spite of fifty years of rule by a native Irish Government which pays lip service to the policy of language revival, in the twenty-six county state of the Irish Republic, Ireland is the only country in Europe pledged to revive its language which has failed utterly in its attempts. Only 27·2 per cent of Ireland's total population spoke Irish in 1970. The spread of Anglo-American capitalist (cocacola) culture has, indeed, created a world after its own image.

From Connolly's attitude towards the Irish language and culture we come to his attitude towards the important part that art and culture plays in revolutionary movements. In his introduction to a collection of verse, containing some of his songs, *Songs of Freedom*, published in New York in 1907, Connolly wrote:

No revolutionary movement is complete without its poetical expression. If such a movement has caught hold of the imagination of the masses, they will seek a vent in song for the aspirations, the fears and hopes, the loves and hatreds engendered by the struggle. Until the movement is marked by the joyous, defiant, singing of revolutionary songs, it lacks one of the most distinct marks of a popular revolutionary movement; it is a dogma of a few, and not the faith of the multitude.

Connolly himself provided many of the revolutionary songs for the socialist movement of his own day. The years 1903–4 were Connolly's most prolific as a verse writer. Many of his songs still exist and are sung by the labour movement of today. It was during this period that he wrote such songs as 'Rebel Song', 'Hymn of Freedom' and 'Watchword of Labour'. These songs were not at first written to Irish airs but to popular Scottish tunes with which Connolly was more familiar. The verses show no great literary merit, Connolly was not another Shelley nor did he have the passionate grave dignity of Ferdinand Freiligrath, one of the original members of Marx's Communist League, and a poet that Friedrich Engels admired and tried to emulate in his own verses. But the sincerity of Connolly's proletarian lyrics is clear – a direct appeal to the heart as well as the head of the workers. While they lacked the technical skill of his mentor, Leslie, or the brilliance of his fellow Irishman John Connell (author of 'The Red Flag') one thing is certain: in common with other great socialist leaders (such as Marx, Engels, Mao Tse-tung, Ho Chi Minh, Che Guevara, etc.) Connolly had a spiritual, creatively poetical side to his nature which, in spite of the social pressures of his life, succeeded in emerging. One of Connolly's most remarkable achievements was the translation of Max Kegel's *Sozialistenmarsch* from German into English verse. In any general collection of Connolly's writings his verse deserves a place and I have included in this selection his poem 'The Legacy', the style of which today's reader might find somewhat passé. It is written in a style popular during the Victorian era, especially in Victorian 'morality poems' which found frequent utterance in music halls. This style, therefore, superficially gives the poem a melodramatic, almost comical quality ... but one must look deeper to the resonant message thundering out in one of Connolly's firmest and fiercest assertions of his Socialist faith.

The creative side of Connolly also manifested itself through essays into purely creative writing, which nevertheless still propagated the beliefs which were near his heart. He wrote at least one short story which was published in the first issue of his *Workers' Republic*, 13 August 1898. It is sad that the scripts of Connolly's two known plays, *The Agitator's Wife*, written in the USA, and *Under Which Flag*, performed at Liberty Hall, Dublin, on 26 March 1916, a few days before the rising, have been lost. Perhaps more systematic searching might bring to light more of his creative writing. Of his literary attempts in the field of playwriting we have a critique by Francis Sheehy-Skeffington.

Writing in *Workers' Republic*, 8 April 1916, Sheehy-Skeffing-ton says that Connolly set *Under Which Flag* during the time of the Fenian uprising 'and it pleasingly blends a picture of simple homely merrymaking Irish song and dance with the serious plot'. The two flags of the title refer to the British flag and the Irish flag. The dramatic conflict centres round a farmer's son called Frank O'Donnell who announces, in Act I, his intention of joining the British army. By Act III his sweetheart, family and an old blind patriot named Brian McMahon have convinced him that his duty lies in joining the revolutionary Irish Republican Brotherhood and fighting for Irish independence. According to Sheehy-Skeffington:

> The dialogue is excellent – entirely unforced and in harmony with the characters depicted. The use of the soliloquy in the second act must, however, be condemned as dramatically inartistic – though Mr Connolly could plead the example of a great English dramatist who is more honoured in Germany than in his own country. Pithy sentences throughout the play embody the author's national creed and drive home the moral; as, for example, 'both soldier and the polisman are traitors; but the polisman is a spy as well', and 'If the soldier is a traitor to Ireland, the emigrant is a deserter'.

Sheehy-Skeffington, in his own newspaper *Irish Citizen* and as correspondent of the *Daily Herald*, provided a significant link between Irish and English socialist journals. Although his pacifism brought him into strong disagreement with Connolly's views on revolutionary warfare, both Sheehy-Skeffington and Connolly enjoyed a strong friendship. According to Dudley Edwards, Connolly had decided to make Sheehy-Skeffington his literary executor while he lay awaiting execution after the 1916 rising. He believed that Sheehy-Skeffington would carry on his gospel and keep the Irish socialist movement to the path he had set for it. According to Dudley Edwards it was Connolly's daughter, Nora, who told her father the terrible news. Sheehy-Skeffington, the pacifist, had been shot during the uprising on the orders of a British officer named Captain J. Bowen-Colthurst. The only part Sheehy-Skeffington had taken in the rising was to organize people in a citizen's police force to prevent the looting which was taking place. He was arrested on the evening of 25

April by a party of military. A raiding party, led by Bowen-Colthurst, then took him as a hostage to be shot if the insurgents fired on them. Returning to Portobello Barracks, Sheehy-Skeffington was witness to Bowen-Colthurst's shooting of a seventeen-year-old boy in cold blood as he lay senseless on the ground. This officer also arrested two other well known Dublin journalists, Thomas Dickson and Patrick McIntyre (both of whom represented violently Loyalist newspapers) and all three were taken to Portobello. On the morning of 26 April, Bowen-Colthurst had the three men taken into the barrack yard and executed. Their bodies were then secretly buried and the wall against which they were shot was immediately repaired. Bowen-Colthurst then conducted a raid on Sheehy-Skeffington's house and placed his wife and seven-year-old son under arrest. Although the Dublin Castle authorities tried to ignore the matter, Major Sir Francis Vane, an army officer, discovering what had occurred, started to press for an inquiry to 'clear the good name of the service'. He took the matter to Lord Kitchener and the Prime Minister but, for his pains, was dismissed from the army on the orders of the GOC of Ireland. Mrs Sheehy-Skeffington, however, pressed the case and because of Sheehy-Skeffington's reputation a court martial was convened on 6 June and accepted that Bowen-Colthurst was of unsound mind at the time of the act. Public opinion finally forced a Royal Commission on the matter which began its sittings on 23 August. Its report was apologetic and Mrs Sheehy-Skeffington was offered financial compensation which she refused. The death of Sheehy-Skeffington was a bitter blow to Connolly in his final hours.

Connolly has been described by his biographer C. D. Greaves as one of the most important figures of 'the middle stage of the world labour history'. He was indeed one of the first great working-class intellectuals. In his magnum opus – *Labour in Irish History*, 1910 – Connolly revealed himself to be an outstanding and original Marxist historian and the first person to apply the Marxist method of analysis to the study of Irish history. Because he was not an academic, one cannot help but be impressed with the effort which went to complete such a work – the research and the scholarship which were involved. The book remains of major importance today. It did not pretend to be an all-embracing treatment and analysis of events; Connolly claimed he was not writing the history of the Irish working class but merely a clarification of their place in Irish history. Connolly, however, had a slight tendency – characteristic of most early Marxist works – to gravitate to a purely economic explanation of historical events. Engels himself warned against this, saying elements in the superstructure can exert an important and often decisive influence on the historical struggle.

As a Marxist Connolly accepted the Marxist analysis of society and nowhere did he attempt to dilute or change it. But to Connolly Marxism was not some dogma or some new plan for a system ... it was a method of analysis, a science, with the objective of taking action. Indeed, Engels saw it as 'nothing more than the science of the general laws of motion and development of nature, human society and thought'. As did Lenin and Mao Tse-tung, Connolly accepted Marxism as a basic philosophy and guide. He set about applying that philosophy and guiding principles to Irish conditions as Lenin and Mao so applied them to their own countries and their own cultures.

In this selection of his writings I have sought merely to provide a general introduction to Connolly's life and work. The fact that Connolly's work is still very much of relevance today does not mean that his writings should be treated as some holy writ and quoted as a solution for all problems. Connolly would be the first to attack unquestioning loyalty and dogmatization. Writing in *Workers' Republic*, 5 August 1899, Connolly said:

We are told to imitate Wolfe Tone, but the greatness of Wolfe Tone lay in the fact that he imitated nobody. The needs of his time called for a man able to shake from his mind the intellectual fetters of the past, and to unite in his own person the hopes of the new revolutionary faith and the ancient aspirations of an oppressed people ...

That was certainly true of Connolly's day and, tragically, still true of today's situation in Ireland. Speaking of the growing interest in Connolly's works in Ireland today, Owen Dudley Edwards writes:

If they are wise, this and later generations will return to Connolly. And, if their wisdom can transcend the petty wisdom of self-interest, they will go forth from his works with a new clarity of thought and a new radicalism of action. But only by its being theirs, taken in the context of their times and applied with their advantages, can it also be his and thus come closer to realizing his aims. Finally, it must be undertaken with laughter and constant self-mockery. If in a sense of righteousness we give ourselves airs, let us remember that in this we are departing hopelessly from the precept and practice of James Connolly. (*The Mind of an Activist – James Connolly*)

They are sentiments that I, in introducing this selection of Connolly's writings, can only wholeheartedly echo.

I

SOCIALISM AND
CATHOLICISM

LABOUR,
NATIONALITY AND RELIGION

*Being a discussion of the Lenten Discourses against
Socialism delivered by Father Kane, SJ, in Gardiner
Street Church, Dublin, 1910*

Nature furnishes its wealth to all men in common. God beneficently
has created all things that their enjoyment be common to all living
beings, and that the earth become the common property of all . . .
Only unjust usurpation has created the right of private property. *St
Ambrose.*

Let the Pope and cardinals, and all the powers of the Catholic world
united make the least encroachment on that (American) constitution,
we will protect it with our lives. Summon a General Council (of the
Church) – let that council interfere in the mode of our electing but
an assistant to a turnkey of a prison – we deny its right; we reject
its usurpation. Let that council lay a tax of one per cent only upon
our churches – we will not pay it. Yet, we are most obedient Papists
– we believe that the Pope is Christ's vicar on earth, supreme visible
head of the Church throughout the world, and lawful successor of
St Peter, prince of the apostles. We believe all this power is in Pope
Leo XII (then reigning), and we believe that a General Council is
infallible in doctrinal decisions. Yet we deny to Pope and Council
united any power to interfere with one title of our political rights, as
firmly as we deny the power of interfering with one tittle of our
spiritual rights to the President and Congress. We will obey each in
its proper place, we will resist any encroachment by one upon the
right of the other. *Rt Rev. John England, Catholic Bishop of
Charleston, USA*, 1824.

FOREWORD

NOTHING is more conducive to the spread of a movement than
the discussions arising out of the efforts of a capable opponent to
refute its principles. Out of such discussions arises clearness of

thought, and the consequent realization on the part of both sides to the controversy of the necessity of considering the movement under discussion in the light of its *essential principles*, rather than of its accidental accompaniments – the basic ideas of the movement itself rather than the ideas of the men or women who may for the moment be its principal exponents or representatives.

Men perish, but principles live. Hence the recent efforts of ecclesiastics to put the Socialist movement under the ban of the Catholic Church, despite the wild and reckless nature of the statements by which the end was sought to be attained, has had a good effect in compelling Catholics to examine more earnestly their position as laymen, and the status of the clergy as such, as well as their relative duties toward each other within the Church and toward the world in general.

One point of Catholic doctrine brought out as a result of such examination is the almost forgotten, and sedulously suppressed one, that the Catholic Church is theoretically a community in which the clergy are but the officers serving the laity in a common worship and service of God, and that should the clergy at any time profess or teach doctrines not in conformity with the true teachings of Catholicity it is not only the right, but it is the absolute duty of the laity to refuse such doctrines and to disobey such teaching. Indeed, it is this saving clause in Catholic doctrine which has again and again operated to protect the Church from the result of the mistaken attempts of the clergy to control the secular activities of the laity.

It seems to be unavoidable, but it is entirely regrettable, that clergymen consecrated to the worship of God, and supposed to be patterned after a Redeemer who was the embodiment of service and humility, should in their relation to the laity insist upon service and humility being rendered to them instead of by them. Their Master served all mankind in patience and suffering; they insist upon all mankind serving them, and in all questions of the social and political relations of men they require the common laity to bow the neck in a meekness, humility and submission which the clergy scornfully reject. They have often insisted that the Church is greater than the secular authority, and acted therefore in flat defiance of the secular powers, but they have forgotten or ignored the fact that the laity are a part of the Church, and that, therefore, the right of rebellion against injustice so freely claimed by the Papacy and the hierarchy is also the inalienable right of the laity. And history proves that in almost every case in which the political or social aspirations of the laity came into opposition to the will of the clergy the laity represented the best interests of the Church as a whole and of mankind in general.

Whenever the clergy succeeded in conquering political power in any country the result has been disastrous to the interests of religion and inimical to the progress of humanity. From whence we arrive at the conclusion that he serves religion best who insists upon the clergy of the Catholic Church taking their proper position as servants of the laity, and abandoning their attempt to dominate the public, as they have long dominated the private life of their fellow Catholics.

The 1910 Lenten Discourses of Father Kane, SJ, in Gardiner Street Church, Dublin, serve to illustrate these, our contentions. The Socialists of Ireland are grateful to those who induced such a learned and eloquent orator in their capital city to attempt combating Socialism. Had it been an antagonist less worthy their satisfaction would not have been so great. But they now feel confident that when an opponent so capable, so wide in his reading, so skilled in his presentation, so admirable in his method of attack, and so eloquent in his language has said his final word upon the question, they may rest satisfied that the best case against their cause has been presented which can ever be forthcoming under similar auspices. In presenting their arguments against the position of the reverend lecturer – as against his reverend co-workers who all over the world are engaged in the same unworthy task of combating this movement for the uplifting of humanity – we desire, in the spirit of our preceding remarks, to place before our readers a brief statement of some of the many instances in which the Catholic laity have been compelled to take political action contrary to the express commands of the Pope and the Catholic hierarchy, and in which subsequent events or the more enlightened conscience of subsequent ages have fully justified the action of the laity and condemned the action of the clergy.

Most of our readers are aware that the first Anglo-Norman invasion of Ireland, in 1169, an invasion characterized by every kind of treachery, outrage, and indiscriminate massacre of the Irish, took place under the authority of a Bull issued by his Holiness, Pope Adrian IV. Doubt has been cast upon the authenticity of the Bull, but it is certain that neither Adrian nor any of his successors in the Papal chair ever repudiated it.

Every Irish man and woman, most enlightened Englishmen, and practically every foreign nation today wish that the Irish had succeeded in preserving their independence against the English king, Henry II, but at a Synod of the Catholic Church, held in Dublin in 1177, according to Rev. P. J. Carew, Professor of Divinity in Maynooth, in his *Ecclesiastical History of Ireland*, the Legate of Pope Alexander III, 'set forth Henry's right to the sovereignty of Ireland in virtue of the Pope's authority, and inculcated the necessity of obeying him *under pain of excommunication*'. The English were not yet eight years in Ireland, the greater part of the country was still closed to them, but already the Irish were being excommunicated for refusing to become slaves.

In Ireland, as in all Catholic countries, a church was a sanctuary in which even the greatest criminal could take refuge and be free from arrest, as the civil authority could not follow upon the consecrated ground. At the Synod of 1177 the Pope, in order to help the English monarch against the Irish, abolished the right of sanctuary in Ireland, and empowered the English to strip the Irish churches, and to hunt the Irish refugees who sought shelter there. The greatest criminals of Europe were safe once they reached the walls of the church, but not an Irish patriot.

In the year 1319 Edward Bruce, brother of Robert the Bruce of Scotland, was invited into Ireland by the Irish chiefs and people to help them in their patriotic war for independence. He accepted the invitation, was joined by vast numbers of people in arms, and together the Irish and Scotch forces swept the English out of Ulster and Connacht. The English king appealed for help to Pope John XXI, and *that Pontiff responded by at once excommunicating all the Irish who were in arms against the English.*

The Battle of the Boyne, fought 1 July 1690, is generally regarded in Ireland as a disaster for the Irish cause – a disaster which made possible the infliction of two centuries of unspeakable degradation upon the Irish people. Yet that battle was the result of an alliance formed by Pope Innocent XI with William, Prince of Orange, against Louis, King of France. King James of England joined with King Louis to obtain help to save his own throne, and the Pope joined in the league with William to curb the power of France. When the news of the defeat of the Irish at the Boyne reached Rome the Vatican was illuminated by order of the new Pope, Alexander VIII, and special masses offered up in thanksgiving. See Von Ranke's *History of the Popes*, and Murray's *Irish Revolutionary History*.

Judge Maguire, of San Francisco, California, writing of this period before the Reformation, says truly:

Under all their Catholic majesties, from Henry II to Henry VIII (nearly 400 years) the Irish people, with the exception of five families, were outlaws. They were murdered at will, like dogs, by their English Catholic neighbours in Ireland, and there was no law to punish the murderers. Yet during all of this unparalleled reign of terror, history fails to show a single instance in which the power of the Catholic Church was ever exerted or suggested by the Pope for the protection of her faithful Irish children.

The Irish people as a whole are proud of the fact that, according to the reported testimony of General Lee of the American army, more than half of the Continental soldiers during the War of the Revolution were from Ireland, yet during the War of Independence Bishop Troy, the Catholic Bishop of Ossory, ordered the Catholics of his diocese to 'observe a day's fast and to humble himself in prayer that they might avert the *divine wrath provoked by their American fellow-subjects who, seduced by the specious notions of liberty* and other illusive expectations of sovereignty, disclaim any dependence upon Great Britain and endeavour by force of arms to distress their mother country'. Quite recently, in 1909, Professor Monaghan, speaking before the Federation of Catholic Societies in America, declared with the approval of the bishop and clergy that the Catholic Hierarchy of the United States would, if need be, sell the sacred vessels of the altar in defence of the American Republic. *Thus the enlightened opinion of the Catholics of our day condemns the Pastoral of the Catholic bishop of the Revolutionary period and endorses the action of the Catholics who disregard it.*

In 1798 an insurrection in favour of an Irish Republic took place in Ireland, assuming most formidable proportions in County Wexford. The insurrection had been planned by the Society of United Irishmen, many of whose leaders were Protestants and Freethinkers. The Catholic hierarchy and most of the priesthood denounced the society and inculcated loyalty to the Government. The more intelligent of the Catholic masses disregarded these clerical denunciations. In the memoirs of his life, Myles Byrne, a staunch Catholic patriot and revolutionist, who took part in the insurrection, says: 'The priests did everything in their power to stop the progress of the Association of United Irishmen, particularly poor Father John Redmond, who refused to hear the confession of any of the United Irish and turned them away from his knees.' Speaking of Father John Murphy, he says he 'was a worthy, simple pious man and one of those Roman Catholic priests who used the greatest exertions and exhortations to oblige the people to give up their pikes and firearms of every description'. The wisdom of the people and the foolishness of the clergy were amply demonstrated by the fact that the soldiers burned Father Murphy's house over his head, and compelled him to take the field as an insurgent. A heroic fight and a glorious martyrdom atoned for his mistake, but the soldier-like qualities he showed in the field were rendered nugatory by the fact that as a priest he had been instrumental in disarming many hundreds of men whom he afterwards commanded. As an insurgent officer he discovered that his greatest hope lay in the men who had disregarded his commands as a priest, and retained the arms with which to fight for freedom.

Dr Troy, when Catholic Archbishop of Dublin, was, according to an incident related in the *Viceroy's Postbag* by Mr Michael MacDonagh, interrogated by the British authorities as to the duty of a priest who discovered in the confessional a plot against the Government, and answered that, 'if in confession any plot against the existing Government was disclosed to the priest, he (the priest) would be bound to give information to the Government that such plot was in agitation, taking care that nothing could in any way lead to a suspicion of the person from whom or the means in which, the information had been obtained'. Chief Secretary Wickham, who reports this conversation with the archbishop, goes on to say, 'I then asked him whether such confession so made to the priest, particularly in the case of a crime against the State, was considered as a full atonement so as to entitle the penitent to absolution without a disclosure of such crime being made to the police or to the Government of the country. To this the Doctor answered very distinctly that he did not consider the confession to the priest alone, under such circumstances, a sufficient atonement, *and that either the priest ought to insist on such confession to the State or to the police being made,* or to enjoin the making of such disclosure subsequent to absolution in like manner as penance is enjoined under similar circumstances'.

There is little doubt in our mind but that Dr Troy misrepresented Catholic doctrine, but it is noteworthy that a parish priest at Mallow, Co. Cork, ordered a member of the United Irishmen, who had sought him in the confessional to give information to the authorities of a plot of the Royal Meath Militia to seize the artillery at that point and turn it over to the revolutionists. This priest, Father Thomas Barry, afterwards drew a pension of £100 per year from the Government for his information; his action was, and is, abhorred by the vast mass of the Irish Catholics, but was in strict accord with his duty as laid down by Archbishop Troy.

All impartial historians recognize that the Legislative Act of Union between Great Britain and Ireland was passed

> By perjury and fraud
> By slaves who sold
> For place or gold
> Their country and their God.

Yet we are informed by Mr Plowden, a Catholic historian, that 'a very great preponderance in favour of the Union existed in the Catholic Body, *particularly in their nobility, gentry and clergy*'. On 1 March 1800, no less than thirty-two Orange lodges protested against the Act of Union, but the Catholic Hierarchy endorsed it.

Every year the members of the Irish race scattered throughout the earth celebrate the memory of Robert Emmet, and cherish him in their hearts as the highest ideal of patriot and martyr; but on the occasion of his martyrdom the Catholic Archbishops of Dublin and Armagh presented an address to the Lord Lieutenant, representative of the British Government in Ireland, denouncing Emmet in the strongest possible terms. That this action was in conformity with the position of the whole Catholic hierarchy was evidenced in 1808 when all the Catholic bishops of Ireland met in Synod on 14 September, and passed the following resolution, as reported in Haverty's *History of Ireland*: 'That the Roman Catholic prelates pledge themselves to adhere to the rules by which they have been *hitherto uniformly guided*, viz., to recommend to his Holiness (for appointment as Irish Roman Catholic bishops) *only such persons as are of unimpeachable loyalty*.'

After Daniel O'Connell and the Catholics of Ireland had wrested Catholic Emancipation from the British Government they initiated a demand for a repeal of the Union. Their service to Catholic Emancipation was a proof positive of their Catholic orthodoxy, but at the urgent request of the British Government Pope Gregory XVI issued a rescript commanding the priests to abstain from attending the repeal meetings. O'Connell said this was an illegal interference with the liberties of the clergy, declared that he would 'take his religion from Rome, but not his politics', and the Catholic opinion of our day emphatically endorses his attitude and condemns the action of the Pope.

In 1847 the Catholics among the Young Irelanders prepared a memorial to be presented to the annual assembly of the Bishops, defending themselves from the charge of infidelity. The Archbishop of Tuam declared he would retire if they were admitted. *They were not admitted.* Today the memory of the Young Irelanders is held close to the heart of every intelligent Irish man or woman.

During the great Irish famine of 1845–6–7–8–9 the Irish people died in hundreds of thousands of hunger, whilst there was food enough in the country to feed three times the population. When the starving peasantry was called upon to refuse to pay rent to idle landlords, and to rise in revolt against the system which was murdering them, the clergy commanded them to pay their rents, instructed them that they would lose their immortal souls should they refuse to do so, and threw all the weight of their position against the revolutionary movement for the freedom of Ireland. Mr A. M. Sullivan, an extremely ardent Catholic, writing in *New Ireland* says of this attitude of the clergy during that crisis that, 'Their antagonism was fatal to the movement – more surely and infallibly fatal to it, than all the powers of the British Crown'.

The Irish revolutionary movement, known popularly as the Fenian Brotherhood, was denounced by all the Catholic hierarchy and most of the clergy, Bishop Moriarty of County Kerry saying that 'Hell was not hot enough nor eternity long enough to punish such miscreants'. The Fenians were represented as being enemies of religion and of morality, yet the three representatives of their cause who died upon the scaffold died with a prayer upon their lips, and Irish men and women the world over today make the anniversary of their martyrdom the occasion for a glorification and endorsement of the principles for which they died – a glorification and endorsement in which many of our clergymen participate.

In January 1871, the Catholic Bishop of Derry denounced the Home Rule movement of Isaac Butt. Today priests and people agree that the movement led by Isaac Butt was the mildest, most inoffensive movement ever known in Ireland.

The Irish Land League, which averted in 1879 a repetition of the famine horrors of 1847, which broke the back of Irish landlordism, and abolished the worst evils of British rule, was denounced by Archbishop McCabe in September 1879, October 1880, and October 1881.

In 1882 the Ladies' Land League, an association of Irish ladies organized for the patriotic and benevolent purpose of raising funds for the relief of distress, of inquiring into cases of eviction, and affording relief to evicted tenants, was denounced by Archbishop McCabe as 'immodest and wicked'. After this attack upon the character of patriotic Irish womanhood, Archbishop McCabe was created a Cardinal.

On 11 May 1883, in the midst of the fight of the Irish peasantry to save themselves from landlord tyranny, his Holiness the Pope issued a rescript *condemning disaffection to the English Government* and also condemning the testimonial to Charles Stewart Parnell. The Irish people answered by more than doubling the subscription to the testimonial. The leader of that fight of the Irish against their ancient tyrants was Michael Davitt, to whose efforts much of the comparative security of peasant life in Ireland is due. Davitt was denied an audience by the Pope, but at his death, priests and people alike united to do tribute to his character and genius.

In 1883 Dr McGlynn, a Catholic priest in America, was invited to deliver a lecture for the purpose of raising funds to save from starvation the starving people of the West of Ireland. The Vatican sent a telegram to Cardinal McCloskey ordering him to 'suspend this priest McGlynn for preaching in favour of the Irish revolution.' The telegram was signed by Cardinal Simeoni. Afterwards Father McGlynn was subjected to the sentence of complete excommunication for preaching revolutionary doctrines upon the land question, but after some years the Vatican acknowledged its error, and revoked the sentence without requiring the victim to change his principles.

In all the examples covered by this brief and very incomplete retrospective glance into history the instincts of the reformers and revolutionists have been right, the political theories of the Vatican and the clergy unquestionably wrong. The verdict of history as unquestionably endorses the former as it condemns the latter. And intelligent Catholics everywhere accept that verdict. Insofar as true religion has triumphed, in the hearts of men it has triumphed, in spite of, not because of, the political activities of the priesthood. That political activity in the past, like the clerical opposition to Socialism at present, was and is an attempt to serve God and mammon – an attempt to combine the service of Him who in His Humbleness rode upon an ass, with the service of those who rode roughshod over the hearts and souls and hopes of suffering humanity.

The capitalist class rose upon the ruins of feudal Catholicism; in the countries where it gained power its first act was to decree the confiscation of the estates of the Church. Yet today that robber class, conceived in sin and begotten in iniquity, asks the Church to defend it, and from the Vatican downwards the clergy respond to the call. Just as the British Government in Ireland on 21 January 1623 published a royal proclamation banishing all priests from Ireland, and in 1795 established a College at Maynooth for the education of priests, and found the latter course safer for British rule than the former, so the capitalist class has also learned its lesson and in the hour of danger enlists as its lieutenants and champions the priesthood it persecuted and despised in the hour of its strength. Can we not imagine some cynical supporter of the capitalist class addressing it today as the great Catholic orator, Richard Lalor Shiel, addressed the British Government on the occasion of the Maynooth Grant of 1845, and saying in his words:

> You are taking a step in the right direction. You must not take the Catholic clergy into your pay, but you can take the Catholic clergy under your care ... Are not lectures at Maynooth cheaper than State prosecutions? Are not professors less costly than Crown Solicitors? Is not a large standing army, and a great constabulary force more expensive than the moral police with which by the priesthood of Ireland you can be thriftily and efficaciously supplied?

THE PROBLEM STATED

It is not to be wondered at that the spirit of restless revolt which has gained such predominating influence over the nations of the world should have passed beyond the arena of politics to assert itself in the domain of practical economy. The causes likely to create a conflict are unmistakable. They are the marvellous discoveries of science, the colossal development of industry, the changed relations between workmen and masters, the enormous wealth of the few and the abject misery of the many, the more defiant self-reliance and the more scientific organization of the workers and finally a widespread depravity in moral principle and practice. The momentous seriousness of the coming crisis fills every thoughtful mind with anxiety and dread. Wise men discuss it, practical men propose schemes; platforms, Parliaments, clubs, kings, all think and talk of it. Nor is there any subject which so completely engrosses the attention of the world. – Encyclical on Labour by Pope Leo XIII, 1891.

In our analysis of the discourses against Socialism which formed the burden of the Lenten Lectures of Father Kane, SJ, we propose to cite at all time the text we are criticizing, and we regret it is not practicable within our space to quote in full the entire series of lectures, and can only trust that our readers before making up their minds upon the question will procure a verbatim report of these discourses in order that they may satisfy themselves upon the correctness of our quotations. As far as it is possible without destroying the unity of our argument we shall follow the plan of the lecture itself, and attempt to answer each objection as it was formulated. But when an objection is merely stated, and no attempt made to follow it by a reasoned argument sustaining the objection we shall not waste our readers' time or our own by wandering off in an attempt to answer. One point stated by our reverend opponent, and then immediately forgotten or systematically ignored, requires to be restated here as the veritable anchor from which the argument should not be allowed to drift. Had our opponent clung to that anchor it would not have been possible for him to introduce so much extraneous matter, so much senseless speculation and foolish slander as he did introduce in the course of his long-drawn-out criticism. That point as stated by Father Kane is: *Once for all we must understand a Socialist to be that man, and only that man, who holds the essential principle of Socialism, i.e., that all wealth-producing power, and all that pertains to it belongs to the ownership and control of the state.* Thus, at the outset of his lectures, in his first discourse, the reverend gentleman makes it clear that Socialists are bound as Socialists only to the acceptance of one great principle – *the ownership and control of the wealth-producing power by the state*, and that therefore totally antagonistic interpretations of the Bible or of prophecy and revelation, theories of marriage, and of history, may be held by Socialists without in the slightest degree interfering with their activities as such, or with their proper classification as supporters of Socialist doctrine. If this great central truth had been made as clear as its importance justifies, and as firmly adhered to by our opponent as the Socialists themselves adhere to it, then it would not be necessary for the present writer to remind our critics of those uncomfortable facts in Irish history to which we have referred in our introduction, nor to those other facts in universal history we shall be forced to cite ere our present survey is finished.

Says our critic:

We now come to examine its principles. One fundamental principle of Socialism is that labour alone is the cause of value, and that labour alone can give any title to ownership. This was first formulated by Saint Simon, and is generally adopted by Socialists. This principle is false. It is founded on an incomplete explanation of the origin of value. We will put it to the test later on. At present we need only remark that a thing may be of real use and therefore of real value to a man who has a right to use it, even independently of any labour spent upon it. Fruit in a forest would have real value for a hungry man, even though no human labour had been given to its growing. Another principle, one invented by Karl Marx, is what he calls the materialistic conception of history. It is an application of the wild philosophic dreams of the German, Hegel: it means, in plain English, that the economic, or broadly speaking, the trade conditions existing in the world, determine the way in which the production of wealth must work out. Now, this working out of production determines what men's social, ethical and religious opinions shall be. But the economic conditions are always in a state of evolution and thus, after a time they come into collision with the previous social, ethical and religious state of things. But these latter do not die without a struggle, and consequently react, and limit to some extent the influence of the material evolution which is going on. I have given this principle as fully as I can in a short space. It assumes that everything in the world depends absolutely and exclusively upon the mere action of mere material causes. It is a principle the only proof of which is in the begging of the question, in supposing that there is no God, no soul, no free will, nothing but mud and the forces of mud.

We are indebted to our critic for his statement of the importance of this doctrine of the materialistic conception of history, although we are amused at his characterization of the doctrine itself. In the beginning of his description, ever mindful of the necessity of prejudicing his hearers, he describes it as an application of the 'wild philosophic dreams' of Hegel; in the middle it is stated that the doctrine rejects dreams as a foundation of religious belief and bases our ideas of religion upon the impression derived from material surroundings, and in the final sentence, so far from it being dreams, it is 'nothing but mud and the forces of mud'.

Let us examine briefly the true context of this doctrine. While remembering that there are many good Socialists who do not hold it, and that a belief in it is *not* an essential to Socialism, it is still accepted as the most reasonable explanation of history by the leading Socialists of this world. It teaches that the ideas of men are derived from their material surroundings, and that the forces which made and make for historical changes and human progress had and have their roots in the development of the tools men have used in their struggle for existence, using the word 'tools' in its broadest possible sense to include all the social forces of wealth-production. It teaches that since the break-up of common ownership and the clan community all human history has turned around the struggle of contending classes in society – one class striving to retain possession, first of the persons of the other class and hold them as chattel slaves, and then of the tools of the other class and hold them as wage-slaves. That all the politics of the world resolved themselves in the last analysis into a struggle for the possession of that portion of the fruits of labour which labour creates, but does not enjoy, i.e., rent, interest, profit. Here let us say that no Socialist claims for Marx the discovery or original formulation of the doctrine of the materialistic conception of history – indeed, the brilliant Irish scholastic, Duns Scotus, taught it in the Middle Ages – but that more precise formulation of the guiding forces of history which relate to the influence of economic factors and which we call economic determinism has indeed Marx as its clearest expositor, although the Irish economist William Thompson, of County Cork, in 1826, had pointed it out before Marx was out of swaddling clothes.

On the first point, viz., the influence of our material surroundings upon our mental processes and conceptions, a few words should be sufficient to establish its substantial truth in the minds of all those who do not fear the light.

Down on the western coast of Ireland the fishermen use, or did until quite recently, as their sole means of sea-going, a little boat made simply of a framework covered with animal hides or tarpaulin, and known as a coracle. At one time in the history of the world such boats represented the sole means of ocean travel. Now, is it not as plain as that two and two makes four that the outlook upon life, the conceptions of Man's relation to nature, the theories of international relations, of politics, of government, of the possibilities of life which characterize the age of the 'Lusitania', the flying machine, and the wireless message, could not possibly have been held by even the wisest men of the age of the coracle. The brains of men were as able then and as subtle in their conceptions as they are today, in fact the philosophers of ancient Asia have never been surpassed and seldom equalled in brain power in the modern world; but the most subtle, acute and powerful mind of the ancient world could not even understand the terms of the social, political or moral problems which confront us today, and are intelligently understood by the average day labourer. We are confronted with a salient instance of this in Holy Scripture. We read the inspired revelation of prophets, judges, and saints giving the world instructions for its future guidance; we read of commands to go forth and convey the gospel to the heathen; but nowhere do we read that those inspired men knew or spoke of a continent beyond the Atlantic in which immortal souls were sitting in darkness, if souls can be said to sit. These wise men of the ancient world, the inspired men of the Holy Land, the brilliant philosophers and scholastics of medieval Europe, were all limited by their material surroundings, could only think in terms of the world with which they were acquainted, and their ideas of what was moral or immoral were fashioned for them by the social system in which they lived. Slavery is held today to be immoral, and no chattel slaveowner would be given absolution; but when Constantine the Great accepted the Christian religion the Pope of the period received him with acclamation, and no one suggested to him the need of surrendering his slaves, of which he held thousands. Queen Elizabeth of England, 'Good Queen Bess', engaged in slave trading and made a good profit in the venture; but no Catholic

historian or pamphleteer of the period ever attacked her for that
offence, although attacks for other causes were made in plenty.
How is it that the point of view as to the morality of slavery has
changed? It cannot be that religion is changed, for we are told
that religion is the same yesterday, today, and for ever. If it is not
because it has been discovered that it is cheaper to hire men and
discharge them when the job is done, than it was to buy men and
be compelled to feed them all the time, working or idle, sick or
well, for what reason has the change in our conceptions come?
Stated brutally, the fact is that slavery is immoral because it is
dearer than wage labour. And so with all our other intellectual
processes. They change with the change in our environment,
particularly our economic or social environment.

A Negro slave in the Southern States of America was told by
his owner to go up and fasten the shingles on top of the roof of
his master's dwelling. 'Boss,' said he to the slave-owner, 'if I go
up there and fall down and get killed you will lose the 500 dollars
you paid for me; but if you send up that Irish labourer and he
falls down and breaks his neck you won't even have to bury him,
and can get another labourer tomorrow for two dollars a day.'
The Irish labourer was sent up. Moral: Slavery is immoral because slaves cost too much.

As man has progressed in his conquest of the secrets of nature,
he has been compelled to accept as eminently natural that from
which his forefathers shrank as a manifestation of the power of
the supernatural; as the progress of commerce has taken wealth,
and the power that goes with wealth, out of the exclusive ownership of kings and put it in the possession of capitalists and merchants, political power has acquired a new basis, and diplomatic
relations from being the expression of the lust for family aggrandizement have become the servants of the need for new markets
and greater profits – kings wait in the ante-chambers of usurers
like Rothschild and Baring to get their consent for war or peace;
Popes have for hundreds of years excommunicated those who put
their money out at usury and have denied them Christian burial,
but now a Pierpoint Morgan, as financier of the Vatican, lends
out at interest the treasures of the Popes. And man caught in the
grasp of changing economic conditions changes his intellectual

conceptions to meet his changed environment. The world moves even although men stand still, and not the least of the changes have been those of the ghostly fathers of the Church towards the world and its problems. Like the girl to the kisses of her sweetheart the Church has ever to the blandishments of the world –

'Swearing she would ne'er consent, consented.'

Our critic proceeds:

The third principle of Socialism is the theory of Karl Marx by which he tries to prove that all capital is robbery. He calls it the theory of Surplus Value. Value is the worth of a thing. Now, the worth of a thing may be in that it satisfies some need, as a piece of bread or a blanket; or the worth of a thing may be in that you can barter it for something else, as if you have more bread than you want, but have not a blanket, you may give some of your bread to a man who has no bread but can spare a blanket. The first kind of value is use value, or own worth. The second kind of value is exchange value, or market worth. Instead of mere direct barter, money is used in civilized nations as an equivalent and standard for exchange value. Now, Karl Marx asserts that exchange value, i.e., the worth of a thing as it may be bought or sold, arises only from the labour spent on it. He goes on to say that a workman only gets his wages according to the market value of his labour – that is to say, he is only paid for his time and toil – whereas the value of his labour, i.e., the worth which results from his labour, may be far in excess of the wages which he gets. Marx calls this value or worth which results from labour over and above the wages of labour, which is equivalent to the labourer's support. Marx calls this overworth surplus value. He states that while it goes to the pocket of the employer, it is really the property of the workman, because it is the result of his labour. This surplus value is really capital, and is used by the employer to create more surplus value – that is to say, more capital. Let me put this in another way: while the value of a thing for a man's own use may depend on the thing itself, the value of a thing in the market arises only from the labour spent on it. But the labour spent on it may also have its market value in winning its wage or it may also have its use value in producing greater value than its wage. But this use value arises from labour as well as the exchange value, and, therefore, belongs to the workman and not to the employer. All this ingenious and intricate system rests absolutely upon the one assumption that exchange value depends only on the labour spent. Now, this assumption is quite false and quite groundless. The worth of a thing in the market will depend first of all upon the nature of the thing's own worth for use. Secondly, upon the demand and other outside circumstances. And thirdly, upon the labour spent. A bottle of good wine will have more exchange value than a bottle of bad wine, even though it may not have cost more labour. A pair of boots carved out of wood with long and careful toil will fetch less in the market than a simple pair of brogues. The principle that labour alone is the source of value and the only title to ownership, was adopted by the American Socialist platform in 1904, with the recommendation that the workmen of the world should gradually seize on all capital.

Now, as to the Socialist system. In the official declaration of the English Socialists we read – the object of Socialism is 'the establishment of a system of society, based upon the common ownership and democratic control of the means and instruments for producing and distributing wealth by, and in the interests of the whole community.'

There is little to refute here that will not have readily occurred to the mind of the intelligent reader. In fact, the haste with which Father Kane left this branch of the subject evinced his knowledge of its dangerous nature. The exposition of the true nature of capital, viz., that it is stored-up, unpaid labour, forms the very basis of the Socialist criticism of modern society, and its method of wealth production; it is the fundamental idea of modern Marxist Socialism, and yet in a discourse covering four columns of small type in the 'Irish Catholic' (what a misnomer!) the full criticism of this really fundamental position takes up only twelve lines. And such a criticism!

'A bottle of good wine will have more exchange value than a bottle of bad wine, even though it may not have cost more labour.' Does the reverend father not know that if good wine can be produced as cheaply as bad wine, and in as great quantity, then good wine will come down to the same price as the inferior article? And if good wine could be produced as cheaply as porter it would be sold at the same price as porter is now – heavenly thought! It is the labour embodied in the respective articles, including the labour of keeping in storage, paying rental for vaults, etc., that determines their exchange value. Wine kept in vaults for years commands higher prices than new wine, but could chemists give new wine the same flavour as is possessed by stored-up wine then the new would bring down the price of the old to a price governed by the amount of labour embodied in the new.

'A pair of boots carved out of wood with long and careful labour will fetch less in the market than a simple pair of brogues.' How illuminating! But what governs the price of the brogues? Why, the amount of labour socially necessary to produce them. The amount of labour necessary to produce an article under average social conditions governs its exchange value. 'Boots carved out of wood with long and careful labour' are not produced under average social conditions; in discussing the economic question we discuss governing conditions, not exceptions. Hence the exchange value of boots such as those instanced by Father Kane is as problematical as the moral value of his hair-splitting. If you do not believe labour cost governs the exchange value of a commodity ask a Dublin master builder to tell you what factors he takes into account when he is asked to give an estimate for building an altar. If he is a Catholic he will cast up his estimate with the same items as if he were a Protestant – that is to say, he will count the cost of labour, including the cost of labour embodied in the raw material, and he will base his estimate upon that cost. Ask any manufacturer, whether employing two men or 2,000, how he determines the price at which he can sell an article, and he will tell you that the cost of labour embodied in it settles that question for the market and for him. Yet it is this simple truth that Father Kane and such enemies of Socialism deny. Altars, beads, cassocks, shoes, buildings, ploughs, books – all articles upon the market, except a politician's conscience – have their exchange value, determined in like manner – by their labour cost.

The learned gentleman winds up this lecture with a sneer at Socialist proposals, and an unwilling admission of the terrible logic of our position in future politics. He says:

The means and methods of the Socialist have now to be considered. Here we have to consider their destructive and constructive methods – what and how they are to knock down, what and how they are to build up. Here, however, we meet with an endless difference of Socialist opinions. As to the knocking down process, some Socialists are very enterprising, and appear to quite fall in with the anarchist programme of the dagger, the firebrand and the bomb. Others prefer to work through parliament by legal voting and by legal measures. Most of them appear from their speeches and writings to be very little troubled with scruples as to the right or wrong of means to be employed. Some fashionable and aesthetic dabblers in Socialism, amongst whom are men of culture, education and wealth – as, for instance, are some prominent members of the Fabian Society – would work very quietly and very gently; they would even contemplate offering some compensation to the owners whose property they stole, but more probably when the real crash came they would gracefully retire with their culture, their education and their money. A man who makes £25,000 a year by amusing the public is not the sort of man who is likely, when the time comes, to willingly give up all that he owns for the honour of sweeping a street crossing as a Socialist. That is only the superficial nonsense which some people pass off as Socialism. Come to the practical point. The way in which Karl Marx explains how all capital is to be confiscated is as follows. On the one hand that fierce competition which is the war of the financial world will result in the survival of a very few and very grasping capitalists. On the other hand, the army of labour will be enlightened, better organized and more scientifically led. It is easy to see what the enormous multitude of the proletariat – with force, votes and law on their side – can do with the few fat but helpless millionaires whose money is wanted. In any case the Socialist intends by one means or another to take private property from all those who have any. As to the constructive methods of the Socialist, we have dreams, visions, castles in the air, fairy tales in which there is much that is amusing, some things that are very sentimental, and some things that are very foul; but in all of them one element is lacking – common sense.

It is surely not necessary to point out that according to the Socialist doctrine the capitalist class are themselves doing much of the constructive work; they, pushed by their economic necessities, concentrate industries, eliminate useless labour and abolish useless plants, and prepare industry for its handling by officials elected by the workers therein. On the other hand the 'army of labour, more enlightened, better organized and more scientifically led', banded into industrial unions patterned after the industry in which they are employed will have prepared the workers to take possession of the productive and distribution forces on the day the incapable capitalist class are forced to surrender to a 'proletariat *with force, votes and law* on their side'.

THE RIGHTS OF MAN

The rights of man is a doctrine popularized by the bourgeois (capitalist) philosophers of the eighteenth century, and has no place in Socialist literature. Although Father Kane is kind enough to credit Socialism with the doctrine, it is in reality the child of that capitalist class he is defending, and was first used by them as a weapon in their fight for power against the kings and hierarchy of France. Now that capitalism has attained to power and made common cause with its old enemies, royalty and hierarchy, it would fain disavow much of the teaching of its earlier days, and hence listens complacently whilst Father Kane attacks the Rights of Man, and sneers at the 'mob', as he elegantly terms the common people for whom his Master died upon the Cross. We do not propose to follow the reverend gentleman into all his excursions away from the subject, but shall content ourselves with citing and refuting those passages which have a real and permanent bearing upon the question at issue.

He begins:

Man's right to live is also the right to take the means wherewith to live. Hence he can make use of such material means as are necessary in order that he should live. But he cannot make use of certain necessary means if others may use them also. Hence his right to use these means is at the same time a right to exclude others from their use. If a man has a right to eat a definite piece of bread, he has a right that no one else shall eat it. We will set this truth in another light. The right of private ownership may be considered either in the abstract, or as it is realized in concrete form. That right in the abstract means that by the very law of nature there is inherent in man a right to take hold of and apply for his own support those material means of livelihood which are not already in the right possession of another man. What those particular means are is not decided in the concrete by Nature's law. Nature gives the right to acquire, and by acquiring to own. But some partial fact is required in order to apply that abstract law to a concrete thing. The fact is naturally the occupying or taking hold of, or entering into possession of, a thing, by which practical action the abstract law of Nature becomes realized in a concrete practical fact. With this, or upon this, follows another right of man, the right to own his labour and the right to what his labour does. Furthermore, this right to exclusive personal ownership is not restricted to the means of one's daily bread from day to day; it is a right to be secure against want, when the needed means may not be at hand. The man who has tilled a field through the winter and spring has a right to hold as his own the harvest which he has earned. Hence the right of ownership is by Nature's law not merely passing, but permanent; it does not come and go at haphazard; it is stable. Hear the teaching of Pope Leo XIII in his Pontifical explanation of this point (Encyclical on Labour): 'The Socialists, working on the poor man's envy of the rich, endeavour to destroy private property, and maintain that personal property should become the common property of all. They are emphatically unjust, because they would rob the lawful possessor ... If one man hires out to another his strength or his industry, he does this in order to receive in return the means of livelihood, with the intention of acquiring a real right, not merely to his wage, but also to the free disposal of it. Should he invest this wage in land, it is only his wage in another form ...

'It is precisely in this power of disposal that ownership consists, whether it be question of land or other property. Socialists ... strike at the liberty of every wage-earner, for they deprive him of the liberty of disposing of his wages. Every man has, by the law of Nature, the right to possess property of his own ...

'It must be within his right to own things, not merely for the use of the moment, not merely things that perish in their use, but such things whose usefulness is permanent and stable ... Man is prior to the state, and he holds his natural rights prior to any right of the State ...

'When man spends the keenness of his mind and the strength of his body in winning the fruits of Nature, he thereby makes his own that spot of Nature's field which he tills, that spot on which he sets the seal of his own personality. It cannot but be just that that spot should be his own, free from outside intrusion ...'

If one of the boys at the national schools could not reason more logically than that he would remain in the dunce's seat all his schooldays. Imagine a priest who defends landlordism as Father Kane and the Pope does, saying, 'The man who has tilled a field through the winter and spring has a right to hold as his own the harvest which he has earned', and imagining that he is putting forward an argument against Socialism. Socialists do not propose to interfere with any man's right 'to hold what he has earned'; but they do emphatically insist that such a man, peasant or worker, shall not be compelled to give up the greater part, or any, of what he has earned, to an idle class whose members 'toil not neither do they spin', but who have attained their hold upon the nation's property by ruthless force, spoliation and fraud.

'Man's right to live is also the right to take the means wherewith to live.'

'His right to use these means is at the same time a right to exclude others from their use.'

That is to say that a man has the right to take the means wherewith to live, and he has also the right to prevent other men taking the means wherewith to live. The one right cancels the other. When the supply of a thing is limited, and that thing is necessary, absolutely necessary, to existence, as is land, water and the means of producing wealth, does it not follow that to allow those things to be made private property enables the owners of them to deny Man 'the right to live', except he agrees to surrender the greater portion of the fruits of his toil to the owners. *Capitalism and Landlordism are based upon the denial to Man of his right to live except as a dependant upon Capitalists and Landlords; they exist by perpetually confiscating the property which the worker has in the fruits of his toil, and establish property for the capitalist by denying it to the labourer.* Why talk about the right to live under capitalism? If a man had all the patriotism of a Robert Emmet or a George Washington, if he had all the genius of a Goldsmith or a Mangan, if he had all the religion of a St Simeon Stylites or a St Francis d'Assisi, if he belongs to the working class he has no effective right to live in this world unless a capitalist can see his way to make a profit out of him. Translated into actual practice these 'natural rights' of which the reverend gentleman discoursed so eloquently means for 23,000 families in Dublin the right to live in one room per family – living, sleeping, eating and drinking and dying in the narrow compass of the four walls of one room.

'When man spends the keenness of his mind and the strength

of his body in winning the fruits of Nature he thereby makes his own that spot of Nature's field which he tills,' so says his Holiness, as quoted by Father Kane. It follows then that the Irish peasantry, like the peasantry of Europe in general, are and were the real owners of the soil, and that the feudal aristocracy, the landlord class, whose proudest boast it was, and is, that they have never soiled their hands by labour, are and were thieves exacting by force tribute from the lawful owners of the soil. Yet those thieves have ever been supported by the hierarchy in their possession of property against the peasants who had made it their own 'by spending the keenness of their mind and the strength of their body' in tilling it.

The working class of the world, by their keenness of mind and their strength of body, have made everything in the world their own – its land, its factories, its ships, its railroads, its houses, everything on earth and sea has been consecrated by the labour of the working class, and therefore belongs to that class; and as factories, ships, railroads and buildings cannot be divided up in pieces, they must be owned in common. If land belongs to those who have tilled it, by what means, other than common ownership, shall we re-establish the right of that 75 per cent of the Irish people who, according to Mulhall, were evicted between 1837 and 1887, or of those agricultural labourers who toil upon the land but own no one foot of it, or of all those labourers in towns and cities whose forefathers have been hunted like wild beasts from the land they had made their own, by the keenness of mind and strength of body applied to labour, and who are now compelled to herd in towns, dependant upon the greed of capitalists for the chance to exist?

Father Kane, in this portion of his address, came to curse Socialism, but his arguments serve to bless it.

Let me bring from another world – the old Pagan world – the greatest philosopher of pure reason, as witness to the truth of the same principle. Aristotle wrote: 'Socialism wears a goodly face and affects an air of philanthropy. The moment it speaks it is eagerly listened to. It speaks of a marvellous love that shall grow out from it between man and man. This impression is emphasized when the speaker rails against the shortcomings of existing institutions, giving as the reason for all our shortcomings the fact that we are not Socialists. These evils of human life are not, however, owing to the absence of Socialism, but to the always inevitable presence of human frailty.'

This is a puzzle. The word Socialism, and the Socialist principles, were unheard of until the beginning of the nineteenth century; and Aristotle flourished in the year 384 B.C. Hence to quote Aristotle as writing about Socialism is like saying that Owen Roe O'Neill sent a telegram to the Catholic Confederation at Kilkenny in 1647, or that George Washington crossed the Delaware in a flying machine. It is an absurd anachronism. For hundreds of years the works of Aristotle were used to combat Christianity, principally by the Arabians in the Middle Ages, and now the same works are used by a Christian priest to combat Socialism. Truly 'misfortune makes strange bedfellows!'

Father Kane says:

We will go back to the old Greek philosopher, Aristotle, the philosopher compared to whom our Kant, Hegel, Comte, Hobbes and Locke are merely dreaming boys or blundering students. Aristotle founded his philosophy on fact, and worked it out through common sense. Our modern philosophers, with marvellous talent, evolve their principles out of their own inner consciousness, and ground their conclusions on their own mental mood.

In a criticism of Draper's 'Conflict between Religion and Science', published by the Catholic Truth Society as the report of a lecture delivered in Cork and Limerick by the Rev. Dr O'Riordan, the author says, 'Owing to the use which the Arabians had made of the name of Aristotle, his name had become a word of offence to Christians, so much so that even Roger Bacon said that his works should be burnt'; and further on, 'St Thomas (Aquinas) took up the philosophy of Aristotle and, purifying it of its Pagan errors, he established Christian truth out of the reasoning of the Greek philosopher.' So that, according to Father Kane, Aristotle 'founded his philosophy on fact, and worked it out through common sense', and according to Dr O'Riordan this philosophy of fact and common sense was subversive of Christianity until it was 'purified of its Pagan errors'. Well, we Socialists, while second to none in our admiration for the encyclopaedic knowledge of Aristotle, will carry the purifying process begun by St Thomas Aquinas a step further. We will purify Aristotle's philosophy of the teaching he derived from the slave-world in which he lived, and make it Socialistic. Let us remind Father Kane that Aristotle's mind was so completely dominated by his economic environment that he was unable to conceive of a world in which there would be no chattel slaves, and so declared that slaves must always exist. A prophecy now falsified for hundreds of years.

We do not propose to follow the reverend gentleman in his wonderful attempt to discredit the Marxist position on Value; that has been dealt with sufficiently already in the passage upon Value in Exchange, in the criticism of the first Discourse, and the attempt to elaborate his position by our opponent in his second Discourse is about as enlightening as an attempt to square the circle generally is. It is summed up in his declaration that 'Labour alone cannot create use value, therefore, Labour alone cannot constitute exchange value.' Which is equivalent to saying that appetite and desire are the real arbiters in civilized life and under normal conditions of the basis on which articles exchange among human beings. The appetite and desire of human beings for water and for bicycles will illustrate to the simplest mind the absurdity of our opponent's position. Water under normal conditions in a modern community will not fetch a halfpenny the bucketful, but bicycles retail easily at £7 and £8 apiece. Yet our desire and appetite for water is based upon a human necessity so imperative that we would die without its satisfaction, but countless millions go through life without even straddling a bicycle. What makes so cheap the article without which we would die? The small amount of labour necessary to convey it from the mountains to our doors, of course. And what makes so costly the article that is not a necessity at all? The comparatively great amount of labour embodied in its production, of course. Then, what fixes the Exchange Value of an article in the normal, modern market. Its cost in labour, certainly.

It is contrary to Divine Law even to covet our neighbour's field. The Church of Christ has always approved, both in principle and in practice, of private and personal property. It is utterly and irreconcilably against the teaching of the Catholic to deny man's right to hold personal property, even independently of the sanction of the State, or to brand such ownership as theft. Pope Leo XIII wrote: 'Christian democracy, by the very fact that it is Christian, must be based upon the principles of Divine Faith in its endeavours for the betterment of the masses. Hence to Christian democracy justice is sacred. It must maintain that the right of acquiring and possessing property cannot be gainsaid, and it must safeguard the various distinctions and degrees which are indispensable in every well-ordered commonwealth. It is clear, therefore, that there is nothing common between Social and Christian democracy. They differ from each other as much as the sect of Socialism differs from the Church of Christ.'

Dear, oh dear! What heretics we must be! And yet we are in good company. Saints and Pontiffs of the Catholic Church have gone before us on this road, and the wildest sayings of modern Socialist agitators are soft and conservative beside some of the doctrines which ere now have been put forth as sound Catholic teachings. Read:

The use of all things that is found in this world ought to be common to all men. Only the most manifest iniquity makes one say to the other, 'This belongs to me, that to you,' *Hence the origin of contention among men*. St Clement.

What thing do you call 'yours'? What thing are you able to say is yours? From whom have you received it? You speak and act like one who upon an occasion going early to the theatre and possessing himself without obstacle of the seats destined for the remainder of the public, pretends to oppose their entrance in due time, and to prohibit them seating themselves, arrogating to his own sole use property that is really destined to common use. And it is precisely in this manner act the rich. St Basil the Great.

Therefore if one wishes to make himself the master of every wealth, to possess it and to exclude his brothers even to the third or fourth part (generation), such a wretch is no more a brother but an inhuman tyrant, a cruel barbarian, or rather a ferocious beast of which the mouth is always open to devour for his personal use the food of the other companions. St Gregory. Nic.

Nature furnishes its wealth to all men in common. God beneficently has created all things that their enjoyment be common to all living beings, and that the earth become the common possession of all. *It is nature itself that has given birth to the right of the community whilst it is only unjust usurpation that has created the right of private property.* St Ambrose.

The earth of which they are born is common to all, and therefore the fruit that the earth brings forth belongs without distinction to all. St Gregory the Great.

The rich man is a thief. St Chrysostom.

Our reverend critic proceeds:

To enchain men with fetters of equality would be to degrade the wise, the good, the energetic, the noble amongst them, to the depths of the men who are nearest to the brute. Freedom must have fair play. Man must be free to make and mould his own life according to his own talent, his own opportunity, his own energy, his own ambition, his own merit, and his own will, according to the circumstances in which Providence has placed him. But you say is it not a pity that, owing to the mere accident of birth, a brainless and worthless creature should wear a ducal crown, while a man of mind and character is sweeping the crossing of a street? Yes, to merely human view it is a pity, just as it is a pity that one girl should be born beautiful while another girl is born ugly; just as it is a pity that one man should be born weak-minded and weak-kneed while another man is born with a treasure trove of talent and with a golden mine of sterling character; just as it is a pity that one more man, by the accident of birth, is born to be himself. There is accident all round, if you wish to call it accident. No man deserves what he gets with him when he is born into the world and no man has deserved anything different. What you may, perhaps, call accident I call Providence. We do not choose our own lot; it is given to us. It is our duty to make the best we can of it.

The first part of this is clap-trap: the second is rank blasphemy. The clap-trap consists in the pretence that the Socialist idea of equality involves the idea that men should be reduced to one moral or intellectual level. Trade unionists are generally and rightfully in favour of a minimum wage – a wage below which no worker shall be depressed. Unscrupulous employers and ignorant journalists and politicians dealing with this demand strive to make the thoughtless believe that a minimum wage will prevent higher wages being paid for extra skill. In other words, they speak as if it were a maximum wage that was demanded. So with the Socialist idea of equality. Like the trade unionist our demand is for a level *below* which no man shall be driven, a common basis of equality of opportunity to all. That whatever promotion, distinction, reward or honour be given to or attained by a man shall not confer upon him the right to exploit, to degrade, to dominate, to rob or humiliate his fellows. And our hope and belief is that in the future sane men and women will find as much delight in, strive as eagerly for, the honour of serving their fellows as they do now for the privilege of plundering them. Men and women are at all times zealous for honour, for the esteem of their fellows; and when the hope of plunder is removed out of the field of human possibility those specially gifted ones who now exhaust their genius in an effort to rule, will as vehemently exert themselves to win the honour accorded to those who serve.

The second part is, we repeat, rankly blasphemous. The reverend gentleman, unable to answer the obvious question he supposes, attempts to draw an analogy between what he would call the 'hand of God' in shaping the faces, forms, minds and characters of His creatures, and the historical and social conditions which have created dukes and crossing-sweepers, brainless aristocrats and intelligent slum-dwellers, morally poisonous kings and Christian-minded hod-carriers, vile ladies idling in mansions and clean-souled women slaving over the washtub. The attempt is an insult to our intelligence. We, as individuals, are not personally responsible for our faces, forms or minds; these are the result of forces over which we had and have no control. But the gross injustices of our social system we are responsible for, in the degree in which we help or acquiesce in their perpetuation. In the degree in which we support them today we become participators in the crimes upon which they were built. And what were those crimes? Need we remind our readers of the origin of private property in Ireland? It had its roots in the adulterous treason of an Irish chief; it was founded upon the betrayal of liberty, and enforced by the wholesale slaughter and enslavement of the Irish people. Must we remind our readers that if they seek for the origin of aristocratic property in Ireland they must seek for it not in the will of a beneficent Deity, as this bold blasphemer alleges, nor in titles won by honest labour on the soil, but in the records of English marauders, in the stories of poisoning and treacheries told in the State Papers of the English ruling class, in the light of the burning homes of Munster in the wake of the armies of Inchiquin,* in the despatches of the English nobleman who boasted to Elizabeth that his army had left in Ulster 'nothing save carcases and ashes', in the piteous tale of the imprisoned jurors of Connaught† who refused to perjure themselves and yield up Irish tribe lands to greedy aristocratic thieves from England, or in the log of the emigrant ships whose course across the Atlantic was marked by the floating corpses of hunted Irishmen, Irish women and Irish children.

Or shall it be necessary to recall to our readers the grim fact that the origin of great estates in England is found in the court records, which tell us that in the reign of Good Queen Bess 72,000 workers were hanged in the name of law and order, hanged as vagrants after they had been driven off the lands they had tilled; that during the Peasant Wars of Germany the nobility slaughtered so many poor peasants that one of the aristocracy eventually called a halt, saying, 'If we kill them all we shall have no one to live upon'; that in Scotland 15,000 people were evicted off one estate in the nineteenth century – the Sutherland clearances; that in fact in every European country the title deeds to aristocratic property have been written in the blood of the poor, and that the tree of capitalism has been watered with the tears of the toilers in every age and clime and country.

Next, wonder of wonders, our clerical friend becomes solicitous for a free press and free speech. He declares:

* Inchiquin was an Irish apostate in the service of the English. Taken as a hostage into England when a child, he was reared up in hatred of the religion and people of his fathers. As an English general in the Irish rebellion of 1641 he became infamous for his cruelties and purposeless massacres; the march of his armies could always be traced by the fire and smoke from burning homes and villages.

† The English Government under Charles I appointed a 'Commission to inquire into defective titles' in Connaught. As all lands in Ireland under the ancient Celtic system were common property it followed that all Irish titles were defective under the feudal law of England. Much land fell into the hands of the English adventurers under this 'Commission', and when the Irish juries refused to be bribed or terrorized into returning verdicts to suit the Commissioners they were promptly imprisoned and their property confiscated.

In Socialism there could be no healthy public opinion, no public opinion at all except that manufactured by officialdom or that artificially cultivated by the demagogues of the mob. There could be no free expression of free opinion. The Press would be only the Press of the officials. Printing machines, publishing firms, libraries, public halls, would be the exclusive property of the State. We do not indeed advocate utter licence for the Press, but we do advocate its legitimate liberty. There would be no liberty of the Press under Socialism; no liberty even of speech, for the monster machine of officialdom would grind out all opposition – for the monster machine would be labelled, 'The Will of the People', and 'The Will of the People' would be nothing more than the whim of the tyrant mob, the most blind and ruthless tyrant of all, because blindly led by blind leaders. Brave men fear no foe, and free men will brook no fetter. You will have thought, in your boyhood, with hot tears, of the deeds of heroes who fought and fell in defence of the freedom of their fatherland. That enthusiasm of your boyhood will have become toned down with maturer years in its outward expression but mature years will have made it more strong and staunch for ever, more ready to break forth with all the energy of your life and with all the sacrifice of your death in defiance of slavery. You may have rough times to face; you may have rough paths to tread, you may have hard taskmasters to urge your toil, and hard paymasters to stint your wage; you may have hard circumstances to limit your life within a narrow field; but after all your life is your own, and your home is your own, and your wage is your own, and you are free. Freedom is your birthright. Even our dilapidated modern nations allow to a man, his birthright – freedom. You would fight for your birthright, freedom, against any man, against any nation, against the world; and if you could not live for your freedom, you would die for it. You would not sell your birthright, freedom, to Satan; and I do not think that you are likely to surrender your birthright, freedom, to the Socialist. Stand back! We are free men. Stand back, Socialist! God has given us the rights of man, to our own life, to our own property, to our own freedom. We will take our chance in the struggle of life. We may have a hard time or a good time, we may be born lucky or unlucky, but we are free men. Stand back, Socialist! God has given us our birthright, freedom and, by the grace of God, we will hold to it in life and in death.

After you have done laughing at this hysterical outburst we will proceed calmly to discuss its central propositions. To take the latter part first, it is very amusing to hear a man, to whom a comfortable living is assured, assure us that we ought to tell the Socialist that 'we will take our chance in the struggle of life'.

He speaks of our 'birthright, freedom', which is allowed us even by dilapidated modern nations, and that we ought not to surrender it to the Socialists. In Ireland 87 per cent of the working class can earn less than 20s. per week; in London, a million of people, according to the non-Socialist investigator, Charles Booth, live below the poverty line – never getting enough to eat; in all civilization, according to Huxley, the lot of the majority of the working class is less desirable than the lot of the mere savage; and this awful condition of the only class in society that is really indispensable is the result of the capitalist system, which mocks the workers with a theoretical freedom and an actual dependence. The freedom of the worker is freedom to sell himself into slavery to the class which controls his supply of food; he is free as the wayside traveller is free of clothes after highwaymen have robbed and stripped him. Says well the poet Shelley.

> What is Freedom? Ye can tell
> That which slavery is too well,
> For its very name has grown
> To an echo of your own.
> 'Tis to work, and have such pay,
> As just keeps life, from day to day,
> In your limbs as in a cell
> For the tyrant's use to dwell.

How can a person, or a class, be free when its means of life are in the grasp of another? How can the working class be free when the sole chance of existence of its individual members depends upon their ability to make a profit for others?

The argument about the freedom of the press – a strange argument from such a source – is too absurd to need serious consideration. Truly, all means of printing will be the common property of all, and if any opposition party, any new philosophy, doctrine, science or even hare-brained scheme has enough followers to pay society for the labour of printing its publications, society will have no more right nor desire to refuse the service than a government of the present day has to refuse the use of its libraries to the political enemies who desire to use those sources of knowledge to its undoing. It will be as possible to hire a printing machine from the community as it will be to hire a hall. Under Socialism the will of the people will be supreme, all officials will be elected from below and hold their position solely during good behaviour, and as the interests of private property, which according to St Clement, are the sole origin of contention among men, will no longer exist, there will be little use of law-making machinery, and no means whereby officialdom can corrupt the people.

This will be the rule of the people at last realized. But says Father Kane, at last showing the cloven foot, 'the will of the people would be nothing more than the whim of the tyrant mob, the most blind and ruthless tyrant of all, because blindly led by blind leaders'. Spoken like a good Tory and staunch friend of despotism! What is the political and social record of the mob in history as against the record of the other classes? There was a time stretching for more than a thousand years, when the mob was without power or influence, when the entire power of the governments of the world was concentrated in the hands of the kings, the nobles and the hierarchy. That was the blackest period in human history. It was the period during which human life was not regarded as being of as much value as the lives of hares and deer; it was the period when freedom of speech was unknown, when trial by jury was suppressed, when men and women were tortured to make them confess crimes before they were found guilty, when persons obnoxious to the ruling powers were arrested and kept in prison (often for a lifetime) without trial; and it was the period during which a vindictive legal code inflicted the death penalty for more than 150 offences – when a boy was hung for stealing an apple, a farmer for killing a hare on the roadside. It was during this undisturbed reign of the kings, the nobles, and the hierarchy that religious persecutions flourished, when Protestants killed Catholics, Catholics slaughtered Protestants and both hunted Jews, when man 'made in God's image' murdered his fellow-man for daring to worship God in a way different from that of the majority; it was then that governments answered their critics by the torture, when racks and thumbscrews pulled apart

the limbs of men and women, when political and religious opponents of the state had their naked feet and legs placed in tin boots
of boiling oil, their heads crushed between the jaws of a vice, their
bodies stretched across a wheel while their bones were broken by
blows of an iron bar, water forced down their throats until their
stomachs distended and burst, and when little children toiled in
mine and factory for 12, 14 and 16 hours per day. But at last,
with the development of manufacturing, came the gathering
together of the mob, and consequent knowledge of its numbers
and power, and with the gathering together also came the possibility of acquiring education. Then the mob started upon its
upward march to power – a power only to be realized in the
Socialist Republic. In the course of that upward march the mob
has transformed and humanized the world. It has abolished religious persecution and imposed toleration upon the bigots of all
creeds; it has established the value of human life, softened the
horrors of war as a preliminary to abolishing it, compelled trial
by jury, abolished the death penalty for all offences save one, and
in some countries abolished it for all; and today it is fighting to
take the children from the factory and mine, and put them to
school. This mob, 'the most blind and ruthless tyrant of all', with
one sweep of its grimy, toil-worn hand swept the rack, the thumb-
screw, the wheel, the boots of burning oil, the torturer's vice and
the stake into the oblivion of history, and they who today would
seek to view those arguments of kings, nobles, and ecclesiastics
must seek them in the lumber room of the museum.

In this civilizing, humanizing work the mob had at all times
to meet and master the hatred and opposition of kings and nobles;
and there is not in history a record of any movement for abolishing torture, preventing war, establishing popular suffrage, or
shortening the hours of labour led by the hierarchy. Against all
this achievement of the mob, its enemies have but one instance of
abuse of power – the French reign of terror – and they suppress
the fact that this classic instance of mob fury lasted but eight
months, whereas the cold-blooded cruelty of the ruling classes
which provoked it had endured for a *thousand years*.

All hail, then, to the mob, the incarnation of progress!

The old pagan idea that the State is everything and owns everything, so as to leave the individual man without any right except such as is conceded to him by the State – that old pagan idea has been adopted by the Socialist. That idea is distinctly contrary to natural law as well as to the law of Christ. That idea is absolutely antagonistic to our ideas of home. It would change our home into a mere lodging-house, where are fed and sheltered the submissive vassals of the State. Socialism has taken up that pagan idea, and pushed it even further than the pagan. For the pagan left the father home's master, and left the wife and child at home. Socialism would ruin the home firstly, because it would rob the father of the home, of his God-given right to be master in the citadel of his own home; secondly, because it would banish home's queen from what ought to be her kingdom, it would break the marriage bond which alone can safeguard the innocence and the stability of the home; it would make the wife of the home practically a tenant at will; thirdly, because it would kidnap the child.

The intelligent reader will note that the reverend critic is entirely incapable of grasping the conception of a state in which the people should rule instead of being creatures of an irresponsible power as the people were under the pagan powers of Rome to whom he is referring. He says, 'It [Socialism] would change our home into a mere lodging-house where are fed and sheltered the *submissive vassals of the State.*' Thus it is that he cannot clear his mind of the monarchial conception of the state; a state which should be a social instrument in the hands of its men and women, where State powers would be wielded as a means *by the* workers instead of being wielded as a repressive force *against the workers* is so strange an idea to him that he simply cannot understand what it signifies. The reader who understands this, and perceives the enormous gap in this clerical reasoning, will understand also that all the terrific bogies which our critics conjure up as a necessary result of the Socialist state – are only bogies.

This attempt to develop this theory of the state plunges him into a mass of contradictions. Read:

The first and most fundamental principle of ethics is that whereas

amongst lesser creatures physical force or animal instinct impels each
thing to act as is befitting its nature, to act in the actual circumstances,
so as to achieve the right order of its kind and the right end of its
existence, man, not flung forward by unreasoning power, but led by
reason's light, contemplates the order of relations that are around him,
and weighing their relative necessity or importance, acts so that his
action shall be in keeping with its own nature and in harmony with
the right conditions in which his life is cast. Now, right and duty are
the moral aspects of these fact-relations, and have their moral force
according to the deeper order and more fundamental necessity of these
fact-relations which are the cause of their existence and the measure of
their power. The reason for man's personal rights is in his actual
existence. Hench such rights are paramount above all. The reason of
the family is in the insufficiency of man alone to secure the right development of human nature. The reason of civil society is in the insufficiency of the family alone to attain that fuller perfection of
human nature which is the heritage of its birth, but which it can
only reach through the help of many homesteads, united into one
common weal. Hence, civil society is only intended by nature to be the
helper of the family, not its master: to be its safeguard, not its
destroyer; to be in a right true sense its servant, but in no sense its
owner. Hence, those Socialistic theories which would hand over the
family and the individual to the supreme command of the state are
false to reason and rebel against right. Rather it is the interest of the
state itself to recognize that its welfare and its security rests upon the
right independence, and deep-rooted stability of the families of which
it is the flower and the fruit.

A State that is tossed about in its social and political existence by
the fluctuating tide of transient individual opinions, ambitions,
actions, cannot have that healthy, hardy, deathless spirit which vivifies
into the same life not merely the chance companions of a day but
the successive generations of a nation.

Surely here is a Daniel come to judgement! We had to read
this passage over several times to satisfy ourselves that it was not
a quotation from a Socialist writer, instead of what it purports
to be – a part of the discourse of the reverend gentleman himself.
For it is the reasoning upon which is built that materialist in-
terpretation of history the lecturer has so eloquently denounced.
If the reader will turn to the first lecture he will see that the
doctrine of Marx, as explained by Father Kane, teaches that the

economic conditions in which man moves, governs or determines his conceptions of right and wrong, his social, ethical and religious opinions. Father Kane there denounced this doctrine in his most violent language. Now, in the part just quoted, he himself affirms the same doctrine. He says: 'The first and most *fundamental* principle of ethics is that ... *man* not flung forward by unreasoning power, but led by reason's light, contemplates the order of relations that are around him, and weighing their relative necessity or importance, *acts so that his action shall be in keeping with his own right nature, and in harmony with the conditions in which his life is cast.* Now, *right and duty,* are the moral aspects of these fact-relations, and *have their normal forces according to the deeper order and more fundamental necessity of those fact-relations which are the cause of their existence and the measure of their power.'* If this is not an affirmation of the Socialist doctrine that our conceptions of right and wrong, and the political and governmental systems built upon them have the 'cause of their existence and the measure of their power' in the 'fact-relation' of man and his fellow-man and not in any divine or philosophical system of mere thought, then language fails to convey any meaning. The remainder of the quotation quite as effectually cuts the ground from under the lecturer's own feet. Observe the last sentence. 'A state that is tossed about in its social and political existence by the fluctuating tide of transient individual opinions, ambitions, actions, cannot have that healthy, hardy, deathless spirit which vivifies into the same life not merely the chance companions of a day, but the successive generations of a nation.' Is not this a lifelike picture of the capitalist State and its endeavour to build a system of society which seeks a healthy national existence and social conscience in 'transient individual opinions, ambitions, and actions' instead of in an ordered co-operation of all for the common good of all. The whole passage we have quoted is essentially Socialist, and opposed to that capitalism its author defends. If the doctrine of economic determinism is heresy then Father Kane was preaching heresy from the pulpit.

As if conscious of his slip our critic immediately makes haste to divert attention by a lurid description of the 'Socialist doctrine of divorce'. Socialists as such have no doctrine of divorce, but a little inconsistency like that does not deter our opponents.

There is no Socialist Government in the world today, but almost every civilized nation has divorce laws, and the least Socialist nations and classes have the most divorces. America and its capitalist class, for example. Our clerical friends proceed upon the maxim of their sister profession, the lawyers: 'When you have a bad case abuse your opponent's attorney', and hence the constant attempt to slander Socialists upon this point. Now, what is the real truth on this matter? It is easily stated. Socialists are bound to agree upon one fundamental, and upon that only. That fundamental is, in the language of Father Kane, 'that all wealth-producing power and all that pertains to it belongs to the ownership and control of the state'. Hence, upon all other subjects there is, and will be, the widest possible diversity of opinion. Divorce is one of those non-essential, non-fundamental points upon which Socialists may and do disagree. But observe this. The law-making authority for Socialists is their national and international congresses; the law-making authority of capitalism is its Parliaments, chambers, congresses, reichstags, etc. Nowhere has a national or international congress of Socialists imposed divorce upon Socialists as something they must accept, but in almost every capitalist State the capitalist law-makers, the spokesmen and defenders of capitalism, have established divorce as a national institution. Who, then, are the chief supporters of divorce? The capitalists. And who can come fresh from the Divorce courts, reeking with uncleanness and immorality, to consummate another marriage, and yet know that he can confidently rely upon Catholic prelates and priests to command the workers to 'order themselves reverently before their superiors', with him as a type? The capitalist.

The divorce evil of today arises not out of Socialist teaching, but out of that capitalist system, whose morals and philosophy are based upon the idea of individualism, and the cash nexus as the sole bond in society. Such teaching destroys the sanctity of the marriage bond, and makes of love and the marriage bed things to be bought and sold. Can it be wondered at that such teaching as that which exalts the *individual* pursuit of riches as the absolutely necessary cement of society should produce a loosening of all *social* bonds, including that of marriage, and threatens to suffocate society with the stench of its own rottenness? Yet it is such capitalist ethics and practice our priests and prelates are defending, and it is of such Father Kane arises as the champion and expounder.

Certain Socialists, horrified at this rising stream of immorality, have sought to find a remedy in the proposal that marriage be regarded as a private matter over which the state shall have no authority. They do so as individuals, and many equally good Socialists believe that such an idea is flatly opposed to the Socialist philosophy; but in itself the proposal carries none of that loathsomeness the critic imputes to it. *It is an insult to the entire human race to say that husbands and wives are only kept together by law, and that women would become mistresses of one man after another if the law did not prevent them.* Yet this is what Father Kane said:

Divorce in the Socialist sense means that women would be willing to stoop to be the mistress of one man after another.

A more unscrupulous slander upon womanhood was never uttered or penned. Remember that this was said in Ireland, and do you not wonder that some Irishwomen – some persons of the same sex as the slanderer's mother – did not get up and hurl the lie back in his teeth, and tell him that it was not law which kept them virtuous, that if all marriage laws were abolished tomorrow, it would not make women 'willing to stoop to be the mistress of one man after another'. Aye, verily, the uncleanness lies not in this alleged Socialist proposal, but in the minds of those who so interpret it. The inability of Father Kane to appreciate the innate morality of womanhood, and the superiority of the morals of the women of the real people to that of the class he is defending, recalls to mind the fact that the Council of the Church held at Macon in the sixth century gravely debated the question as to whether woman had or had not a soul, and that the affirmation that she had was only carried by a small majority. Many of the early Fathers of the Church were, indeed, so bitter in their denunciation of women and of marriage that their opinions read like the expressions of madmen when examined in the cold light of the twentieth century. Origen said: 'Marriage is unholy and unclean – a means of sensual lust.' St Jerome declared, 'Marriage is at the least a vice; all that we can do is to excuse and justify it'; and Tertullian, in his hatred of women, thundered forth boldly that which Father Kane dared only insinuate, 'Woman,' he preaches, 'thou oughtest always to walk in mourning and rags, thine eyes filled with tears of repentance to make men forget that thou hast been the destruction of the race. Woman! thou art the Gates of Hell.' Thus throughout the centuries persists the idea of the Churchmen that women can only be kept virtuous by law.

In his further quotation Father Kane is equally disingenuous. Thus:

Listen now to one of the great German Socialist authorities, Bebel, who in his famous book, *Die Frau*, wrote: 'Every child that comes into the world, whether male or female, is a welcome addition to society; for society beholds in every child the continuation of itself and its own further development. It, therefore, perceives from the very outset that its duty, according to its power, is to provide for the new-born child ... It is evident that the mother herself must nurse the child as long as possible and necessary ... When the child waxes stronger, the other children await it for common amusement under public direction.' Behold their plan: All boys and girls, as soon as they are weaned, are to be taken from their parents and brought up, boys and girls together, first in state nurseries, and then, boys and girls together, in state boarding schools, but brought up without any religion whatever. Thus the child would grow up a stranger to its father and mother, without the hallowed influence of a happy home.

The reader will observe there is nothing whatever in the words quoted from Bebel which justifies this statement that the child is to be taken from the parents, or brought up a stranger to its father and mother, or without the influence of a home. There is simply the statement that it is the duty of the state to provide for the care, education and physical and mental development of the child. All the rest is merely read into the statement by the perverted malevolence of our critic. And yet this same critic had declared, as already quoted in this chapter, 'the reason of civil society is in the *insufficiency of the family alone* to attain that fuller perfection of human nature which is the heritage of its birth'. But when he comes across the Socialist proposal to supplement and help out that 'insufficiency' he forthwith makes it the occasion for the foulest slanders.

THE SUICIDE OF A NATION

Most scientific Socialists appear to follow Karl Marx in his theory that economic forces alone determine the evolution of all else in the world. In other words, to put the matter in a broad, blunt way, they assert that financial or business or trade conditions determine and decide the inevitable course and development of all other matters – intellectual, moral, social and religious. Marx says: 'The sum total of the conditions of wealth production constitutes the economic structure of society, the real basis on which is raised an ethical and political superstructure to which correspond certain forms of social consciousness ... It is not the mind of man which determines his life in society, but it is this material economic life that determines his mind.' The world has beheld one fact which gives the lie to all that flimsy theory. Christ brought into the world so deep and wide and lasting a change that there has been no other ever like it. That change was hostile to economic causes; it came from outside the business world. But it determined a new world of thought and conduct, and through these moral causes it changed the social and economic lives of men. It brought into the civilized world the duty and honour of labour, the breaking of the fetters of the slave, the lifting up of woman to be man's helpmate and equal, not his mere plaything or his property, the recognition of the rights of the poor to the ownership of the superabundance of the wealthy.

Such a statement as that Christ brought into the world a change hostile to economic causes could only be made by a lecturer who presumed either upon lack of historical knowledge on the part of his audience, or upon the fact that as he spoke from a pulpit none of his immediate listeners would dare to point out his errors upon the spot. All but the merest dabblers in Scriptural history know that the economic oppression of the Jewish people was so great immediately before the coming of Christ that the whole nation had been praying and hoping for the promised

Redeemer, and it was just at the psychological moment of their bondage as a nation and their slavery as a race that Christ appeared. And it is equally well known that the priests and comfortable classes – the 'canting, fed classes' – refused to acknowledge His message and intrigued to bring about His crucifixion, whereas it was the 'common people' who 'heard Him gladly' in Judea, as it was the slaves and labourers who formed the bulk of His believers throughout the Gentile world until the fury of the persecutions had passed. Roman and Jewish historians alike speak contemptuously of early Christianity as a religion of slaves and labourers. These early Christians had been socially enslaved. Christ and His disciples spoke to them of redemption, of freedom. They interpreted, rightly or wrongly, the words to mean an earthly redemption, a freedom here and now as a prelude possibly to the freedom hereafter; and hence they joined with enthusiasm the sect hated by their oppressors. We have had a similar experience in Ireland. The passionate adherence of the Irish to Catholicity in Reformation times was no doubt largely due to the fact that the English Government had embraced Protestantism.

For the last portion of the part quoted it should not be necessary to point out to anyone other than Father Kane that of all those things which he asserts Christianity has 'brought into the world', most are not here yet. The 'duty and honour of labour.' The greatest honours of Church and State are reserved for those classes whose members do not labour, and highest honours of all for those who claim that their ancestors have not laboured for a hundred generations. 'The lifting up of women to be man's helpmate and equal, not his plaything or his property.' She has not yet attained to that elevation in fact, and the Socialists are the only ones who claim it for her in their programmes, whereas his Holiness the Pope has recently denounced her for seeking the right to vote. 'The rights of the poor to the superabundance of the wealthy' is so far from being recognized that a starving man would be sent for seven years to prison for stealing a loaf of bread, and a rich man sent to the House of Lords for stealing a nation's liberty.

Universal ownership by the state of all means of wealth production is the one cardinal doctrine of Socialism. The Erfurt platform lays

down: 'Private property in the means of production has become incompatible with their proper utilization and full development.' The
platform of the Socialists of the United States lays down: 'The aim
of Socialism is the organization of the working classes for the purpose
of transforming the present system of private ownership of the means
of production into collective ownership by the entire people.' The
International Socialist Convention at Paris, 1900, lays down as an
essential condition of membership the admission of the essential
principles of Socialism; amongst them, 'the socialization of the means
of production and distribution'.

Now consider the colossal magnitude of such a scheme. The taking
of a census entails a strange amount of time and trouble. Try to
imagine what it would mean to ascertain the wants, needs, desires,
helps or difficulties of every man, woman and child in a nation, not
merely in one branch, but in every possible branch of human life; all
possible food stuffs, all possible dress stuffs, all possible lodging
accommodation, all possible means of transit, travel or communication. Then imagine what it would mean that all this should be catered
for; that all the possible labour should be applied in the right time,
place and manner; that all the possible materials and tools for work
should be made ready beforehand; that all possible difficulties or
accidents should be anticipated. Surely so vast, so unending, so com-
plex, so intricate a task would require many men of most surpassing
genius. Further, consider the enormous multitude of officials which
all this would require. The percentage of officials amongst the people
would be really alarming, and these flunkeys would grow fat on the
labour of the common fellows. It is absurd to suggest that every man
would get his turn at being a full-blown flunkey with a pet position,
or a full private with hard and nasty work to do.

With a childishness born of a training in a profession 'not
concerned with this world', the reverend gentleman does not
realize that the task of ascertaining and catering for the 'wants,
needs, desires', etc., of the nation is done every day by the common everyday men and women he sees around him – done in a
blundering, imperfect manner it is true, but still it is done. And
what is done imperfectly by the competing forces of capitalism
today, can be done more perfectly by the organized forces of
industry under Socialism. Government under Socialism will be
largely a matter of statistics. The chief administrative body of
the nation will be a collection of representatives from the various

industries and professions. From the industries they represent these administrators will learn of the demand for the articles they manufacture; the industries will learn from the storekeepers of the national stores and warehouses what articles are demanded by the general public who purchase at these stores, and the cumulative total of the reports given by storekeepers and industries will tell the chief administrative body (Congress, if you will) how much to produce, and where to place it to meet the demand. Likewise the reports brought to the representatives from their Industrial Union as to the relative equipment and power of their factories in each district will enable them to place their orders in the places most suited to fill them, and to supervise and push forward the building and development of new factories and machinery. All this is so obvious to a mind acquainted with the processes of modern industry that it gives the Socialist a feeling of talking to the baby class when he has to step aside in order to explain it. All the talk of Socialist flunkies, bosses, corruption, favouritism, etc., is the product of minds who are imagining the mechanism of capitalist business at work in a Socialist commonwealth, which is as absurd as to suppose that an Atlantic liner of the present day could be handled on the methods of a fishing boat on the sea of Galilee in the days of St Peter. When the workers elect their foreman and superintendents, and retain them only during effective supervision and handling of their allotted duties, when industries elect their representatives in the National Congress and the Congress obeys the demand emanating from the public for whom it exists, corruption and favouritism will be organically impossible. Being a merely human society there will be faults and imperfections of course, but it has also been whispered that faults and imperfections exist even in the Society of Jesus. And yet that institution does its work.

Father Kane says:

They suppose that they could avoid class distinctions, but unless the State should lapse into barbarism it must have its specialists, its great engineers, its great doctors, its great scientists, its great writers, its great statisticians, its great inventors, its great administrators, and, above all, its great officials. All these men should have their lives devoted to their profession with material comfort and studious ease, with high incentive to their talents' use, and with right reward for their labour done.

Observe the phrase, 'with high incentive to their talents' use', and its implied meaning, with great *monetary* reward. It is a strange fact that when Socialists preach the necessity and duty of the men and women of genius *serving* their fellows, instead of using their God-given genius to *rob* their 'fellow brothers and sisters of Christ', it is always a paid servant of Christ who gets up to denounce the idea, and to insists that progress will cease unless men gifted by God get the right to plunder their fellow-men. And yet Christ said, 'Give, hoping for nothing in return'. Fortunately, history knows and teaches us better than the Churchmen. It teaches us that the greatest 'engineers, doctors, scientists, writers, statisticians and inventors' reaped nothing but their labour for their pains, that for the most part they died in poverty, and that the highest incentive they ever possessed was the inward desire to give outward expression to the divine passion to create planted in their bosoms by Him who knew better than Father Kane. Under Socialism all will enjoy a full, free and abundant life, with every possibility and appliance provided them to serve well their fellows. And what more could the 'specialists' desire?

At present the two great Socialist organizations in the United States are at war. Among other choice epithets bandied between them one stigmatized the other as a party of 'scabs'. Among German Socialists there are signs of a cleavage, which must inevitably split in twain any Socialist state. A fierce jealousy between the educated and the proletarians; between, on the one hand, writers or speakers of good family, mostly the madcaps of atheistic universities and, on the other hand, the mere workmen, who are suspicious of any leaders who do not belong to the labour class. This is easily understood for Socialism must logically work out into a solid class organism to steady it, must oscillate wildly between a despotism, an oligarchy, and universal muddle; for a pure democracy has no other standard of right than the will of the masses, and the will of the masses is at the mercy of wire-pullers and demagogues. Thus a Socialist state would in theory be under the sovereignty of the mob in the street, but in reality it would be under the slavery of the conspirators in their den.

In previous portions of his tirade the reverend lecturer has been insisting vehemently that Socialism will inevitably mean a despotism in which political freedom will be impossible, and all must conform to the common mould. In this portion he finds fault with the Socialists because while in perfect agreement as to their object they quarrel over other matters. He says this 'must inevitably split in twain the Socialist State', but he carefully avoids explaining how the existence of two or more parties will destroy Socialism any more than it destroys capitalism. There are two, and more than two, purely capitalist parties in every nation in the civilized world. The fact that Socialists are as a rule men and women of strong individuality who fiercely contest for their rights, while it makes occasional unseemly squabbles in the Socialist ranks today, is the best guarantee that they are not likely to be working for a system which will crush their individuality or destroy their personal or political liberty. Also if splits in the party, harsh words among the members, and even hatred could destroy the movement, it would have died long ago, instead of growing stronger and more rapidly every day. And surely when we remember how fiercely hatreds have developed within the Christian fold – how Dominicans have fought the Jesuits, and the Jesuits have denounced the Dominicans, how the Lutherans have burned Calvinists and the Calvinists have burned the Lutherans – we have no right to demand from an organization of mere earthly origin more than was shown by organizations claiming Divine inspiration. Quarrels among Socialists, forsooth! Have we not had quarrels among Catholics? For sixty-eight years the Christian world saw two Popes directing and claiming its allegiance. The Pope at Avignon, supported by half of the bishops and clergy of the world, excommunicated the Pope at Rome and all his supporters; and his Holiness at Rome hurled back his curse in return. In 1604 Henry III of Germany entered Italy and found three Popes in Rome – all claiming the allegiance of the Catholic world, and denouncing each other worse than Socialists are denounced today. In 1527 an army of 30,000 troops under the Catholic Constable of Bourbon attacked and captured Rome, killed the Pope's soldiers, imprisoned his Holiness Clement VIII in the Castle of St Angelo, and put the sacred city to the sack. They were all Catholic soldiers under Catholic officers, and they plundered and ravished the centre of Catholicity. But, it will be said, these were only quarrels; they were not disputes over doctrine. Father Kane is a Jesuit; the majority of priests who at present are in the forefront of the attack upon Socialism are also Jesuits. Let us remind our reverend critics of a few incidents in the history of their own order – instances of the fierce disputes between the Jesuits and other Catholics on points of important Catholic doctrine:

In India, Jesuit missionaries adopted the life and practices of the Brahmins in 1609 in order to make converts, and in their desire to conciliate that caste *they even refused the Holy Sacrament to no-caste pariah converts*. This outrage upon Catholic teaching and practice was reported to the Pope by a Capuchin Friar, Norbert, and by the Bishop of Rosalia, and condemned in the strongest terms by Pope Innocent X in 1645, by Clement IX in 1669, by Clement XII in 1734 and 1739, and by Benedict XIV in 1745. Pope Benedict XIV in 1741 denounced the Jesuits as 'disobedient contumacious, captious and reprobate persons'. Melchior Cano, Bishop of the Canary Islands, banished the Jesuits from his diocese for teaching false doctrines, and for the same reason St Charles Borromeo expelled them from the diocese of Milan, as did also his successor, Cardinal Frederick Borromeo. We do not presume to say which side was right in these controversies, but we submit that if Popes and Jesuits could be wrong then on a point of doctrine they can be wrong now on Socialism – a point of economics and politics.

At the beginning of the seventeenth century a Jesuit missionary, Father Ricci, gained the favour of the Chinese Emperor, and he appointed Catholics to all high positions. The Catholic religion gained a strong foothold in China, established scientific observatories, and founded schools and universities. But the Dominican Fathers accused the Jesuits of allowing their converts to practise their old idolatry, and a fight started between the Jesuits and Dominicans over this question of what were called the 'Chinese Rites'. Nine different Popes condemned these 'Chinese Rites', but the Jesuits *refused to obey the Popes*, and in 1710 imprisoned the Papal Legate of Clement XI in the prison of the Inquisition at Macao, where he died. Sixtus V, Urban VIII and Clement VIII all died so soon after opposing the Jesuits that popular prejudice accused the Society of having had them assassinated. The Bishop of Pastoia, Scipio de Ricci, accused the Jesuits of having poisoned Pope Clement XIV, as did also Cardinal de Bernis, and the Spanish ambassador to the Court of Madrid declared that several Jesuits had told the Vicar-General of Padua the approximate date on which the Pope would die. In China the Jesuits in 1700 got an edict from the Pagan Emperor defending them against the charges of heresy brought by the Pope, but eventually the fight between the Catholics became so scandalous that all the heathens withdrew their toleration and suppressed the Christian religion in the empire. In 1661 the Jesuits alone had possessed 151 churches and 28 residences in China, had written 131 works upon religion, 103 on mathematics, and 53 on physical and moral science. All this was lost to Catholicity because of Jesuit perversion of Catholic doctrine, and consequent disgraceful feuds between Catholics. As the Jesuits perverted Catholic doctrine in India and China to gain the support of the great and powerful, is it wonderful if some think that they and other ecclesiastics are now again perverting Catholic doctrine for a like purpose?

The reader who has studied the facts set forth in our little excursion into Irish history in the introduction will appraise at its full value our reverend opponent's disquisition upon patriotism in the next passage:

There is a patriotism that is false. It is a mere morbid, hysterical idolatry of a fetish, with an unreasoning rancorous hatred of those people who are not of its own ilk. But there is a patriotism that is true. It is a thoughtful, manly worship for the nation of which one is the son; it is a chivalrous allegiance to her honour, a disinterested service of her fortune, a prayerful veneration for her name, a devotedness unto death to her life. The Socialist will say that that is sentiment. No wonder, then, that the Socialist is the enemy of his country. The French Socialists are the worst enemies of France. The German Socialists are the worst enemies of Germany. The English Socialists are the worst enemies of the power, the greatness and the empire of England. But our sentiment is the heartbeat of men true to their country; their Socialism is the heartburn of traitors to their Fatherland. If it be sentiment that a child should love its mother, that a man should love his home, then it is sentiment that a citizen should love his country, that a patriot should love his nature. But if this be sentiment, then I say that is the power which makes a nation. Ah! there is something in your inmost nature that affirms the truth and re-echoes the enthusiasm of what the poet sang:

> Breathes there a man with soul so dead,
> Who never to himself hath said,
> This is my own, my native land.

The Socialist doctrine teaches that all men are brothers, that the same red blood of a common humanity flows in the veins of all races, creeds, colours and nations, that the interests of Labour are everywhere identical, and that wars are an abomination. Is not this also good Catholic doctrine – the doctrine of a Church which prides itself upon being universal or Catholic? How, then, can that doctrine which is high and holy in theory on the lips of a Catholic become a hissing and a blasphemy when practised by the Socialist? The Socialist does not cease to love his country when he tries to make that country the common property of its people; he rather shows a greater love of country than is shown by those who wish to perpetuate a system which makes the great majority of the people of a country exiles and outcasts, living by sufferance of capitalists and landlords in their native land. Under Socialism we can all voice the saying of the poet, at present 'our' native land is in pawn to landlords and capitalists.

When the reverend lecturer hurls at the Socialists the taunt that they are the worst enemies of their own country, whatever that country be, he is only repeating against us the accusation made more truly in times past against the order of which he is such an ornament. The Jesuits have been expelled from every Catholic country in Europe, and the grounds on which they have been expelled were everywhere the same, viz., that they were the worst enemies of their country, and were constantly intriguing against the government and national welfare, that their teaching made bad subjects, and all their influence was against the welfare of the state – just what they allege against Socialists today. They were expelled from Venice during the first half of the seventeenth century, from Portugal in 1759, from the French dominions in 1764 and 1767, from Spain in 1767, from Naples, Parma and Modena about the same time. Maria Theresa of Austria and Emperor Joseph, her son, also expelled them. The kings of Spain, Portugal and France united in an ultimatum to the Pope threatening to withdraw their countries from fealty to Rome and to create a schism unless the Pope suppressed them, and finally in a Brief issued 21 July 1773, his Holiness, Pope Clement XIV, suppressed the Jesuits 'in all the States of Christendom'. As the Catholic author of the article on the Jesuits in the Encyclopaedia Americana truly says, 'They have been expelled over and over again from almost every Catholic country in Europe.' In 1601 the secular priests of England issued a pamphlet entitled 'Important Considerations', in which they laid the blame of the Penal Laws against Catholics upon the Jesuits. The author of this work, William Watson, afterwards died a martyr for the Catholic faith. The Papal Brief, Dominus ac Redemptor, speaks of their defiance of their own constitution expressly revised by Pope Paul V, *forbidding them to interfere in politics*, of the great ruin to souls caused by their quarrels with local ordinaries and other religious orders, *their conformity to heathen usages in the East*, and the disturbances resulting in persecution of the Church which they have stirred up even in Catholic countries, so that several Popes have been obliged to punish them. It is instructive to recall that upon their suppression the Jesuits took refuge in Russia under Catherine, and in Prussia under Frederick, both sovereigns being freethinkers. Not until the French Revolution had frightened all liberal ideas out of the crowned heads of Europe, and the fall of Napoleon enabled the sceptred tyrants of England and the Continent to place their iron heels upon the necks of the people did the Jesuits once more receive an invitation to resume their activity and their existence as an order. That invitation was coincident with the suppression of all popular liberties, and the enthronement of absolute power.

Is it not, then, a joke to see Socialists accused of being unpatriotic, and accused by a Jesuit?

In his fifth lecture our reverend critic simply refurbishes and places upon exhibition all the individual opinions of individual Socialists he can find antagonistic to religion, and tells us that their individual opinions are orthodox Socialist doctrines. After having for four weeks beaten the air in a wild endeavour to convince us that the Church is and always was against Socialism, that Socialists were and are beasts of immorality, uncleanness and treason, he affects to be horrified at the idea of those Socialists thinking and saying harsh things about the religion whose priests have been so busy slandering and vilifying them. We would say to him, and all others, that if the pioneers of the Socialist movement were indeed freethinkers, so much the more shame to the Church that by neglecting its obvious duty left freethinkers to do the work in which Churchmen ought to have been their leaders.

Sufficient to remind our readers, that, even according to the oft-repeated assertion of Father Kane, Socialism means a state of society in which the will of the people should be supreme, that therefore Marx and Bebel and Liebknecht and Vandervelde and Blatchford were not and are not working for the establishment of a system in which they would be able to force their theories about religion upon the people, but for a system in which the people would be free to accept only that of which their conscience approved. In the light of that central truth how absurd seems the following passage:

Now, in Socialism there are principles which no real Catholic can hold. First, Socialists hold that private ownership is in itself wrong; that, no Catholic can admit. Secondly, Socialists maintain that the child is the property of the State as against the father's right; that, no Catholic can admit. Thirdly, Socialists recognize divorce as a breaking of the marriage bond; that, no Catholic can admit. Fourth, Socialists limit and confine religion to mere personal private worship; that, no Catholic can admit.

We have seen that saints and Popes denounced private ownership of the means of life. We challenge the reverend father to produce from any Socialist congress or party a declaration that

Socialists desire to take the child from the father or mother, but we will produce many declarations that it is the right of the State to help fathers and mothers to support their children, and finally, we flatly deny, and brand as an unqualified falsehood, the statement ,that the Socialist programme declares for the breaking of the marriage bond. Our reverend and holy critics make it appear that the Socialist idea of society must be responsible for the other ideas held by some of its sponsors. Why not apply this to the Catholic Church then? When King Edward VII of England ascended the throne he swore that the Mass was blasphemous and idolatrous; and when he died the Vatican went into mourning. Did the Vatican believe that the institution of monarchy was not to be blamed for the official declaration of its supporters? And if so, why blame Socialism for the private, non-official declaration of a few of its supporters.

Recently there died in Europe a king – King Leopold of Belgium – whose private life was so disgracefully immoral that it was the scandal of Europe. A married man with a grown-up family, he kept a Parisian actress as his mistress, and led so scandalous a life that the females of his family refused to follow his body to the grave. Yet when he died the whole official Catholic world went into mourning for him. He was more of a representative of the institution of monarchy than any private individual can ever be of Socialism; but the Rev. Father Kane or his Holiness the Pope did not therefore deliver sermons against the wickedness of supporting kings. And what is true in these two striking examples is also true of kings, nobles and capitalists all the world over. In the United States the divorce rate for 100,000 of the population rose from 23 in 1880 to 73 in 1900. Between 1887 and 1906 the total number of divorces was 945,625. *This enormous increase of divorces was almost entirely among the classes least affected by Socialist teaching* – the middle and upper capitalist class. That is to say, among the class our reverend opponent is defending. Why all this howl about supposed Socialist theories of divorce, and all this silence about the capitalist practice thereof?

Is there any logical connection between Socialism and atheism? This question has two aspects; first, does atheism logically lead to

Socialism? And, secondly, does Socialism logically lead to atheism?
As regards the first question it is very evident that a wealthy atheist
is little likely to be a genuine Socialist. For him his wealth and
pleasure will be the only objects of his worship, and he will not
sacrifice them in order to secure the honour of being a Socialist
labourer. But with the atheist who is penniless it is quite another
matter. For him there is no moral law, because there is no law without a lawgiver, and there is no lawgiver but God; hence, there is no
right that can restrain him from taking all the wealth on which he
can lay his hands, and Socialism supplies him with the means of
doing this. A beggar atheist is a Socialist, unless he be a fool. The
answer to the second question is not so clear. Does Socialism logically
lead to atheism? *If we understand Socialism exclusively in its real
and essential sense as a social system, which would give exclusively to
the state all ownership of capital, of means of wealth production, and
kindred powers, with also the exclusive right of distribution and
administration of such goods, then we admit that Socialism is not
logically the same thing as atheism.* However wrong a man may be in
ethical or economic matters, he may yet be right in recognizing God.
This, however, is vague and abstract. Is Socialism logically incompatible with Catholicity? To this we must fearlessly answer this; a
true Catholic cannot be a real Socialist. Understand what this does
not mean and what it does mean. It does not mean that the Catholic
who calls himself a Socialist is thereby a heretic. It does not even
follow that a Catholic who is a real Socialist is thereby a heretic; but
it does logically follow that a real Catholic cannot be a real Socialist.
Do not push this statement unfairly towards one side or towards the
other.

When he makes the damaging admission he does in the point
we have put in *italic type*, our reverend friend knocks the feet
from under his own case; and when he goes on to wriggle still
further in an attempt to cloud the issue he reveals that his purpose is not to discuss Socialism so much as to traduce it. He
admits that logically there is no connection between Socialism
and atheism, and yet his whole discourse was a long-drawn-out
attempt to prove such a connection. In what other walk of life
would a man be tolerated who indulged in such senseless hair-
splitting as the foregoing, or in such vilification as the following:

What will you then have in your Socialist paradise? A herd of
human cattle, some of them intelligent, educated, cultured, a very

suspected lot in the Socialistic state, most of them, practically all of them, a Godless, unprincipled, immoral crowd. In our Christian commonwealth there are many criminals, but they are the exception. They are an offence against our principles and rebels against our right. Under Socialism criminals would be the authorized spokesmen of your principles and the ruthless henchmen of your lawlessness. Again and again, without God there is no morality, and without morality there is only left the God of the Socialist – irreligion, immorality, degradation of the man and suicide of the nation.

Note the words, 'Under Socialism criminals would be the authorized spokesman of your principles.' He has repeatedly asserted that under Socialism the will of the people would rule, and now he asserts that the people would choose criminals as their spokesmen. Yet such a thing as a Socialist criminal is practically unknown in the records of the police courts of the world. Can any sane man believe that if the 'means of wealth production and kindred powers' were common property that the people would be so debased by the enjoyment of the full fruits of their labour that they would elect criminals to be their spokesmen and rulers? Or that a man cannot worship God unless he concedes the right of a capitalist to three fourths or more of the fruits of his labour? Or that a people cannot love their country if they own it as their common property? Or that a nation would commit suicide if it refused to allow a small class to monopolize all its natural resources and means of life? Or that the nation which refused to allow a class to use the governmental machinery for personal aggrandizement, to stir up wars and slaughter thousands of men 'made in the image of God' for the sake of more profits for a few, that the nation which should refuse to allow this would be 'powerless in the moral order', and hastening on to decay? Yet it is this monstrous farrago of nonsense Rev. Father Kane attempts to establish in his fifth lecture.

THE FIREBRAND OR THE OLIVE LEAF

Socialists will not shrink from resorting to brute force. A Socialist ring will not scruple when there is a question of finally superseding the old order of society to snatch up anarchist weapons – the dagger, the torch, the bomb. Listen to the candid utterances of the great founder of Socialism. Karl Marx, with his henchman, Engels, declared in their manifesto 'that their purpose can be obtained only by a violent subversion of the existing order. Let the ruling classes tremble at the Communist revolution.'

Again, at the Congress of The Hague, Karl Marx, as the mouthpiece of Socialists, officially declared: 'In most countries of Europe violence must be the lever of our social reform. This violent upheaval must be universal. A proof of this was witnessed in the Commune of Paris, which only failed because in other capitals — Berlin and Madrid — a simultaneous revolutionary movement did not break out in connection with the mighty upheaval of the proletariat in Paris.' Again, Bebel, one of the greatest leaders of Socialist thought, dared to say in the German Reichstag: 'The Commune in Paris was only a slight skirmish in the war which the proletariat is prepared to wage against all palaces.' Again, Bebel said elsewhere this Socialistic change cannot be brought about by 'sprinkling rose-water'. At the Socialist Convention at Ghent in 1877 one of their leaders said: 'When our day comes, rifle and cannon will face about to mow down the foes of the Socialist people.' At a public meeting during the recent elections in England an MP supporter of the Liberal Government is reported to have said: 'I honour the man or woman who throws a bomb.'

That some Socialists believe that force may be used to inaugurate the new social order only indicates their conviction that the criminal capitalist and ruling classes will not peacefully abide by the verdict of the ballot, but will strive by violence to perpetuate their robber rule in spite of the declared will of the majority of the people. In this conviction such Socialists are strengthened by the record of all the revolutions of the world's history. It is a well-established fact that from the earliest revolutionary outbreak known down to the Commune of Paris, or Red Sunday in Russia, the first blood has been shed, the first blow struck, by the possessing conservative classes. And we are not so childish as to imagine that the capitalist class of the future will shrink from the shedding of the blood of the workers in order to retain their ill-gotten gains. They shed more blood, destroy more working class lives every year, by the criminal carelessness with which they conduct industry and drive us to nerve-racking speed, than is lost in the average international war. In the United States there are killed on the railroads in one year more men than died in the Boer War on both sides. When the capitalists kill us so rapidly for the sake of a few pence extra profit it would be suicidal to expect that they would hesitate to slaughter us wholesale when their very existence as parasites was at stake. Therefore the Socialists anticipate violence only because they know the evil nature of the beast they contend with. But with a working class thoroughly organized and already as workers in possession of the railroads, shops, factories and ships we do not need to fear their violence. The hired assassin armies of the capitalist class will be impotent for evil when the railroad men refuse to transport them, the miners to furnish coal for their ships of war, the dock labourers to load or coal these ships, the clothing workers to make uniforms, the sailors to provision them, the telegraphists to serve them, or the farmers to feed them. In the vote, the strike, the boycott and the *lockout exercised against the master class* the Socialists have weapons that will make this social revolution comparatively bloodless and peaceable despite the tigerish instincts or desires of the capitalist enemy, and the doleful Cassandra-like prophecies of our critic.

And if the capitalists do abide the issue of the ballot and allow this battle to be fought out on lines of peaceful political and economic action, gladly we will do likewise. But if not –

But the real point is this: it is not merely the Rothschilds or other millionaires who are to be robbed; it is not merely the fashionable people who live in palaces and drive in motor-cars who are to be robbed, but the shopkeepers are also to be robbed; it is not merely the great big shopkeepers who are to be robbed, but every small business house will be robbed. The professional classes, the barristers and the doctors will be robbed. The small farmer, the small cottager will be evicted. The cabman's horse and cab will be taken from him. The poor woman who sells apples in the street will have her basket seized upon. These are all ways of making money, and the Socialist says that nobody has any right to make money except the Socialist state. Do you think that men would stand for this? Do you think that a tenant who has bought out his land will willingly give it up to the Socialist who promises to spoon-feed him? Do you think that any respectable shopkeeper would give up his shop for the honour of being the shop-boy of a Socialist flunkey? Do you think that any manly man would give up the few shillings that are his own in order to become an irresponsible easy-going loafer in an idealized work-house? No.

This argument is brought in after telling a silly story about a Socialist who wanted Rothschild to divide up, and the story is told despite the fact that the reverend and pious lecturer has frequently explained that Socialism has nothing to do with dividing up. In fact Socialists want to stop dividing up with the 'irresponsible easy-going loafers' called aristocrats and capitalists, in the 'idealized work-houses' known as palaces and mansions. All of those poor workers whom he mentions – the small farmer, the cottager, the cabman, the apple-woman, the doctor – all are compelled to divide up with the capitalist, speculator and landlord, and Socialism proposes to them that instead of wearing life out working night and day as in the case of the doctor, or shivering and suffering as in the case of the farmer, the cottager, the cabman and the apple-woman, they shall help to establish a system of society where the functions they now perform shall be performed better through more perfect organization, with equipment supplied by the community, and where they shall be honoured co-workers with all their fellow-workers with an old age guaranteed against the want and privation they know awaits them under the present order. And they are hearkening to this Socialist promise of relief from their present social purgatory.

Father Kane next proceeds to quote Socialists to prove the beneficence of medieval Catholicism. He says:

The contrast is reproduced under a different aspect when we compare the Church of Christ with the Church of Luther, King Harry and Queen Bess. Whoever studies Socialism will find that there is much to learn from this contrast. We read in Professor Nitti, of Naples: 'An English Socialist Hyndman, whose profound historical and economic learning cannot be questioned even by his adversaries, has understood and admirably expressed the many benefits society has derived from the Church of the Middle Ages.' Hyndman wrote: 'It is high time that the nonsense that has been foisted on to the public by men interested in suppressing the facts should be exposed. It is not true that the Church of our ancestors was the organized fraud which it suits fanatics to represent it. The monasteries and priests did far more for elementary education than is at all known ... As to university education, where would Oxford be today but for the munificence of bishops, monks, and nuns? Fourteen of her finest colleges were founded by Churchmen or abbots for the benefit of the children of the people. The Reformation converted these colleges into luxurious preserves for the sons of the aristocracy.' He tells us how the Reformation converted the lands of the monastries into the properties of rack-renting landlords. Abbots and priors were the best landlords in England. While the Church had power, permanent or general pauperism was unknown. One third of all tithes, one third of all ecclesiastical revenue was first set aside to be given to the poor. The monks were the roadmakers, almsgivers, teachers, doctors, nurses of the country. They built, furnished and attended the hospitals, and gave the poor relief out of their own funds. While the monasteries stood, the poor or unemployed were always sure of food and shelter. Look at the other side of the contrast. When Harry VIII was king in Merrie England he wanted to get rid of his wife and he wanted to get money. Both motives moved him to break away from the Church of Christ, and to confiscate the monasteries. One sad and most pitiful result was that thousands and thousands were driven out on the roads to beg. They were all able men and willing to work, but the monasteries had disappeared, and with them work and shelter and food. These 'sturdy beggars', or 'stalwart vagabonds', as they were called, thronged the road. They had been able to earn their bread under the old Church of Christ, but under the new church of King Hal and his merry men these 'sturdy beggars' were a nuisance. In 1547 a law was passed that these 'sturdy beggars' should be branded with hot irons and handed over as slaves to the person who denounced them, or if again caught, they were to be hanged. Under good Queen Bess unlicensed beggars over fourteen were flogged and branded on the left ear unless someone would take them into service for two years. If they begged again, all over eighteen were executed unless someone was willing to take them into service for two years; caught a third time, death was the penalty, without reprieve. Hollingshead asserts that in the reign of the good King Henry VIII 72,000 sturdy beggars were hanged for begging. That was the contrast between the Reformation and the love of Christ's Church for Christ's poor. It was the way in which the Reformation solved the difficulty of the unemployed. Queen Bess, the 'virgin queen', the good sweet Queen Bess, found a woman's way of following her father's mood. She had her 'stalwart vagabonds' strung up in batches, like flitches of bacon along the rafters, in order to teach the people the godly way in which they should walk – the way of her Reformation of the Church of Christ. The Church of Christ has always protected the poor.

This long extract should be enlightening and illuminating to our readers. It shows that the Socialists have been uniformly fair in their treatment of the attitude of the Catholic Church of the past towards the poor, that they have defended that Church from the attacks of unscrupulous Protestant historians, upon that point, so that our reverend friend has to admit that a correct knowledge of the contrast between the attitude of the Church and that of the Protestant reformers can be best attained by whoever studies Socialist literature. But, as we pointed out in a previous chapter, when Father Kane is recounting the numberless murders, outrages and barbarities practised upon the poor by the aristocracy of the Reformation he is telling also where we are to find the title deeds of the landed estates of England and Ireland. And it is just those landed estates, gained by such means, that Father Kane and his like are fighting to perpetuate in the ownership of the English and Irish aristocracy today. How do the Catholic clergy dare to defend the possessors in the present possession of their stolen property, when they publicly proclaim from the altar their knowledge of the inhuman crimes against God and man by which that property passed out of the hands of Church and people? The Reformation was the capitalist idea appearing in the religious field; as capitalism teaches that the social salvation of man depends solely upon his own individual effort, so Protestantism, echoing it, taught that the spiritual salvation of man depends solely upon his own individual appeal to God; as capitalism abolished the idea of social interdependence which prevailed under feudalism, and made men isolated units in a warring economic world, so Protestantism abolished the independent links of priests, hierarchy and pontiffs which in the Catholic system unites man with his Creator, and left man at the mercy of his own interpretations of warring texts and theories. In fine, as capitalism taught the doctrine of every man for himself, and by its growing power forced such doctrines upon the ruling class, it created its reflex in the religious world, and that reflex, proclaiming that individual belief was the sole necessity of salvation, appears in history as the Protestant Reformation. Now, the Church curses the Protestant Reformation – the child; and blesses capitalism – its parent.

Now listen to the peroration of our critic:

Nothing will do but Socialism.

Not so! not so! The Church of Christ teaches both men and masters that for their own sake they should be friends not foes, that their mutual interests are inseparably interwoven, and that they are bound together not merely by the duties or rights of justice, but by a sacred bond of kindliness, which is the same virtue that moves a man to fondly love his home and nobly love his fatherland. Still, still! – that misery! that most sad poverty, that despairing wretchedness of utter want! Surely! surely! were the kind Christ here, Whose heart was moved to tender pity for the hungering crowd; surely He would give them food. He is not here, but in His stead He has placed you, Christian men and women, that you may do His blessed work. Have pity! have pity on the poor. We cannot stand idly by with folded arms while so many starve, nor can we suffer, while we have wealth to spare, that such multitudes who are brothers and sisters of our human blood should eke out in lingering death a life that is not worth the living. There is no need, no excuse for Socialism. But there is sore need of social reform. The state is indeed bound to enforce such remedial measures as are needed, and of these, whatever be our politics or party, we must all approve. But in our own way and in our own measure we should recognize in actual practice that Christians should be like the great Christ Who had pity on the poor.

And so he concludes – with an appeal for pity for the poor. After all his long discourse, after again and again admitting the tyranny, the extortions, the frauds, the injustices perpetrated in our midst every day by those who control and own our means of existence he has no remedy to offer but pity! After all his brave appeal to individuality, to national honour, to the heroic spirit in poor men and women, he shrinks from appealing to that individuality, to that national honour, to that heroic spirit in the poor and asking them to so manifest themselves as to rescue their lives from the control of the forces of mammon. Professing to denounce mammon, he yet shrinks from leading the forces of righteousness against it, and by so shrinking shows that all his professed solicitude for justice, all his vaunted hatred of tyranny, were 'mere sound and fury, signifying nothing'.

Is not this attitude symbolic of the attitude of the Church for hundreds of years? Ever counselling humility, but sitting in the seats of the mighty; ever patching up the diseased and broken wrecks of an unjust social system, but blessing the system which made the wrecks and spread the disease; ever running divine discontent and pity into the ground as the lightning rod runs and dissipates lightning, instead of gathering it and directing it for socal righteousness as the electric battery generates and directs electricity for social use.

The day has passed for patching up the capitalist system; it must go. And in the work of abolishing it the Catholic and the Protestant, the Catholic and the Jew, the Catholic and the Freethinker, the Catholic and the Buddhist, the Catholic and the Mahometan will co-operate together, knowing no rivalry but the rivalry of endeavour towards an end beneficial to all. For, as we have said elsewhere, Socialism is neither Protestant nor Catholic, Christian nor Freethinker, Buddhist, Mahometan, nor Jew; it is only HUMAN. *We of the Socialist working class realize that as we suffer together we must work together that we may enjoy together*. We reject the firebrand of capitalist warfare and offer you the olive leaf of brotherhood and justice to and for all.

First published as a pamphlet in 1910

2

NATIONALISM AND IMPERIALISM

SOCIALISM AND NATIONALISM

In Ireland at the present time there are at work a variety of agencies seeking to preserve the national sentiment in the hearts of the people.

These agencies, whether Irish Language movements, Literary Societies or Commemoration Committees, are undoubtedly doing a work of lasting benefit to this country in helping to save from extinction the precious racial and national history, language and characteristics of our people.

Nevertheless, there is a danger that by too strict an adherence to their present methods of propaganda, and consequent neglect of vital living issues, they may only succeed in stereotyping our historical studies into a worship of the past, or crystallizing nationalism into a tradition – glorious and heroic indeed, but still only a tradition.

Now traditions may, and frequently do, provide materials for a glorious martyrdom, but can never be strong enough to ride the storm of a successful revolution.

If the national movement of our day is not merely to re-enact the old sad tragedies of our past history, it must show itself capable of rising to the exigencies of the moment.

It must demonstrate to the people of Ireland that our nationalism is not merely a morbid idealizing of the past, but is also capable of formulating a distinct and definite answer to the problems of the present and a political and economic creed capable of adjustment to the wants of the future.

This concrete political and social ideal will best be supplied, I believe, by the frank acceptance on the part of all earnest nationalists of the Republic as their goal.

Not a Republic as in France, where a capitalist monarchy with an elective head parodies the constitutional abortions of England, and in open alliance with the Muscovite despotism brazenly flaunts its apostasy to the traditions of the Revolution.

Not a Republic as in the United States, where the power of the purse has established a new tyranny under the forms of freedom; where, one hundred years after the feet of the last British red-coat polluted the streets of Boston, British landlords and financiers impose upon American citizens a servitude compared with which the tax of pre-Revolution days was a mere trifle.

No! the Republic I would wish our fellow-countrymen to set before them as their ideal should be of such a character that the mere mention of its name would at all times serve as a beacon-light to the oppressed of every land, at all times holding forth promise of freedom and plenteousness as the reward of their efforts on its behalf.

To the tenant farmer, ground between landlordism on the one hand and American competition on the other, as between the upper and the nether millstone; to the wage-workers in the towns, suffering from the exactions of the slave-driving capitalist, to the agricultural labourer, toiling away his life for a wage barely sufficient to keep body and soul together; in fact to every one of the toiling millions upon whose misery the outwardly-splendid fabric of our modern civilization is reared, the Irish Republic might be made a word to conjure with – a rallying point for the disaffected, a haven for the oppressed, a point of departure for the Socialist, enthusiastic in the cause of human freedom.

This linking together of our national aspirations with the hopes of the men and women who have raised the standard of revolt against that system of capitalism and landlordism, of which the British Empire is the most aggressive type and resolute defender, should not, in any sense, import an element of discord into the ranks of earnest nationalists, and would serve to place us in touch with fresh reservoirs of moral and physical strength sufficient to lift the cause of Ireland to a more commanding position than it has occupied since the day of Benburb.

It may be pleaded that the ideal of a Socialist Republic, implying, as it does, a complete political and economic revolution, would be sure to alienate all our middle-class and aristocratic supporters, who would dread the loss of their property and privileges.

What does this objection mean? That we must conciliate the privileged classes in Ireland!

But you can only disarm their hostility by assuring them that in a *free* Ireland their 'privileges' will not be interfered with. That is to say, you must guarantee that when Ireland is free of foreign domination, the green-coated Irish soldiers will guard the fraudulent gains of capitalist and landlord from 'the thin hands of the poor' just as remorselessly and just as effectually as the scarlet-coated emissaries of England do today.

On no other basis will the classes unite with you. Do you expect the masses to fight for this ideal?

When you talk of freeing Ireland, do you only mean the chemical elements which compose the soil of Ireland? Or it is the Irish people you mean? If the latter, from what do you propose to free them? From the rule of England?

But all systems of political administration or governmental machinery are but the reflex of the economic forms which underlie them.

English rule in Ireland is but the symbol of the fact that English conquerors in the past forced upon this country a property system founded upon spoliation, fraud and murder: that, as the present-day exercise of the 'rights of property' so originated involves the continual practice of legalized spoliation and fraud, English rule is found to be the most suitable form of government by which the spoliation can be protected, and an English army the most pliant tool with which to execute judicial murder when the fears of the propertied classes demand it.

The Socialist who would destroy, root and branch, the whole brutally materialistic system of civilization, which like the English language we have adopted as our own, is, I hold, a far more deadly foe to English rule and tutelage than the superficial thinker who imagines it possible to reconcile Irish freedom with those insidious but disastrous forms of economic subjection – landlord tyranny, capitalist fraud and unclean usury; baneful fruits of the Norman Conquest, the unholy trinity, of which

Strongbow and Diarmuid MacMurchadha – Norman thief and Irish traitor – were the fitting precursors and apostles.

If you remove the English army tomorrow and hoist the green flag over Dublin Castle, unless you set about the organization of the Socialist Republic your efforts would be in vain.

England would still rule you. She would rule you through her capitalists, through her landlords, through her financiers, through the whole array of commercial and individualist institutions she has planted in this country and watered with the tears of our mothers and the blood of our martyrs.

England would still rule you to your ruin, even while your lips offered hypocritical homage at the shrine of that Freedom whose cause you had betrayed.

Nationalism without Socialism – without a reorganization of society on the basis of a broader and more developed form of that common property which underlay the social structure of Ancient Erin – is only national recreancy.

It would be tantamount to a public declaration that our oppressors had, so far, succeeded in inoculating us with their perverted conceptions of justice and morality that we had finally decided to accept those conceptions as our own, and no longer needed an alien army to force them upon us.

As a Socialist I am prepared to do all one man can do to achieve for our motherland her rightful heritage – independence; but if you ask me to abate one jot or tittle of the claims of social justice, in order to conciliate the privileged classes, then I must decline.

Such action would be neither honourable nor feasible. Let us never forget that he never reaches Heaven who marches thither in the company of the Devil. Let us openly proclaim our faith: the logic of events is with us.

Shan Van Vocht, January 1897

SOCIALISM AND IRISH NATIONALISM

THE public life of Ireland has been generally so much identified with the struggle for political emancipation, that, naturally, the economic side of the situation has only received from our historians and public men a very small amount of attention.

Scientific Socialism is based upon the truth incorporated in this proposition of Karl Marx, that, 'the economic dependence of the workers on the monopolists of the means of production is the foundation of slavery *in all its forms*, the cause of nearly all social misery, modern crime, mental degradation and political dependence'. Thus this false exaggeration of purely political forms which has clothed in Ireland the struggle for liberty, must appear to the Socialist an inexplicable error on the part of a people so strongly crushed down as the Irish.

But the error is more in appearance than in reality.

The reactionary attitude of our political leaders notwithstanding, the great mass of the Irish people know full well that if they had once conquered that political liberty which they struggle for with so much ardour, it would have to be used as a means of social redemption before their well-being would be assured.

In spite of occasional exaggeration of its immediate results one must remember that by striving determinedly, as they have done, towards this definite political end, the Irish are working on the lines of conduct laid down by modern Socialism as the indispensable condition of success.

Since the abandonment of the unfortunate insurrectionism of the early Socialists whose hopes were exclusively concentrated on the eventual triumph of an uprising and barricade struggle, modern Socialism, relying on the slower, but surer method of the ballot-box, has directed the attention of its partisans toward the peaceful conquest of the forces of government in the interests of the revolutionary ideal.

The advent of Socialism can only take place when the revolutionary proletariat, in possession of the organized forces of the nation (the political power of government) will be able to build up a social organization in conformity with the natural march of industrial development.

On the other hand, non-political co-operative effort must infallibly succumb in face of the opposition of the privileged classes, entrenched behind the ramparts of law and monopoly. This is why, even when he is from the economic point of view intensely conservative, the Irish Nationalist, even with his false reasoning, is an active agent in social regeneration, in so far as he seeks to invest with full power over its own destinies a people actually governed in the interests of a feudal aristocracy.

The section of the Socialist army to which I belong, the Irish Socialist Republican Party, never seeks to hide its hostility to those purely bourgeois parties which at present direct Irish politics.

But, in inscribing on our banners an ideal to which they also give lip-homage, we have no intention of joining in a movement which could debase the banner of revolutionary Socialism.

The Socialist parties of France oppose the mere Republicans without ceasing to love the Republic. In the same way the Irish Socialist Republican Party seeks the independence of the nation, while refusing to conform to the methods or to employ the arguments of the chauvinist Nationalist.

As Socialists we are not imbued with national or racial hatred by the remembrance that the political and social order under which we live was imposed on our fathers at the point of the sword; that during 700 years Ireland has resisted this unjust foreign domination; that famine, pestilence and bad government have made this western isle almost a desert and scattered our exiled fellow-countrymen over the whole face of the globe.

The enunciation of facts such as I have just stated is not able today to inspire or to direct the political energies of the militant working class of Ireland; such is not the foundation of our resolve to free Ireland from the yoke of the British Empire. We recognize rather that during all these centuries the great mass of the British people had no political existence whatever; that England was, politically and socially, terrorized by a numerically

small governing class; that the atrocities which have been perpetrated against Ireland are only imputable to the unscrupulous
ambition of this class, greedy to enrich itself at the expense of
defenceless men; that up to the present generation the great
majority of the English people were denied a deliberate voice in
the government of their own country; that it is, therefore, mani-
festly unjust to charge the English people with the past crimes of
their Government; and that at the worst we can but charge them
with a criminal apathy in submitting to slavery and allowing
themselves to be made an instrument of coercion for the enslavement of others. An accusation as applicable to the present as to
the past.

But whilst refusing to base our political action on hereditary
national antipathy, and wishing rather comradeship with the
English workers than to regard them with hatred, we desire with
our precursors the United Irishmen of 1798 that our animosities
be buried with the bones of our ancestors – there is not a party
in Ireland which accentuates more as a vital principle of its
political faith the need of separating Ireland from England and
of making it absolutely independent. In the eyes of the ignorant
and of the unreflecting this appears an inconsistency, but I am
persuaded that our Socialist brothers in France will immediately
recognize the justice of the reasoning upon which such a policy
is based.

1. We hold 'the economic emancipation of the worker requires
the conversion of the means of production into the common
property of Society'. Translated into the current language and
practice of actual politics this teaches that the necessary road to
be travelled towards the establishment of Socialism requires the
transference of the means of production from the hands of
private owners to those of public bodies directly responsible to
the entire community.

2. Socialism seeks then in the interest of the democracy to
strengthen popular action on all public bodies.

3. Representative bodies in Ireland would express more
directly the will of the Irish people than when those bodies
reside in England.

An Irish Republic would then be the natural depository of

popular power; the weapon of popular emancipation, the only power which would show in the full light of day all these class antagonisms and lines of economic demarcation now obscured by the mists of bourgeois patriotism.

In that there is not a trace of chauvinism. We desire to preserve with the English people the same political relations as with the people of France, or Germany, or of any other country; the greatest possible friendship, but also the strictest independence. Brothers, but not bedfellows. Thus, inspired by another ideal, conducted by reason not by tradition, following a different course, the Socialist Republican Party of Ireland arrives at the same conclusion as the most irreconcilable Nationalist. The governmental power of England over us must be destroyed; the bonds which bind us to her must be broken. Having learned from history that all bourgeois movements end in compromise, that the bourgeois revolutionists of today become the conservatives of tomorrow, the Irish Socialists refuse to deny or to lose their identity with those who only half understand the problem of liberty. They seek only the alliance and the friendship of those hearts who, loving liberty for its own sake, are not afraid to follow its banner when it is uplifted by the hands of the working class who have most need of it. Their friends are those who would not hesitate to follow that standard of liberty, to consecrate their lives in its service even should it lead to the terrible arbitration of the sword.

L'Irlande Libre, Paris, 1897

PATRIOTISM AND LABOUR

WHAT is Patriotism? Love of country, someone answers. But what is meant by 'love of country'? 'The rich man,' says a French writer, 'loves his country because he conceives it owes him a duty, whereas the poor man loves his country as he believes he owes it a duty.' The recognition of the duty we owe our country is, I take it, the real mainspring of patriotic action; and our 'country', properly understood, means not merely the particular spot on the earth's surface from which we derive our parentage, but also comprises all the men, women and children of our race whose collective life constitutes our country's political existence. True patriotism seeks the welfare of each in the happiness of all, and is inconsistent with the selfish desire for worldly wealth which can only be gained by the spoliation of less favoured fellow-mortals.

Viewed in the light of such a definition, what are the claims to patriotism possessed by the moneyed class of Ireland? The percentage of weekly wages of £1 per week and under received by the workers of the three kingdoms is stated by the Board of Trade report to be as follows: England, 40; Scotland, 50; and Ireland, 78 per cent. In other words, three out of every four wage-earners in Ireland receive less than £1 per week. Who is to blame? What determines the rate of wages? The competition among workers for employment. There is always a large surplus of unemployed labour in Ireland, and owing to this fact the Irish employer is able to take advantage of the helplessness of his poorer fellow-countrymen and compel them to work for less than their fellows in England receive for the same class of work.

The employees of our municipal Corporations and other public bodies in Ireland are compelled by our middle-class town-councillors – their compatriots – to accept wages of from 4s. to 8s. per week less than English Corporations pay in similar branches of public service. Irish railway servants receive from

5s. to 10s. per week less than English railway servants in the same departments, although shareholders in Irish railways draw higher dividends than are paid on the most prosperous English lines. In all private employment in Ireland the same state of matters prevails. Let us be clear upon this point. There is no law upon the statute book, no power possessed by the Privy Council, no civil or military function under the control of Prime Minister, Lord Lieutenant, or Chief Secretary which can, does or strives to compel the employing class in Ireland to take advantage of the crowded state of the labour market and use it to depress the wages of their workers to the present starvation level.

To the greed of our moneyed class, operating upon the social conditions created by landlordism and capitalism and maintained upon foreign bayonets, such a result is alone attributable, and no amount of protestations should convince intelligent workers that the class which grinds them down to industrial slavery can, at the same moment, be leading them forward to national liberty. True patriotism seeks the welfare of each in the happiness of all, and is inconsistent with the selfish desire for worldly wealth which can only be gained by the spoliation of less favoured fellow-mortals. It is the mission of the working class to give to patriotism this higher, nobler, significance. This can only be done by our working class, as the only universal, all-embracing class, organizing as a distinct political party, recognizing in Labour the cornerstone of our economic edifice and the animating principle of our political action.

Hence the rise of the Irish Socialist Republican Party. We are resolved upon national independence as the indispensable groundwork of industrial emancipation, but we are equally resolved to have done with the leadership of a class whose social charter is derived from oppression. Our policy is the outcome of long reflection upon the history and peculiar circumstances of our country. In an independent country the election of a majority of Socialist representatives to the Legislature means the conquest of political power by the revolutionary party, and consequently the mastery of the military and police forces of the State, which would then become the ally of revolution instead of its enemy.

In the work of social reconstruction which would then ensue, the State power – created by the propertied classes for their own class purposes – would serve the new social order as a weapon in its fight against such adherents of the privileged orders as strove to resist the gradual extinction of their rule.

Ireland not being an independent country, the election of a majority of Socialist Republicans would not, unfortunately, place the fruits of our toil so readily within our grasp. But it would have another, perhaps no less important, effect. It would mean that for the first time in Irish history a clear majority of the responsible electorate of the Irish nation – men capable of bearing arms – had registered at the ballot-boxes their desire for separation from the British Empire. Such a verdict, arrived at not in the tumultuous and, too often, fickle enthusiasm of monster meetings, but in the sober atmosphere and judicial calmness of the polling-booth, would ring like a trumpet-call in the ears alike of our rulers and of every enemy of the British imperial system. That would not long survive such a consummation. Its enemies would read in the verdict thus delivered at the ballot-box a passionate appeal for help against the oppressor, the *moral* insurrection of the Irish people, which a small expeditionary force and war material might convert into such a *military* insurrection as would exhaust the power of the empire at home and render its possessions an easy prey abroad. How long would such an appeal be disregarded?

Meanwhile, there is no temporary palliative of our misery, no material benefit which Parliament can confer that could not be extorted by the fear of a revolutionary party seeking to create such a situation as I have described, sooner than by any action of even the most determined Home Rule or other constitutional party. Thus, alike for present benefits and for future freedom, the revolutionary policy is the best. A party aiming at a merely political Republic and proceeding upon such lines, would always be menaced by the danger that some astute English Statesman might, by enacting a sham measure of Home Rule, disorganize the Republican forces by an appearance of concessions, until the critical moment had passed. But the Irish Socialist Republican Party, by calling attention to evils inherent in that social system of which the British Empire is but the highest political expression, founds its propaganda upon discontent with social iniquities which will only pass away when the Empire is no more, and thus implants in all its followers an undying, ineradicable hatred of the enemy, which will remain undisturbed and unmollified by any conceivable system of political quackery whatever.

An Irish Socialist Republic ought, therefore, to be the rallying cry of all our countrymen who desire to see the union and triumph of Patriotism and Labour.

Editorial Note:

Whilst in full sympathy with Mr Connolly's views on the labour and social questions, we are absolutely opposed to the scheme he puts forward for the formation of an Irish Republican party in the British Parliament. Any conscientious Republican would stick at the oath of allegiance and no reliance could be placed on what John O'Leary calls 'double-oathed' men. John Mitchel allowed himself to be returned as a representative, but absolutely refused to entertain the idea of claiming his seat. He looked upon his election merely as a declaration in favour of his unalterable rebel principles. We would like to have this question debated.

Shan Van Vocht, August 1897

SOCIALISM AND IMPERIALISM

As Socialists – and therefore anxious at all times to throw the full weight of whatever influence we possess upon the side of the forces making most directly for Socialism – we have often been somewhat disturbed in our mind by observing in the writings and speeches of some of our foreign comrades a tendency to discriminate in favour of Great Britain in all the international complications in which that country may be involved over questions of territorial annexations, spheres of influence, etc., in barbarous or semi-civilized portions of the globe. We are, we repeat, disturbed in our mind because we ourselves do not at all sympathize with this pro-British policy, but, on the contrary, would welcome the humiliation of the British arms in any one of the conflicts in which it is at present engaged, or with which it has been lately menaced. This we freely avow. But the question then arises: is this hostility to the British Empire due to the fact of our national and racial subjection by that Power, or is it consistent with the doctrine we hold as adherents of the Marxist propaganda, and believers in the Marxist economics?

...The English Socialists are apparently divided over the question of the war on the Transvaal; one section of the Social Democratic Federation going strongly for the Boers and against the war; another also declaring against the war, but equally denouncing the Boers; and finally, one English Socialist leader, Mr Robert Blatchford, editor of *The Clarion* and author of *Merrie England*, coming out bluntly for the war and toasting the health of the Queen, and the success of the British arms. On the other hand, all the journals of the party on the continent of Europe and in America, as far as we are aware, come out in this instance wholeheartedly on the side of the Transvaal and against what the organ of our Austrian comrades fittingly terms England's act of 'blood-thirsty piracy'... Our esteemed comrade, H. M. Hyndman* ... took the position that England ought not to have given way to Russia at Port Arthur, but ought to have fought her and asserted British supremacy in the Far East. His reason for so contending being the greater freedom enjoyed under British than under Russian rule ...

... That we may not be accused of criticizing the attitude of others without stating our own, we hereby place on record our position on all questions of international policy:

Scientific revolutionary Socialism teaches us that Socialism can only be realized when capitalism has reached its zenith of development; that consequently the advance of nations industrially undeveloped into the capitalistic stage of industry is a thing highly to be desired, since such an advance will breed a revolutionary proletariat in such countries and force forward there the political freedom necessary for the speedy success of the Socialist movement; and finally, that as colonial expansion and the conquest of new markets are necessary for the prolongation of the life of capitalism, the prevention of colonial expansion and the loss of markets to countries capitalistically developed, such as England, precipitates economic crises there, and so gives an impulse to revolutionary thought and helps to shorten the period required to develop backward countries and thus prepare the economic conditions needed for our triumph ...

Comrade Hyndman claims that we should oppose Russia because her people are ruled despotically, and favour England because her people are politically free. But that is the reasoning of a political radical, not the dispassionate analysis of contemporary history we have a right to expect from an economist and a Socialist of Hyndman's reputation ... Russia is not yet a capitalist country, therefore her people bow beneath the yoke of an autocrat ... Drive the Russian out of Poland! By all means! Prevent his extension towards Europe! Certainly! But favour his extension and acquisition of new markets in Asia (at the expense of England if need be) if you would see capitalism hurry forward to its death.

It may be argued that our Irish nationality plays a large part

* H. M. Hyndman (1842–1921), English Socialist leader.

in forming this conception of international politics. We do not plead guilty, but even if it were so the objection would be puerile. As Socialists we base our political policy on the class struggle of the workers, because we know that the self-interest of the workers lies our way. That the self-interest may sometimes be base does not affect the correctness of our position. The mere fact that the inherited (and often unreasoning) anti-British sentiment of a chauvinist Irish patriot impels him to the same conclusion as we arrived at as the result of our economic studies does not cause us to shrink from proclaiming our position. It rather leads us to rejoice that our propaganda is thus made all the easier by this none too common identity of aim established as a consequence of what we esteem strong and irreconcilable hostility between English imperialism and Socialism.

Workers' Republic, 4 November 1899

LET US FREE IRELAND!

LET us free Ireland! Never mind such base carnal thoughts as concern work and wages, healthy homes, or lives unclouded by poverty.

Let us free Ireland! The rack-renting landlord; is he not also an Irishman, and wherefore should we hate him? Nay, let us not speak harshly of our brother, yea, even when he raises our rent.

Let us free Ireland! The profit-grinding capitalist, who robs us of three fourths of the fruit of our labour, who sucks the very marrow of our bones when we are young, and then throws us out in the street like a worn-out tool when we are grown prematurely old in his service, is he not an Irishman, and mayhap a patriot, and wherefore should we think harshly of him?

Let us free Ireland! 'The land that bred and bore us.' And the landlord who makes us pay for permission to live upon it. Whoop it up for liberty!

'Let us free Ireland,' says the patriot who won't touch Socialism. Let us all join together, and cr-r-rush the br-r-rutal Saxon. Let us all join together, says he, all classes and creeds. And, says the town worker, after we have crushed the Saxon and freed Ireland, what will we do? Oh, then you can go back to your slums, same as before. Whoop it up for liberty!

And, says the agricultural worker, after we have freed Ireland, what then? Oh, then you can go scraping around for the land-lord's rent or the money-lenders' interest same as before. Whoop it up for liberty!

After Ireland is free, says the patriot who won't touch Socialism, we will protect all classes, and if you won't pay your rent you will be evicted same as now. But the evicting party, under the command of the sheriff, will wear green uniforms and the Harp without the Crown, and the warrant turning you out on the roadside will be stamped with the arms of the Irish Republic. Now isn't that worth fighting for?

And when you cannot find employment, and, giving up the struggle for life in despair, enter the poorhouse, the band of the nearest regiment of the Irish army will escort you to the poorhouse door to the tune of 'St Patrick's Day'. Oh! it will be nice to live in those days.

'With the Green Flag floating o'er us' and an ever-increasing army of unemployed workers walking about under the Green Flag, wishing they had something to eat. Same as now! Whoop it up for liberty!

Now, my friend, I also am Irish, but I'm a bit more logical. The capitalist, I say, is a parasite on industry; as useless in the present stage of our industrial development as any other parasite in the animal or vegetable world is to the life of the animal or vegetable upon which it feeds.

The working class is the victim of this parasite – this human leech, and it is the duty and interest of the working class to use every means in its power to oust this parasite class from the position which enables it to thus prey upon the vitals of labour.

Therefore, I say, let us organize to meet our masters and destroy their mastership; organize to drive them from their hold upon public life through their political power; organize to wrench from their robber clutch the land and workshops on and in which they enslave us; organize to cleanse our social life from the stain of social cannibalism, from the preying of man upon his fellow man.

Organize for a full, free and happy life FOR ALL OR FOR NONE.

Workers' Republic, 1899
also reproduced in *Socialism Made Easy,* 1908

WHAT IS A FREE NATION?

WE are moved to ask this question because of the extraordinary confusion of thought upon the subject which prevails in this country, due principally to the pernicious and misleading newspaper garbage upon which the Irish public has been fed for the past twenty-five years.

Our Irish daily newspapers have done all that human agencies could do to confuse the public mind upon the question of what the essentials of a free nation are, what a free nation must be, and what a nation cannot submit to lose without losing its title to be free.

It is because of this extraordinary newspaper-created ignorance that we find so many people enlisting in the British army under the belief that Ireland has at long last attained to the status of a free nation, and that therefore the relations between Ireland and England have at last been placed upon the satisfactory basis of freedom. Ireland and England, they have been told, are now sister nations, joined in the bond of Empire, but each enjoying equal liberties – the equal liberties of nations equally free. How many recruits this idea sent into the British army in the first flush of the war it would be difficult to estimate, but they were assuredly numbered by the thousand.

The Irish Parliamentary Party, which at every stage of the Home Rule game has been outwitted and bulldozed by Carson and the Unionists, which had surrendered every point and yielded every advantage to the skilful campaign of the aristocratic Orange military clique in times of peace, behaved in equally as cowardly and treacherous a manner in the crisis of war.

There are few men in whom the blast of the bugles of war do not arouse the fighting instinct, do not excite to some chivalrous impulses if only for a moment. But the Irish Parliamentary Party must be reckoned amongst that few. In them the bugles of war only awakened the impulse to sell the bodies of their countrymen as cannon fodder in exchange for the gracious smiles of the rulers of England. In them the call of war sounded only as a call to emulate in prostitution. They heard the call of war – and set out to prove that the nationalists of Ireland were more slavish than the Orangemen of Ireland, would more readily kill and be killed at the bidding of an Empire that despised them both.

The Orangemen had at least the satisfaction that they were called upon to fight abroad in order to save an Empire they had been prepared to fight to retain unaltered at home; but the nationalists were called upon to fight abroad to save an Empire whose rulers in their most generous moments had refused to grant their country the essentials of freedom in nationhood.

Fighting abroad the Orangeman knows that he fights to preserve the power of the aristocratic rulers whom he followed at home; fighting abroad the nationalist soldier is fighting to maintain unimpaired the power of those who conspired to shoot him down at home when he asked for a small instalment of freedom.

The Orangeman says: 'We will fight for the Empire abroad if its rulers will promise not to force us to submit to Home Rule.' And the rulers say heartily: 'It is unthinkable that we should coerce Ulster for any such purpose.'

The Irish Parliamentary Party and its press said: 'We will prove ourselves fit to be in the British Empire by fighting for it, in the hopes that after the war is over we will get Home Rule.' And the rulers of the British Empire say: 'Well, you know what we have promised Carson, but send out the Irish rabble to fight for us, and we will, ahem, consider your application after the war.' Whereat, all the Parliamentary leaders and their press call the world to witness that they have won a wonderful victory!

James Fintan Lalor spoke and conceived of Ireland as a 'discrowned queen, taking back her own with an armed hand'. Our Parliamentarians treat Ireland, their country, as an old prostitute selling her soul for the promise of favours *to come*, and in the spirit of that conception of their country they are conducting their political campaign.

That they should be able to do so with even the partial success that for a while attended their apostasy was possible only because so few in Ireland really understood the answer to the question that stands at the head of this article.

What is a free nation? A free nation is one which possesses absolute control over all its own internal resources and powers, and which has no restriction upon its intercourse with all other nations similarly circumstanced except the restrictions placed upon it by nature. Is that the case of Ireland? If the Home Rule Bill were in operation would that be the case of Ireland? To both questions the answer is: no, most emphatically, NO!

A free nation must have complete control over its own harbours, to open them or close them at will, or shut out any commodity, or allow it to enter in, just as it seemed best to suit the well-being of its own people, and in obedience to their wishes, and entirely free of the interference of any other nation, and in complete disregard of the wishes of any other nation. Short of that power no nation possesses the first essentials of freedom.

Does Ireland possess such control? No. Will the Home Rule Bill give such control over Irish harbours in Ireland? It will not. Ireland must open its harbours when it suits the interests of another nation, England, and must shut its harbours when it suits the interests of another nation, England; and the Home Rule Bill pledges Ireland to accept this loss of national control for ever.

How would you like to live in a house if the keys of all the doors of that house were in the pockets of a rival of yours who had often robbed you in the past? Would you be satisfied if he told you that he and you were going to be friends for ever more, but insisted upon you signing an agreement to leave him control of all your doors, and custody of all your keys? This is the condition of Ireland today, and will be the condition of Ireland under Redmond and Devlin's precious Home Rule Bill.

That is worth dying for in Flanders, the Balkans, Egypt or India, is it not?

A free nation must have full power to nurse industries to health, either by government encouragement or by government prohibition of the sale of goods of foreign rivals. It may be foolish to do either, but a nation is not free unless it has that power, as all free nations in the world have today. Ireland has no such power, will have no such power under Home Rule. The nourishing of industries in Ireland hurts capitalists in England, therefore this power is expressly withheld from Ireland.

A free nation must have full power to alter, amend, or abolish or modify the laws under which the property of its citizens is held in obedience to the demand of its own citizens for any such alteration, amendment, abolition, or modification. Every free nation has that power; Ireland does not have it, and is not allowed it by the Home Rule Bill.

It is recognized today that it is upon the wise treatment of economic power and resources, and upon the wise ordering of social activities that the future of nations depends. That nation will be the richest and happiest which has the foresight to marshal the most carefully its natural resources to national ends. But Ireland is denied this power, and will be denied it under Home Rule. Ireland's rich natural resources, and the kindly genius of its children, are not to be allowed to combine for the satisfaction of Irish wants, save in so far as their combination can operate on lines approved of by the rulers of England.

Her postal service, her telegraphs, her wireless, her customs and excise, her coinage, her fighting forces, her relations with other nations, her merchant commerce, her property relations, her national activities, her legislative sovereignty – all the things that are essential to a nation's freedom are denied to Ireland now, and are denied to her under the provisions of the Home Rule Bill. And Irish soldiers in the English Army are fighting in Flanders to win for Belgium, we are told, all those things which the British Empire, now as in the past, denies to Ireland.

There is not a Belgian patriot who would not prefer to see his country devastated by war a hundred times rather than accept as a settlement for Belgium what Redmond and Devlin have accepted for Ireland. Have we Irish been fashioned in meaner clay than the Belgians?

There is not a pacifist in England who would wish to end the war without Belgium being restored to full possession of all those national rights and powers which Ireland does not possess, and which the Home Rule Bill denies to her. But these same pacifists never mention Ireland when discussing or suggesting terms of settlement. Why should they? Belgium is fighting for her independence, but Irishmen are fighting for the Empire that denies Ireland every right that Belgians think worth fighting for.

And yet Belgium as a nation is, so to speak, but a creation of yesterday – an artificial product of the schemes of statesmen. Whereas, the frontiers of Ireland, the ineffaceable marks of the separate existence of Ireland, are as old as Europe itself, the handiwork of the Almighty, not of politicians. And as the marks of Ireland's separate nationality were not made by politicians so they cannot be unmade by them.

As the separate individual is to the family, so the separate nation is to humanity. The perfect family is that which best draws out the inner powers of the individual, the most perfect world is that in which the separate existence of nations is held most sacred. There can be no perfect Europe in which Ireland is denied even the least of its national rights; there can be no worthy Ireland whose children brook tamely such denial. If such denial has been accepted by soulless slaves of politicians then it must be repudiated by Irish men and women whose souls are still their own.

The peaceful progress of the future requires the possession by Ireland of all the national rights now denied to her. Only in such possession can the workers of Ireland see stability and security for the fruits of their toil and organization. A destiny not of our fashioning has chosen this generation as the one called upon for the supreme act of self-sacrifice – to die if need be that our race might live in freedom.

Are we worthy of the choice? Only by our response to the call can that question be answered.

Workers' Republic, 12 February 1916

THE IRISH FLAG

THE Council of the Irish Citizen Army has resolved, after grave and earnest deliberation, to hoist the green flag of Ireland over Liberty Hall, as over a fortress held for Ireland by the arms of Irishmen.

This is a momentous decision in the most serious crisis Ireland has witnessed in our day and generation. It will, we are sure, send a thrill through the hearts of every true Irish man and woman, and send the red blood coursing fiercely along the veins of every lover of the race.

It means that in the midst of and despite the treasons and backslidings of leaders and guides, in the midst of and despite all the weaknesses, corruption and moral cowardice of a section of the people, in the midst of and despite all this there still remains in Ireland a spot where a body of true men and women are ready to hoist, gather round, and to defend the flag made sacred by all the sufferings of all the martyrs of the past.

Since this unholy war first started we have seen every symbol of Irish freedom desecrated to the purposes of the enemy, we have witnessed the prostitution of every holy Irish tradition. That the young men of Ireland might be seduced into the service of the nation that denies every national power to their country, we have seen appeals made to our love of freedom, to our religious instincts, to our sympathy for the oppressed, to our kinship with suffering.

The power that for seven hundred years has waged bitter and unrelenting war upon the freedom of Ireland, and that still declares that the rights of Ireland must forever remain subordinate to the interests of the British Empire, hypocritically appealed to our young men to enlist under her banner and shed their blood 'in the interests of freedom'.

The power whose reign in Ireland has been one long carnival

of corruption and debauchery of civic virtue, and which has rioted in the debasement and degradation of everything Irish men and women hold sacred, appealed to us in the name of religion to fight for her as the champion of christendom.

The power which holds in subjection more of the world's population than any other power on the globe, and holds them in subjection as slaves without any guarantee of freedom or power of self-government, this power that sets Catholic against Protestant, the Hindu against the Mohammedan, the yellow man against the brown, and keeps them quarrelling with each other whilst she robs and murders them all – this power appeals to Ireland to send her sons to fight under England's banner for the cause of the oppressed. The power whose rule in Ireland has made of Ireland a desert, and made the history of our race read like the records of a shambles, as she plans for the annihilation of another race appeals to our manhood to fight for her because of our sympathy for the suffering, and of our hatred of oppression.

For generations the shamrock was banned as a national emblem of Ireland, but in her extremity England uses the shamrock as a means for exciting in foolish Irishmen loyalty to England. For centuries the green flag of Ireland was a thing accurst and hated by the English garrison in Ireland, as it is still in their inmost hearts. But in India, in Egypt, in Flanders, in Gallipoli, the green flag is used by our rulers to encourage Irish soldiers of England to give up their lives for the power that denies their country the right of nationhood. Green flags wave over recruiting offices in Ireland and England as a bait to lure on poor fools to dishonourable deaths in England's uniform.

The national press of Ireland, the true national press, uncorrupted and unterrified, has largely succeeded in turning back the tide of demoralization, and opening up the minds of the Irish public to a realization of the truth about the position of their country in the war. The national press of Ireland is a real flag of freedom flying for Ireland despite the enemy, but it is well that also there should fly in Dublin the green flag of this country as a rallying point of our forces and embodiment of all our hopes. Where better could that flag fly than over the unconquered citadel of the Irish working class, Liberty Hall, the fortress of the militant working class of Ireland.

We are out for Ireland for the Irish. But who are the Irish? Not the rack-renting, slum-owning landlord; not the sweating, profit-grinding capitalist; not the sleek and oily lawyer; not the prostitute pressman – the hired liars of the enemy. Not these are the Irish upon whom the future depends. Not these, but the Irish working class, the only secure foundation upon which a free nation can be reared.

The cause of labour is the cause of Ireland, the cause of Ireland is the cause of labour. They cannot be dissevered. Ireland seeks freedom. Labour seeks that an Ireland free should be the sole mistress of her own destiny, supreme owner of all material things within and upon her soil. Labour seeks to make the free Irish nation the guardian of the interests of the people of Ireland, and to secure that end would vest in that free Irish nation all property rights as against the claims of the individual, with the end in view that the individual may be enriched by the nation, and not by the spoiling of his fellows.

Having in view such a high and holy function for the nation to perform, is it not well and fitting that we of the working class should fight for the freedom of the nation from foreign rule, as the first requisite for the free development of the national powers needed for our class? It is so fitting. Therefore on Sunday, 16 April 1916, the green flag of Ireland will be solemnly hoisted over Liberty Hall as the symbol of our faith in freedom, and as a token to all the world that the working class of Dublin stands for the cause of Ireland, and the cause of Ireland is the cause of a separate and distinct nationality.

In these days of doubt, despair, and resurgent hope we fling our banner to the breeze, the flag of our fathers, the symbol of our national redemption, the sunburst shining over an Ireland re-born.

Workers' Republic, 8 April 1916

3

INDUSTRIAL UNIONISM
AND TRADE UNIONISM

INDUSTRIAL UNIONISM
AND CONSTRUCTIVE SOCIALISM

There is not a Socialist in the world today who can indicate with any degree of clearness how we can bring about the co-operative commonwealth except along the lines suggested by industrial organization of the workers.

Political institutions are not adapted to the administration of industry. Only industrial organizations are adapted to the administration of a co-operative commonwealth that we are working for. Only the industrial form of organization offers us even a theoretical constructive Socialist programme. There is no constructive Socialism except in the industrial field.

THE above extracts from the speech of Delegate Stirton, editor of the *Wage Slave*, of Hancock, Michigan, so well embody my ideas upon this matter that I have thought well to take them as a text for an article in explanation of the structural form of Socialist society. In a previous chapter I have analysed the weakness of the craft or trade union form of organization alike as a weapon of defence against the capitalist class in everyday conflict on the economic field, and as a generator of class consciousness on the political field, and pointed out the greater effectiveness for both purposes of an industrial form of organization.

Organizing Constructively

In the present article I desire to show how they who are engaged in building up industrial organizations for the practical purpose of today are at the same time preparing the framework of the society of the future. It is the realization of that fact that indeed marks the emergence of Socialism as a revolutionary force from the critical to the positive stage. Time was when Socialists, if asked how society would be organized under Socialism, replied invariably, and airily, that such things would be left to the future to decide. The fact was that they had not considered the matter, but the development of the Trust and Organized Capital in general, making imperative the Industrial Organizations of Labour on similar lines, has provided us with an answer at once more complete to ourselves and more satisfying to our questioners.

Now to analyse briefly the logical consequences of the position embodied in the above quotation.

'Political institutions are not adapted to the administration of industry.'

Here is a statement that no Socialist with a clear knowledge of the essentials of his doctrine can dispute. The political institutions of today are simply the coercive forces of capitalist society: they have grown up out of, and are based upon, territorial divisions of power in the hands of the ruling class in past ages, and were carried over into capitalist society to suit the needs of the capitalist class when that class overthrew the dominion of its predecessors.

The Old Order and the New

The delegation of the function of government into the hands of representatives elected from certain districts, States or territories, represents no real natural division suited to the requirements of modern society, but is a survival from a time when territorial influences were more potent in the world than industrial influences, and for that reason is totally unsuited to the needs of the new social order, which must be based upon industry.

The Socialist thinker, when he paints the structural form of the new social order, does not imagine an industrial system directed or ruled by a body of men or women elected from an indiscriminate mass of residents within given districts, said residents working at a heterogeneous collection of trades and industries. To give the ruling, controlling, and directing of industry into the hands of such a body would be too utterly foolish.

What the Socialist does realize is that under a social democratic form of society the administration of affairs will be in the hands of representatives of the various industries of the nation;

that the workers in the shops and factories will organize themselves into unions, each union comprising all the workers at a given industry; that said union will democratically control the workshop life of its own industry, electing all foremen etc., and regulating the routine of labour in that industry in subordination to the needs of society in general, to the needs of its allied trades, and to the departments of industry to which it belongs; that representatives elected from these various departments of industry will meet and form the industrial administration or national government of the country.

Begin in the Workshop

In short, social democracy, as its name implies, is the application to industry, or to the social life of the nation, of the fundamental principles of democracy. Such application will necessarily have to begin in the workshop, and proceed logically and consecutively upward through all the grades of industrial organization until it reaches the culminating point of national executive power and direction. In other words, social democracy must proceed *from the bottom upward*, whereas capitalist political society is organized *from above downward*.

Social democracy will be administered by a committee of experts elected from the industries and professions of the land; capitalist society is governed by representatives elected from districts, and is based upon territorial division.

The local and national governing, or rather administrative, bodies of Socialists will approach every question with impartial minds, armed with the fullest expert knowledge born of experience; the governing bodies of capitalist society have to call in an expensive professional expert to instruct them on every technical question, and know that the impartiality of said expert varies with, and depends upon, the size of his fee.

No 'Servile State'

It will be seen that this conception of Socialism destroys at one blow all the fears of a bureaucratic State, ruling and ordering the lives of every individual from above, and thus gives assurance that the social order of the future will be an extension of the freedom of the individual, and not the suppression of it. In short, it blends the fullest democratic control with the most absolute expert supervision, something unthinkable of any society built upon the political State.

To focus the idea properly in your mind you have but to realize how industry today transcends all limitations of territory and leaps across rivers, mountains and continents; then you can understand how impossible it would be to apply to such far-reaching intricate enterprises the principle of democratic control by the workers through the medium of political territorial divisions.

Under Socialism, States, territories, or provinces will exist only as geographical expressions, and have no existence as sources of governmental power, though they may be seats of administrative bodies.

Now, having grasped the idea that the administrative force of the Socialist republic of the future will function through unions industrially organized, that the principle of democratic control will operate through the workers correctly organized in such industrial unions, and that the political territorial State of capitalist society will have no place or function under Socialism, you will at once grasp the full truth embodied in the words of this member of the Socialist Party whom I have just quoted, that *'only the industrial form of organization offers us even a theoretical constructive Socialist programme.'*

The Political State and its Uses

To some minds constructive Socialism is embodied in the work of our representatives on the various public bodies to which they have been elected. The various measures against the evils of capitalist property brought forward by, or as a result of, the agitation of Socialist representatives on legislative bodies are figured as being of the nature of constructive Socialism.

As we have shown, the political State of capitalism has no place under Socialism; therefore, measures which aim to place industries in the hands of, or under the control of, such a political State are in no sense steps towards that ideal; they are but useful measures to restrict the greed of capitalism and to familiarize the workers with the conception of common ownership. This latter is, indeed, their chief function.

But the enrolment of the workers in unions patterned closely after the structure of modern industries, and following the organic lines of industrial development, is *par excellence* the swiftest, safest, and most peaceful form of constructive work the Socialist can engage in. It prepares within the framework of capitalist society the working forms of the Socialist republic, and thus, while increasing the resisting power of the worker against present encroachments of the capitalist class, it familiarizes him with the idea that the union he is helping to build up is destined to supplant that class in the control of the industry in which he is employed.

The Union Can Build Freedom

The power of this idea to transform the dry detail work of trade union organization into the constructive work of revolutionary Socialism, and thus make of the unimaginative trade unionist a potent factor in the launching of a new system of society, cannot be over-estimated. It invests the sordid details of the daily incidents of the class struggle with a new and beautiful meaning, and presents them in their true light as skirmishes between the two opposing armies of light and darkness.

In the light of this principle of industrial unionism every fresh shop or factory organized under its banner is a fort wrenched from the control of the capitalist class and manned with the soldiers of the revolution to be held by them for the workers.

On the day that the political and economic forces of Labour finally break with capitalist society and proclaim the Workers' Republic, these shops and factories so manned by industrial unionists will be taken charge of by the workers there employed, and force and effectiveness be thus given to that proclamation. Then and thus the new society will spring into existence, ready equipped to perform all the useful functions of its predecessor.

Socialism Made Easy, Chicago, 1908

THE FUTURE OF LABOUR

IN choosing for the subject of this chapter such a title as 'The Future of Labour' I am aware that I run the risk of arousing expectations that I shall not be able to satisfy. The future of Labour is a subject with which is bound up the future of civilization and therefore a comprehensive treatment of the subject might be interpreted as demanding an analysis of all the forces and factors which will influence humanity in the future, and also their resultant effect.

Needless to say, my theme is a less ambitious one. I propose simply to deal with the problem of Labour in the immediate future, with the marshalling of Labour for the great conflict that confronts us, and with a consideration of the steps to be taken in order that the work of aiding the transition from Industrial Slavery to Industrial Freedom might be, as far as possible, freed from all encumbering and needless obstacles and expense of time, energy and money.

But first, and as an aid to a proper understanding of my position, let me place briefly before you my reading of the history of the past struggles against social subjugation, my reading of the mental development undergone by each revolting class in the different stages of their struggle, from the first period of their bondage to the first dawn of their freedom. As I view it, such struggles had three well-marked mental stages, corresponding to inception, development, and decay of the oppressing powers, and as I intend to attempt to apply this theory to the position of Labour as a subject class today, I hope you will honour me by at least giving me your earnest attention to this conception and aid by your discussions in determining at which period or stages the working class, the subject class of today, has arrived. My reading, then, briefly is this: that in the first period of bondage the eyes of the subject class are always turned towards the past, and all efforts in revolt are directed to the end of destroying the social system in order that it might march backwards and re-establish the social order of ancient times – 'the good old days'. That the goodness of those days was largely hypothetical seldom enters the imagination of men on whose limbs the fetters of oppression still sit awkwardly.

In the second period the subject class tends more and more to lose sight and recollection of any pre-existent state of society, to believe that the social order in which it finds itself always did exist, and to bend all its energies to obtaining such amelioration of its lot within existent society as will make that lot more bearable. At this stage of society the subject class, as far as its own aspirations are concerned, may be reckoned as a conservative force.

In the third period the subject class becomes revolutionary, recks little of the past for inspiration, but, building itself upon the achievements of the present, confidently addresses itself to the conquest of the future. It does so because the development of the framework of society has revealed to it its relative importance, revealed to it the fact that within its grasp has grown, unconsciously to itself, a power which, if intelligently applied, is sufficient to overcome and master society at large.

As a classic illustration of this conception of the history of the mental development of the revolt against social oppression, we might glance at the many peasant revolts recorded in European history. As we are now aware, common ownership of land was at one time the basis of society all over the world. Our fathers not only owned their land in common, but in many ways practised a common ownership of the things produced. In short, tribal communism was at one time the universally existent order. In such a state there existed a degree of freedom that no succeeding order has been able to parallel, and that none will be able to until the individualistic order of today gives way to the Industrial Commonwealth, the Workers' Republic of the future. How that ancient order broke up it is no part of my task to tell. What I do wish to draw your attention to is that for hundreds, for a thousand years after the break up of that tribal communism, and the reduction to serfdom of the descendants of the formerly free tribesmen, all the efforts of the revolting serfs were directed to a destruction of the new order of things and to a rehabilitation of the old. Take, as an example, the various peasant wars of Germany, the Jacquerie of France, or the revolt of Wat Tyler and John Ball in England as being the best known; examine their rude literature in such fragments as have been preserved, study their speeches, as they have been recorded even by their enemies, read the translations of their songs, and in all of them you will find a passionate harking back to the past, a morbid idealizing of the status of their fathers, and a continual exhortation to the suffering people to destroy the present in order that, in some vague and undefined manner, they may reconstruct the old.

The defeat of the peasantry left the stage clear for the emergence of the bourgeoisie as the most important subject class and for the development of that second period of which I have spoken. Did it develop? Well, in every account we read of the conflict between the nobility and the burghers in their guilds and cities we find that the aggressive part was always taken by the former and that wherever a revolt took place the revolting guild merchants and artisans justified their act by an appeal to past privileges which had been abrogated and the restoration of which formed the basis of their claims, and their only desire if successful in revolt. One of the most curious illustrations of this mental condition is to be found in the *History of the Rise of the Dutch Republic* by Motley, in which that painstaking historian tells how the Netherlands in their revolt against the Spanish Emperor continued for a generation to base their claims upon the political status of the provinces under a former emperor, made war upon the Empire with troops levied in the name of the Emperor, and led by officers whose commissions were made out by the rebel provinces in the name of the sovereign they were fighting against. This mental condition lasted in England until the great Civil War, which ended by leaving Charles I without a head, and the bourgeoisie, incarnated in Cromwell, firmly fixed in the saddle; in France it lasted until the Revolution. In both countries it was abandoned not because of any *a priori* reasoning upon its absurdity nor because some great thinker had evolved a better scheme — but because the growth of the industrial system had made the capitalist class realize that they could at any moment stop the flow of its life blood, so to speak, and from so realizing it was but a short mental evolution *to frame a theory of political action which proclaimed that the capitalist class was the nation,* and all its enemies the enemies of the nation at large. The last period of that social evolution had been reached from feudal ownership to capitalist property.

Now, let me apply this reading of history to the development of the working class under capitalism and find out what lessons it teaches us, of value in our present struggle. Passing by the growth of the working class under nascent capitalism, as it belongs more to the period I have just dealt with than to the present subject, and taking up working-class history from the point marked by the introduction of machinery to supplant hand labour – a perfectly correct standpoint for all practical purposes – we find in the then attitude of the workers an exemplification of the historical fidelity of our conception. Suffering from the miseries attendant on machine labour, the displacement of those supplanted and the scandalous overworking of those retained, the workers rioted and rebelled in a mad effort to abolish machinery and restore the era of hand labour. In a word, they strove to revert to past conditions, and their most popular orators and leaders were they who pictured in most glowing terms the conditions prevalent in the days of their fathers.

They were thus on the same mental plane as those medieval peasants who, in their revolt, were fired by the hope of restoring the primitive commune. And just as in the previously cited case, the inevitable failure of the attempt to reconstruct the past was followed in another generation by movements which accepted the social order of their day as permanent, and looked upon their social status as wage slaves as fixed and immutable in the eternal order of things. To this category belongs the trade union movement in all its history. As the struggles of the serfs and burghers in the middle ages were directed to no higher aim than the establishment of better relations between these struggling classes and their feudal overlords, as during those ages the division of society into ruling classes of king, lord and church resting upon a basis of the serfdom of the producers was accepted by all in spite of the perpetual recurrences of civil wars between the various classes, so, in capitalist society, the trade unionist, despite strikes, lock-outs, and black lists, accepted the employing class as part and parcel of a system which was to last through all eternity.

The rise of Industrial Unionism is the first sign that the second stage of the mental evolution of our class is rapidly passing away. And the fact that it had its inception amongst men actually engaged in the work of trade union organization, and found its inspiration in a recognition of the necessities born of the struggles of the workers, and not in the theories of any political party – this fact is the most cheering sign of the legitimacy of its birth and the most hopeful augury of its future. For we must not forget that it is not the theorist who makes history; it is history in its evolution that makes the theorists. And the roots of history are to be be found in the workshops, fields and factories. It has been remarked that Belgium was the cockpit of Europe because within its boundaries have been fought out many of the battles between old dynasties; in like manner we can say that the workshop is the cockpit of civilization because in the workshops has been and will be fought out those battles between the new and the old methods of production, the issues of which change the face and the history of the world.

I have said that the capitalist class became a revolutionary class when it realized that it held control of the economic heart of the nation. I may add when the working class is in the same position it will also as a class become revolutionary, it will also give effective political expression to its economic strength. The capitalist class grew into a political party when it looked around and found itself in control of the things needed for the life of the individual and the State, when it saw that the ships carrying the commerce of the nation were its own, when it saw that the internal traffic of the nation was in the hands of its agents, when it saw that the feeding, clothing, and sheltering of the ruling class depended on the activities of the subject class, when it saw itself applied to furnish finance to equip the armies and fleets of the king and nobles; in short, when the capitalist class found that all the arteries of commerce, all the agencies of production, all the mainsprings of life in fact, passed through their hands as blood flows through the human heart – then and only then did capital raise the banner of political revolt and from a class battling for concession become a class leading its forces to the mastery of society at large.

This leads me to the last axiom of which I wish you to grasp the significance. It is this, that the fight for the conquest of the political state is not the battle, it is only the echo of the battle. The real battle is the battle being fought out every day for the power to control industry, and the gauge of the progress of that battle is not to be found in the number of votes making a cross beneath the symbol of a political party, but in the number of these workers who enrol themselves in an industrial organization with the definite purpose of making themselves masters of the industrial equipment of society in general.

That battle will have its political echo, that industrial organization will have its political expression. *If we accept the definition of working-class political action as that which brings the workers as a class into direct conflict with the possessing class AS A CLASS, and keeps them there, then we must realize that NOTHING CAN DO THAT SO READILY AS ACTION AT THE BALLOT-BOX.* Such action strips the working-class movement of all traces of such sectionalism as may, and indeed must, cling to strikes and lock-outs, and emphasizes the class character of the Labour Movement. IT IS THEREFORE ABSOLUTELY INDISPENSABLE FOR THE EFFICIENT TRAINING OF THE WORKING CLASS ALONG CORRECT LINES THAT ACTION AT THE BALLOT-BOX SHOULD ACCOMPANY ACTION IN THE WORKSHOP.

I am convinced that this will be the ultimate formation of the fighting hosts of Labour. The workers will be industrially organized on the economic field, and until that organization is perfected, whilst the resultant feeling of class consciousness is permeating the minds of the workers, the Socialist Labour Party will carry on an independent campaign of education and attack upon the political field, and as a consequence will remain the sole representative of the Socialist idea in politics. But as industrial organization grows, feels its strength, and develops the revolutionary instincts of its members, there will grow also the

desire for a closer union and identification of the two wings of
the army of Labour. Any attempt prematurely to force this
identification would only defeat its own purpose, and be fraught
with danger alike to the economic and the political wing. Yet it
is certain that such attempts will be of continual recurrence and
multiply in proportion to the dissatisfaction felt at the waste of
energy involved in the division of forces. Statesmanship of the
highest kind will be required to see that this union shall take
place only under the proper conditions and that at the moment
for effective action. Two things must be kept in mind – viz., that
a Socialist Political Party not emanating from the ranks of
Labour is, as Karl Marx phrased it, simply a Socialist sect,
ineffective for the final revolutionary act, but that also the
attempt of craft organized unions to create political unity before
they have laid the foundation of industrial unity in their own,
the economic field, would be an instance of putting the cart
before the horse. But when the foundation of the industrial union
is finally secured then nothing can prevent the union of the
economic and political forces of Labour. I look forward to the
time when every economic organization will have its Political
Committee, just as it has its Organizational Committee or its
Strike Committee, and when it is counted to be as great a crime,
as much an act of scabbery, to be against the former as against
any of the latter. When that time comes we will be able to count
our effective vote before troubling the official ballot-box, simply
by counting our membership in the allied organizations; we will
be able to estimate our capacity for the revolutionary act of
Social Transformation simply by taking stock of the number of
industries we control and their importance relative to the whole
system, and when we find that we control the strategic industries
in society, then society must bend to our will – or break. In our
organization we will have Woman Suffrage, whether governments like it or not, we will also have in our organizations a pure
and uncorrupted ballot, and if the official ballot of capitalist
society does not purify itself of its own accord, its corruption can
only serve to blind the eyes of our enemies and not hide our
strength from ourselves.

Compare the political action of such a body with that of any party we know. Political parties are composed of men and women who meet together to formulate a policy and programme to vote upon. They set up a political ticket in the hope of getting people, most of whom they do not know, to vote for them, and when the vote is at last cast, it is cast by men whom they have not organized, do not know, and cannot rely on to use in their own defence. We have proven that such a body can make propaganda, for Socialist principles, but it can never function as the weapon of an industrially organized working class. To it such a party will always be an outside body, a body not under its direct control, but the political weapon of the *Industrial Organized Working Class will be a weapon of its own forging* and wielded by its own hand. I believe it to be incumbent upon organized Labour to meet the capitalist class upon every field where it can operate to our disadvantage. Therefore I favour direct attacks upon the control of governmental powers through the ballot-box, but I wish to see these attacks supported by economic organization. In short, I believe that there is no function performed by a separate political party that the economic organization cannot help it perform much better and with greater safety to working-class interests. Let us be clear as to the function of Industrial Unionism. That function is to build up an industrial republic inside the shell of the political State, in order that when the industrial republic is fully organized it may crack the shell of the political State and step into its place in the scheme of the universe. But in the process of upbuilding, during the period of maturing, the mechanism of the political State can be utilized to assist in the formation of the embryo Industrial Republic. Or, to change the analogy, we might liken the position of the Industrial Republic in its formative period towards political Society to the position of the younger generation towards the generations passing away. The younger accepts the achievements of the old, but gradually acquires strength to usurp its functions until the new generation is able to abandon the paternal household and erect its own. While doing so it utilizes to the fullest all the principles of its position. So the Industrial Unionist will function in a double capacity in a capitalist society. In his position as a citizen in a given geographical area he will use his political voting power in attacks upon the political system of capitalism, and in his position as a member of the Industrial Union he will help in creating the economic power which in the fullness of time will overthrow that political system and replace it by the Industrial Republic.

My contentions along these lines do not imply by any means that I regard immediate action at the ballot-box by the economic organization as essential, although I may regard it as advisable. As I have already indicated, the proletarian revolution will in that respect most likely follow the lines of the capitalist revolution in the past.

In Cromwellian England, in Colonial America, in Revolutionary France, the real political battle did not begin until after the bourgeoisie, the capitalist class, had become the dominant class in the nation. Then they sought to conquer political power in order to allow their economic power to function freely. It was no mere coincidence, but a circumstance born of the very nature of things, woven so to speak in the warp and woof of fate, that in the three countries the signal for the revolution was given by the ruling class touching the bourgeoisie in the one part that was calculated to arouse them as a class, and at the same time demonstrate their strength. That one sensitive part was their finance, their ownership of the sinews of war. In England it was over the question of taxes, of ship money, that Hampden raised the standard of revolt, whose last blow was struck at Whitehall when the king's head rolled in the gutter. In America it was over the question of taxes, and again the capitalist class were united, until a new nation was born to give them power. In France it was the failure of the king to raise taxes that led to the convocation of the States General, which assembly first revealed to the French capitalists their power as a class and set their feet on the revolutionary path. In all three countries the political rebellion was but the expression of the will of a class already in possession of economic power. This is in conformity with the law of human evolution, that the new system can never overthrow the old until it itself is fully matured and able to assume all the useful functions of the one they seek to dethrone.

In the light of such facts, and judging by such reasoning, we need not exercise our souls over the question of the date of the appearance of the Industrial Organization of Labour upon the electoral field. Whether we believe, as I believe, that the electoral field offers its opportunities it would be criminal to ignore, or believe, as some do, that electoral action on the part of the economic organization is at present premature, one thing we can be agreed upon, if we accept the outline of history I have just sketched – viz. that it is necessary to remember that at the present stage of development all actions of our class at the ballot-box are in the nature of preliminary skirmishes, or educational campaigns, and that *the conquest of political power by the working class waits upon the conquest of economic power* and must function through the economic organization.

Hence, reader, if you belong to the working class your duty is clear. Your union must be perfected until it embraces everyone who toils in the service of your employer or as a unit in your industry. The fact that your employers find it necessary to secure the services of any individual or worker is or ought to be that individual's highest and best title to be a member of your union. If the boss needs him you need him more. You need *open union* and the *closed shop* if you ever intend to control the means and conditions of life. And, as the champion of your class upon the political field, as the ever active propagandist of the idea of the working class, as the representative and embodiment of the social principle of the future, you need the Socialist Labour Party. The future of Labour is bound up with the harmonious development of those twin expressions of the forces of progress; the freedom of Labour will be born of their happily consummated nation.

Socialism Made Easy, Chicago, 1908

INDUSTRIALISM AND THE
TRADE UNIONS

IN the second part of my book *Socialism Made Easy*, I have
endeavoured to establish two principles in the minds of my
readers as being vitally necessary to the upbuilding of a strong
revolutionary Socialist movement. Those two principles are:
First, that the working class as a class cannot become permeated
with a belief in the unity of their class interests unless they have
first been trained to a realization of the need of industrial unity;
second, that the revolutionary act – the act of taking over the
means of production and establishing a social order based upon
the principles of the working class (labour) – cannot be achieved
by a disorganized, defeated and humiliated working class, but
must be the work of that class *after* it has attained to a commanding position on the field of economic struggle. It has been
a pleasure to me to note the progress of Socialist thought towards
acceptance of these principles, and to believe that the publication
of that little work helped to a not inconsiderable degree in
shaping that Socialist thought and in accelerating its progress.
In the following article I wish to present one side of the discussion which inevitably arises in our Socialist party branches upon
the mooting of this question. But as a preliminary to this presentation I would like to decry, and ask my comrades to decry and
dissociate themselves from, the somewhat acrid and intolerant
manner in which this discussion is often carried on. Believing
that the Socialist Party is part and parcel of the labour movement of the United States, and that in the growth of that movement to true revolutionary clearness and consciousness it, the
Socialist Party, is bound to attract to itself and become mentor
and teacher of elements most unclear and lacking in class consciousness, we should recognize that it is as much our duty to be
patient and tolerant with the erring brother or sister within our
ranks as with the rank heathen outside the fold. No good purpose

can be served by wildly declaiming against 'intellectuals', nor yet by intriguing against and misrepresenting 'impossibilists'. The comrades who think that the Socialist Party is run by 'compromisers' should not jump out of the organization and leave the revolutionists in a still more helpless minority; and the comrades who pride themselves upon being practical Socialist politicians should not too readily accuse those who differ with them of being potential disrupters. Viewing the situation from the standpoint of an industrialist I am convinced that both the industrialist and those estimable comrades who pander to the old style trade unions to such a marked degree as to leave themselves open to the suspicion of coquetting with the idea of a 'labour' party, both, I say, have the one belief, both have arrived at the one conclusion from such different angles that they appear as opposing instead of aiding, auxiliary forces. That belief which both share in common is that the triumph of Socialism is impossible without the aid of labour organized upon the economic field. It is their common possession of this one great principle of action which impels me to say that there is a greater identity of purpose and faith between those two opposing (?) wings of the Socialist Party than either can have with any of the intervening schools of thought. Both realize that the Socialist Party must rest upon the economic struggle and the forces of labour engaged therein, and that the Socialism which is not an outgrowth and expression of that economic struggle is not worth a moment's serious consideration.

There, then, we have found something upon which we agree, a ground common to both, the first desideratum of any serious discussion. The point upon which we disagree is: *Can the present form of American trade unions provide the Socialist movement with the economic force upon which to rest?* Or can the American Federation of Labour develop towards industrialism sufficiently for our needs? It is the same problem stated in different ways. I propose to state here my reasons for taking the negative side in that discussion.

Let it be remembered that we are not, as some good comrades imagine, debating whether it is possible for a member of the American Federation of Labour to become an industrialist, or for all its members, but we are to debate whether the organization of the American Federation of Labour is such as to permit of a modification of its structural formation to keep pace with the progress of industrialist ideas amongst its members. Whether the conversion of the membership of the American Federation of Labour to industrialism would mean the disruption of the Federation and the throwing of it aside as the up-to-date capitalist throws aside a machine, be it ever so costly, when a more perfectly functioning machine has been devised.

At this point it is necessary for the complete understanding of our subject that we step aside for a moment to consider the genesis and organization of the American Federation of Labour and the trade unions patterned after it, and this involves a glance at the history of the labour movement in America. Perhaps of all the subjects properly pertaining to Socialist activity this subject has been the most neglected, the least analysed. And yet it is the most vital. Studies of Marx and popularizing (*sic*) of Marx, studies of science and popularizing of science, studies of religion and application of same with Socialist interpretations, all these we have without limit. But of attempts to apply the methods of Marx and of science to an analysis of the laws of growth and incidents of development of the organizations of labour upon the economic field the literature of the movement is almost, if not quite, absolutely barren. Our Socialist writers seem in some strange and, to me, incomprehensible manner to have detached themselves from the everyday struggles of the toilers and to imagine they are doing their whole duty as interpreters of Socialist thought when they bless the economic organization with one corner of their mouth and insist upon the absolute hopelessness of it with the other. They imagine, of course, that this is the astutest diplomacy, but the net result of it has been that the organized working class has never looked upon the Socialist Party as a part of the labour movement, and the en-rolled Socialist Party member has never found in American Socialist literature anything that helped him in strengthening his economic organization or leading it to victory.

Perhaps some day there will arise in America a Socialist writer who in his writing will live up to the spirit of the Communist

Manifesto that the Socialists are not apart from the labour movement, are not a sect, but are simply that part of the working class which pushes on all others, which most clearly understands the line of march. Awaiting the advent of that writer permit me to remind our readers that the Knights of Labour preceded the American Federation of Labour, that the structural formation of the Knights was that of a mass organization, that they aimed to organize all toilers into one union and made no distinction of craft, *nor of industry,* and that they cherished revolutionary aims. When the American Federation of Labour was organized it was organized as a dual organization, and although at first it professed a desire to organize none but those then unorganized, it soon developed opposition to the Knights and proceeded to organize wherever it could find members, and particularly to seek after the enrolment of those who were already in the Knights of Labour. In this it was assisted by the good will of the master class, who naturally preferred its profession of conservatism and identity of interest between capital and labour to the revolutionary aims and methods of the Knights. But even this assistance on the part of the master class would not have assured its victory were it not for the fact that its method of organization, *into separate crafts,* recognized a certain need of the industrial development of the time which the Knights of Labour had failed up to that moment to appraise at its proper significance.

The Knights of Labour, as I have pointed out, organized all workers into one union, an excellent idea for teaching the toilers their ultimate class interests, but with the defect that it made no provision for the treating of special immediate craft interests by men and women with the requisite technical knowledge. The scheme was the scheme of an idealist, too large-hearted and noble-minded himself to appreciate the hold small interests can have upon men and women. It gave rise to jealousies. The printer grumbled at the jurisdiction of a body comprising tailors and shoemakers over his shop struggles, and the tailors and shoemakers fretted at the attempts of carpenters and bricklayers to understand the technicalities of their disputes with the bosses.

To save the Knights of Labour and to save the American working class a pilgrimage in the desert of reaction, it but required the advent of some practical student of industry to propose that, instead of massing all workers together irrespective of occupation, they should, keeping the organization intact and remaining bound in obedience to one supreme head, *for administrative purposes only*, group all workers together according to their industries, and subdivide their industries again according to crafts. That the allied crafts should select the ruling body for the industry to which they belonged, and that the allied industries again should elect the ruling body for the whole organization. This could have been done without the slightest jar to the framework of the organization; it would have recognized all technical differences and specialization of function in actual industry; it would have kept the organization of labour in line with the actual progress of industrial development; and would still have kept intact the idea of the unity of the working class by its common bond of brotherhood, a universal membership card, and universal obligation to recognize that an injury to one was an injury to all.

Tentative steps in such a direction were already being taken when the American Federation of Labour came upon the scene. The promoters of this organization, seizing upon this one plank in the Knights of Labour organization, specialized its work along that line, and, instead of hastening to save the unity of the working class on the lines above indicated, they made the growing realization of the need of representation of craft differences the entering wedge for disrupting and destroying the earlier organization of that class.

Each craft was organized as a distinct body having no obligation to strike or fight beside any other craft, and making its own contracts with the bosses heedless of what was happening between these bosses and their fellow-labourers of another craft in the same industry, building, shop or room. The craft was organized on a national basis, to be governed by the vote of its members throughout the nation, and with a membership card good only in that craft and of no use to a member who desired to leave one craft in order to follow another. The fiction of national unity was and is still paid homage to, as vice always pays homage to virtue, by annual congresses in which many resolutions are gravely debated, to be forgotten as soon as congress adjourns. But the unifying (?) qualities of this form of organization are best revealed by the fact that the main function of the congress seems to be to provide the cynical master class with the, to them, pleasing spectacle of allied organizations fiercely fighting over questions of jurisdiction.

This policy of the American Federation of Labour coupled with the unfortunate bomb incident of Chicago,* for which the Knights of Labour received much of the blame, completed the ruin of the latter organization and destroyed the growing unity of the working class for the time being. The industrial union, as typified today in the Industrial Workers of the World, could have, as I have shown, developed out of the Knights of Labour as logically and perfectly as the adult develops from the child. No new organization would have been necessary, and hence we may conclude that the Industrial Workers of the World is the legitimate heir of the native American labour movement, the inheritor of its principles, and the ripened fruit of its experiences. On the other hand the American Federation of Labour may truly be regarded as a usurper on the throne of labour, a usurper who occupies the throne by virtue of having strangled its predecessor, and now, like all usurpers, raises the cry of 'treason' against the rightful heir when it seeks to win its own again. It is obvious that the sway of the American Federation of Labour in the American labour movement is but a brief interregnum between the passing of the old revolutionary organization and the ascension into power of the new.

But, I fancy I hear some one say, granting that all that is true, may we not condemn the methods by which the American Federation of Labour destroyed, or helped to destroy, the Knights of Labour, and still believe that out of the American Federation of Labour we may now build up an industrial organization such as we need, such as the Industrial Workers of the World aims to be?

This we can only answer by clearly focusing in our mind the

* A bomb explosion in Haymarket Square, Chicago, 4 May 1886, during a labour demonstration. Four anarchists, the 'Chicago Martyrs', were arrested and subsequently executed.

American Federation of Labour system of organization in actual practice. A carpenter is at work in a city. He has a dispute with the bosses, or all his fellow-carpenters have. They will hold meetings to discuss the question of a strike, and finding the problem too big for them they will pass it on to the headquarters, and the headquarters pass it on to the general membership. The general membership, from San Francisco to Rhode Island, and from Podunk to Kalamazoo, will have a vote and say upon the question of the terms upon which the Chicago carpenters work, and if said carpenters are called out they will expect all these widely scattered carpenters to support them by financial and moral help. But while they are soliciting and receiving the support of their fellow-carpenters they are precluded from calling out in sympathy with them the painters who follow them in their work, the plumbers whose pipes they cover up, the steamfitters who work at their elbows, or the plasterer who precedes them. Yet the co-operation of these workers with them in their strikes is a thousandfold more important than the voting of strike funds which would keep them out on strike – until the building season is over and the winter sets in. In many cities today there is a Building Trades' Council which is looked upon by many as a beginning of industrialism within the American Federation of Labour. It is not only the beginning but it is as far as industrialism can go within that body, and its sole function is to secure united action in remedying petty grievances and enforcing the observance of contracts, but it does not take part in the really important work of determining hours or wages. It cannot for the simple reason that each of the thirty-three unions in the building industry are international organizations with international officers, and necessitating international referendums before any strikes, looking to the fixing of hours or wages, are permissible. Hence, although all the building trade branches in a given district may be satisfied that the time is ripe for obtaining better conditions, they cannot act before they obtain the consent of the membership throughout the entire country, and before that is obtained the moment for action is passed. The bond that is supposed to unite the carpenter in New York with the carpenter in Kokomo, Indiana, is converted into a wall of isolation which prevents him uniting, except in the most perfunctory fashion, with the men of other crafts who work beside him. The industrial union and the craft union are mutually exclusive terms. Suppose all the building trades branches of Chicago resolved to unite industrially to form an industrial union. Every branch which became an integral part of said union, pledged to obey its call to action, would by so doing forfeit its charter in the craft union and in the American Federation of Labour, and outside Chicago its members would be considered as scabs. The Brewers Union has been fighting for years to obtain the right to organize *all* brewery employees. It is hindered from doing so, not only by the rules of the American Federation of Labour, but by the form of organization of that body. Breweries, for instance, employ plumbers. Now if a plumber, so employed, would join the Brewers Union and obey its call to strike he would be expelled from his craft union, and if he ever lost his job in the brewery would be considered as a scab if he went to work where union plumbers were employed. A craft union cannot recognize the right of another association to call its members out on a strike. A machinist works today in a machine shop; a few months from now he may be employed in a clothing factory attending to the repairs of sewing machines. If the clothing industry resolves itself into an industrial union and he joins them, as he needs must if he believes in industrialism, he loses his membership in the International Association of Machinists. And if ever he loses his factory job and seeks to return to the machine shop he must either do so as a non-union man or pay a heavy fine if he is permitted to re-enter the International Association of Machinists. A stationary engineer works today at the construction of a new building, three months from now he is in a shipyard, six months from now he is at the mouth of a coal mine. Three different industries, requiring three different industrial unions.

The craft card is good today in all of them, but if any of them chose to form industrial unions, and called upon him to join, he could only do so on penalty of losing his craft card and his right to strike benefits from his old organization. And if he did join, his card of membership in the one he joined would be of no value when he drifted to any of the others. How can the American Federation of Labour avoid this dilemma? Industrialism requires that all the workers in a given industry be subject to the call of the governing body, or of the vote of the workers in that industry. But if these workers are organized in the American Federation of Labour they must be subject only to the call of their national or international craft body; and if at any time they obey the call of the industry in preference to the craft they are ordered peremptorily back to scab upon their brothers.

If in addition to this organic difficulty, and it is the most insuperable, we take into consideration the system of making contracts or trade agreements on a craft basis pursued by old style unions we will see that our unfortunate brothers in the American Federation of Labour are tied hand and foot, handcuffed and hobbled, to prevent their advance into industrialism. During the recent shirt-waist makers' strike in New York when the question was mooted of a similar strike in Philadelphia our comrade Rose Pastor Stokes, according to our Socialist press, was continually urging upon the shirt-waist makers of Philadelphia the wisdom of striking before Christmas, and during the busy season. No more sensible advice could have been given. It was of the very essence of industrialist philosophy. Industrialism is more than a method of organization – it is a science of fighting. It says to the worker: fight only at the time you select, never when the boss wants a fight. Fight at the height of the busy season, and in the slack season when the workers are in thousands upon the sidewalk absolutely refuse to be drawn into battle. Even if the boss insults and vilifies your union and refuses to recognize it, take it lying down in the slack season but mark it up in your little note book. And when work is again rushing and master capitalist is pressed for orders squeeze him, and squeeze him till the most sensitive portion of his anatomy, his pocket-book, yells with pain. That is the industrialist idea of the present phase of the class war as organized labour should conduct it. But, whatever may have been the case with the shirt-waist makers, that policy so ably enunciated by comrade Rose Pastor Stokes is utterly opposed to the whole philosophy and practice of the American Federation of Labour. Contracts almost always expire when there is little demand for labour. For instance the United Mine Workers' contract with the bosses expires in the early summer when they have before them a long hot season with a minimum demand for coal. Hence the expiration of the contract generally finds the coal operators spoiling for a fight, and the union secretly dreading it. Most building trade contracts with the bosses expire in the winter. For example, the Brotherhood of Carpenters in New York, their contract expires in January. A nice time for a fight, in the middle of a northern winter, when all work in their vicinity is suspended owing to the rigours of the climate!

The foregoing will, I hope, give the reader some food for consideration upon the problem under review. That problem is intimately allied with the future of the Socialist Party in America. Our party must become the political expression of the fight in the workshop, and draw its inspiration therefrom. Everything which tends to strengthen and discipline the hosts of labour tends irresistibly to swell the ranks of the revolutionary movement, and everything which tends to divide and disorganize the hosts of labour tends also to strengthen the forces of capitalism. *The most dispersive and isolating force at work in the labour movement today is craft unionism, the most cohesive and unifying force, industrial unionism.* In view of that fact all objections which my comrades make to industrial unionism on the grounds of the supposedly, or truly, anti-political bias of many members of the Industrial Workers of the World is quite beside the mark. That question at the present stage of the game is purely doctrinaire. The use or non-use of political action will not be settled by the doctrinaires who may make it their hobby today, but will be settled by the workers who use the Industrial Workers of the World in their workshop struggles. And if at any time the conditions of a struggle in shop, factory, railroad or mine necessitate the employment of political action those workers so organized will use it, all theories and theorists to the contrary notwithstanding. In their march to freedom the workers will use every weapon they find necessary.

As the economic struggle is the preparatory school and training ground for Socialists it is our duty to help guide along right lines the effort of the workers to choose the correct kind of organization to fight their battles in that conflict. According as they choose aright or wrongly, so will the development of class consciousness in their minds be hastened or retarded by their everyday experience in class struggles.

International Socialist Review, February 1910

OLD WINE IN NEW BOTTLES

SCRIPTURE tells us in a very notable passage about the danger of putting new wine in old bottles. I propose to say a few words about the equally suicidal folly of putting old wine into new bottles. For I humbly submit that the experiment spoken of is very popular just now in the industrial world, has engaged the most earnest attention of most of the leaders of the working class, and received the practically unanimous endorsement of the Labour and Socialist press. I have waited in vain for a word of protest.

The Idea Behind Industrial Unionism

In the year of grace 1905 a convention of American Labour bodies was held in Chicago for the purpose of promoting a new working-class organization on more militant and scientific lines. The result of that convention was the establishment of the Industrial Workers of the World – the first Labour organization to organize itself with the definite idea of taking over and holding the economic machinery of society. The means proposed to that end – and it is necessary to remember that the form of organization adopted was primarily intended to accomplish that end, and only in the second degree as a means of industrial warfare against capitalism – was the enrolment of the working class in unions built upon the lines of the great industries. It was the idea of the promoters of the new organization that craft interests and technical requirements should be met by the creation of branches, that all such branches should be represented in a common executive, that all united should be members of an industrial union which should embrace all branches and be co-extensive with the industry, that all industrial unions should be linked as members of one great union, and that one membership card should cover the whole working-class organization. Thus was to be built up a working-class administration which should be capable of the revolutionary act of taking over society, and whose organizers and officers should in the preliminary stages of organizing and fighting constantly remember, and remembering, teach, that no new order can replace the old until it is capable of performing the work of the old, and performing it more efficiently for human needs.

Fighting Spirit More than Mass Organization

As one of the earliest organizers of that body, I desire to emphasize also that, as a means of creating in the working class the frame of mind necessary to the upbuilding of this new order within the old, we taught, and I have yet seen no reason to reconsider our attitude upon this matter, that the interests of one were the interests of all, and that no consideration of a contract with a section of the capitalist class absolved any section of us from the duty of taking instant action to protect other sections when said sections were in danger from the capitalist enemy. Our attitude always was that in the swiftness and unexpectedness of our action lay our chief hopes of temporary victory, and since permanent peace was an illusory hope until permanent victory was secured, temporary victories were all that need concern us. We realized that every victory gained by the working class would be followed by some capitalist development that in the course of time would tend to nullify it, but that until development was perfect the fruits of our victory would be ours to enjoy, and the resultant moral effect would be of incalculable value to the character and to the mental attitudes of our class towards their rulers. It will thus be seen that in our view – and now I am about to point the moral I may personally appropriate it and call it my point of view – the spirit, the character, the militant spirit, the fighting character of the organization, was of the first importance. I believe that the development of the fighting spirit is of more importance than the creation of the theoretically perfect organization; that, indeed the most theoretically perfect organization may, because of its very perfection and vastness, be of the greatest possible danger to the revolutionary movement if it tends, or is used, to repress and curb the fighting spirit of comradeship in the rank and file.

Success of the Sympathetic Strike in 1911

Since the establishment in America of the organization I have just sketched, and the initiation of propaganda on the lines necessary for its purpose, we have seen in all capitalist countries, and notably in Great Britain, great efforts being made to abolish sectional division, and to unite or amalgamate kindred unions. Many instances will arise in the minds of my readers, but I propose to take as a concrete example the National Transport Workers Federation. Previous to the formation of this body, Great Britain was the scene of the propagandist activities of a great number of irregular and unorthodox bodies, which, taking their cue in the main from the Industrial Workers of the World, made great campaigns in favour of the new idea. Naturally their arguments were in the main directed towards emphasizing the absurdity implied in one body of workers remaining at work whilst another body of workers were on strike in the same employment. As a result of this campaign, frowned upon by the leading officials in Great Britain, the Seamen's strike of 1911 was conducted on, and resulted in, entirely new lines of action. The sympathetic strike sprang into being; every group of workers stood by every allied group of workers: and a great wave of effective solidarity caught the workers in its grasp and beat the terrified masters. Let me emphasize the point that the greatest weapon against capital was proven in those days to be the sporadic strike. It was its very sporadic nature, its swiftness and unexpectedness, that won. It was ambush, the surprise attack of our industrial army, before which the well trained battalions of the capitalist world crumpled up in panic, against which no precautions were available.

Weakness of the National Transport Workers Federation

Since that time we have had all over these countries a great wave of enthusiasm for amalgamations, for more cohesion in the working-class organizations. In the transport industry all unions are being linked up until the numbers now affiliated have become imposing enough to awe the casual reader and silence the cavilling objector at trade union meetings. But I humbly submit that, side by side with that employment and affiliation of organization, there has proceeded a freezing up of the fraternal spirit of 1911, there is now, despite the amalgamations, less solidarity in the ranks of Labour than was exhibited in that year of conflict and victory.

If I could venture an analysis of the reason for this falling off in solidarity, I would have to point out that the amalgamations and federations are being carried out in the main by officials absolutely destitute of revolutionary spirit, and that as a consequence the methods of what should be militant organizations having the broad working-class outlook are conceived and enforced in the temper and spirit of the sectionalism those organizations were meant to destroy.

Into the new bottles of industrial organization is being poured the old, cold wine of Craft Unionism.

The much condemned small unions of the past had at least this to recommend them, viz. that they were susceptible to pressure from the sudden fraternal impulses of their small membership. If their members worked side by side with scabs, or received tainted goods from places where scabs were employed, the shame was all their own, and proved frequently too great to be borne. When it did so, we had the sympathetic strike and the fraternization of the working class. But when the workers handling tainted goods, or working vessels loaded by scabs, are members of a nation wide organization with branches in all great centres or ports, the sense of personal responsibility is taken off the shoulders of each member and local official, and the spirit of solidarity is destroyed. The local official can conscientiously order the local member to remain at work with the scab, or to handle tainted goods, 'pending action by the General Executive'.

Recent Events Foretold in 1914

As the General Executive cannot take action pending a meeting of delegates, and as the delegates at that meeting have to report back to their bodies and those bodies to meet, discuss, and then report back to the General Executive, which must meet, hear their report, and then, perhaps, order a ballot vote of the entire membership, after which another meeting must be held to tabulate the result of the vote and transmit it to the local branches, which must meet again to receive it, the chances are, of course, a million to one that the body of workers in distress will be starved into subjection, bankrupted, or disrupted, before the leviathan organization will allow their brothers on the spot to lift a finger or drop a tool in their aid. Readers may, perhaps, think that I am exaggerating the danger. But who will think so that remembers the vindictive fine imposed by the NUR upon its members in the North of England for taking swift action on behalf of a persecuted comrade instead of going through all this red tape whilst he was suffering. Or who will think so that knows that Dublin and Belfast members of the Irish Transport Workers Union have been victimized ever since the end of the lock-out by the Head Line Company, whose steamers have been and are regularly coaled in British ports and manned by Belfast and British members of the Seamen's and Firemen's Union?

Tactics That Will Win

The amalgamations and federations that are being built today are, without exception, being used in the old spirit of the worst type of sectionalism, each local union or branch finds in the greater organization, of which it is a part, a shield and excuse for refusing to respond to the call of brothers and sisters in distress, for the handling of tainted goods, for the working of scab boats. A main reason for this shameful distortion of the Greater Unionism from its true purpose is to be found in the campaign against 'sporadic strikes'.

I have no doubt that Robert Williams of the National Transport Workers Federation is fully convinced that his articles and speeches against such strikes are and were wise; I have just a little doubt that they were the best service performed for the capitalist by any labour leader of late years. The big strike, the vast massed battalions of Labour against the massed battalions of Capital on a field every inch of which has been explored and mapped out beforehand, is seldom successful, for very obvious reasons. The sudden strike, and the sudden threat to strike suddenly, has won more for labour than all the great labour conflicts in history. In the Boer War the long line of communication was the weak point of the British army; in a Labour War the ground covered by the goods of the capitalist is his line of communication. The larger it is the better for the attacking forces of labour. But these forces must be free to attack or refuse to attack, just as their local knowledge guides them. But, it will be argued, their action might imperil the whole organization. Exactly so, and their inaction might imperil that working-class spirit which is more important than any organization. Between the horns of a dilemma what can be done? In my opinion, we must recognize that the only isolation of that problem is the choice of officers, local or national, from the standpoint of their responsiveness to the call for solidarity, and, having got such officials, to retain them only as long as they can show results in the amelioration of the conditions of their members and the development of their union as a weapon of class warfare.

Advance or Retreat

If we develop on those lines, then the creation of a great Industrial Union, such as I have rudely sketched in my opening reminiscences, or the creation of those much more clumsy federations and amalgamations now being formed, will be of immense revolutionary value to the working class; if, on the contrary, we allow officialism of the old, narrow sectional kind to infuse its spirit into the new organizations, and to strangle these with rules suited only to a somnolent working class, then the Greater Unionism will but serve to load us with great fetters. It will be to real Industrial Unionism what the servile state would be to our ideal Co-operative Commonwealth.

The New Age, 30 April 1914

THE PROBLEM OF TRADE UNION
ORGANIZATION

RECENTLY I have been complaining in this column and elsewhere of the tendency in the Labour movement to mistake mere
concentration upon the industrial field for essentially revolutionary advance. My point was that the amalgamation or federation of unions, unless carried out by men and women with the
proper revolutionary spirit, was as likely to create new obstacles
in the way of effective warfare, as to make that warfare possible.
The argument was reinforced by citations of what is taking place
in the ranks of the railwaymen and in the transport industry.
There we find that the amalgamations and federations are
rapidly becoming engines for steam-rolling or suppressing all
manifestations of revolutionary activity, or effective demonstrations of brotherhood. Every appeal to take industrial action on
behalf of a union in distress is blocked by insisting upon the
necessity of 'first obtaining the sanction of the Executive', and in
practice it is found that the process of obtaining that sanction is
so long, so cumbrous, and surrounded with so many rules and
regulations that the union in distress is certain to be either disrupted or bankrupted before the Executive can be moved. The
Greater Unionism is found in short to be forging greater fetters
for the working class; to bear to the real revolutionary industrial
unionism the same relation as the servile State would bear to the
Co-operative Commonwealth of our dreams.

This argument of mine, which to many people may appear as
far-fetched, gains new strength from the circumstances related
by our friend Robert Williams of the Transport Workers Federation, in the weekly report of that body for the 9 May. After
describing how the Head Line Company played with the above
Federation in connection with its protest against the continued
victimization of the members of the Irish Transport Workers
Union, and how he was powerless to effect anything as the other

unions involved still continued to work the scab ships, he goes on to tell of a similar state of affairs in the Port of London. The quotation is long, but it is so valuable an instructive lesson to all your readers that I do not hesitate to give it as an ample confirmation of my argument.

This week, again, there has been a recrudescence of the trouble existing between the Seamen's Union at Tilbury and the Anglo-American Oil Company. This Company has a fleet of oil-tank steamers running between America and various ports in this country.

As a result of the protest made by the crew of the SS *Narragansett* against the chief steward, who acted in the most inhumane manner towards one of the crew who received a severe injury, this Company displaced union men and took on Shipping Federation scabs. Further than this, they have replaced all union men by obtaining Federation scabs in ship after ship since the commencement of the trouble. On Sunday last the *Narragansett* arrived once more at Purfleet, on the lower reaches of the Thames, and the Tilbury Secretary of the Seamen's Union, Mr E. Potton, naturally commenced to hustle. He communicated with Mr Harry Gosling, Mr Havelock Wilson, and the Secretary of this Federation, in order, if possible, to bring pressure upon the Company by preventing the ship from being bunkered.

After consultation with Messrs Gosling and Wilson, the Secretary telephoned, and further, wrote the Anglo-American Oil Company asking them to confer with one or more of these three, in order to avoid a possible extension of the dispute to the 'coalies' and the tugboatmen, etc. (Purfleet steamers are bunkered from lighters.) As in the case of the Head Line, the Secretary specifically drew the attention of the Anglo-American Oil Company to the nature of the complaints, and also sent a written request, following upon a telephone message, by a special messenger for the purpose of saving time. It should be remembered that the bunkers would all be aboard by Tuesday, and this was written on Monday. The Secretary was not very much surprised, however, to receive a reply asking him 'what exactly the complaints are, and on whose behalf they are made'. The reply was strangely in keeping with the replies received from the Head Line Company. The inference is that both these replies received inspiration from the same source.

We are writing these words in the hope that they will be read by all those responsible for the guidance and control of the Transport

Workers in all our seaports. On the face of it, it seems that the one course of action was to call off the men who were working on this ship. If the Company are asking for a fight, what earthly use is it to fight with a portion of your men, leaving all the others to render service to your enemy? This Company has made an open attack on all their employees who are members of the Seamen's Union. At the same time the cargo of oil was being pumped into reservoirs ashore by Trade Union engineers, the men employed ashore are members of an affiliated Union in the Federation, the ship is bunkered by members of an affiliated Union, the tugboats and lighters are staffed by members of an affiliated Union, and still we are *powerless*.

We are not so fatuous as to suggest that continuous warfare shall be waged by general strikes whenever a member considers he has a grievance, or whenever an official encounters a difficulty, but we feel that we are drifting back to the position we were in prior to 1911. A Federation with 29 Unions as its constituents, but with no ties more binding than the payment of 3d. per member per year, will not, and *cannot*, meet the requirements of modern industry. We are responsible to a quarter of a million men, and the existing methods are utterly incapable of protecting them from the insidious attacks of the employers. The organization that is afraid of making a massed attack will experience a series of isolated disasters. The workers' organization secures respect and consideration in proportion to the extent to which it can hamper and embarrass the employers against whom it is pitted.

When co-operation is sought from one Union by another, the men involved say – Consult an official. The official says – Get the consent of my E.C. The Executive officers say – Communicate with the Transport Workers' Federation. The Federation waits on the decision of its own Executive, and by this inconsequent fiddling of time and opportunity, a thousand Romes would have burned to extinction.

The employers move, strike, move, and strike again with the rapidity of a serpent, while we are turning about and contorting with the facility of an alligator. We have at once to determine whether the future is to mean for us efficiency, aptitude, *capacity and *life*, or muddle, incompetence, decay and *death*.

Just what is the real remedy for this state of matters, it would be hard to say. But it is at least certain that the organizations I have been speaking of have not discovered the true methods of working-class organizations. They may be on the road to discovering it; they may also be on the road to foisting upon the working class a form of organization which will make our last state infinitely worse than our first. It is the old story of adopting the letter but rejecting the spirit. The letter of industrial concentration is now accepted by all trade union officials, but the spirit of working-class solidarity is woefully absent. Each union and each branch of each union desires above all things to show a good balance sheet, and that that might be done every nerve is strained to keep their members at work, and in a condition to pay subscriptions. Hence the pitiful dodges to avoid taking sympathetic action in support of other unions, and hence also the constant victories of the master class upon the industrial field.

I have often thought that we of the working class are too slow, or too loath, to take advantage of the experience of our rulers. Perhaps if upon all questions of industrial or other war we followed more closely after them we would be able to fight them more successfully. Here is one suggestion I make on those lines. I am not welded to it, but I would like to see it discussed:

In the modern State the capitalist class has evolved for its own purposes of offence what it calls a Cabinet. This Cabinet controls its fighting forces, which must obey it implicitly. If the Cabinet thinks the time and opportunity is ripe for war, it declares war at the most favourable moment, *and explains its reasons in Parliament afterwards.*

Can we trust any of our members with such a weapon as the capitalist class trusts theirs? I think so. Can we not evolve a system of organization which will leave to the unions the full local administration, but invest in a Cabinet the power to call out the members of any union when such action is desirable, and explain their reasons for it afterwards? Such a Cabinet might have the right to call upon all affiliated unions to reimburse the union whose members were called out in support of another, but such unions so supported would be under the necessity of obeying instantly the call of the Cabinet, or whatever might be the name of the board invested with the powers indicated.

Out of such an arrangement the way would be opened for a more thorough organization of the working class upon the lines of real Industrial Unionism. At present we are too much afraid of each other. Whatever be our form of organization, the spirit of sectionalism still rules and curses our class.

Forward, 23 May 1914

4

WOMEN'S RIGHTS

WOMAN

IN our chapter dealing with the industrial conditions of Belfast, it was noted that the extremely high rate of sickness in the textile industry, the prevalence of tuberculosis and cognate diseases, affected principally the female workers, as does also the prevalence of a comparative illiteracy amongst the lower-paid grades of labour in that city.

The recent dispute in Dublin also brought out in a very striking manner the terrible nature of the conditions under which women and girls labour in the capital city, the shocking insanitary conditions of the workshops, the grinding tyranny of those in charge, and the alarmingly low vitality which resulted from the inability to procure proper food and clothes with the meagre wages paid. Consideration of such facts inevitably leads to reflection on the whole position of women in modern Ireland, and their probable attitude towards any such change as that we are forecasting.

It will be observed by the thoughtful reader, that the development in Ireland of what is known as the women's movement has synchronized with the appearance of women upon the industrial field, and that the acuteness and fierceness of the women's war has kept even pace with the spread amongst educated women of a knowledge of the sordid and cruel nature of the lot of their suffering sisters of the wage-earning class.

We might say that the development of what, for want of a better name, is known as sex-consciousness, has waited for the spread amongst the more favoured women of a deep feeling of social consciousness, what we have elsewhere in this work described as a civic conscience. The awakening amongst women of a realization of the fact that modern society was founded upon force and injustice, that the highest honours of society have no relations to the merits of the recipients, and that acute human sympathies were rather hindrances than helps in the world, was a phenomenon due to the spread of industrialism and to the merciless struggle for existence which it imposes.

Upon woman, as the weaker physical vessel, and as the most untrained recruit, that struggle was inevitably the most cruel; it is a matter for deep thankfulness that the more intellectual women broke out into revolt against the anomaly of being compelled to bear all the worst burdens of the struggle, and yet be denied even the few political rights enjoyed by the male portion of their fellow-sufferers.

Had the boon of political equality been granted as readily as political wisdom should have dictated, much of the revolutionary value of woman's enfranchisement would probably have been lost. But the delay, the politicians' breach of faith with the women, a breach of which all parties were equally culpable, the long-continued struggle, the ever-spreading wave of martyrdom of the militant women of Great Britain and Ireland, and the spread amongst the active spirits of the Labour movement of an appreciation of the genuineness of the women's longings for freedom, as of their courage in fighting for it, produced an almost incalculable effect for good upon the relations between the two movements.

In Ireland the women's cause is felt by all Labour men and women as their cause; the Labour cause has no more earnest and whole-hearted supporters than the militant women. Rebellion, even in thought, produces a mental atmosphere of its own; the mental atmosphere the women's rebellion produced, opened their eyes and trained their minds to an understanding of the effects upon their sex of a social system in which the weakest must inevitably go to the wall, and when a further study of the capitalist system taught them that the term 'the weakest' means in practice the most scrupulous, the gentlest, the most humane, the most loving and compassionate, the most honourable, and the most sympathetic, then the militant women could not fail to see that capitalism penalized in human beings just those characteristics of which women supposed themselves to be the most complete embodiment. Thus the spread of industrialism makes for the awakening of a social consciousness, awakes in women a feeling of self-pity as the greatest sufferers under social and political injustice; the divine wrath aroused when that self-pity is met with a sneer, and justice is denied, leads women to revolt, and revolt places women in comradeship and equality with all the finer souls whose life is given to warfare against established iniquities.

The worker is the slave of capitalist society, the female worker is the slave of that slave. In Ireland that female worker has hitherto exhibited, in her martyrdom, an almost damnable patience. She has toiled on the farms from her earliest childhood, attaining usually to the age of ripe womanhood without ever being vouchsafed the right to claim as her own a single penny of the money earned by her labour, and knowing that all her toil and privation would not earn her that right to the farm which would go without question to the most worthless member of the family, if that member chanced to be the eldest son.

The daughters of the Irish peasantry have been the cheapest slaves in existence – slaves to their own family, who were, in turn, slaves to all social parasites of a landlord and gombeen-ridden community. The peasant, in whom centuries of servitude and hunger had bred a fierce craving for money, usually regarded his daughters as beings sent by God to lighten his burden through life, and too often the same point of view was as fiercely insisted upon by the clergymen of all denominations. Never did the idea seem to enter the Irish peasant's mind, or be taught by his religious teachers, that each generation should pay to its successors the debt it owes to its forerunners; that thus, by spending itself for the benefit of its children, the human race ensures the progressive development of all. The Irish peasant, in too many cases, treated his daughters in much the same manner as he regarded a plough or a spade – as tools with which to work the farm. The whole mental outlook, the entire moral atmosphere of the countryside, enforced this point of view. In every chapel, church or meeting-house the insistence was ever upon duties – duties to those in superior stations, duties to the Church, duties to the parents. Never were the ears of the young polluted (?) by any reference to 'right', and, growing up in this atmosphere, the women of Ireland accepted their position of social inferiority. That, in spite of this, they have ever proven valuable assets in every progressive movement in Ireland, is evidence of the great value their co-operation will be, when to their self-sacrificing acceptance of duty they begin to unite its necessary counterpoise, a high-minded assertion of rights.

We are not speaking here of rights, in the thin and attenuated meaning of the terms to which we have been accustomed by the Liberal or other spokesmen of the capitalist class, that class to whom the assertion of rights has ever been the last word of human wisdom. We are rather using it in the sense in which it is used by, and is familiar to, the Labour movement.

We believe, with that movement, that the serene performance of duty, combined with and inseparable from the fearless assertion of rights, unite to make the highest expression of the human soul. That soul is the grandest which most unquestionably acquiesces in the performance of duty, and most unflinchingly claims its rights, even against a world in arms. In Ireland the soul of womanhood has been trained for centuries to surrender its rights, and as a consequence the race has lost its chief capacity to withstand assaults from without, and demoralization from within. Those who preached to Irish womankind fidelity to duty as the only ideal to be striven after, were, consciously or unconsciously, fashioning a slave mentality, which the Irish mothers had perforce to transmit to the Irish child.

The militant women who, without abandoning their fidelity to duty, are yet teaching their sisters to assert their rights, are re-establishing a sane and perfect balance that makes more possible a well-ordered Irish nation.

The system of private capitalist property in Ireland, as in other countries, has given birth to the law of primogeniture under which the eldest son usurps the ownership of all property to the exclusion of the females of the family. Rooted in a property system founded upon force, this iniquitous law was unknown to the older social system of ancient Erin, and, in its actual workings out in modern Erin, it has been and is responsible for the moral murder of countless virtuous Irish maidens. It has meant that, in the continual dispersion of Irish families, the first to go was not the eldest son, as most capable of bearing the burden and heat of a struggle in a foreign country, but was rather the younger and least capable sons, or the gentler and softer daughters. Gentle Charles Kickham sang:

> O brave, brave Irish girls,
>   We well might call you brave;
> Sure the least of all your perils
>   Is the stormy ocean wave.

Everyone acquainted with the lot encountered by Irish emigrant girls in the great cities of England or America, the hardships they had to undergo, the temptations to which they were subject, and the extraordinary proportion of them that succumbed to these temptations, must acknowledge that the poetic insight of Kickham correctly appreciated the gravity of the perils that awaited them. It is humiliating to have to record that the overwhelming majority of those girls were sent out upon a conscienceless world, absolutely destitute of training and preparation, and relying solely upon their physical strength and intelligence to carry them safely through. Laws made by men shut them out of all hope of inheritance in their native land; their male relatives exploited their labour and returned them never a penny as a reward, and finally, when at last their labour could not wring sufficient from the meagre soil to satisfy the exactions of all, these girls were incontinently packed off across the ocean with, as a parting blessing, the adjuration to be sure and send some money home. Those who prate glibly about the 'sacredness of the home' and the 'sanctity of the family circle' would do well to consider what home in Ireland today is sacred from the influence of the greedy mercenary spirit, born of the system of capitalist property; what family circle is unbroken by the emigration of its most gentle and loving ones.

Just as the present system in Ireland has made cheap slaves or untrained emigrants of the flower of our peasant women, so it has darkened the lives and starved the intellect of the female operatives in mills, shops and factories. Wherever there is a great demand for female labour, as in Belfast, we find that the woman tends to become the chief support of the house. Driven out to work at the earliest possible age, she remains fettered to her wage-earning – a slave for life. Marriage does not mean for her a rest from outside labour, it usually means that, to the outside labour, she has added the duty of a double domestic toil. Throughout her life she remains a wage-earner; completing each day's work, she becomes the slave of the domestic needs of her family; and when at night she drops wearied upon her bed, it is with the knowledge that at the earliest morn she must find her way again into the service of the capitalist, and at the end of that coming day's service for him hasten homeward again for another round of domestic drudgery. So her whole life runs – a dreary pilgrimage from one drudgery to another; the coming of children but serving as milestones in her journey to signalize fresh increases to her burdens. Overworked, underpaid, and scantily nourished because underpaid, she falls easy prey to all the diseases that infect the badly-constructed 'warrens of the poor'. Her life is darkened from the outset by poverty, and the drudgery to which poverty is born, and the starvation of the intellect follows as an inevitable result upon the too early drudgery of the body.

Of what use to such sufferers can be the re-establishment of any form of Irish State if it does not embody the emancipation of womanhood. As we have shown, the whole spirit and practice of modern Ireland, as it expresses itself through its pastors and masters, bear socially and politically hardly upon women. That spirit and that practice had their origins in the establishment in this country of a social and political order based upon the private ownership of property, as against the older order based upon the common ownership of a related community.

Whatever class rules industrially will rule politically, and impose upon the community in general the beliefs, customs and ideas most suitable to the perpetuation of its rule. These beliefs, customs, ideas become then the highest expression of morality and so remain until the ascent to power of another ruling industrial class establishes a new morality. In Ireland since the Conquest, the landlord-capitalist class has ruled; the beliefs, customs, ideas of Ireland are the embodiment of the slave morality we inherited from those who accepted that rule in one or other of its forms; the subjection of women was an integral part of that rule.

Unless women were kept in subjection, and their rights denied, there was no guarantee that field would be added unto field in the patrimony of the family, or that wealth would accumulate even although men should decay. So, down from the landlord to the tenant or peasant proprietor, from the monopolist to the small business man eager to be a monopolist, and from all above to all below, filtered the beliefs, customs, ideas establishing a slave morality which enforces the subjection of women as the standard morality of the country.

None so fitted to break the chains as they who wear them, none so well equipped to decide what is a fetter. In its march towards freedom, the working class of Ireland must cheer on the efforts of those women who, feeling on their souls and bodies the fetters of the ages, have arisen to strike them off, and cheer all the louder if in its hatred of thraldom and passion for freedom the women's army forges ahead of the militant army of Labour.

But whosoever carries the outworks of the citadel of oppression, the working class alone can raze it to the ground.

The Reconquest of Ireland, Dublin, 1915

5

WAR AND REVOLUTIONARY WARFARE

THE ROOTS OF MODERN WAR

THE Cabinets who rule the destinies of nations from the various capitals of Europe are but the tools of the moneyed interest. Their quarrels are not dictated by sentiments of national pride or honour, but by the avarice and lust of power on the part of the class to which they belong. The people who fight under their banners in the various armies or navies do indeed imagine they are fighting the battles of their own country, but in what country has it ever happened that the people have profited by foreign conquest?

The influence which impels towards war today is the influence of capitalism. Every war now is a capitalist move for new markets, and it is a move capitalism must make or perish. The mad scramble for wealth which this century has witnessed has resulted in lifting almost every European country into the circle of competition for trade. New machinery, new inventions, new discoveries in the scientific world have all been laid under contribution as aids to industry, until the wealth producing powers of society at large have far outstripped the demand for goods, and now those very powers we have conjured up from the bosom of nature threaten to turn and rend us ... Every new labour-saving machine at one and the same time, by reducing the number of workers needed, reduces the demand for goods which the worker cannot buy, while increasing the power of producing goods, and thus permanently increases the number of un-employed, and shortens the period of industrial prosperity. Competition between capitalists drives them to seek for newer and more efficient wealth-producing machines, but as the home market is now no longer able to dispose of their produce they are driven to foreign markets ... So it is in China today. The great industrial nations of the world, driven on by their respective moneyed classes, themselves driven on by their own machinery, now front each other in the far East, and, with swords in hand, threaten to set the armed millions of Europe in terrible and bloody conflict, in order to decide which shall have the right to force upon John Chinaman the goods which his European brother produces. Laveleye* says somewhere that capitalism came into the world covered with blood and tears and dirt. We might add that if this war cloud now gathering in the East does burst, it will be the last capitalist war, so the death of that baneful institution will be like its birth, bloody, muddy and ignominious.

Workers' Republic, 20 August 1898

* Emile de Laveleye (1822–92), Belgian critic of Socialism.

BALLOTS, BULLETS, OR – ?

NOT the least of the services our comrade Victor Berger* has rendered to the Socialist cause must be accounted the writing and publishing of that now famous article in which he draws the attention of his readers to the possibility that the ballot will yet be stricken from the hands of the Socialist Party, and raises the question of the action our party must take in such an emergency.

It must be confessed, however, that the question has not been faced at all squarely by the majority of the critics who have unburdened themselves upon the matter. We have had much astonishment expressed, a great deal of deprecation of the introduction of the question at the present time, and not a little sly fun poked at our comrade. But one would have thought that a question of such a character brought up for discussion by a comrade noted for his moderation – a moderation by some thought to be akin to compromise – would have induced in Socialists a desire to seriously consider the elements of fact and probability behind and inspiring the question. What are these facts?

Briefly, the facts as they are known to us all are that all over the United States the capitalist class is even now busily devising ways and means by which the working class can be disfranchised. In California it is being done by exacting an enormous sum for the right to place a ticket upon the ballot; in Minnesota the same end is sought by a new primary law; in the south by an educational (?) test to be imposed only upon those who possess no property; in some States by imposing a property qualification upon candidates; and all over by wholesale counting out of Socialist ballots, and wholesale counting in of fraudulent votes. In addition to this we have had in Colorado and elsewhere many cases where the hired thugs of the capitalists forcibly occupied

* American Socialist Congressman.

the polling-booths, drove away the real voters and themselves voted in the name of every citizen on the list.

These are a few of the facts. Now what are the probabilities? One is that the capitalist class will not wait until we get a majority at the ballot-box, but will precipitate a fight upon some fake issue whilst the mass of the workers are still undecided as to the claims of capitalism and Socialism.

Another is that even if the capitalist class were law-abiding enough, or had miscalculated public opinion enough, to wait until the Socialists had got a majority at the ballot-box in some presidential election, they would then refuse to vacate their offices, or to recognize the election, and with the Senate and the military in their hands would calmly proceed to seat those candidates for president, etc. who had received the highest votes from the capitalist electorate. As to the first of these probabilities, the issue upon which a Socialist success at the ballot-box can be averted from the capitalist class is already here, and I expect at any time to see it quietly but effectually materialize. It is this: we have often seen the capitalist class invoke the aid of the Supreme Court in order to save it some petty annoyance by declaring unconstitutional some so-called labour or other legislation. Now I can conceive of no reason why this same Supreme Court cannot be invoked to declare unconstitutional any or all electoral victories of the Socialist Party. Some may consider this far-fetched. I do not consider it nearly as far-fetched as the decision which applied the anti-trust laws solely to trade unions,* or used the Inter-State Commerce Acts to prevent strikes upon railways.

I consider that if the capitalist class appealed to the Supreme Court and interrogated it to declare *whether a political party which aimed at overthrowing the constitution of the United States could legally operate to that end within the constitution* of the United States the answer in the negative which that Court would undoubtedly give would not only be entirely logical, but would also be extremely likely to satisfy every shallow thinker and financial ancestor-worshipper in the country.

* 1890 Sherman Anti-Trust Act which forbade 'combinations in restraint of trade'.

And, if such an eventuality arose, and the ballot was, in comrade Berger's words, stricken out of our hands, it would be too late then to propound the query which our comrade propounds now, and ask our friends and supporters: what are you going to do about it?

But even while admitting, nay, urging all this on behalf of the pertinency of our comrade's query, it does not follow that I therefore endorse or recommend his alternative. The rifle is, of course, a useful weapon under certain circumstances, but these circumstances are little likely to occur. This is an age of complicated machinery in war as in industry, and confronted with machine guns and artillery which kill at seven miles distance, rifles are not likely to be of much material value in assisting in the solution of the labour question in a proletarian manner. It would do comrade Berger good to read a little of the conquests of his countryman, Count Zeppelin, over the domain of the air, and thus think of the futility of opposing even an armed working class to such a power as the airship. Americans have been so enamoured of the achievements of the Wright brothers that too little attention has been paid to the development of the balloon by Zeppelin. Yet in his hands it has evolved into the most perfect and formidable fighting machine ever dreamt of. The words 'dirigible balloon' seem scarcely applicable to his creation. It is a floating ship, divided into a large number of separate compartments, so that the piercing of one even by a shell leaves the others intact and the machine still floating. Nothing less than fire can menace it with immediate destruction. It can carry seventeen tons and with that weight on board can be guided at will, perform all sorts of figures and evolutions, rise or descend, travel fast or remain stationary. It has already been equipped with a quick-firing Krupp gun and shells made for its own special use, and at the tests of the German army has proven itself capable of keeping up a rapid and sustained fire without interfering with its floating or manoeuvring powers. No army on earth, even of highly trained and disciplined men, could withstand an attack from ten of those monsters for as many minutes. It is more than probable that the development of these machines will eventuate in an armed truce from military conquest by the international capitalist class, the consecration of the flying machine to the cold task of holding in check the working class, and the making safe and profitable all sorts of attacks upon social and political rights. In facing such a weapon in the hands of our remorseless and unscrupulous masters the gun of comrade Victor Berger will be as ineffective as the paper ballot in the hands of a reformer.

Is the outlook, then, hopeless? No! We still have the opportunity to forge a weapon capable of winning the fight for us against political usurpation and all the military powers of earth, sea or air. That weapon is to be forged in the furnace of the struggle in the workshop, mine, factory or railroad, and its name is industrial unionism.

A working class organized on the lines on which the capitalist class has built its industrial plants today, regarding every such plant as the true unit of organization and society as a whole as the sum total of those units, and ever patiently indoctrinated with the idea that the mission of unionism is to take hold of the industrial equipment of society, and erect itself into the real holding and administrative force of the world; such a revolutionary working class would have a power at its command greater than all the achievements of science can put in the hands of the master class. An injunction forbidding the workers of an industrial union to do a certain thing in the interest of labour would be followed by every member of the union doing that thing until jails became eagerly sought as places of honour and the fact of having been in one would be as proudly vaunted as is now service on the field of Gettysburg; a Supreme Court decision declaring invalid a Socialist victory in a certain district, supported by the organization all over the country, and by a relentless boycott extending into the private life of all who supported fraudulently elected officials. Such a union would revive and apply to the class war of the workers the methods and principles so successfully applied by the peasants of Germany in the *Vehmgericht*, and by those of the Land League in the land war in Ireland in the eighties.

And eventually, in the case of a Supreme Court decision rendering illegal the political activities of the Socialist Party, or instructing the capitalist officals to refuse to vacate their offices after a national victory by that party, the industrially organized workers would give the usurping government a Roland for its Oliver by refusing to recognize its officers, to transport or feed its troops, to transmit its messages, to print its notices, or to chronicle its doings by working in any newspaper which upheld it. Finally, after having thus demonstrated the helplessness of capitalist officialdom in the face of united action by the producers (by attacking said officialdom with economic paralysis instead of rifle bullets) the industrially organized working class could proceed to take possession of the industries of the country after informing the military and other coercive forces of capitalism that they could procure the necessaries of life by surrendering themselves to the lawfully elected government and renouncing the usurpers at Washington. Otherwise they would have to try and feed and maintain themselves. In the face of such organization the airships would be as helpless as pirates without a port of call, and military power a broken reed.

The discipline of the military forces before which comrade Berger's rifles would break like glass would dissolve, and the authority of officers would be non-effectual if the soldiery were required to turn into uniformed banditti scouring the country for provisions.

Ireland during the Land League, Paris during the strike of the postmen and telegraphers, the strike of the peasants at Parma, Italy, all were miniature demonstrations of the effectiveness of this method of warfare, all were so many rehearsals in part for this great drama of social revolution, all were object lessons teaching the workers how to extract the virtue from the guns of the political masters.

International Socialist Review, October 1909

PHYSICAL FORCE IN IRISH POLITICS

IRELAND occupies a position among the nations of the earth unique in a great variety of its aspects, but in no one particular is this singularity more marked than in the possession of what is known as a 'physical force party' – a party, that is to say, whose members are united upon no one point, and agree upon no single principle, except upon the use of physical force as the sole means of settling the dispute between the people of this country and the governing power of Great Britain.

Other countries and other peoples have, from time to time, appealed to what the first French Revolutionists picturesquely described as the 'sacred right of insurrection', but in so appealing they acted under the inspiration of, and combated for, some great governing principle of political or social life upon which they, to a man, were in absolute agreement. The latter-day high falutin 'hillside' man, on the other hand, exalts into a principle that which the revolutionists of other countries have looked upon as a weapon, and in his gatherings prohibits all discussion of those principles which formed the main strength of his proto-types elsewhere and made the successful use of that weapon possible. Our people have glided at different periods of the past century from moral force agitation, so-called, into physical force rebellion, from constitutionalism into insurrectionism, meeting in each the same failure and the same disaster and yet seem as far as ever from learning the great truth that neither method is ever likely to be successful until they first insist that a perfect agreement *upon the end to be attained* should be arrived at as a starting-point of all our efforts.

To the reader unfamiliar with Irish political history such a remark seems to savour almost of foolishness, its truth is so apparent; but to the reader acquainted with the inner workings of the political movements of this country the remark is pregnant with the deepest meaning. Every revolutionary effort in Ireland has drawn the bulk of its adherents from the ranks of the disappointed followers of defeated constitutional movements. After having exhausted their constitutional efforts in striving to secure such a modicum of political power as would justify them to their own consciences in taking a place as loyal subjects of the British Empire, they, in despair, turned to thoughts of physical force as a means of attaining their ends. Their conception of what constitutes freedom was in no sense changed or revolutionized; they still believed in the political form of freedom which had been their ideal in their constitutional days; but no longer hoping for it from the acts of the British Parliament, they swung over into the ranks of the 'physical force' men as the only means of attaining it.

The so-called physical force movement of today in like manner bases its hopes upon the disgust of the people over the failure of the Home Rule movement; it seeks to enlist the people under its banners, not so much by pointing out the base ideals of the constitutionalists or the total inadequacy of their pet measures to remedy the evils under which the people suffer, as by emphasizing the greater efficacy of physical force as a national weapon. Thus, the one test of an advanced Nationalist is, in their opinion, one who believes in physical force. It may be the persons so professing to believe are Republicans; it may be they are believers in monarchy; it may be that Home Rule would satisfy them; it may be that they despise Home Rule. No matter what their political faith may be, if only they are prepared to express belief in the saving grace of physical force, they are acclaimed as advanced Nationalists – worthy descendants of 'the men of '98'. The '98 Executive, organized in the commencement by professed believers in the physical force doctrine, started by proclaiming its adherence to the principle of national independence 'as understood by Wolfe Tone and the United Irishmen', and in less than twelve months from doing so, deliberately rejected a similar resolution and elected on its governing body men notorious for their Royalist proclivities. As the '98 Executive represents the advanced Nationalists of Ireland, this repudiation of the Republican faith of the United Irishmen is an interesting corroboration of the truth of our statement that the advanced

Nationalists of our day are utterly regardless of principle and only attach importance to methods – an instance of putting the cart before the horse, absolutely unique in its imbecility and unparalleled in the history of the world.

It may be interesting, then, to place before our readers the Socialist Republican conception of the functions and uses of physical force in a popular movement. We neither exalt it into a principle nor repudiate it as something not to be thought of. Our position towards it is that the use or non-use of force for the realization of the ideas of progress always has been and always will be determined by the attitude, not of the party of progress, but of the governing class opposed to that party. If the time should arrive when the party of progress finds its way to freedom barred by the stubborn greed of a possessing class entrenched behind the barriers of law and order; if the party of progress has indoctrinated the people at large with the new revolutionary conception of society and is therefore representative of the will of a majority of the nation; if it has exhausted all the peaceful means at its disposal for the purpose of demonstrating to the people and their enemies that the new revolutionary ideas do possess the suffrage of the majority; then, but not till then, the party which represents the revolutionary idea is justified in taking steps to assume the powers of government, and in using the weapons of force to dislodge the usurping class or government in possession, and treating its members and supporters as usurpers and rebels against the constituted authorities always have been treated. In other words, Socialists believe that the question of force is of very minor importance; the really important question is of the principles upon which is based the movement that may or may not need the use of force to realize its object.

Here, then, is the immense difference between the Socialist Republicans and our friends the physical force men. The latter, by stifling all discussions of principles, earn the passive and fleeting commendation of the unthinking multitude; the former, by insisting upon a thorough understanding of their basic principles, do not so readily attract the multitude, but do attract and hold the more thoughtful amongst them. It is the difference betwixt a mob in revolt and an army in preparation. The mob who cheer a speaker referring to the hopes of a physical force movement would, in the very hour of apparent success, be utterly disorganized and divided by the passage through the British Legislature of any trumpery Home Rule Bill. The army of class-conscious workers organizing under the banner of the Socialist Republican Party, strong in their knowledge of economic truth and firmly grounded in their revolutionary principles, would remain entirely unaffected by any such manoeuvre and, knowing it would not change their position as a subject class, would still press forward, resolute and undivided, with their faces set towards their only hope of emancipation – the complete control by the working-class democracy of *all the powers of National Government*.

Thus the policy of the Socialist Republicans is seen to be the only wise one. 'Educate that you may be free'; principles first, methods afterwards. If the advocacy of physical force failed to achieve success or even to effect an uprising when the majority were unenfranchised and the secret ballot unknown, how can it be expected to succeed now that the majority are in possession of voting power and the secret ballot safeguards the voter?

The ballot-box was given us by our masters for their purpose; let us use it for our own. Let us demonstrate at that ballot-box the strength and intelligence of the revolutionary idea; let us make the hustings a rostrum from which to promulgate our principles; let us grasp the public powers in the interest of the disinherited class; let us emulate our fathers and, like the 'true men of '98', place ourselves in line with the most advanced thought of our age, and drawing inspiration and hope from the spectacle presented by the world-wide revolt of the workers, prepare for the coming of the day when the Socialist working class of Ireland will, through its elected representatives, present its demand for freedom from the yoke of a governing master class or nation – the day on which the question of moral or physical force shall be finally decided.

Workers' Republic, 22 July 1899

CAN WARFARE BE CIVILIZED?

THE progress of the great war and the many extraordinary developments accompanying it are rapidly tending to bring home to the minds of the general public the truth of the Socialist contention that all war is an atrocity, and that the attempt to single out any particular phase of it as more atrocious than another is simply an attempt to confuse the public mind.

We in this journal and in our predecessor, the *Irish Worker*, have consistently stood upon that principle. We have held, and do hold, that war is a relic of barbarism only possible because we are governed by a ruling class with barbaric ideas; we have held, and do hold, that the working class of all countries cannot hope to escape the horrors of war until in all countries that barbaric ruling class is thrown from power; and we have held, and do hold, that the lust for power on the part of that ruling class is so deeply rooted in the nature and instinct of its members, that it is more than probable that nothing less than superior force will ever induce them to abandon their throttling grasp upon the lives and liberties of mankind.

Holding such views we have at all times combated the idea of war; held that we have no foreign enemies outside of our own ruling class; held that if we are compelled to go to war we had much rather fight that ruling class than any other, and taught in season and out of season that it is the duty of the working class in self-protection to organize its own force to resist the force of the master class. The force available to the working class is two-fold, industrial and political, which latter includes military organization to protect political and industrial rights. 'Those who live by the sword shall perish by the sword' say the Scriptures, and it may well be that in the progress of events the working class of Ireland may be called upon to face the stern necessity of taking the sword (or rifle) against the class whose rule has brought upon them and upon the world the hellish horror of the present European war. Should that necessity arise it would be well to realize that the talk of 'humane methods of warfare', of the 'rules of civilized warfare', and all such homage to the finer sentiments of the race are hypocritical and unreal, and only intended for the consumption of stay-at-homes. There are no humane methods of warfare, there is no such thing as civilized warfare; all warfare is inhuman, all warfare is barbaric; the first blast of the bugles of war ever sounds for the time being the funeral knell of human progress.

A few illustrations will suffice to drive home these points. One concerns the outcry over the alleged use of what are known as dum-dum bullets. It is alleged by both sides that the others are using those bullets and that they inflict a most grievous wound, and as they inflict such a serious wound they are opposed to the rules of 'civilized and humane warfare'. The same persons who raise this cry will calmly read of the firing of shrapnel into a body of troops and will exult in the result. Yet a shrapnel shell contains 340 bullets which scatter in all directions, tearing off legs and arms, rending and bursting the human bodies, and in general creating wounds which no surgical science can hope to cure. How hypocritical, then, is the pretence of horror over the grievous wound inflicted by a dum-dum bullet!

Of like character is the outcry over the bombardment of undefended towns. One would think to read such diatribes that it was not a recognized practice of all naval warfare. For generations the public of these islands have been reading of Great Britain sending punitive expeditions against native tribes in Africa, the islands of the ocean, or parts of Asia. It may be that some benighted native has stolen a cask of rum from the compound of a missionary, and thrown a stone at the holy man of God when the latter demanded the return of the cask in question. Immediately a British man-of-war is ordered to that coast, opens fire upon and destroys the whole town, indiscriminately massacring the majority of its inhabitants, women and old men, and babes yet unborn, all to punish one or two persons for a slight upon a British subject. That thousands of British subjects are subjected to worse slights at home every day of their lives is a matter of not enough consequence to move a policeman, let alone a battleship. Yet up and down the world the British fleet has gone carrying out such orders, and bombarding such undefended places without ever moving the inkslingers of the jingo press to protest.

It all depends, it appears, upon whose houses are being bombarded, whose people are being massacred, whose limbs are torn from the body, whose bodies are blown to a ghastly mass of mangled flesh and blood and bones. The crime of the Germans seems to consist in believing that what is sauce for the goose is sauce for the gander.

But what is the theory of the matter? We have before us the work of M. Bloch on *Modern weapons and modern war*, the famous work in which the methods and results of modern warfare were analysed and foretold long before they had been brought to the test of practical trial on modern battlefields. This author, a Pole but a Russian subject, foretold most of the phenomena accompanying modern campaigns, and has lived to see the results he predicted in a large measure embodied in the practice of armies actually in conflict.

To arrive at such a wonderful accuracy in prediction he was compelled to undertake a systematic investigation of all the conditions of modern warfare on land and sea with modern weapons. On the question of undefended towns he has this to say, and all who have read his works bear witness to his scrupulous impartiality and freedom from national bias:

It must be remembered that, as is shown by the practice of manoeuvres, the principle that undefended towns are not subject to bombardment is not acknowledged, and in a future war no towns will be spared. As evidence of this the following case may be cited. On 24 August 1889, the following letter was addressed by the commander of the *Collingwood* to the Mayor of Peterhead:

'By order of the Vice-Admiral commanding the 11th Division of the Fleet, I have to demand from your town a contribution of £150,000 sterling... I must add that in case the officers who deliver this letter do not return within the course of two hours the town will be burnt, the shipping destroyed, and factories ruined.'

This letter was printed in all the newspapers and called forth no protest... It is evident then that England will not refrain from such action when convenient, and as her voice is the most important in naval matters, the other Powers will certainly follow her example.

M. Bloch here cites as an example the course taken by a British fleet in the course of naval manoeuvres, and as such manoeuvres are always carried out strictly according to official handbooks it is safe to assume that in the bombardment of undefended towns we have a practice authorized by the British Admiralty. Yet whether authorized by British or German practice or theory, how brutal, how repulsive, how murderous it is.

Up to the present no such bombardment has yet taken place, for, of course, the East Coast towns bombarded were all defended by entrenchments and garrison artillery, but what lover of humanity can view with anything but horror the prospect of this ruthless destruction of human life.

Yet this is war: war for which all the jingoes are howling, war to which all the hopes of the world are being sacrificed, war to which a mad ruling class would plunge a mad world.

No, there is no such thing as humane or civilized war! War may be forced upon a subject race or subject class to put an end to subjection of race, of class, or sex. When so waged it must be waged thoroughly and relentlessly, but with no delusions as to its elevating nature, or civilizing methods.

The Worker, 30 January 1915

A WAR FOR CIVILIZATION

WE are hearing and reading a lot just now about a war for civilization. In some vague, ill-defined manner we are led to believe that the great empires of Europe have suddenly been seized with a chivalrous desire to right the wrongs of mankind, and have sallied forth to war, giving their noblest blood and greatest measures to the task of furthering the cause of civilization.

It seems unreal, but it may be possible. Great emotions sometimes master the most cold and calculating individuals, pushing them on to do that which in their colder moments they would have sneered at. In like manner great emotions sometimes master whole communities of men and women, and nations have gone mad, as in the Crusades, over matters that did not enter into any scheme of selfish calculation.

But in such cases the great emotions manifested themselves in at least an appropriate manner. Their actions under the influence of great emotions had a relation to the cause or the ideal for which they were ostensibly warring.

In the case of the war for civilization, however, we look in vain for any action which in itself bears the mark of civilization. As we count civilization it means the ascendancy of industry and the arts of industry over the reign of violence and pillage. Civilization means the conquest by ordered law and peaceful discussion of the forces of evil, it means the exaltation of those whose strength is only in the righteousness of their cause over those whose power is gained by a ruthless seizing of domination founded on force.

Civilization necessarily connotes the gradual supplanting of the reign of chance and muddling by the forces of order and careful provision for the future; it means the levelling up of classes, and the initiation of the people into a knowledge and enjoyment of all that tends to soften the natural hardships of life and to make that life refined and beautiful.

But the war for civilization has done none of those things – aspires to do none of these things. It is primarily a war upon a nation whose chief crime is that it refuses to accept a position of dependence, but insists instead upon organizing its forces so that its people can co-operate with nature in making their lives independent of chance, and independent of the goodwill of others.

The war for civilization is a war upon a nation which insists upon organizing its intellect so as to produce the highest and best in science, in art, in music, in industry; and insists more-over upon so co-ordinating and linking up all these that the final result shall be a perfectly educated nation of men and women.

In the past civilization has been a heritage enjoyed by a few upon a basis of the brutalization of the vast multitude; that nation aims at a civilization of the whole resting upon the whole, and only made possible by the educated co-operation of an educated whole.

The war for civilization is waged by a nation like Russia, which has the greatest proportion of illiterates of any European power, and which strives sedulously to prevent education where it is possible, and to poison it where prohibition is impossible.

The war for civilization is waged by a nation like Britain which holds in thrall a sixth of the human race, and holds as a cardinal doctrine of its faith that none of its subject races may, under penalty of imprisonment and death, dream of ruling their own territories. A nation which believes that all races are subject to purchase, and which brands as perfidy the act of any nation which, like Bulgaria, chooses to carry its wares and its arms to any other than a British market.

This war for civilization in the name of neutrality and small nationalities invades Persia and Greece, and in the name of the interests of commerce seizes the cargo of neutral ships, and flaunts its defiance of neutral flags.

In the name of freedom from militarism it establishes military rule in Ireland, battling for progress it abolishes trial by jury, and waging war for enlightened rule it tramples the freedom of the press under the heel of a military despot.

Is it any wonder then that that particular war for civilization arouses no enthusiasm in the ranks of the toiling masses of the Irish nation?

But there is another war for civilization in which these masses are interested. That war is being waged by the forces of organized labour.

Civilization cannot be built upon slaves; civilization cannot be secured if the producers are sinking into misery; civilization is lost if they whose labour makes it possible share so little of its fruits that its fall can leave them no worse than its security.

The workers are at the bottom of civilized society. That civilization may endure they ought to push upward from their poverty and misery until they emerge into the full sunlight of freedom. When the fruits of civilization, created by all, are enjoyed in common by all, then civilization is secure. Not till then.

Since this European war started the workers as a whole have been sinking. It is not merely that they have lost in comfort – have lost a certain standard of food and clothing by reason of the increase of prices – but they have lost in a great measure, in Britain at least, all those hard won rights of combination and freedom of action, the possession of which was the foundation upon which they hoped to build the greater freedom of the future.

From being citizens with rights the workers were being driven and betrayed into the position of slaves with duties. Some of them may have been well-paid slaves, but slavery is not measured by the amount of oats in the feeding trough to which the slave is tied. It is measured by his loss of control of the conditions under which he labours.

We here in Ireland, particularly those who follow the example of the Irish Transport and General Workers Union, have been battling to preserve those rights which others have surrendered; we have fought to keep up our standards of life, to force up our wages, to better our conditions.

To that extent we have been truly engaged in a war for civilization. Every victory we have gained has gone to increase the security of life amongst our class, has gone to put bread on the tables, coals in the fires, clothes on the backs of those to whom food and warmth and clothing are things of ever pressing moment.

Some of our class have fought in Flanders and the Dardanelles; the greatest achievement of them all combined will weigh but a feather in the balance for good compared with the achievements of those who stayed at home and fought to secure the rights of the working class against invasion.

The carnival of murder on the continent will be remembered as a nightmare in the future, will not have the slightest effect in deciding for good the fate of our homes, our wages, our hours, our conditions. But the victories of labour in Ireland will be as footholds, secure and firm, in the upward climb of our class to the fulness and enjoyment of all that labour creates, and organized society can provide.

Truly, labour alone in these days is fighting the real *war for civilization*.

Workers' Republic, 30 October 1915

WHAT IS OUR PROGRAMME?

WE are often asked the above question. Sometimes the question is not too politely put, sometimes it is put in frantic bewilderment, sometimes it is put in wrathful objurgation, sometimes it is put in tearful entreaty, sometimes it is put by Nationalists who affect to despise the Labour movement, sometimes it is put by Socialists who distrust the Nationalists because of the anti-Labour record of many of their friends, sometimes it is put by our enemies, sometimes by our friends, and always it is pertinent, and worthy of an answer.

The Labour movement is like no other movement. Its strength lies in being like no other movement. It is never so strong as when it stands alone. Other movements dread analysis and shun all attempts to define their objects. The Labour movement delights in analysing, and is perpetually defining and re-defining its principles and objects. The man or woman who has caught the spirit of the Labour movement brings that spirit of analysis and definition into all his or her public acts, and expects at all times to answer the call to define his or her position. They cannot live on illusions, nor thrive by them; even should their heads be in the clouds they will make no forward step until they are assured that their feet rest upon the solid earth.

In this they are essentially different from the middle or professional classes, and the parties or movements controlled by such classes in Ireland. These always talk of realities, but nourish themselves and their followers upon the unsubstantial meat of phrases; always prate about being intensely practical but nevertheless spend their whole lives in following visions.

When the average non-Labour patriot in Ireland who boasts of his practicality is brought in contact with the cold world and its problems he shrinks from the contact. Should his feet touch the solid earth he effects to despise it as a 'mere material basis', and strives to make the people believe that true patriotism needs no foundation to rest upon other than the brainstorms of its poets, orators, journalists and leaders.

Ask such people for a programme and you are branded as a carping critic; refuse to accept their judgement as the last word in human wisdom and you become an enemy to be carefully watched; insist that in the crisis of your country's history your first allegiance is to your country and not to any leader, executive, or committee, and you are forthwith a disturber, a factionist, a wrecker.

What is our programme? We at least, in conformity with the spirit of our movement, will try and tell it. Our programme in time of peace was to gather into Irish hands in Irish trade unions the control of all the forces of production and distribution in Ireland. We never believed that freedom would be realized without fighting for it. From our earliest declaration of policy in Dublin in 1896 the editor of this paper has held to the dictum that our ends should be secured 'peacefully if possible, forcibly if necessary'. Believing so, we saw what the world outside Ireland is realizing today, that the destinies of the world and the fighting strength of armies are at the mercy of organized Labour as soon as that Labour becomes truly revolutionary. Thus we strove to make Labour in Ireland organized – and revolutionary.

We saw that should it come to a test in Ireland, (as we hoped and prayed it might come), between those who stood for the Irish nation and those who stood for the foreign rule, the greatest civil asset in the hand of the Irish nation for use in the struggle would be the control of Irish docks, shipping, railways and production by unions that gave sole allegiance to Ireland.

We realized that the power of the enemy to hurl his forces upon the forces of Ireland would lie at the mercy of the men who controlled the transport system of Ireland; we saw that the hopes of Ireland as a nation rested upon the due recognition of the identity of interest between that ideal and the rising hopes of Labour.

In Europe today we have seen the strongest governments of the world exerting every effort, holding out all possible sorts of inducement, to organized Labour to use its organization on the side of those governments in time of war. We have spent the best part of our lifetime striving to create in Ireland the working class spirit that would create an Irish organization of Labour willing to do voluntarily for Ireland what those governments of Europe are beseeching their trade unions to do for their countries. And we have partly succeeded.

We have succeeded in creating an organization that will willingly do more for Ireland than any trade union in the world has attempted to do for its national government. Had we not been attacked and betrayed by many of our fervent advanced patriots, had they not been so anxious to destroy us, so willing to applaud even the British Government when it attacked us, had they stood by us and pushed our organization all over Ireland it would now be in our power at a word to crumple up and demoralize every offensive move of the enemy against the champions of Irish freedom. Had we been able to carry out all our plans, as such an Irish organization of Labour alone could carry them out, we could at a word have created all the conditions necessary to the striking of a successful blow whenever the military arm of Ireland wished to move.

Have we a programme? We are the only people that had a programme – that understood the mechanical conditions of modern war, and the dependence of national power upon industrial control. What is our programme now? At the grave risk of displeasing alike the perfervid Irish patriot and the British 'competent military authority', we shall tell it.

We believe that in times of peace we should work along the lines of peace to strengthen the nation, and we believe that whatever strengthens and elevates the working class strengthens the nation. But we also believe that in times of war we should act as in war. We despise, entirely despise and loathe, all the mouthings and mouthers about war who infest Ireland in time of peace, just as we despise and loathe all the cantings about caution and restraint to which the same people treat us in times of war.

Mark well then our programme. While the war lasts and Ireland still is a subject nation we shall continue to urge her to fight for her freedom.

We shall continue, in season and out of season, to teach that the 'far-flung battle line' of England is weakest at the point nearest its heart, that Ireland is in that position of tactical advantage, that a defeat of England in India, Egypt, the Balkans or Flanders would not be so dangerous to the British Empire as any conflict of armed forces in Ireland, that the time for Ireland's battle is NOW, the place for Ireland's battle is HERE. That a strong man may deal lusty blows with his fists against a host of surrounding foes, and conquer, but will succumb if a child sticks a pin in his heart.

But the moment peace is once admitted by the British Government as being a subject ripe for discussion, *that moment our policy will be for peace* and in direct opposition to all talk or preparation for armed revolution. We will be no party to leading out Irish patriots to meet the might of an England at peace. The moment peace is in the air we shall strictly confine ourselves, and lend all our influence to the work of turning the thought of Labour in Ireland to the work of peaceful reconstruction.

That is our programme. You can now compare it with the programme of those who bid you hold your hand now, and thus put it in the power of the enemy to patch up a temporary peace, turn round and smash you at his leisure, and then go to war again with the Irish question settled – in the graves of Irish patriots.

We fear that is what is going to happen. It is to our mind inconceivable that the British public should allow conscription to be applied to England and not to Ireland. Nor do the British Government desire it. But that Government will use the cry of the necessities of war to force conscription upon the people of England, and will then make a temporary peace, and turn round to force Ireland to accept the same terms as have been forced upon England.

The English public will gladly see this done – misfortune likes company. The situation will then shape itself thus: the Irish Volunteers who are pledged to fight conscription will either need to swallow their pledge, and see the young men of Ireland conscripted, or will need to resist conscription, and engage the military force of England at a time when England is at peace.

This is what the diplomacy of England is working for, what the stupidity of some of our leaders who imagine they are Wolfe Tones is making possible. It is our duty, it is the duty of all who wish to save Ireland from such shame or such slaughter to strengthen the hand of those of the leaders who are for action as against those who are playing into the hands of the enemy.

We are neither rash nor cowardly. We know our opportunity when we see it, and we know when it has gone. We know that at the end of this war England will have at least an army of one million men, *or more than two soldiers for every adult male in Ireland.* And these soldiers veterans of the greatest war in history.

We shall not want to fight those men. We shall devote our attention to organizing their comrades who return to civil life, to organizing them into trade unions and Labour parties to secure them their rights in civil life.

Unless we emigrate to some country where there are men.

Workers' Republic, 22 January 1916

MOSCOW INSURRECTION OF 1905

In the year 1905, the fires of revolution were burning very brightly in Russia. Starting with a parade of unarmed men and women to the palace of the Tsar, the flames of insurrection spread all over the land. The peaceful parades were met with volleys of shrapnel and rifle fire, charged by mounted Cossacks, and cut down remorselessly by cavalry of the line, and in answer to this attack, general strikes broke out all over Russia. From strikes the people proceeded to revolutionary uprisings, soldiers revolted and joined the people in some cases, and in others the sailors of the navy seized the ironclads of the Tsar's fleet and hoisted revolutionary colours. One incident in this outburst was the attempted revolution in Moscow. We take it as our task this week because, in it, the soldiers remained loyal to the Tsar, and therefore it resolved itself into a clean-cut fight between a revolutionary force and a government force. Thus we are able to study the tactics of (a) a regular army in attacking a city defended by barricades, and (b) a revolutionary force holding a city against a regular army.

Fortunately for our task as historians, there was upon the spot an English journalist of unquestioned ability and clearsightedness, as well as of unrivalled experience as a spectator in warfare. This was H. W. Nevinson, the famous war-correspondent. From his book *The Dawn of Russia* as well as from a close intimacy with many refugees who took part in the revolution, this description is built up.

The revolutionists of Moscow had intended to postpone action until a much later date in the hope of securing the co-operation of the peasantry, but the active measures of the government precipitated matters. Whilst the question of 'Insurrection' or 'No Insurrection yet' was being discussed at a certain house in the city, the troops were quietly surrounding the building and the first intimation of their presence received by the revolutionists was the artillery opening fire on the building at point-blank range. A large number of the leaders were killed or arrested, but next morning the city was in insurrection.

Of the numbers engaged on the side of the revolutionists, there is considerable conflict of testimony. The government estimate, anxious to applaud the performance of the troops, is 15,000. The revolutionary estimate, on the other hand, is only 500. Mr Nevinson states that a careful investigator friendly to the revolutionists, and with every facility for knowing, gave the number as approximately 1,500. The deductions we were able to make from the stories of the refugees aforementioned makes the latter number seem the most probable. The equipment of the revolutionists was miserable in the extreme. Among the 1,500 there was only a total of 80 rifles, and a meagre supply of ammunition for same. The only other weapons were revolvers and automatic pistols, chiefly Brownings. Of these latter a goodly supply seems to have been on hand as at one period of the fighting the revolutionists advertised for volunteers, and named Browning pistols as part of the 'pay' for all recruits.

Against this force, so pitifully armed, the government possessed in the city, 18,000 seasoned troops, armed with magazine rifles, and a great number of batteries of field artillery.

The actual fighting which lasted nine days, during which time the government troops made practically no progress, is thus described by the author we have already quoted.

Of the barricades, he says that they were erected everywhere, even the little boys and girls throwing them up in the most out-of-the-way places, so that it was impossible to tell which was a barricade with insurgents to defend it and which was a mock barricade, a circumstance which greatly hindered the progress of the troops, who had always to spend a considerable period in finding out the real nature of the obstruction before they dared to pass it.

The very multitude of these barricades (early next morning I counted one hundred and thirty of them, and I had not seen half) made it difficult to understand the main purpose of all the fighting.

As far as they had any definite plan at all, their idea seems to have been to drive a wedge into the heart of the city, supporting the advance by barricades on each side so as to hamper the approach of troops.

The four arms of the cross roads were blocked with double or even treble barricades about ten yards apart. As far as I could see along the curve of the Sadavoya, on both sides, barricade succeeded barricade, and the whole road was covered with telegraph wire, some of it lying loose, some tied across like netting. The barricades enclosing the centre of the cross roads like a fort were careful constructions of telegraph poles or the iron supports to the overhead wires of electric trams, closely covered over with doors, railings and advertising boards, and lashed together with wire. Here and there a tram-car was built in to give solidity, and on the top of every barricade waved a little red flag.

Men and women were throwing them (the barricades) up with devoted zeal, sawing telegraph poles, wrenching iron railings from their sockets, and dragging out the planks from builders' yards.

Noteworthy as an illustration of how all things, even popular revolutions, change their character as the conditions change in which they operate, is the fact that no barricade was defended in the style of the earlier French or Belgian revolutions.

Mr Nevinson says:

But it was not from the barricades themselves that the real opposition came. From first to last no barricade was 'fought' in the old sense of the word. The revolutionary methods were far more terrible and effective. By the side-street barricades, and wire entanglements they had rid themselves of the fear of cavalry. By the barricades across the main streets, they had rendered the approach of troops necessarily slow. To the soldiers, the horrible part of the street fighting was that they could never see the real enemy. On coming near a barricade or the entrance to a side street, a few scouts would be advanced a short distance before the guns. As they crept forward, firing as they always did, into the empty barricades in front, they might suddenly find themselves exposed to a terrible revolver fire, at about fifteen paces range, from both sides of the street. It was useless to reply, for there was nothing visible to aim at. All they could do was to fire blindly in almost any direction. Then the revolver fire would suddenly cease, the guns would trundle up and wreck the houses on both sides. Windows fell crashing on the pavement, case-shot burst into the bedrooms, and round-shot made holes through three or four walls. It was bad for furniture, but the revolutionists had long ago escaped through a labyrinth of courts at the back, and were already preparing a similar attack on another street.

The troops did not succeed in overcoming the resistance of the insurgents but the insurrection rather melted away as suddenly as it had taken form. The main reason for this sudden dissolution lay in receipt of discouraging news from St Petersburg from which quarter help had been expected, and was not forthcoming, and in the rumoured advance of a hostile body of peasantry eager to co-operate with the soldiery against the people who were 'hindering the sale of agricultural produce in the Moscow market'.

Criticism

The action of the soldiery in bringing field-guns, or indeed any kind of artillery, into the close quarters of street fighting was against all the teaching of military science, and would infallibly have resulted in the loss of the guns had it not been for the miserable equipment of the insurgents. Had any body of the latter been armed with a reasonable supply of ammunition the government could only have taken Moscow from the insurgents at the cost of an appalling loss of life.

A regular bombardment of the city would only have been possible if the whole loyalist population had withdrawn outside the insurgent lines, and apart from the social reasons against such an abandonment of their business and property, the moral effect of such a desertion of Moscow would have been of immense military value in strengthening the hands of the insurgents and bringing recruits to their ranks. As the military were thus compelled to fight in the city and against a force so badly equipped, not much fault can be found with their tactics.

Of the insurgents also it must be said that they made splendid use of their material. It was a wise policy not to man the barricades and an equally wise policy not to open fire at long range where the superior weapons of the enemy would have been able with impunity to crush them, but to wait before betraying their whereabouts until the military had come within easy range of their inferior weapons.

Lacking the co-operation of the other Russian cities, and opposed by the ignorant peasantry, the defeat of the insurrection was inevitable, but it succeeded in establishing the fact that even under modern conditions the professional soldier is, in a city, badly handicapped in a fight against really determined civilian revolutionaries.

Workers' Republic, 29 May 1915
from *Revolutionary Warfare*

STREET FIGHTING – SUMMARY

A COMPLETE summary of the lessons to be derived from the military events we have narrated in these chapters during the past few months would involve the writing of a very large volume. Indeed it might truly be urged that the lessons are capable of such infinite expansion that no complete summary is possible.

In the military sense of the term what after all is a *street*? A street is a defile in a city. A defile is a narrow pass through which troops can only move by narrowing their front, and therefore making themselves a good target for the enemy. A defile is also a difficult place for soldiers to manoeuvre in, especially if the flanks of the defile are held by the enemy.

A mountain pass is a defile the sides of which are constituted by the natural slopes of the mountain sides, as at the Scalp. A bridge over a river is a defile the sides of which are constituted by the river. A street is a defile the sides of which are constituted by the houses in the street.

To traverse a mountain pass with any degree of safety the sides of the mountain must be cleared by flanking parties ahead of the main body; to pass over a bridge the banks of the river on each side must be raked with gun or rifle fire whilst the bridge is being rushed; to take a street properly barricaded and held on both sides by forces in the houses, these houses must be broken into and taken by hand to hand fighting. A street barricade placed in position where artillery cannot operate from a distance is impregnable to frontal attack. To bring artillery within a couple of hundred yards – the length of the average street – would mean the loss of the artillery if confronted by even imperfectly drilled troops armed with rifles.

The Moscow revolution, where only 80 rifles were in the possession of the insurgents, would have ended in the annihilation of the artillery had the number of insurgent rifles been 800.

The insurrection of Paris in June, 1848, reveals how districts of towns, or villages, should be held. The streets were barricaded at tactical points *not on the main streets* but commanding them. The houses were broken through so that passages were made inside the houses along the whole length of the streets. The party walls were loopholed, as were also the front walls, the windows were blocked by sandbags, boxes filled with stones and dirt, bricks, chests, and other pieces of furniture with all sorts of odds and ends piled up against them.

Behind such defences the insurgents poured fire upon the troops through loopholes left for the purpose.

In the attack upon Paris by the allies fighting against Napoleon a village held in this manner repulsed several assaults of the Prussian allies of England. When these Prussians were relieved by the English these latter did not dare attempt a frontal attack, but instead broke into an end house on one side of the village street, and commenced to take the houses one by one. Thus all the fighting was inside the houses, and musket-fire played but a small part. On one side of the street they captured all the houses, on the other they failed, and when a truce was declared the English were in possession of one side of the village, and their French enemies of the other.

The truce led to a peace. When peace was finally proclaimed the two sides of the village street were still held by opposing forces.

The defence of a building in a city, town or village is governed by the same rules. Such a building left unconquered is a serious danger even if its supports are all defeated. If it had been flanked by barricades, and these barricades were destroyed, no troops could afford to push on and leave the building in the hands of the enemy. If they did so they would be running the danger of perhaps meeting a check further on, which check would be disastrous if they had left a hostile building manned by an unconquered force in their rear. Therefore, the fortifying of a strong building, as a pivot upon which the defence of a town or village should hinge, forms a principal object of the preparations of any defending force, whether regular army or insurrectionary.

In the Franco–German War of 1870 the château, or castle, of Geissberg formed such a position in the French lines on 4 August. The Germans drove in all the supports of the French party occupying this country house, and stormed the outer courts, but were driven back by the fire from the windows and loopholed walls. Four batteries of artillery were brought up to within 900 yards of the house and battered away at its walls, and battalion after battalion was hurled against it. The advance of the whole German army was delayed until this one house was taken. To take it caused a loss of 23 officers and 329 men, yet it had only a garrison of 200.

In the same campaign the village of Bazeilles offered a similar lesson in the tactical strength of a well-defended line of houses. The German Army drove the French off the field and entered the village without a struggle. But it took a whole army corps seven hours to fight its way through to the other end of the village.

A mountainous country has always been held to be difficult for military operations owing to its passes or glens. A city is a huge mass of passes or glens formed by streets and lanes. Every difficulty that exists for the operation of regular troops in mountains is multiplied a hundredfold in a city. And the difficulty of the commissariat which is likely to be insuperable to an irregular or popular force taking to the mountains, is solved for them by the sympathies of the populace when they take to the streets.

The general principle to be deducted from a study of the examples we have been dealing with, is that the defence is of almost overwhelming importance in such warfare as a popular force like the Citizen Army might be called upon to participate in. Not a mere passive defence of a position valueless in itself, but the active defence of a position whose location threatens the supremacy or existence of the enemy. The genius of the commander must find such a position, the skill of his subordinates must prepare and fortify it, the courage of all must defend it. Out of this combination of genius, skill and courage alone can grow the flower of military success.

The Citizen Army and the Irish Volunteers are open for all those who wish to qualify for the exercise of these qualities.

Workers' Republic, 24 July 1915
from *Revolutionary Warfare*

6

THE FIRST WORLD WAR

OUR DUTY IN THIS CRISIS

WHAT should be the attitude to the working-class democracy of Ireland in face of the present crisis? I wish to emphasize the fact that the question is addressed to the 'working-class democracy' because I believe that it would be worse than foolish – it would be a crime against all our hopes and aspirations – to take counsel in this matter from any other source.

Mr John E. Redmond has just earned the plaudits of all the bitterest enemies of Ireland and slanderers of the Irish race by declaring, in the name of Ireland, that the British Government can now safely withdraw all its garrisons from Ireland, and that the Irish slaves will guarantee to protect the Irish estate of England until their masters come back to take possession – a statement that announces to all the world that Ireland has at last accepted as permanent this status of a British province. Surely no inspiration can be sought from that source.

The advanced Nationalists have neither a policy nor a leader. During the Russian Revolution such of their press as existed in and out of Ireland, as well as their spokesmen, orators and writers vied with each other in laudation of Russia and vilification of all the Russian enemies of Tsardom. It was freely asserted that Russia was the natural enemy of England; that the heroic revolutionalists were in the pay of the English Government and that every true Irish patriot ought to pray for the success of the armies of the Tsar. Now, as I, amongst other Irish Socialists, predicted all along, when the exigencies of diplomacy makes it suitable, the Russian bear and the English lion are hunting together and every victory for the Tsar's Cossacks is a victory for the paymasters of those King's Own Scottish Borderers who, but the other day, murdered the people of Dublin in cold blood. Surely such childish intellects that conceived of the pro-Russian campaign of nine years ago cannot give us light and leading in any campaign for freedom from the British allies of Russia today? It is well to remember also that in this connection since 1909 the enthusiasm for the Russians was replaced in the same quarter by as blatant a propaganda in favour of the German War Lord. But since the guns did begin to speak in reality this propaganda had died out in whispers, whilst without a protest, the manhood of Ireland was pledged to armed warfare against the very power our advanced Nationalist friends have wasted so much good ink in acclaiming.

Of late, sections of the advanced Nationalist press have lent themselves to a desperate effort to misrepresent the position of the Carsonites, and to claim for them the admiration of Irish Nationalists on the grounds that these Carsonites were fearless Irishmen who had refused to take dictation from England. A more devilishly mischievous and lying doctrine was never preached in Ireland. The Carsonite position is indeed plain – so plain that nothing but sheer perversity of purpose can misunderstand it, or cloak it with a resemblance to Irish patriotism. The Carsonites say that their fathers were planted in this country to assist in keeping the natives down in subjection that this country might be held for England. That this was God's will because the Catholic Irish were not fit for the responsibilities and powers of free men and that they are not fit for the exercise of these responsibilities and powers till this day. Therefore, say the Carsonites, we have kept our side of the bargain; we have refused to admit the Catholics to power and responsibility; we have manned the government of this country for England, we propose to continue to do so, and rather than admit that these Catholics – these 'mickies and teagues' – are our equals, we will fight, in the hope that our fighting will cause the English people to revolt against their government and re-establish us in our historic position as an English colony in Ireland, superior to, and unhampered by, the political institutions of the Irish natives.

How this can be represented as the case of Irishmen refusing to take dictation from England passeth all comprehension. It is rather the case of a community in Poland, after 250 years colonization, still refusing to adopt the title of natives, and obstinately clinging to the position and privileges of a dominant colony. Their programme is summed up in the expression which forms the dominant note of all their speeches, sermons and literature:

We are loyal British subjects. We hold this country for England. England cannot desert us.

What light or leading then can Ireland get from the hysterical patriots who so egregiously misrepresent this fierce contempt for Ireland as something that ought to win the esteem of Irishmen?

What ought to be the attitude of the working-class democracy of Ireland in face of the present crisis?

In the first place, then, we ought to clear our minds of all the political cant which would tell us that we have either 'natural enemies' or 'natural allies' in any of the powers now warring. When it is said that we ought to unite to protect our shores against the 'foreign enemy' I confess to be unable to follow that line of reasoning, as I know of no foreign enemy of this country except the British Government and know that it is not the British Government that is meant.

In the second place we ought to seriously consider that the evil effects of this war upon Ireland will be simply incalculable, that it will cause untold suffering and misery amongst the people, and that as this misery and suffering have been brought upon us because of our enforced partisanship with a nation whose government never consulted us in the matter, we are therefore perfectly at liberty morally to make any bargain we may see fit, or that may present itself in the course of events.

Should a German army land in Ireland tomorrow we should be perfectly justified in joining it if by doing so we could rid this country once and for all from its connection with the Brigand Empire that drags us unwillingly into this war.

Should the working class in Europe, rather than slaughter each other for the benefit of kings and financiers, proceed to-morrow to erect barricades all over Europe, to break up bridges and destroy the transport service that war might be abolished, we should be perfectly justified in following such a glorious example and contributing our aid to the final dethronement of the vulture classes that rule and rob the world.

But pending either of these consummations it is our manifest duty to take all possible action to save the poor from the horrors this war has in store.

Let it be remembered that there is no natural scarcity of food in Ireland. Ireland is an agricultural country, and can normally feed all her people under any sane system of things. But prices are going up in England and hence there will be an immense demand for Irish produce. To meet that demand all nerves will be strained on this side, the food that ought to feed the people of Ireland will be sent out of Ireland in greater quantities than ever and *famine prices will come in Ireland to be immediately followed by famine itself.* Ireland will starve, or rather the townspeople of Ireland will starve, that the British army and navy and jingoes may be fed. Remember, the Irish farmer like all other farmers will benefit by the high prices of the war, but these high prices will mean starvation to the labourers in the towns. But without these labourers the farmers' produce cannot leave Ireland without the help of a garrison that England cannot now spare. We must consider at once whether it will not be our duty to refuse to allow agricultural produce to leave Ireland until provision is made for the Irish working class.

Let us not shrink from the consequences. This may mean more than a transport strike, it may mean armed battling in the streets to keep in this country the food for our people. But whatever it may mean it must not be shrunk from. It is the immediately feasible policy of the working-class democracy, the answer to all the weaklings who in this crisis of our country's history stand helpless and bewildered crying for guidance, when they are not hastening to betray her.

Starting thus, Ireland may yet set the torch to a European conflagration that will not burn out until the last throne and the last capitalist bond and debenture will be shrivelled on the funeral pyre of the last war-lord.

Irish Worker, 8 August 1914

A CONTINENTAL REVOLUTION

THE outbreak of war on the continent of Europe makes it impossible this week to write to *Forward* upon any other question. I have no doubt that to most of my readers Ireland has ere now ceased to be, in colloquial phraseology, the most important place on the map, and that their thoughts are turning gravely to a consideration of the position of the European Socialist movement in the face of this crisis.

Judging by developments up to the time of writing, such considerations must fall far short of affording satisfying reflections to the Socialist thinker. For, what is the position of the Socialist movement in Europe today? Summed up briefly it is as follows:

For a generation at least the Socialist movement in all the countries now involved has progressed by leaps and bounds, and more satisfactory still, by steady and continuous increase and development.

The number of votes recorded for Socialist candidates has increased at a phenomenally rapid rate, the number of Socialist representatives in all legislative chambers has become more and more of a disturbing factor in the calculations of governments. Newspapers, magazines, pamphlets and literature of all kinds teaching Socialist ideas have been and are daily distributed by the million amongst the masses; every army and navy in Europe has seen a constantly increasing proportion of Socialists amongst its soldiers and sailors, and the industrial organizations of the working class have more and more perfected their grasp over the economic machinery of society, and more and more proved responsive to the Socialist conception of their duties. Along with this, hatred of militarism has spread through every rank of society, making everywhere its recruits, and raising an aversion to war even amongst those who in other things accepted the capitalist order of things. Anti-militarist societies and anti-militarist campaigns of Socialist societies and parties, and anti-militarist resolutions of Socialist and international trade union conferences have become part of the order of the day and are no longer phenomena to be wondered at. The whole working-class movement stands committed to war upon war – stands so committed at the very height of its strength and influence.

And now, like the proverbial bolt from the blue, war is upon us, and war between the most important, because the most Socialist, nations of the earth. And we are helpless!!

What then becomes of all our resolutions; all our protests of fraternization; all our threats of general strikes; all our carefully-built machinery of internationalism; all our hopes for the future? Were they all as sound and fury, signifying nothing? When the German artilleryman, a Socialist serving in the German army of invasion, sends a shell into the ranks of the French army, blowing off their heads; tearing out their bowels, and mangling the limbs of dozens of Socialist comrades in that force, will the fact that he, before leaving for the front, 'demonstrated' against the war be of any value to the widows and orphans made by the shell he sent upon its mission of murder? Or, when the French rifleman pours his murderous rifle-fire into the ranks of the German line of attack, will he be able to derive any comfort from the probability that his bullets are murdering or maiming comrades who last year joined in thundering 'hochs' and cheers of greeting to the eloquent Jaurès, when in Berlin he pleaded for international solidarity? When the Socialist pressed into the army of the Austrian Kaiser, sticks a long, cruel bayonet-knife into the stomach of the Socialist conscript in the army of the Russian Tsar, and gives it a twist so that when pulled out it will pull the entrails out along with it, will the terrible act lose any of its fiendish cruelty by the fact of their common theoretical adhesion to an anti-war propaganda in times of peace? When the Socialist soldier from the Baltic provinces of Russia is sent forward into Prussian Poland to bombard towns and villages until a red trail of blood and fire covers the homes of the unwilling Polish subjects of Prussia, as he gazes upon the corpses of those he has slaughtered and the homes he has destroyed, will he in his turn be comforted by the thought that the Tsar whom he serves sent other soldiers a few years ago to carry the same devastation and murder into his own home by the Baltic Sea?

But why go on? Is it not as clear as the fact of life itself that no insurrection of the working class; no general strike; no general uprising of the forces of Labour in Europe, could possibly carry with it, or entail a greater slaughter of Socialists, than will their participation as soldiers in the campaigns of the armies of their respective countries? Every shell which explodes in the midst of a German battalion will slaughter some Socialists; every Austrian cavalry charge will leave the gashed and hacked bodies of Serbian or Russian Socialists squirming and twisting in agony upon the ground; every Russian, Austrian, or German ship sent to the bottom or blown sky-high will mean sorrow and mourning in the homes of some Socialist comrades of ours. If these men must die, would it not be better to die in their own country fighting for freedom for their class, and for the abolition of war, than to go forth to strange countries and die slaughtering and slaughtered by their brothers that tyrants and profiteers might live?

Civilization is being destroyed before our eyes; the results of generations of propaganda and patient heroic plodding and self-sacrifice are being blown into annihilation from a hundred cannon mouths; thousands of comrades with whose souls we have lived in fraternal communion are about to be done to death; they whose one hope it was to be spared to co-operate in building the perfect society of the future are being driven to fratricidal slaughter in shambles where that hope will be buried under a sea of blood.

I am not writing in captious criticism of my continental comrades. We know too little about what is happening on the continent, and events have moved too quickly for any of us to be in a position to criticize at all. But believing as I do that any action would be justified which would put a stop to this colossal crime now being perpetrated, I feel compelled to express the hope that ere long we may read of the paralysing of the internal transport service on the continent, even should the act of paralysing necessitate the erection of Socialist barricades and acts of rioting by Socialist soldiers and sailors, as happened in Russia in 1905.

Even an unsuccessful attempt at social revolution by force of arms, following the paralysis of the economic life of militarism, would be less disastrous to the Socialist cause than the act of Socialists allowing themselves to be used in the slaughter of their brothers in the cause.

A great continental uprising of the working class would stop the war; a universal protest at public meetings will not save a single life from being wantonly slaughtered.

I make no war upon patriotism; never have done. But against the patriotism of capitalism – the patriotism which makes the interest of the capitalist class the supreme test of duty and right – I place the patriotism of the working class, the patriotism which judges every public act by its effect upon the fortunes of those who toil. That which is good for the working class I esteem patriotic, but that party or movement is the most perfect embodiment of patriotism which most successfully works for the conquest by the working class of the control of the destinies of the land wherein they labour.

To me, therefore, the Socialist of another country is a fellow-patriot, as the capitalist of my own country is a natural enemy. I regard each nation as the possessor of a definite contribution to the common stock of civilization, and I regard the capitalist class of each nation as being the logical and natural enemy of the national culture which constitutes that definite contribution.

Therefore, the stronger I am in my affection for national tradition, literature, language, and sympathies, the more firmly rooted I am in my opposition to that capitalist class which in its soulless lust for power and gold would bray the nations as in a mortar.

Reasoning from such premises, therefore, this war appears to me as the most fearful crime of the centuries. In it the working class are to be sacrificed that a small clique of rulers and armament makers may sate their lust for power and their greed for wealth. Nations are to be obliterated, progress stopped, and international hatreds erected into deities to be worshipped.

Forward, 15 August 1914

THE WAR UPON THE GERMAN NATION

Now that the first drunkenness of the war fever is over, and the contending forces are locked in deadly combat upon the battle-field, we may expect that the sobering effect of the reports from the front will help to restore greater sanity to the minds of the people. There are thousands of Irish homes today from which, deluded by the foolish declaration of Mr Redmond that Ireland was as one with the Empire in this struggle, and the still more foolish and criminal war whoops of the official Home Rule press, there went forth sons and fathers to recruit the armies of England. If to those thousands of Irish homes from which Mr Redmond drew forth young Irishmen we add the tens of thousands of homes from which reservists were drawn, we have a vast number of Irish homes in which from this day forward gibbering fear and heartbreaking anxiety will be constantly present – forever present at the fireside, unbidden guests at the table, loathsome spectres in the darkness grinning from the pillows and the coverlet.

Each day some one of these homes, some days thousands of these homes will be stricken from the field of battle, and news will come home that this young son or that loving father has met his doom, and out there under a foreign sky the mangled remains, twisted, blown and gashed by inconceivable wounds will lie, each of them in all their ghastly horror crying out to Heaven for vengeance upon the political tricksters who lured them to their fate.

Poor and hunger-harassed as are the members of the Irish Transport and General Workers Union, is there one of them who today has not a happier position and a clearer conscience than the so-called leaders of the Irish race, who are responsible for deluding into enlisting to fight England's battles the thousands of Irish youths whose corpses will ere many months be manuring the soil of a foreign country, or whose mangled bodies will be contemptuously tossed home to starve – a burden and a horror to all their kith and kin?

Read this report from the *Daily News and Leader* of the 25th inst. of the statement of an Alsatian peasant who saw some of the fighting in Alsace. He says:

The effects of artillery fire are terrific. The shells burst, and where you formerly saw a heap of soldiers you then see a heap of corpses or a number of figures writhing on the ground, torn and mutilated by the exploded fragments.

And when you have read that then think of the many thousands of our boys – for God help us and them, they are still our brave Irish boys though deluded into fighting for the oppressor – around whom such shells will be falling by day and by night for many a long month to come. Think of them, and think also of the multitude of brave German boys who never did any harm to them or to us, but who rather loved us and our land, and our tongue and our ancient literature, and consider that those boys of ours will be busy sending shot and shell and rifle-ball into their midst, murdering and mangling German lives and limbs, widowing humble German women, orphaning helpless German children.

Such reflections will perhaps open the way for the more sane frame of mind I spoke of at the beginning of this article. To help in clarifying the thought of our people that such sanity may be fruitful in greater national as well as individual wisdom, permit me, then, to present a few facts to those whose attitude upon the war has been so far determined by the criminal jingoism of the daily press. I wish to try and trace *the real origin of this war upon the German nation*, for despite the truculent shouts of a venal press and conscienceless politicians, this war is not a war upon German militarism, but upon the industrial activity of the German nation.

If the reader was even slightly acquainted with the history of industry in Europe he would know that as a result of the discovery of steam as a motive power, and the consequent development of machine industry depending upon coal, Great Britain towards the close of the eighteenth century began to dominate the commercial life of the world. Her large coal supply helped her to this at a time when the coal supply of other countries had not yet been discovered or exploited. Added to this was the fact that the ruling class of England by a judicious mixing in European struggles, by a dexterous system of alliances and a thoroughly unscrupulous use of her sea power was able to keep the Continent continually embroiled in war whilst her own shores were safe. While the cities and towns of other countries were constantly the prey of rival armies, their social life crushed under the cannon wheels of contending forces, and their brightest young men compelled to give to warfare the intellect that might have enriched their countries by industrial achievements, England was able peacefully to build up her industries, to spread her wings of commerce, and to become the purveyor-general of manufactured goods to the civilized and uncivilized nations of the world. In her own pet phrase she was 'the workshop of the world', and other nations were but as so many agricultural consumers of the products of England's factories and workshops.

Obviously such a state of matters was grossly artificial and unnatural. It could not be supposed by reasonable men that the civilized nations would be content to remain for ever in such a condition of tutelage or dependence. Rather was it certain that self-respecting nations would begin to realize that the industrial over-lordship by England of Europe meant the continued dependence of Europe upon England – a most humiliating condition of affairs.

So other nations began quietly to challenge the unquestioned supremacy of England in the markets. They began first to produce for themselves what they had hitherto relied upon England to produce for them, and passed on from that to enter into competition with English goods in the markets of the world. Foremost and most successful European nation in this endeavour to escape from thraldom of dependence upon England's manufactures stands the German nation. To this contest in the industrial world it brought all the resources of science and systematized effort. Early learning that an uneducated people is necessarily an inferior people, the German nation attacked the work of educating its children with such success that it is now universally admitted that the Germans are the best educated people in Europe. Basing its industrial effort upon an educated working class, it accomplished in the workshop results that this half-educated working class of England could only wonder at. That English working class trained to a slavish subservience to rule-of-thumb methods, and under managers wedded to traditional processes saw themselves gradually outclassed by a new rival in whose service were enrolled the most learned scientists co-operating with the most educated workers in mastering each new problem as it arose, and unhampered by old traditions, old processes or old equipment. In this fruitful marriage of science and industry the Germans were pioneers, and if it seemed that in starting both they became unduly handicapped it was soon realized that if they had much to learn they had at least nothing to unlearn, whereas the British remained hampered at every step by the accumulated and obsolete survivals of past industrial traditions.

Despite the long hold that England has upon industry, despite her pre-emption of the market, despite the influence of her far-flung empire, German competition became more and more a menace to England's industrial supremacy; more and more German goods took the place of English. Some few years ago the cry of 'Protection' was raised in England in the hopes that English trade would be thus saved by a heavy customs duty against imported commodities. But it was soon realized that as England was chiefly an exporting country a tax upon imported goods would not save her industrial supremacy. From the moment that realization entered into the minds of the British capitalist we may date the inception of this war.

It was determined that since Germany could not be beaten in fair competition industrially, it must be beaten unfairly in organizing a military and naval conspiracy against her. British methods and British capitalism might be inferior to German methods and German capitalism; German scientists aided by German workers might be superior to British workers and tardy British science, but the British fleet was still superior to the

German in point of numbers and weight of artillery. Hence it was felt that if the German nation could be ringed round with armed foes upon its every frontier until the British fleet could strike at its ocean-going commerce, then German competition would be crushed and the supremacy of England in commerce ensured for another generation. The conception meant calling up the forces of barbaric powers to crush and hinder the development of the peaceful powers of industry. It was a conception worthy of fiends, but what do you expect? You surely do not expect the roses of honour and civilization to grow on the thorn tree of capitalist competition – and that tree planted in the soil of a British ruling class.

But what about the independence of Belgium? Aye, what about it?

Remember that the war found England thoroughly prepared, Germany totally unprepared. That the British fleet was already mobilized on a scale never attempted in times of peace, and the German fleet was scattered in isolated units all over the seven seas. That all the leading British commanders were at home ready for the emergency, and many German and Austrian officers, such as Slatin Pasha, have not been able to get home yet. Remember all this and realize how it reveals that the whole plan was ready prepared; and hence that the cry of 'Belgium' was a mere subterfuge to hide the determination to crush in blood the peaceful industrial development of the German nation. Already the British press is chuckling with joy over the capture of German trade. All capitalist journals in England boast that the Hamburg-America Line will lose all its steamers, valued at twenty millions sterling. You know what that means! It means that a peaceful trade built up by peaceful methods is to be struck out of the hands of its owners by the sword of an armed pirate. You remember the words of John Mitchel descriptive of the British Empire, as 'a pirate empire, robbing and plundering upon the high seas'.

Understand the game that is afoot, the game that Christian England is playing, and when next you hear apologists for capitalism tell of the wickedness of Socialists in proposing to 'confiscate' property remember the plans of British and Irish capitalists to steal German trade – the fruits of German industry and German science.

Yes, friends, governments in capitalist society are but committees of the rich to manage the affairs of the capitalist class. The British capitalist class have planned this colossal crime in order to ensure its uninterrupted domination of the commerce of the world. To achieve that end it is prepared to bathe a continent in blood, to kill off the flower of the manhood of the three most civilized great nations of Europe, to place the iron heel of the Russian tyrant upon the throat of all liberty-loving races and peoples from the Baltic to the Black Sea, and to invite the blessing of God upon the spectacle of the savage Cossacks ravishing the daughters of a race at the head of Christian civilization.

Yes, this war is the war of a pirate upon the German nation.

And up from the blood-soaked graves of the Belgian frontiers the spirits of murdered Irish soldiers of England call to Heaven for vengeance upon the Parliamentarian tricksters who seduced them into the armies of the oppressor of their country.

Irish Worker, 29 August 1914

THE FRIENDS OF SMALL
NATIONALITIES

THE 'war on behalf of small nationalities' is still going merrily on in the newspapers. That great champion of oppressed races, Russia, is pouring her armies into East Prussia and offering freedom and deliverance to all and sundry if they will only take up arms on her behalf – without undue delay. She is to be the judge after the war as to whether they did or did not delay unduly . . .

. . . The Russian Socialists have issued a strong manifesto denouncing the war, and pouring contempt upon the professions of the Tsar in favour of oppressed races, pointing out his suppression of the liberties of Finland, his continued martyrdom of Poland, his atrocious tortures and massacres in the Baltic provinces, and his withdrawal of the recently granted parliamentary liberties of Russia. And to that again add the fact that the Polish Nationalists have warned the Poles against putting any faith in a man who has proven himself incapable of keeping his solemnly pledged faith with his own people, and you will begin to get a saner view of the great game that is being played than you can ever acquire from the lying press of Ireland and England.

Of course, that should not blind you to the splendid stand which the British Government, we are assured, is making against German outrages and brutality and in favour of small nationalities. The Russian Government is admitted by every publicist in England to be a foul blot upon civilization. It was but the other day that when the Russian Duma was suppressed by force and many of its elected representatives imprisoned and exiled, an English Cabinet Minister defiantly declared in public, in spite of international courtesies:

The Duma is dead! Long live the Duma!

But all that is forgotten now, and the Russian Government and the British Government stand solidly together in favour of small nationalities everywhere except in countries now under Russian and British rule.

Yes, I seem to remember a small country called Egypt, a country that through ages of servitude has painfully evolved to a conception of national freedom, and under leaders of its own choosing essayed to make that conception a reality. And I think I remember how this British friend of small nationalities bombarded its chief seaport, invaded and laid waste its territory, slaughtered its armies, imprisoned its citizens, led its chosen leaders away in chains, and reduced the new-born Egyptian nation into a conquered, servile British province.

And I think I remember how, having murdered this new-born soul of nationality amongst the Egyptian people, it signalized its victory by the ruthless hanging at Denshawai of a few helpless peasants who dared to think their pigeons were not made for the sport of British officers.

Also, if my memory is not playing me strange tricks, I remember reading of a large number of small nationalities in India, whose evolution towards a more perfect civilization in harmony with the genius of their race, was ruthlessly crushed in blood, whose lands were stolen, whose education was blighted, whose women were left to the brutal lusts of the degenerate soldiery of the British Raj.

Over my vision comes also grim remembrances of two infant republics in South Africa, and I look on the map in vain for them today. I remember that the friend of small nationalities waged war upon them – a war of insolent aggression at the instance of financial bloodsuckers. Britain sent her troops to subjugate them, to wipe them off the map; and although they resisted until the veldt ran red with British and Boer blood, the end of the war saw two small nationalities less in the world.

When I read the attempts of the prize Irish press to work up feeling against the Germans by talk of German outrages at the front, I wonder if those who swallow such yarns ever remember the facts about the exploits of the British generals in South Africa. When we are told of the horrors of Louvain, when the only damage that was done was the result of civilians firing upon German troops from buildings which those troops had in consequence to attack, I remember that in South Africa Lord Roberts issued an order that whenever there was an attack upon the railways in his line of communication every Boer house and farmstead within a radius of ten square miles had to be destroyed.

When I hear of the unavoidable killing of civilians in a line of battle 100 miles long in a densely populated country, being of, as it were, part of the German plan of campaign, I remember how the British swept up the whole non-combatant Boer population into concentration camps, and kept it there until the little children died in thousands of fever and cholera; so that the final argument in causing the Boers to make peace was the fear that at the rate of infant mortality in those concentration camps there would be no new generation left to inherit the republic for which their elders were fighting.

This vicious and rebellious memory of mine will also recur to the recent attempt of Persia to form a constitutional government, and it recalls how, when that ancient nation shook off the fetters of its ancient despotism, and set to work to elaborate the laws and forms in the spirit of a modern civilized representative state, Russia, which in solemn treaty with England had guaranteed its independence, at once invaded it, and slaughtering all its patriots, pillaging its towns and villages, annexed part of its territories, and made the rest a mere Russian dependency. I remember how Sir Edward Grey, who now gushes over the sanctity of treaties, when appealed to to stand by and make Russia stand by the treaty guaranteeing the independence of Persia, coolly refused to interfere.

Oh, yes, they are great fighters for small nationalities, great upholders of the sanctity of treaties!

And the Irish Home Rule press knows this, knows all these things that a poor workman like myself remembers, knows them all, and is cowardly and guiltily silent, and viciously and fiendishly evil.

Let us hope that all Ireland will not some day have to pay an awful price for the lying attacks of the Home Rule press upon the noble German nation.

Let our readers encourage and actively spread every paper, circular, leaflet or manifesto which in these dark days dares to tell the truth.

Thus our honour may be saved; thus the world may learn that the Home Rule press is but a sewer-pipe for the pouring of English filth upon the shores of Ireland.

Irish Worker, 12 September 1914

REVOLUTIONARY UNIONISM AND WAR

SINCE the war broke out in Europe, and since the Socialist forces in the various countries failed so signally to prevent or even delay the outbreak, I have been reading everything in American Socialist papers or magazines that came to hand; to see if that failure and the reasons therefor, were properly understood among my old comrades in the United States.

But either I have not seen the proper publications, or else the dramatic side of the military campaigns has taken too firm a hold upon the imagination of Socialist writers to allow them to estimate properly the inner meaning of that debacle of political Socialism witnessed in Europe when the bugles of war rang out upon our ears.

I am going then to try, in all calmness, to relate the matter as it appears to us who believe that *the signal of war ought also to have been the signal for rebellion*, that when the bugles sounded the first note for actual war, their notes should have been taken as the tocsin for social revolution. And I am going to try to explain why such results did not follow such actions. My explanation may not be palatable to some; I hope it will be at least interesting to all.

In the first place let me be perfectly frank with my readers as to my own position, now that that possibility has receded out of sight. As the reader will have gathered from my opening remarks, I believe that the Socialist proletariat of Europe in *all* the belligerent countries ought to have refused to march against their brothers across the frontiers, and that such refusal would have prevented the war and all its horrors even though it might have led to civil war. Such a civil war would not, could not possibly have resulted in such a loss of Socialist life as this international war has entailed, and each Socialist who fell in such a civil war would have fallen knowing that he was battling for the cause he had worked for in days of peace, and that there was no possibility of the bullet or shell that laid him low having been sent on its murderous way by one to whom he had pledged the 'life-long love of comrades' in the international army of labour.

But seeing that the Socialist movement did not so put the faith of its adherents to the test, seeing that the nations are now locked in this death grapple, and the issue is knit, I do not wish to disguise from anyone my belief that there is no hope of peaceful development for the industrial nations of continental Europe whilst Britain holds the dominance of the sea. The British fleet is a knife held permanently at the throat of Europe; should any nation evince an ability to emerge from the position of a mere customer for British products, and to become a successful competitor of Britain in the markets of the world, that knife is set in operation to cut that throat.

By days and by nights the British Government watches and works to isolate its competitor from the comity of nations, to ring it around with hostile foes. When the time is propitious, the blow is struck, the allies of Britain encompass its rival by land and the fleet of Britain swoops upon its commerce by sea. In one short month the commerce-raiding fleet of Great Britain destroys a trade built up in forty years of slow, peaceful industry, as it has just done in the case of Germany.

Examining the history of the foreign relations of Great Britain since the rise of the capitalist class to power in that country, the continuity of this policy becomes obvious and as marvellous as it is obvious.

Neither religion nor race affinity nor diversity of political or social institutions availed to save a competitor of England. The list of commercial rivals or would-be rivals is fairly large, and gives the economic key to the reasons for the great wars of Britain. In that list we find Spain, Holland, France, Denmark and now Germany. Britain must rule the waves, and when the continental nations wished to make at the Hague a law forbidding the capture of merchant vessels during war, Britain refused her assent. Naturally! It is her power to capture merchant ships during war that enables Britain to cut the throat of a commercial rival at her own sweet will.

If she had not that power she would need to depend upon her

superiority in technical equipment and efficiency; and the uprise in other countries of industrial enterprise able to challenge and defeat her in this world market has amply demonstrated that she has not that superiority any longer.

The United States and Germany lead in crowding Britain industrially; the former cannot be made a target for the guns of militarist continental Europe, therefore escapes for the time being as Britain never fights a white power single-handed. But Germany is caught within the net and has to suffer for her industrial achievements.

The right to capture merchant ships for which Britain stood out against the public opinion of all Europe is thus seen to be the trump card of Britain against the industrial development of the world outside her shores – against the complete freedom of the seas by which alone the nations of the world can develop that industrial status which Socialists maintain to be an indispensable condition for Socialist triumph.

I have been thus frank with my readers in order that they may perfectly understand my position and the reasons therefor, and thus anticipate some of the insinuations that are sure to be levelled against me as one who sympathizes neither with the anti-German hysteria of such comrades as Professor George D. Herron nor with the suddenly developed belief in the good faith of Tsars shown by Prince Peter Kropotkin.*

I believe the war could have been prevented by the Socialists; as it was not prevented and as the issues are knit, I want to see England beaten so thoroughly that the commerce of the seas will henceforth be free to all nations – to the smallest equally with the greatest.

But *how could this war have been prevented*, which is another way of saying how and why did the Socialist movement fail to prevent it?

The full answer to that question can only be grasped by those who are familiar with the propaganda that from 1905 onwards

* Professor George D. Herron, American Socialist. Prince Peter Kropotkin (1842–1921), Russian revolutionary exile, author of *The Conquest of Bread, Fields, Factories and Workshops*, etc.

has been known as 'industrialist' in the United States and, though not so accurately, has been called 'syndicalist' in Europe.

The essence of that propaganda lay in two principles. To take them in the order of their immediate effectiveness these were: First, that labour could only enforce its wishes by organizing its strength at the point of production, i.e., the farms, factories, workshops, railways, docks, ships – where the work of the world is carried on, the effectiveness of the political vote depending primarily upon the economic power of the workers organized behind it. Secondly, that the process of organizing that economic power would also build the industrial fabric of the Socialist Republic, build the new society within the old.

It is upon the first of these two principles I wish my readers to concentrate their attention in order to find the answer to the question we are asking.

In all the belligerent countries of western and central Europe the Socialist vote was very large; in none of these belligerent countries was there an organized revolutionary industrial organization directing the Socialist vote nor a Socialist political party directing a revolutionary industrial organization.

The Socialist voters having cast their ballots were helpless, as voters, until the next election; as workers, they were indeed in control of the forces of production and distribution, and by exercising that control over the transport service could have made the war impossible. But the idea of thus co-ordinating their two spheres of activity had not gained sufficient lodgment to be effective in the emergency.

No Socialist Party in Europe could say that rather than go to war it would call out the entire transport service of the country and thus prevent mobilization. No Socialist Party could say so, because no Socialist Party could have the slightest reasonable prospect of having such a call obeyed.

The executive committee of the Socialist movement was not in control of the labour-force of the men who voted for the Socialist representatives in the legislative chambers of Europe, nor were the men in control of the supply of labour-force in control of the Socialist representatives. In either case there would have been an organized power immediately available against war. Lacking either, the socialist parties of Europe, when they had protested against war, had also *fired their last shot* against militarism and were left like 'children crying in the night'.

Had the Socialist Party of France been able to declare that rather than be dragged into war to save the Russian Tsar from the revolutionary consequences which would have followed his certain defeat by Germany, they would declare a railway strike, there would have been no war between France and Germany, as the latter country saved from the dread of an attack in the west whilst defending itself in the east could not have coerced its Socialist population into consenting to take the offensive against France.

But the French government knows, the German government knows, all cool observers in Europe know, that the Socialist and syndicalist organization of France could not have carried out such a threat even had they made it. Both politically and industrially the revolutionary organizations of France are mere skeleton frameworks, not solid bodies.

Politically large numbers roll together at elections around the faithful few who keep the machinery of the party together; industrially, more or less, large numbers roll together during strikes or lock-outs. But the numbers of either are shifting, uncertain and of shadowy allegiance. From such no revolutionary action of value in face of modern conditions of warfare and state organization could be expected. And none came.

Hence the pathetic failure of French Socialism – the Socialist battalion occupying the position of the most tactical importance on the European battlefield. For neither Russia nor Britain could have fought had France held aloof; Russia because of the fear of internal convulsions; Britain, because Britain never fights unless the odds against her foe are overwhelming. And Britain needed the aid of the French fleet.

To sum up then, the failure of European Socialism to avert the war is primarily due to the divorce between the industrial and political movements of labour. The Socialist voter, as such, is helpless between elections. He requires to organize power to enforce the mandate of the elections and the *only power he can so organize is economic power* – the power to stop the wheels of commerce, to control the heart that sends the life blood pulsating through the social organism.

International Socialist Reveiw, March 1915

THE GERMAN OR THE BRITISH EMPIRE?

NOTHING warms the cockles of my old heart so much as when some British Socialist kind-heartedly approves of my attitude – approves of it 'except', 'but', and 'only for'. Especially am I pleased when I learn from his letter that he has only read one copy of the *Workers' Republic*, is only just arrived in Ireland, but nevertheless understands our position thoroughly, and is only filled with pity for the 'sweet innocence' that inspires our little mistakes in such matters as a desire to vindicate the character of the enemies of the British capitalist Government.

Perhaps after he has been here as many years as he has been days he will begun to understand that the instinct of the slave to take sides with whoever is the enemy of his own particular slave-driver is a healthy instinct, and makes for freedom. That every Socialist who knows what he is talking about must be in favour of freedom of the seas, must desire that private property shall be immune from capture at sea during war, must realize that as long as any one nation dominates the water highways of the world neither peace nor free industrial development is possible for the world. If the capitalists of other nations desire the freedom of the seas for selfish reasons of their own that does not affect the matter. Every Socialist anxiously awaits and prays for that full development of the capitalist system which can alone make Socialism possible, but can only come into being by virtue of the efforts of the capitalists inspired by selfish reasons.

The German Empire is a homogeneous Empire of self-governing peoples; the British Empire is a heterogeneous collection in which a very small number of self-governing communities connive at the subjugation, by force, of a vast number of despotically ruled subject populations.

We do not wish to be ruled by either empire, but we certainly believe that the first named contains in germ more of the possibilities of freedom and civilization than the latter.

Workers' Republic, 18 March 1916

7

PARTITION
OF IRELAND

NORTH-EAST ULSTER

A DUBLIN Comrade once remarked to the writer of these notes that as two things cannot occupy the same space at the same time, so the mind of the working class cannot take up two items at the same time. Meaning thereby that when that working class is obsessed with visions of glory, patriotism, war, loyalty, or political or religious bigotry, it can find no room in its mind for considerations of its own interests as a class.

Somewhere upon these lines must be found the explanation of the fact that whereas Dublin and Nationalist Ireland generally is seething with rebellion against industrial conditions and manifesting that rebellion by a crop of strikes, in Belfast and the quarter dominated by the loyal element, class feeling or industrial discontent is at present scarcely manifested at all.

For Dublin and its Nationalist allies, the Home Rule question has long gone beyond the stage of controversy; it is regarded as out of the region of dispute and consequently the mind of the working class is no more excited over that question than it can be considered to be excited over the general proposition that the whole is greater than its parts.

In North-East Ulster, on the other hand, the question of Home Rule is not a settled question in men's minds, much less settled politically, and hence its unsettled character makes it still possible for that question to so possess the minds of the multitude that all other questions such as wages, hours and conditions of labour, must take a subordinate place and lose their power to attract attention, much less to compel action.

According to all Socialist theories North-East Ulster, being the most developed industrially, ought to be the quarter in which class lines of cleavage, politically and industrially, should be the most pronounced and class rebellion the most common.

As a cold matter of fact, it is the happy hunting ground of the slave-driver and the home of the least rebellious slaves in the industrial world.

Dublin, on the other hand, has more strongly developed working-class feeling, more strongly accentuated instincts of loyalty to the working class than any city of its size in the globe.

I have explained before how the perfectly devilish ingenuity of the master class had sought its ends in North-East Ulster. How the land was stolen from Catholics, given to Episcopalians, but planted by Presbyterians; how the latter were persecuted by the Government, but could not avoid the necessity of defending it against the Catholics, and how out of this complicated situation there inevitably grew up a feeling of common interests between the slaves and the slave-drivers.

As the march of the Irish towards emancipation developed, as step by step they secured more and more political rights and greater and greater recognition, so in like ratio the disabilities of the Presbyterians and other dissenters were abolished.

For a brief period during the closing years of the eighteenth century, it did indeed seem probable that the common disabilities of Presbyterians and Catholics would unite them all under the common name of Irishmen. Hence the rebel society of that time took the significant name of 'United Irishmen'.

But the removal of the religious disabilities from the dissenting community had, as its effect, the obliteration of all political difference between the sects and their practical political unity under the common designation of Protestants, as against the Catholics, upon whom the fetters of religious disability still clung.

Humanly speaking, one would have confidently predicted that as the Presbyterians and Dissenters were emancipated as a result of a clamorous agitation against religious inequality, and as that agitation derived its chief force and menace from the power of Catholic numbers in Ireland, then the members of these sects would unite with the agitators to win for all an enjoyment of these rights the agitators and rebels had won for them.

But the prediction would have missed the mark by several million miles. Instead, the Protestants who had been persecuted joined with the Protestants who had persecuted them against the menace of an intrusion by the Catholics into the fold of political and religious freedom – 'Civil and religious liberty'.

There is no use blaming them. It is common experience in history that as each order fought its way upward into the circle of governing classes, it joined with its former tyrants in an endeavour to curb the aspirations of these orders still unfree.

That in Ireland religious sects played the same game as elsewhere was played by economic or social classes does not prove the wickedness of the Irish players, but does serve to illustrate the universality of the passions that operate upon the stage of the world's history.

It also serves to illustrate the wisdom of the Socialist contention that as the working class has no subject class beneath it, therefore, to the working class of necessity belongs the honour of being the class destined to put an end to class rule, in emancipating itself, it cannot help emancipating all other classes.

Individuals out of other classes must and will help as individual Protestants have helped in the fight for Catholic emancipation in Ireland; but on the whole, the burden must rest upon the shoulders of the most subject class.

If the North-East corner of Ireland is, therefore, the home of a people whose minds are saturated with conceptions of political activity fit only for the atmosphere of the seventeenth century, if the sublime ideas of an all-embracing democracy equally as insistent upon its duties as upon its rights have as yet found poor lodgment here, the fault lies not with this generation of toilers, but with those pastors and masters who deceived it and enslaved it in the past – and deceived it in order that they might enslave it.

But as no good can come of blaming it, so also no good, but infinite evil, can come of truckling to it. Let the truth be told, however ugly. Here, the Orange working class are slaves in spirit because they have been reared up among a people whose conditions of servitude were more slavish than their own. In Catholic Ireland the working class are rebels in spirit and democratic in feeling because for hundreds of years they have found no class as lowly paid or as hardly treated as themselves.

At one time in the industrial world of Great Britain and Ireland the skilled labourer looked down with contempt upon the unskilled and bitterly resented his attempt to get his children taught any of the skilled trades; the feeling of the Orangemen of

Ireland towards the Catholics is but a glorified representation on a big stage of the same passions inspired by the same unworthy motives.

An atavistic survival of a dark and ignorant past!

Viewing Irish politics in the light of this analysis, one can see how futile and vain are the criticisms of the Labour Party in Parliament which are based upon a comparison of what was done by the Nationalist group in the past and what is being left undone by the Labour group today. I am neither criticizing nor defending the Labour group in Parliament; I am simply pointing out that any criticism based upon an analogy with the actions, past or present, of the Irish party, is necessarily faulty and misleading.

The Irish party had all the political traditions and prejudices of centuries to reinforce its attitude of hostility to the Government, nay, more, its only serious rival among its own constituents was a party more uncompromisingly hostile to the Government than itself – the republican or physical force party.

The Labour Party, on the other hand, has had to meet and overcome all the political traditions and prejudices of its supporters in order to win their votes, and knows that at any time it may lose these suffrages so tardily given.

The Irish party never needed to let the question of retaining the suffrages of the Irish electors enter into their calculations. They were almost always returned unopposed. The Labour Party knows that a forward move on the part of either Liberal or Tory will always endanger a certain portion of Labour votes.

In other words, the Irish group was a party to whose aid the mental habits formed by centuries of struggle came as a reinforcement among its constituents at every stage of the struggle. But the Labour Party is a party which, in order to progress, must be continually breaking with and outraging institutions which the mental habits of its supporters had for centuries accustomed them to venerate.

I have written in vain if I have not helped the reader to realize that the historical backgrounds of the movement in England and Ireland are so essentially different that the Irish Socialist movement can only be truly served by a party indigenous to the soil, and explained by a literature having the same source: that the phrases and watchwords which might serve to express the soul of the movement in one country may possibly stifle its soul and suffocate its expression in the other.

One great need of the movement in Ireland is a literature of its very own. When that is written people will begin to understand why it is that the Irish Catholic worker is a good democrat and a revolutionist, though he knows nothing of the fine spun theories of democracy or revolution; and how and why it is that the doctrine that because the workers of Belfast live under the same industrial conditions as do those of Great Britain, they are therefore subject to the same passions and to be influenced by the same methods of propaganda, is a doctrine almost screamingly funny in its absurdity.

Forward, 2 August 1913

THE LIBERALS AND ULSTER

THIS is the fateful week when, according to all the authorities, the drums of war are really to beat in Ulster. Everybody is on the tip-toe of expectation, and many worthy souls are not able to sleep at nights listening anxiously for the first rattle of musketry.

It is all very weird and puzzling. Had some writer gifted with the powers of prophecy attempted four years ago, or fourteen years ago, to sketch in a novel the outlines of the political developments of the past two years in Ulster, he would have been branded as a foul libeller of the British governing classes or else as an idiot who failed to understand the passion for order and constitutional methods of procedure that inspires those set in authority in these islands. Not in all Europe would he have found one who would have accepted his prophecy as an indication of the probable trend of events.

Permit me briefly to recapitulate the chief marvels that have astounded the world in this political struggle.

A Cabinet Minister, Mr Winston Churchill, announces that he has accepted an invitation from Ulster Liberals to address a Home Rule meeting in the Ulster Hall in Belfast. A meeting of the Ulster Unionist Council, with a noble lord in the chair, publicly announces that it will take steps to prevent Mr Churchill's meeting. Up to that point nobody in Ulster who knows the Ulstermen had taken in the least degree seriously the threats of fighting on their part. All recognized that the rank and file were probably ready enough to fight, but all also recognized that the economic position of the leaders of the Orange forces, their standing as holders of capitalist stock, land, coal mines, shipping, etc., made the suggestion that they should rebel against the Government that guaranteed their investments – a very ridiculous suggestion indeed. It was generally felt that a firm application of the power of the police force would suffice to quell in a few days all the Orange resistance, and nobody dreamt that the Government would hesitate in firmly applying that force upon the first opportunity. Any open defiance of the law, any open declaration of an intention to break the laws, supplied just that opportunity for the Government to act with all the traditions of law and order at its back.

This projected meeting of Mr Winston Churchill and the Unionist threat to prevent it came almost as a providential gift to a Government desirous, before it should act, to have its opponents entirely in the wrong. All the traditions of British constitutional procedure were outraged; even the most hardened Tories in Great Britain looked askance at this Orange proposal to deny a Cabinet Minister that right of public meeting theoretically allowed to even the most responsible agitator. The occasion called, and called loudly, for a firm application of force to establish, once and for all, the right of public meeting in Ulster; to convince the Orange hosts that henceforth unpopular opinion must be met by arguments and not by bolts, rivets, nuts or weapons of war.

But, lo and behold! the Government ran away. Mr Winston Churchill abandoned his right to hold his meeting in the place advertised, and slunk away to the outskirts of the city to hold a meeting surrounded by more soldiers and police than would have sufficed to capture the city if held by the whole Orange forces in battle array. We in Ulster gasped with astonishment at this pitiful surrender of public liberties, and we realized that a direct encouragement had been given to all the forces of reaction to pursue the path of violence.

Mr Winston Churchill's meeting was for the Ulster Orange leaders a glorious opportunity; it gave them the excuse for a daring experiment in lawlessness. That experiment was a success; it stood and stands to the succeeding events in the same relation as a trial trip of a newly-launched vessel stands to all its following voyages. Such a trial trip demonstrates the amount of pressure that can be safely put upon the boilers; Mr Churchill's meeting demonstrated how, in what manner, and to what extent, pressure can be successfully applied to the Liberal Government by a reactionary class.

Suppose that the declaration of an intention to take steps to prevent the meeting had been made by a committee representing the Labour movement, do you think that Mr Churchill would have abandoned his meeting, even although the Committee represented an overwhelming majority of the inhabitants of the city? You know that he would have held that meeting at all costs, under such circumstances.

Next in importance to the abandonment of the right of public meeting came the tacit permission given to the Ulster Volunteers to arm themselves with the avowed object of resisting the law.

For two years this arming went on, accompanied by drilling and organizing upon a military basis, and no effort was made to still the drilling or to prevent the free importation of arms until the example of the Ulster Volunteers began to be followed through the rest of Ireland. The writer of these notes established a Citizen Army at Dublin in connection with the Irish Transport and General Workers Union, and this was followed by the establishment of Irish Volunteer Corps all through Nationalist Ireland. Hardly had the first of these corps been organized, and the desirability of having them armed been mooted, than the Liberal Government rushed out a proclamation forbidding the importation of arms into Ireland. What had been freely allowed whilst Orangemen alone were arming was immediately made illegal when Labour men and Nationalists thought of obtaining the same weapons. Then having allowed the Unionist to drill and arm, the Government made the fact of their military preparations an excuse for proposing the dismemberment of Ireland as a sop to those whom it had allowed to arm against it. Ulster, where democracy had suffered most because of religious ascendancy, was to be handed over to those whose religious ascendancy, principles and practices had made democracy suffer.

Then we had the revolt, or mutiny, at the Curragh. Some regiments were ordered North, and the Liberal Minister humbly inquired of the officers if these gentlemen would kindly consent to go. The Orange leaders, their ladies and the royal family itself, had, it is believed, been usually engaged for two years in seducing these officers from all sense of duty – in teaching them to believe that they should refuse to act against the poor dupes who were being humbugged by the brothers, uncles, fathers, cousins and other relatives of those officers. And hence, as the ties of class are stronger than the ties of governments, the officers very quickly told your backboneless Liberal War Minister that they would not proceed against their fellow landlords and capitalists in the North, nor against the poor wretches who had surrendered their political initiative to them. And the Liberal War Minister, instead of promptly cashiering those officers, or ordering them to be tried by court-martial, humbly crawled to them, asked their pardon, so to speak, for daring to suggest such a thing, and gave them a guarantee that their services would not be called for against the Orange leaders. The guarantee was afterwards repudiated, but the rebellious officers are still in high favour with royalty, and still in command of their regiments. And the Liberal Government itself allowed the men who had corrupted the army to put it upon the defensive, and stand it in the dock, pitifully denying that it did the very thing that it is not fit to hold office if it fears to do, viz., to use its armed forces to make an ascendancy clique beaten at the polls recognize the machinery of the law from which it derived its powers in the past.

A final consummation to all this pitiful compromise and treachery to a people's hopes is the gun-running of the past few weeks. A ship sails into Larne Harbour one fine Friday evening, and immediately the Ulster Volunteers take possession of that town and seaport, the Royal Irish Constabulary are imprisoned in their barracks, the roads are held up by armed guards, the railway stations of Park Road, Belfast, of Larne, Bangor and Donaghadee are seized by the Ulster Volunteers and thousands of stands of rifles are landed together with a million rounds of ammunition. Along with the landing at Larne vessels are used to tranship arms and ammunition from the original gun-running steamer and land the cargo so transhipped at Bangor and Donaghadee. Some hundreds of motor cars were used to convey the arms and ammunition to safe places, that night, and the same motor cars worked all day on Saturday conveying them from temporary resting places to more secure and handy depots throughout Ulster.

In a few days afterwards the affair came up for discussion in the House of Commons. The Liberals stormed and raved, and the Tories laughed. Why should they not? All the laugh was on their side. Then up rose again the hero of the Ulster Hall – Winston Churchill. He screeched and shouted and perorated and declaimed about law and order until one might have thought that, at last, a wrathful government was about to put forth its mighty powers to crush its unscrupulous enemy. And then, having attained to almost Olympic heights, Mr Churchill ended by cooing more gently than a sucking dove and blandly assured the Orange law-breakers that he had not yet reached the limits of concession – he was willing to betray the Irish some more. If they would only let him know how much degradation of the mere Irish would satisfy them, he would try and work it for them. And Parliament adjourned, wondering what it all meant.

Now let me put the situation re the gun-running to any un-prejudiced reader. Can anyone believe that the gun-ship, the *Fanny*, which had been reported at Hamburg a month before its appearance at Larne and the nature of its cargo known, could keep hovering around these coasts for a month without the Government having it under close supervision?

Can anyone believe that if this gun-running feat had been attempted at Tralee, Waterford, Skibbereen or Bantry and Nationalists had attempted to imprison armed Royal Irish Constabularymen in their barracks that no shots would have been fired and no lives lost?

Can anyone believe that if railway stations were seized, roads held up, coastguards imprisoned and telegraph systems interfered with by Nationalists or Labour men, that at least 1,000 arrests would not have been made the next morning? Evidence is difficult to get, they say. Evidence be hanged! If Nationalists or Labour men were the culprits, the Liberal Government would have made the arrests first and looked for evidence afterwards. And been in no hurry about it either.

My firm conviction is that the Liberal Government wish to betray the Home Rulers, that they connive at these illegalities that they might have an excuse for their betrayal, and that the Home Rule party through its timidity and partly through its hatred of Labour in Ireland is incapable of putting the least pressure upon its Liberal allies and must now dance to the piping of its treacherous allies.

Who can forecast what will come out of such a welter of absurdities, betrayals and crimes?

Forward, 30 May 1914

LABOUR AND THE PROPOSED
PARTITION OF IRELAND

THE recent proposals of Messrs Asquith, Devlin, Redmond and Co. for the settlement of the Home Rule question deserve the earnest attention of the working-class democracy of this country. They reveal in a most striking and unmistakeable manner the depths of betrayal to which the so-called Nationalist politicians are willing to sink. For generations the conscience of the civilized world has been shocked by the historical record of the partition of Poland; publicists, poets, humanitarians, patriots, all lovers of their kind and of progress have wept over the unhappy lot of a country torn asunder by the brute force of their alien oppressors, its unity ruthlessly destroyed and its traditions trampled into the dust.

But Poland was disrupted by outside forces, its enemies were the mercenaries of the tyrant kingdoms and empires of Europe; its sons and daughters died in the trenches and on the battlefields by the thousands rather than submit to their beloved country being annihilated as a nation. But Ireland, what of Ireland? It is the trusted leaders of Ireland that in secret conclave with the enemies of Ireland have agreed to see Ireland as a nation disrupted politically and her children divided under separate political governments with warring interests.

Now, what is the position of Labour towards it all? Let us remember that the Orange aristocracy now fighting for its supremacy in Ireland has at all times been based upon a denial of the common human rights of the Irish people; that the Orange Order was not founded to safeguard religious freedom, but to deny religious freedom, and that it raised this religious question, not for the sake of any religion, but in order to use religious zeal in the interests of the oppressive property rights of rack-renting landlords and sweating capitalists. That the Irish people might be kept asunder and robbed whilst so sundered and divided, the

Orange aristocracy went down to the lowest depths and out of
the lowest pits of hell brought up the abominations of sectarian
feuds to stir the passions of the ignorant mob. No crime was too
brutal or cowardly; no lie too base; no slander too ghastly, as
long as they served to keep the democracy asunder.

And now that the progress of democracy elsewhere has somewhat muzzled the dogs of aristocratic power, now that in
England as well as in Ireland the forces of labour are stirring
and making for freedom and light, this same gang of well-fed
plunderers of the people, secure in Union held upon their own
dupes, seek by threats of force to arrest the march of ideas and
stifle the light of civilization and liberty. And, lo and behold,
the trusted guardians of the people, the vaunted saviours of the
Irish race, agree in front of the enemy and in face of the world
to sacrifice to the bigoted enemy the unity of the nation and
along with it the lives, liberties and hopes of that portion of the
nation which in the midst of the most hostile surroundings have
fought to keep the faith in things national and progressive.

Such a scheme as that agreed to by Redmond and Devlin, the
betrayal of the national democracy of industrial Ulster, would
mean a carnival of reaction both North and South, would set
back the wheels of progress, would destroy the oncoming unity
of the Irish Labour movement and paralyse all advanced
movements whilst it endured.

To it Labour should give the bitterest opposition, against it
Labour in Ulster should fight even to the death, if necessary, as
our fathers fought before us.

Irish Worker, 14 March 1914

PARTITION

HERE in Ireland the proposal of the Government to consent to the partition of Ireland – the exclusion of certain counties in Ulster – is causing a new line of cleavage. Not one of the supporters of Home Rule accepts this proposal with anything like equanimity, but rather we are already hearing in North-East Ulster rumours of a determination to resist it by all means. It is felt that the proposal to leave the Home Rule minority at the mercy of an ignorant majority with the evil record of the Orange party is a proposal that should never have been made, and that the establishment of such a scheme should be resisted with armed force if necessary.

Personally I entirely agree with those who think so; Belfast is bad enough as it is; what it would be under such rule the wildest imagination cannot conceive. Filled with the belief that they were defeating the Imperial Government and the Nationalists combined, the Orangemen would have scant regards for the rights of the minority left at their mercy.

Such a scheme would destroy the Labour movement by disrupting it. It would perpetuate in a form aggravated in evil the discords now prevalent, and help the Home Rule and Orange capitalists and clerics to keep their rallying cries before the public as the political watchwords of the day. In short, it would make division more intense and confusion of ideas and parties more confounded.

Forward, 21 March 1914

IRELAND AND ULSTER: AN APPEAL
TO THE WORKING CLASS

IN this great crisis of the history of Ireland, I desire to appeal to the working class – the only class whose true interests are always on the side of progress – to take action to prevent the betrayal of their interests contemplated by those who have planned the exclusion of part of Ulster from the Home Rule Bill. Every effort is now being made to prevent the voice of the democracy being heard in those counties and boroughs which it is callously proposed to cut off from the rest of Ireland. Meetings are being rushed through in other parts of Ireland, and at those meetings wirepullers of the United Irish League and the Ancient Order of Hibernians (Board of Erin) are passing resolutions approving of the exclusion, whilst you who will suffer by this dastardly proposal are never even consulted, but, on the contrary, these same organizations are working hard to prevent your voice being heard, and have done what they could to prevent the calling of meetings, of holding of demonstrations at which you could register your hatred of their attempt to betray you into the hand of the sworn enemies of democracy, of labour, and of nationality.

An instance of this attempt to misrepresent you may be quoted from the Irish press of 26 March. In a letter from the Irish Press Agency it says:

The proposal, representing the limit of concession and made 'as the price of peace' would only mean, if accepted, that the Counties of Down, Derry, Antrim and Armagh would remain as they are for six years at the end of which time they would come in automatically under Home Rule. They know, too, that the Nationalists in these four counties are perfectly willing to assent to this arrangement and that they are the Nationalists most concerned.

Remember that this is a quotation from a letter sent out by the Irish Press Agency and that copies of it are supplied by the agents of the Irish Parliamentary Party to every newspaper in Ireland and to Liberal papers in England, and you will see how true is my statement that you are being betrayed, that the men whom you trusted are busily engaged in rigging up a fake sentiment in favour of this betrayal of your interests. For the statements contained in the letter just quoted are, in the first part, deliberately misleading and, and, in the second part, an outrageous falsehood.

The statement that the counties excluded would come in automatically at the end of six years is deliberately misleading because, as was explained in the House of Commons, two General Elections would take place before the end of that time. If at either of these General Elections the Tories got a majority – and it is impossible to believe that the Liberals can win the other two elections successively – it would only require the passage of a small Act of not more than three or four lines to make the exclusion perpetual. And the Tories would pass it. What could prevent them? You can prevent them getting the chance by insisting upon the Home Rule Bill and no exclusion, being passed *now*. If you do not act *now*, your chance is gone.

The second part of the statement I have quoted is an outrageous falsehood, as every one knows. The Nationalists of the four countries have not been asked their opinion, and if any politician would dare to take a plebiscite upon this question of exclusion or no exclusion, the democracy of Ulster would undoubtedly register a most emphatic refusal to accept this proposal. And yet so-called Home Rule journals are telling the world that you are quite willing to be cut off from Ireland and placed under the heel of the intolerant gang of bigots and enemies of progress who for so long have terrorized Ulster.

Men and women, consider! If your lot is a difficult one now, subject as you are to the rule of a gang who keep up the fires of religious bigotry in order to divide the workers, and make united progress impossible; if your lot is a difficult one, even when supported by the progressive and tolerant forces of all Ireland, how difficult and intolerable it will be when you are cut off from Ireland, and yet are regarded as alien to Great Britain, and left at the tender mercies of a class who knows no mercy, of a mob poisoned by ignorant hatred of everything national and democratic.

Do not be misled by the promises of politicians. Remember that Mr Birrell, Chief Secretary, solemnly promised that a representative of Dublin Labour would sit upon the Police Inquiry Commission in Dublin, and that he broke his solemn promise. Remember that Mr Redmond pledged his word at Waterford that the Home Rule Bill would go through without the loss of a word or a comma, and almost immediately afterwards he agreed to the loss of four counties and two boroughs. Remember that the whole history of Ireland is a record of betrayals by politicians and statesmen, and remembering this, spurn their lying promises and stand up for a United Ireland – an Ireland broad based upon the union of Labour and Nationality.

You are not frightened by the mock heroics of a pantomime army. Nobody in Ulster is. If the politicians in Parliament pretend to be frightened, it is only in order to find an excuse to sell you. Do not be sold. Remember that when soldiers were ordered out to shoot you down in the Belfast Dock Strike of 1907 no officer resigned then rather than shed blood in Ulster, and when some innocent members of our class were shot down in the Falls Road, Belfast, no Cabinet Ministers apologized to the relatives of the poor workers they had murdered. Remember that more than a thousand Dublin men, women and children were brutally beaten and wounded by the police a few months ago, and three men and one girl killed, but no officer resigned, and neither Tory nor Home Rule press protested against the coercion of Dublin. Why, then, the hypocritical howl against compelling the pious sweaters of Ulster and their dupes to obey the will of the majority? Remember the AOH, the UIL and the Irish Parliamentary Party cheered on the government when it sent its police to bludgeon the nationalist workers of Dublin. Now the same organization and the same party cheers on the same treacherous government when it proposes to surrender you into the hands of the Carsonite gang. As the officers of the Curragh have stood by their class, so let the working-class democracy of Ulster stand by its class, and all Irish workers from Malin Head to Cape Clear and from Dublin to Galway will stand by you.

Let your motto be that of James Fintan Lalor, the motto which the working-class Irish Citizen Army has adopted as its aim and object, viz.:

That the entire ownership of Ireland [all Ireland] – moral and material – is vested of right in the entire people of Ireland.

And, adopting this as your motto, let it be heard and understood that Labour in Ireland stands for the unity of Ireland – an Ireland united in the name of progress, and who shall separate us?

Irish Worker, 4 April 1914

THE EXCLUSION OF ULSTER

SOCIALISTS and Labour people generally in Great Britain have had good reason to deplore the existence of the Irish question and to realize how disastrous upon the chances of their candidates has been the fact of the existence in the constituencies of a large mass of organized voters whose political activities were not influenced solely or even largely by the domestic issues before the electors. Our British comrades have had long and sore experience of contests in which all the arguments and all the local feeling were on the side of the Socialist or Labour candidate, and yet that local candidate was ignominiously defeated because there existed in the constituency a large Irish vote – a large mass of voters who supported the Liberal, not because they were opposed to Labour, but because they wanted Ireland to have Home Rule.

Our British comrades have learned that the existence of that Irish vote and the knowledge that it would be cast for the Home Rule official candidate, irrespective of his record on or his stand upon Labour matters, caused hundreds of thousands who otherwise would have voted Labour to vote Liberal in dread that the Irish defection would 'let the Tory in'. For a generation now the Labour movement in Great Britain has been paralysed politically by this fear; and all hands have looked forward eagerly to the time when the granting of Home Rule would remove their fear and allow free expression to all the forces that make for a political Labour movement in that country. Even many of the actions and votes of the Labour Party in the House of Commons which have been strenuously complained of have been justified by that Party on the plea that it was necessary to keep in power the government that would get Home Rule out of the way. Now, in view of this experience of the Socialist movement in Great Britain, we can surely not view with any complacency a proposal that will keep that question to the front as a live issue at British elections for six years longer or rather for a totally indefinite period. We know that this 'six years' period' so glibly spoken of by politicians has no background of reality to justify the belief that that term can be considered as more than a mere figure of speech.

In the *Daily News and Leader* of 6 April, Mr H. W. Massingham, writing of the 'Ulster Limit', says, and the saying is valuable as indicative of the trend of Liberal thought:

> Should we, therefore, make an absolutely dead halt at the six years' milestone? Both parties implicitly admit that that is impossible, for one Parliament cannot bind another.

And in the previous week the Liberal Solicitor General declared in Parliament that if within the six years' period

> ... the other side brought in a Bill to exclude Ulster, it would have a royal and triumphant procession to the foot of the throne.

Thus we have it clearly foreshadowed that there is no such thing as a six years' limit which can be binding upon future Parliaments and that therefore the question of Home Rule for the Ulster Counties will be a test question at future elections in Great Britain, and will then play there the same disastrous role for the Labour movement as the question of Home Rule does now. The political organization of the Home Rule party will be kept alive in every industrial constituency on the pretext of working for a 'United Ireland', and in the same manner the Unionist Party will also keep up its special organizations, Orange Lodges, etc., in order to keep alive the sectarian appeal to the voters from Ireland who will be asked to 'vote against driving Ulster under the heels of the Papish Dublin Parliament'.

Labour men in and out of Ireland have often declared that if Home Rule was wanted for no other purpose, it was necessary in order to allow of the solidifying of the Labour vote in Great Britain, and the rescue of the Irish voters in that country from their thraldom to the Liberal caucus. It might not be far from the truth to surmise that the Liberal Party managers have seen the same point as clearly as we did ourselves, and have quietly resolved that such a good weapon as the Nationalist Party sentiment should not be entirely withdrawn from their armoury. The reader will also see that with a perfectly Mephistophelian subtlety the question of exclusion is not suggested to be voted upon by any large area where the chances for or against might be fairly equal, where exclusion might be defeated as it might be if all Ulster were the venue of the poll, and all Ulster had to stay out or come in as a result of the verdict of the ballot-box. No, the counties to be voted on the question are the counties where the Unionists are in an overwhelming majority, and where therefore the vote is a mere farce – a subterfuge to hide the grossness of the betrayal of the Home Rule electors. Then again each county or borough enters or remains outside according to its own vote, and quite independent of the vote of its neighbours in Ulster. Thus the Home Rule question as far as Ulster is concerned, may be indefinitely prolonged and kept alive as an issue to divide and disrupt the Labour vote in Great Britain.

The effect of such exclusion upon Labour in Ireland will be at least equally, and probably more, disastrous. All hopes of uniting the workers, irrespective of religion or old political battle cries will be shattered, and through North and South the issue of Home Rule will be still used to cover the iniquities of the capitalist and landlord class. I am not speaking without due knowledge of the sentiments of the organized Labour movement in Ireland when I say that we would much rather see the Home Rule Bill defeated than see it carried with Ulster or any part of Ulster left out. . .

Meanwhile, as a study in political disparity, watch the manoeuvres of the Home Rule party on this question. The deal is already, I believe, framed up, but when the actual vote is to be taken in the Counties of Down, Antrim, Derry and Armagh and the Boroughs of Belfast and Derry, Messrs Redmond, Devlin and Co. will tour these counties and boroughs letting loose floods of oratory asking for votes against exclusion and thus will delude the workers into forgetting the real crime, viz., consenting to make the unity of the Irish Nation a subject to be decided by the votes of the most bigoted and passion-blinded reactionaries in these four counties where such reactionaries are in the majority. The betrayal is agreed upon, I repeat, the vote is only a subterfuge to hide the grossness of the betrayal.

It still remains to be seen whether the working-class agitation cannot succeed in frightening these vampires from the feast they are promising themselves upon the corpse of a dismembered Ireland. . .

Forward, 11 April 1914

8

CULTURE

THE LANGUAGE MOVEMENT

I DO believe in the necessity, and indeed in the inevitability, of an universal language; but I do not believe it will be brought about, or even hastened, by smaller races or nations consenting to the extinction of their language. Such a course of action, or rather of slavish inaction, would but lead to the intensification of the struggle for mastery between the languages of the greater powers.

On the other hand, a large number of small communities, speaking different tongues, are more likely to agree upon a common language as a common means of communication than a small number of great empires, each jealous of its own power and seeking its own supremacy.

I have heard some doctrinaire Socialists arguing that Socialists should not sympathize with oppressed nationalities or with nationalities resisting conquest. They argue that the sooner these nationalities are suppressed the better, as it will be easier to conquer political power in a few big empires than in a number of small states. This is the language argument over again.

It is fallacious in both cases. It is even more fallacious in the case of nationalities than in the case of languages, because the emancipation of the working class will function more through economic power than through the political state. The first act of the workers will be through their economic organizations seizing the organized industries; the last act the conquest of political power.

In this the working class will, as they needs must, follow in the lines traversed by the capitalist revolutions of Cromwellian England, of Colonial and Revolutionary America, of Republican France, in each of whom the capitalist class had developed their economic power before they raised the banner of political revolt.

The working class in their turn must perfect their organizations, and when such organizations are in a position to control, seize and operate the industries, they will find their political power equal to the task.

But the preparatory work of the revolutionary campaign must lie in the daily and hourly struggles in the workshop, the daily and hourly perfectioning of the industrial organization.

And these two factors for freedom take no heed to political frontiers, nor to the demarcations of political states. They march side by side with the capitalist; where capitalism brings its machinery it brings the rebels against itself, and all its governments and all its armies can establish no frontier the revolutionary idea cannot pass.

Let the great truth be firmly fixed in your mind that the struggle for the conquest of the political state of the capitalist is not the battle, it is only the echo of the battle. The real battle is being fought out, and will be fought out, on the industrial field.

Because of this and other reasons the doctrinaire Socialists are wrong in this as in the rest of their arguments. It is not necessary that Irish Socialists should hostilize those who are working for the Gaelic language, nor whoop it up for territorial aggrandizement of any nation. Therefore, in this, we can wish the Sinn Féiners, good luck.

Besides, it is well to remember that nations which submit to conquest or races which abandon their language in favour of that of an oppressor do so, not because of the altruistic motives, or because of a love of brotherhood of man, but from a slavish and cringing spirit.

From a spirit which cannot exist side by side with the revolutionary idea.

This was amply evidenced in Ireland by the attitude of the Irish people towards their language.

For six hundred years the English strove to suppress that mark of the distinct character of the Gael – their language, and failed. But in one generation the politicians did what England had failed to do.

The great Daniel O'Connell, the so-called liberator, conducted his meetings entirely in English. When addressing meetings in Connaught where, in his time, everybody spoke Gaelic and over 75 per cent of the people nothing else but Gaelic, O'Connell spoke exclusively in English. He thus conveyed to the simple people the impression that Gaelic was something to be ashamed of – something fit for only ignorant people. He pursued the same course all over Ireland.

As a result of this and similar actions the simple people turned their backs upon their own language and began to ape 'the gentry'. It was the beginning of the reign of the toady and the crawler, the *seoinín** and the slave.

The agitator for revenue came into power in the land.

It is not ancient history, but the history of yesterday that old Irish men and women would speak Irish to each other in the presence of their children, but if they caught son or daughter using the language the unfortunate child would receive a cuff on the ear accompanied with the adjuration:

'Speak English, you rascal; speak English like a gintleman!'

It is freely stated in Ireland that when the Protestant evangelizers, soupers they call them at home, issued tracts and Bibles in Irish in order to help the work of proselytizing, the Catholic priesthood took advantage of the incident to warn their flocks against reading all literature in Gaelic. Thus still further discrediting the language.

I cannot conceive of a Socialist hesitating in his choice between a policy resulting in such self-abasement and a policy of defiant self-reliance and confident trust in a people's own power of self-emancipation by a people.

The Harp, April 1908

---

* *Seoinín* – jackeen or johnnie, an aper of foreign ways, a flunkey.

9

SONGS OF FREEDOM

WE ONLY WANT THE EARTH

Some men, faint-hearted, ever seek
    Our programme to retouch,
And will insist, whene'er they speak
    That we demand too much.
'Tis passing strange, yet I declare
    Such statements give me mirth,
For our demands most moderate are,
    We only want the earth.

'Be moderate,' the trimmers cry,
    Who dread the tyrants' thunder.
'You ask too much and people fly
    From you aghast in wonder.'
'Tis passing strange, for I declare
    Such statements give me mirth,
For our demands most moderate are,
    We only want the earth.

Our masters all a godly crew,
    Whose hearts throb for the poor,
Their sympathies assure us, too,
    If our demands were fewer.
Most generous souls! But please observe,
    What they enjoy from birth
Is all we ever had the nerve
    To ask, that is, the earth.

The 'labour fakir' full of guile,
    Base doctrine ever preaches,
And whilst he bleeds the rank and file
    Tame moderation teaches.
Yet, in despite, we'll see the day
    When, with sword in its girth,

Labour shall march in war array
  To realize its own, the earth.

For labour long, with sighs and tears,
  To its oppressors knelt.
But never yet, to aught save fears,
  Did the heart of tyrant melt.
We need not kneel, our cause no dearth
  Of loyal soldiers' needs
And our victorious rallying cry
  Shall be we want the earth!

Songs of Freedom, 1907

A REBEL SONG

Come workers sing a rebel song,
A song of love and hate,
Of love unto the lowly
And of hatred to the great.
The great who trod our fathers down,
Who steal our children's bread,
Whose hands of greed are stretched to rob
The living and the dead.

chorus:

Then sing our rebel song as we
  proudly sweep along
To end the age-old tyranny
  that makes for human tears.
Our march is nearer done, with
  each setting of the sun.
And the tyrants' might is passing
  with the passing of the years.

We sing no more of wailing
And no songs of sighs or tears;
High are our hopes and stout our hearts
And banished all our fears.
Our flag is raised above us
So that all the world may see,
'Tis Labour's faith and Labour's arm
Alone can Labour free.

chorus:

Out of the depths of misery
We march with hearts aflame;
With wrath against the rulers false
Who wreck our manhood's name.

The serf who licks the tyrant's rod
May bend forgiving knee;
The slave who breaks his slavery's chain
A wrathful man must be.

chorus:

Our army marches onward
With its face towards the dawn,
In trust secure in that one thing
The slave may lean upon.
The might within the arm of him
Who knowing freedom's worth,
Strikes hard to banish tyranny
From off the face of earth.

chorus:

The Socialist, May 1903

THE WATCHWORD OF LABOUR

Oh, hear ye the watchword of Labour,
　　the slogan of those who'd be free,
That no more to any enslaver
　　must Labour bend suppliant knee,
That we on whose shoulders are borne
　　the pomp and the pride of the great,
Whose toil they repay with their scorn,
　　must challenge and master our fate.

chorus:

Then send it aloft on the breeze boys,
That watchword the grandest we've known
That Labour must rise from its knees, boys,
And claim the broad earth as its own.

Aye, we who oft won by our valour,
　　empires for our rulers and lords,
Yet knelt in abasement and squalor
　　to things we had made with our swords,
Now valour with worth will be blending,
　　when answering Labour's command,
We arise from our knees and ascending
　　to manhood for freedom take stand.

chorus:

Then out from the field and the city
　　from workshop, from mill and from mine,
Despising their wrath and their pity,
　　we workers are moving in line,
To answer the watchword and token
　　that Labour gives forth as its own,
Nor pause till our fetters we've broken,
　　and conquered the spoiler and drone.

The Legacy and Songs of Freedom, 1918

LOVE OF FREEDOM

I love you, I love you, though toil may obscure
   And make dimmer the light of my eye,
Though slow runs my blood, and my heart, if as pure
   Beats calmer when women are nigh.
Yet out from my heart comes a passionate wail
   With a note of sincerity true,
The protest of my heart, though its vigour may fail,
   Yet beats stronger its love, dear, for you.

I love you, I love you, no swain to his dear,
   Nor mother to first fruit of her womb,
Nor thinker to thought he has garnered in tear,
   From the deserts where Truth hid in gloom,
Hath love more devoted, more unfailing than he
   Now laying this poor wreath at thy shrine
In hope that accepted this offering will be
   And remembered when victory is thine.

Yes, Freedom, I love you, my soul thou has fired
   With the flame that redeems from the clay,
Thou hast given to me, as to Moses inspired,
   A glimpse of that land, bright as day,
Which Labour must journey, though each foot of road
   Sweated blood from the graves of our best,
Where built upon Justice and Truth the abode
   Thou preparest awaits the opprest.

Workers' Republic, 8 April 1915

THE LEGACY

The Dying Socialist to His Son

Come here my son, and for a time put up your childish play,
Draw nearer to your father's bed, and lay your games away.
No sick man's 'plaint is this of mine, ill-tempered at your noise,
Nor carping at your eagerness to romp with childish toys.
Thou'rt but a boy and I, a man outworn with care and strife,
Would not deprive you of one joy thou canst extract from life;
But o'er my soul comes creeping on death's shadow, and my lips
Must give to you a message ere life meets that eclipse.
Slow runs my blood, my nether limbs I feel not, and my eyes
Can scarce discern, here in this room, that childish form I prize.

Aye, death's grim hand is on my frame, and helpless it lies here
But to my mental vision comes the power of a seer,
And time and space are now as nought as with majestic sweep
I feel my mind traverses the land and encompasses the deep;
Search backward over history's course, or with prophetic view,
And sounding lines of hope and fear gauge man's great destiny
    too.
The chasm deep twixt life and death I bridge at last tonight,
And with a foot on either side absorb their truths and light.
And thus, my son, though reft of strength, my limbs slow turn
    to clay,
Fired by this light I call you here to hear my legacy.

'My legacy!' Ah, son of mine! wert thou a rich man's pride
He'd crown thee with his property, possessions far and wide
And golden store to purchase slaves, whose aching brain and limb
Would toil to bring you luxury as such had toiled for him.
But thy father is a poor man, and glancing round you here
Thou canst see all his property – our humble household gear,
No will we need by lawyers drawn, no witnesses attest
To guard for you your legacy, your father's last bequest.

'Thy father is a poor man' mark well what that may mean
On the tablets of thy memory that truth write bright and clean.
Thy father's lot it was to toil from earliest boyhood on
And know his latent energies for a master's profit drawn;
Or else, ill-starred, to wander round and huxter-like to vend
His precious store of brain and brawn to all whom fate may send
And cross his path with gold enough to purchase Labour's
    power
To turn it into gold again, and fructify the hour.
With sweat and blood of toiling slaves, like unto us, my son,
Aye, through our veins since earliest days, 'tis poor man's blood
    has run.
Yes, son of mine, since History's dawn two classes stand revealed,
The Rich and Poor, in bitterest war, by deadliest hatred steeled.
The one, incarnate greed and crime, disdaining honest toil
Had grasped man's common birthright and treasure house, the
    soil.
And standing twixt their fellow man and all that earth could give
Had bade them render tribute if they would hope to live.
And, building crime on top of crime, had pushed their conquests
    on
Till, arbiters of life and death, they stood with weapons drawn.
And blades athirst to drink the blood, on land and over-sea,
Of him who dared for human rights to stem their tyranny.
They held our lands, our bodies ruled, and strove to rule the
    mind
And Hell itself could not surpass their evil to mankind –
And all who strove for human rights to break their cursed yoke –
The noblest of our race, my child, went down beneath their
    stroke.
And where'er earth's sweetest spots, in nature's loveliest haunt
Each built his fort or castle grim the poor of earth to daunt.
And issuing forth from walls of stone, high over cliff and pass,
With sword in hand, would gather tribute for his class.
And given emblems of their rule, flaunting to humankind
The pit to drown our women, the gibbet for our men,
Stood, aye, beside their fortresses; and underneath the moat
Tier upon tier of noisome cells for those the tyrant smote.

Thumbscrews and rack and branding rod, and each device of
    Hell
Perverted genius could devise to torture men to sell
(For brief respite from anguish dire to end their wretched lives)
The secret of their comradeship, the honour of their wives.

As the fabled upas tree of old, by ancient poets sung,
Consumed with blight each living thing then 'neath its branches
    sprung,
The rich man's power o'er all the earth had spread its baleful
    blight
Respecting neither age nor sex to sate its lust and might.
It stole the harvest from the field, the product of the loom,
Struck down the old man in his age, the young man in his bloom.
It robbed the carrier on the road, the sailor on the tide
And from the bridegroom of the hour it took the new-made
    bride.
Such crimes it wrought not Hell itself and its satanic school
Could fashion crimes to equal those wrought by the rich man's
    rule.

'The past?' Aye, boy, the method's past, the deed is still the same,
And robbery is robbery, yet though cloaked in gentler name.
Our means of life are still usurped, the rich man still is lord,
And prayers and cries for justice still meet one reply – the sword!
Though hypocrites for rich men's gold may tell us we are free,
And oft excel in speech and print our vaunted liberty,
But freedom lies not in a name, and he who lacks for bread
Must have that bread tho' he should give his soul for it instead.
And we, who live by Labour, know that while they rule we must
Sell freedom, brain and limb to win for us and ours a crust.
The robbers made our fathers slaves then chained them to the
    soil,
For a little larger chain – a wage – we must exchange our toil.
But open force gave way to fraud but force again behind
Prepares to strike if fraud should fail to keep men deaf and blind.
Our mothers see their children's limbs they fondled as they grew
And doted on, caught up to make for rich men profits new,

Whilst strong men die for lack of work and cries of misery swell
And women's souls in city streets creep shuddering to Hell.
These things belong not to the past but to the present day
And they shall last till in our wrath we sweep them all away.

'We sweep them.' Ah, too well I know my work on earth is done,
Even as I speak my chilling blood tells me my race is run.
But you, my last-born child, take the legacy I give
And do as your father did whilst he was spared to live.
Treasure ye in your inmost heart this legacy of hate
For those who on the poor man's back have climbed to high
   estate.
The lords of land and capital – the slave lords of our age,
Who of this smiling earth of ours have made for us a cage
Where golden bars fetter men's souls, and noble thoughts are
   flame
To burn with vain desire, and virtue yields to shame.
Each is your foe, foe of your class, of human rights the foe,
Be it your thought by day and night to work their overthrow.
And howsoe'er you earn your wage, and wheresoe'er you go,
Be it beneath the tropic heat or mid the northern snow
Or closely penn'd in factory walls or burrowing in the mine
Or scorching in the furnace hell of steamers cross the brine
Or on a railroad's shining track you guide the flying wheel
Or clambering up buildings high to weld the frames of steel
Or use the needle, or the type, the hammer or the pen,
Have you one thought, one speech alone, to all your fellow-men.
The men and women of your class, tell them their wrongs and
   yours,
Plant in their hearts that hatred deep that suffers and endures,
And treasure up each deed of wrong, each scornful word and
   look
Inscribe it in the memory, as others in a book,
And wait and watch through galling years the ripening of time
Yet deem to strike before that hour were worse than folly – crime.

This be your task, oh son of mine, the rich man's hate to brave
And consecrate your noblest part to rouse each fellow slave.

To spread the day the world awaits when Labour long opprest
Shall rise and strike for Freedom true and from the tyrant wrest
The power they have abused so long. Oh ever glorious deed!
The crowning point of history, yet child, the bitterest need.

Ah, woe is me, thy father's eyes shall not behold the day
I faint and die; child, hold my hand,
Keep thou my legacy.

Irish Worker, 23 May 1914
(but first published in an American newspaper
some years before)

CHRONOLOGY OF CONNOLLY'S LIFE

1868 5 June, James Connolly born at 107 Cowgate, Edinburgh, Scotland, the third son of Irish emigrants John Connolly (1833–1900), a manure carter for Edinburgh Corporation, and Mary McGinn (1833–1892).

1878/9 Starts work as 'printers' devil' in Edinburgh *Evening News* where his brother Thomas works as a compositor's labourer. Factory inspector discovers his age and he is dismissed.

1880 Works in bakery.

1881 Works in mosaic tiling factory.

1882 Joins First Battalion of King's Liverpool Regiment. In July the regiment is sent to Ireland which Connolly sees for the first time. Serves in Youghal, Castlebar, The Curragh and Dublin. During period in Ireland he meets his future wife Lillie Reynolds, a domestic servant working in Rathmines.

1889 February, regiment returns to Aldershot, England. His father John in accident and given work as caretaker of a public convenience. Connolly leaves army and returns to Scotland. 13 April, marries Lillie Reynolds in Perth and is employed as a carter by Edinburgh Cleansing Dept. Becomes active in socialist politics as member of the Socialist League and later the Scottish Socialist Federation, SSF.

1892 Mother dies of acute bronchitis. Succeeds his eldest brother John as secretary of the SSF and begins his first writings in *Justice*, journal of the Social Democratic Federation.

1894 First public speech at Independent Labour Party meeting in Edinburgh. November, stands as socialist candidate for St Giles Ward, Edinburgh, in municipal elections. Result, he comes third. Starts contributions to *Labour Chronicle* under pseudonym R. Ascal (rascal).

1895 February, sets up as a cobbler at 73 Buccleuch Street, Edinburgh. April, stands as socialist candidate in Poor Law election for St Giles Ward, again comes third. June, becomes full-time socialist organizer and propagandist.

1896 May, settles in Ireland as organizer of the Dublin Socialist Club. 29 May, prime mover in the foundation of the Irish Socialist Republican Party (ISRP) and is appointed secretary. 7 June, first public meeting of the ISRP. September, ISRP issues manifesto. Connolly takes job as labourer with Dublin Corporation. October, Connolly's first major political essay 'Ireland for the Irish' published in *Labour Leader*, London. Edits excerpts from writings of James Fintan Lalor, *The Rights of Ireland* and *The Faith of a Felon*.

1897 March, *Erin's Hope: the End and the Means* published. June, arrested during a demonstration against Queen Victoria's Diamond Jubilee. October, lectures in Edinburgh. December, Rank and File '98 Club (to commemorate the 1798 Irish Rising) founded by Connolly and opened to general public. 1897/8 edits *'98 Readings*, five numbers issued fortnightly.

1898 12 March, lecture in Dublin on Paris Commune. March issues manifesto *The Rights of Life and the Rights of Property* (drafted by Connolly and Maud Gonne) due to impending Irish famine. Spends three weeks in Kerry reporting on famine for *Weekly People* (New York). June, travels to Scotland seeking financial aid for projected ISRP journal. Keir Hardie gives £50. 13 August, first issue of the *Workers' Republic*. 14 August, lecture in Dublin on 'Wolfe Tone and the Irish Social Revolution'.

1899 14 February, lecture in Cork on 'Labour and the Irish Revolution'. 27 August, organizes first public protest against Boer War.

1900 ISRP sends delegates to International Socialist Congress in Paris.

1901 *The New Evangel* published. June–October lecture tour in Britain. October, elected to Dublin Trades Council by United Labourers Union.

1902 January, stands as Labour candidate in Wood Quay Ward in Dublin municipal elections and is defeated. February, American Socialist Labour Party (SLP) republishes *Erin's Hope: the End and the Means* in New York. May Day address at meeting held by Social Democratic Federation in Edinburgh. August, leaves for USA lecture tour at invitation of SLP. September–December, tour from New York to Los Angeles and visits Canada. Contributes articles to *Weekly People* (New York).

1903 2 January, farewell meeting at Manhattan Lyceum Annex, New York. January, unsuccessful candidate for Wood Quay Ward in Dublin municipal elections. April, lecture tour in

Scotland. May, poem 'A Rebel Song' set to music by Gerald Crawford appears in May issue of *The Socialist* (Edinburgh). 1903/4 prolific year of writing verse. 7 June, chairman at inaugural meeting of Socialist Labour Party, Edinburgh (breakaway from SDF) and is appointed national organizer. June–July, lecture tour of Scotland. August, returns to Dublin where ISRP proclaims itself Irish section of SLP. 18 September, emigrates to America and takes up residence in Troy, New York, working as insurance collector. Joins SLP.

1904 Eldest child, Mona, dies aged 13 from severe burns in an accident. August, is joined in USA by his wife and five children, Nora, Aideen, Ina, Maire and Ruaidhre (Roderick). 1904/5 lectures at Clark's Hall, New York. Begins to learn Italian, having mastered French and German.

1906 Joins the Industrial Workers of the World ('Wobblies'). Active in Newark and Elizabeth (New Jersey) where he organizes Singer factory.

1907 5 January, elected to National Executive of SLP. 29 March, forms Irish Socialist Federation. Becomes secretary of Building and Constructional Workers Industrial Union and is soon organizing tramwaymen, moulders, garment workers, milkmen and dockers for the IWW. Becomes New York correspondent of *Industrial Union Bulletin*. October, resigns from SLP. Completes *Labour in Irish History*.

1908 January, launches first issue of *The Harp* as organ of ISF in New York. Founds IWW Propaganda League at McMahon Hall, New York. July, lecture tour of USA. Delegate to fourth IWW Convention in Chicago. December, *Socialism Made Easy* published in Chicago.

1909 May Day address at IWW May Day meeting in New York. June, appointed national organizer of the Socialist Party of America.

1910 January, *The Harp* published in Dublin with Jim Larkin as Dublin editor. March, Larkin launches fund to bring Connolly on lecture tour of Ireland. June–July, takes part in Free Speech Campaign in New Castle, Pennsylvania led by 'Big Bill' Hayward, edits *New Castle Free Press* when editor is jailed. June, final issue of *The Harp*. 14 July, farewell banquet at Cavanagh's Restaurant, New York. 16 July, sails for Ireland. 26 July, arrives in Derry. 17 July, visits Larkin in Mountjoy Jail, Dublin. August, joins Socialist Party of

Ireland and establishes branches in Belfast and Cork. *Labour, Nationality and Religion* published. October, SPI manifesto issue. November, *Labour in Irish History* published. Campaigns with Maud Gonne McBride for extension to Ireland of the act providing meals for school children, appointed National Organizer of the SPI.

1911 March, moves to Belfast and joins Irish Transport and General Workers Union. July, appointed secretary and Ulster district organizer of ITGWU and addresses mass meeting of locked-out coal-trade workers in Dublin. October, leads millgirls' strike in Belfast. November, founds Textile Workers section of ITGWU. Delegate from ITGWU to Belfast Trades Council.

1912 30 January, arrives in Wexford to lead strikers and locked-out workers following arrest of P. T. Daly. Easter, establishes Independent Labour Party of Ireland and drafts programme. April, Home Rule for Ireland Bill introduced in House of Commons. Connolly demands proportional representation, excision of proposal for a senate and suffrage for women. May, Irish TUC meeting in Clonmel, Connolly proposes the TUC involve itself with labour politics. Debates with Hilaire Belloc at Irish Club in London.

1913 Contests Dock Ward in municipal elections in Belfast unsuccessfully. Delegate to Irish TUC in Cork. 26 August, Dublin tramway strike led by Larkin begins. 29 August, Connolly speaks with Larkin at mass meeting outside Liberty Hall. 30 August, Connolly arrested and sentenced to three months imprisonment. 31 August, 'Bloody Sunday' when police attack crowds in O'Connell Street. September, Keir Hardie visits Connolly in prison. 7 September, Connolly goes on hunger strike. 14 September, he is released. October, Connolly prepares statement of workers' case for Board of Trade Inquiry. Tours Scotland seeking support for Dublin workers. 27 October, Larkin imprisoned. November, Connolly organizes campaign for his release. 12 November, issues *Manifesto to British Working Class*. 13 November, Larkin released and Connolly drafts appeal to British workers calling for a general strike in support of Irish workers. 14 November, Larkin leaves for Britain on 'Fiery Cross' campaign. Speaks with Larkin at monster meeting in Free Trade Hall, Manchester. 19 November, speaks at Albert Hall with Larkin, George Bernard Shaw, Sylvia

Pankhurst, George Lansbury and George Russell. 23
November, Citizen Army named to protect workers.

1914 14 March, denounces proposal to partition Ireland in *Irish
Worker*. 22 March, Irish Citizen Army reorganized and
constitution is adopted. It becomes the first 'Red Guard' in
Europe. 17 April, organizes protest meeting against proposed partition in Belfast. 1 June, Irish TUC meets in
Dublin and becomes Irish TUC and Labour Party. Connolly elected to National Executive Committee. 5 July,
speaks in Limerick in support of striking members of United
Carmen's and Storemen's Union. August, denounces the
war in *Irish Worker*. 10 August, Irish TUC declares that 'a
European war for the aggrandizement of the capitalistic
class has been declared'. October, becomes president of Irish
Neutrality League and becomes involved with members of
the Irish Republican Brotherhood with the intention of
organizing an uprising in Ireland. 24 October, Larkin leaves
for USA and Connolly becomes acting General Secretary
of the ITGWU, editor of *Irish Worker* and Commandant
of the Irish Citizen Army. 5 December, last issue of *Irish
Worker* before suppression by authorities.

1915 30 May, addresses Labour Day demonstration in Phoenix
Park. 18 July, addresses anti-conscription meeting outside
Liberty Hall. Writes a series of articles on guerrilla warfare
to prepare Irish Citizen Army and Irish Volunteers for the
uprising. Connolly also lectures Irish Volunteers on street
fighting. 13 March, plans for the rising explained, Connolly
to command Dublin area. *The Reconquest of Ireland*
published 14 December, speaks at all Ireland rally against
conscription at Mansion House, Dublin.

1916 19–22 January, meets with Military Council of Irish Republican Brotherhood and date for the rising is agreed,
Easter Sunday, 23 April. Connolly becomes a member of
the Military Council. 24 March, Irish Citizen Army resists
police raid on Liberty Hall. 26 March, Connolly's second
play *Under Which Flag* performed in Liberty Hall. 23 April,
countermanding orders stop rising. Military Council meet
in Liberty Hall and decide on rising on Easter Monday.
Proclamation of the Republic printed in basement of Liberty
Hall. 24 April, appointed vice-president of the Provisional
Government of the Irish Republic and Commandant-
General of the Dublin Division of the Army of the Irish

Republic ('From the moment the first shot is fired there will be no longer Volunteers or Citizen Army but only the Army of the Irish Republic'). 27 April, Connolly wounded in foot and also suffers a wound in the arm. 29 April, 3.45 p.m., the Provisional Government surrenders, 1,351 people killed or severely wounded in the week of bloody fighting. 1 May, gangrene sets in and Connolly sends for the Capuchin Father Aloysius. Reiterates his belief that one can be a Marxist and a Catholic. 9 May, Connolly propped up in bed, court-martialled and sentenced to death. 12, May, carried to yard at Kilmainham Jail in a stretcher, sat up in a chair, to which he is strapped to keep him upright, and executed by British firing squad.

BIBLIOGRAPHY

CONNOLLY'S WRITINGS

Erin's Hope: The End and the Means, first published by the Irish Socialist Republican Party, March 1897.

The New Evangel, 1901.

Socialism and Nationalism, 1901.

Songs of Freedom, New York, 1907.

Socialism Made Easy, first published by C. H. Kerry & Co., Chicago, December 1908.

Labour, Nationality and Religion, The Harp Library, Dublin, August 1910.

Labour in Irish History, Maunsel & Co., Dublin, November 1910.

The Reconquest of Ireland, Liberty Hall, Dublin, 1915.

The Legacy and Songs of Freedom, Socialist Party of Ireland, Liberty Hall, Dublin, 1918.

COLLECTIONS (BOOKS)

Labour in Ireland (containing *Labour in Irish History* and *The Reconquest of Ireland*), Maunsel & Co., Dublin, 1917.

A Socialist and War 1914–1916, ed. P. J. Musgrove, Lawrence & Wishart, London, 1941.

Socialism and Nationalism, ed. Desmond Ryan, Sign of Three Candles, Dublin, 1948.

Labour and Easterweek, ed. Desmond Ryan, introduction by William O'Brien, Sign of Three Candles, Dublin, 1949.

The Workers' Republic, ed. Desmond Ryan, introduction by William McMullen, Sign of Three Candles, Dublin, 1951.

The Best of Connolly, ed. Proinsias Mac Aonghusa and Liam Ó Reagáin, Mercier Press, Cork, 1967.

COLLECTIONS (PAMPHLETS)

Erin's Hope & The New Evangel, New Books, Dublin, 1968.

Revolutionary Warfare, New Books, Dublin, 1968.

Yellow Unions in Ireland, Connolly Books, Cork, 1968.

Press Poisoners in Ireland, Connolly Books, Cork, 1968.

Connolly-Walker Controversy, Connolly Books, Cork, 1969.

Socialism Made Easy, New Writers' Press, Dublin, 1968.

Workshop Talks (extracts from Socialism Made Easy), Saor Éire Press, 1969.

Workshop Talks, Republican Education Department ('Official Sinn Féin'), Dublin, 1971.

Ireland Upon the Dissecting Table, Cork Workers' Club, 1972.

Quotations from James Connolly, Derry Kelleher (ed.), Vanguard Publications, Dublin, 1972.

The James Connolly Songbook, Cork Workers' Club, 1972.

PAMPHLETS EDITED BY CONNOLLY

The Rights of Ireland and The Faith of a Felon, by James Fintan Lalor, Dublin, 1896.

'98 Readings (five numbers), Dublin, 1897–98.

PERIODICALS EDITED BY CONNOLLY

The *Workers' Republic*, Dublin, August 1898–May 1903 (not continuous – 85 issues).

The Harp, New York, 1908–1910 (monthly).

The Irish Worker, Dublin, 24 October–5 December 1914 (paper suppressed).

Irish Work, Dublin, 19 December 1914 (one issue only).

The Worker, Dublin, December 1914–January 1915 (weekly, suppressed February 1915).

The Workers' Republic, Dublin, 29 May 1915–22 April 1916 (weekly).

BIOGRAPHIES AND STUDIES

James Connolly, G. O'Connor (Seán Mac Giollarnarth and J. Forde), Dublin, 1917.

The Social Teachings of James Connolly, Father Lambert McKenna SJ, Dublin, 1920.

James Connolly, Desmond Ryan, Talbot Press, Dublin, 1924.

Reminiscences of Connolly, P. Quinlan, *New York Monitor*, 1932.

Portrait of a Rebel Father, Nora Connolly O'Brien, Talbot Press, Dublin, 1935.

Under the Banner of Connolly, Pat Dooley, Irish Freedom Pamphlet, London, 1945.

Connolly the Forerunner, R. M. Fox, Kerryman, Tralee, 1946.

Connolly of Ireland, Noëlle Davies, Swyddfa'r Blaid, Caernarvon, 1946.

Fifty Years of Liberty Hall, ed. Cathal O'Shannon, ITGWU, Dublin, 1959.

The Life and Times of James Connolly, C. Desmond Greaves, Lawrence & Wishart, 1961.

Leaders and Workers, ed. John Boyle (text of Radio Éireann Thomas Davies lecture on Connolly by Desmond Ryan), Mercier Press, Cork, 1963.

Tart na Córa – Saol agus Saothar Sheamais Ui Chonghaile, Proinsias Mac an Bheatha, Foilseacháin Náisiúnta Teo, Baile Átha Cliath, 1963.

James Connolly – A Biography, Ina Heron Connolly, eight instalments in *Liberty* (March–October 1966), ITGWU journal Dublin.

Leaders and Men of the Easter Rising, ed. F. X. Martin (includes essay on Connolly by Edward MacLysaght), Methuen, London, 1967.

The Teachings of James Connolly, Joseph Deasy, New Books, Dublin, 1968.

Connolly Bibliography, D. Nevin, Trade Union Information, Irish TUC, Dublin, April, 1968.

James Connolly, D. Nevin (Thomas Davies lecture on Radio Éireann 27 October 1968, full report in *Irish Times* 28 October 1969).

The Mind of an Activist – James Connolly, Owen Dudley Edwards, Gill & Macmilland, Dublin, 1971.

Connolly in America, Manus O'Riordan, Irish Communist Organization, Belfast, 1972.

INDEX

MORE ABOUT PENGUINS
AND PELICANS

Penguinews, which appears every month, contains details of all the new books issued by Penguins as they are published. From time to time it is supplemented by *Penguins in Print*, which is a complete list of all available books published by Penguins. (There are well over four thousand of these.)

A specimen copy of *Penguinews* will be sent to you free on request. For a year's issues (including the complete lists) please send 30p if you live in the United Kingdom, or 60p if you live elsewhere. Just write to Dept EP, Penguin Books Ltd, Harmondsworth, Middlesex, enclosing a cheque or postal order, and your name will be added to the mailing list.

Note: *Penguinews* and *Penguins in Print* are not available in the U.S.A. or Canada

DIVIDED ULSTER

Liam de Paor

The violence which erupted in Northern Ireland in 1969 and has been continuing sporadically since then was, in Liam de Paor's opinion, easily predictable from the turbulent history of the region.

The issue on civil rights for the Roman Catholic minority produced widespread sympathy, but this is basically more than just a religious dispute. Almost equally deprived in Ulster are the poor Protestants, yet they oppose the Catholics with as much ferocity as the Paisleyite extremists.

Liam de Paor is the author of several books on Ireland and is a lecturer at University College, Dublin. In this skilful and perceptive analysis he takes us through the long and difficult history of Ireland since the great settlement of the seventeenth century and through the struggle for independence. He shows how the Six Counties came to be treated separately and how the religious divisions of the north have been used as an instrument of policy.

In this Pelican edition Liam de Paor has added an introduction and revised his final chapter to cover the more recent events down to the resignation of Major Chichester-Clark.

'By far the most comprehensive, best written and most rewarding book yet published on the Northern Ireland situation and its full background' – *New Statesman*

'The best short summary of the Ulster problem to appear so far' – *Guardian*